Renee Richardson

Renee Richardson

THE
SENSITIVE

a novel

RENEE RICHARDSON

Renee Richardson

THE
SENSITIVE

Instagram: @reneerichardsonbooks

E-mail: reneerichardsonbooks@gmail.com

Website: reneerichardsonbooks.com

Cover design by Dustin Lee Richardson.

Cover drawing and photographs by Renee Richardson.

Author photograph by Dustin Lee Richardson.

First Edition. 2023.

BEFORE YOU READ

The following contains scenes and words that some readers may find disturbing, triggering, and/or may not be suitable for readers under the age of 18, including the use of explicit language with detailed descriptions and/or mention of rape, sexual assault, self-harm, suicide, homicide, and drug and alcohol use.

Reader discretion is advised.

Renee Richardson

Special Thanks

This page is dedicated to those of you who showed your support by making a generous pledge to my project via Kickstarter. Thank you for sticking around for all of my updates, for being patient, and for having faith in this novel.

Derek

Ed

Edina

The Marlows

Renee & George

Rob

Silk Rhode Books

I am forever grateful for your kindness.

Much love,

Renee

Renee Richardson

To Paisley-
Though we have never met in this world, I know you so well.
Thank you for guiding and inspiring me from wherever you are.
Everything Lynette is is what I've imagined you would've been.
I love you.

To Grandpa-
Your kind soul and contagious laugh deserved much more
time here. Thank you for watching over me on the road and for
reminding me to drive safely whenever your favorite songs
come on.

To Newport-
The best memories of my childhood come from you. Thank
you for your beauty, history, and impact on who I am today. I
can't wait to visit you again soon.

...

And to those of you who have ever forgotten your purpose or
felt truly lost. No amount of trauma could ever make you
worthless. There is always a reason for you to be here. Find that
special something or somewhere that makes you feel safe, and
use that to rediscover your peace and power. I hope this book
reminds you that change is necessary for growth, and that you
can't experience the miraculous without the miserable. And
please, remember to breathe through it all.

Renee Richardson

THE
SENSITIVE

1

JULY

1.

TO NOTHING

I knew something was very wrong the first time it happened, but I buried it in denial. I hid that realization under the excuse of grief and exhaustion. Sometimes my mind wanders and I think about how things would've been different if I'd acknowledged it all sooner, but then I remind myself that there's no such thing as "different if." There's no use in looking back on the past except to tell a good story, because that's all we really are.

The nightmares started the third night I spent in the house, and after that, they repeated every single sleep. I always ran through a rainy forest at night. My head pounded, heat rushing through it. I glanced down a few times to see that my dress was covered in mud. I panted, feeling small and weak, tasting my tears as they mixed with raindrops on my lips. As I weaved through the shadows in the woods, tree branches scratched my arms.

I reached a clearing, only to be beckoned by one tree in particular, whose twisted limbs seemed to reach out, offering refuge. Feeling no other option, I darted toward the tree and shimmied up the branches as high as my little legs could before hearing heavy footsteps enter the clearing. I hid back, clinging to the trunk and the thick branch that cradled me away.

A dark blurred figure entered the center of the clearing and remained motionless, huffing for several seconds until backing out slowly and splashing into a puddle on the way out.

Once the footsteps faded, I felt a brief sense of relief and let out the breath I'd held in since the moment I'd desperately settled into my hiding place. With hesitation, I began making my way down the tree, solidly landing two branches in the pouring rain. Though in a flash, my short-lived sense of safety vanished. My foot just…slipped, and didn't have the strength to catch myself. I hit every branch in my path on the fall down, each hit causing a bright flash in my eyes. The leaves and mud might've caught my fall if it weren't for the sizable rock situated just beneath the tree.

I felt my head crack on it and bounce off. I landed on my side in the mud, unable to feel any pain- only dizziness paired with the sensation of floating. A wet warmth trickled down the side of my head as all of my perceptions started to drift away. The faint smells of night air and rain on wood disappeared. The jarring taste of iron in my mouth and throat went away gradually. My fear faded, replaced with sadness and confusion. Soon after, I could no longer see the dark silhouettes of leaves on the ground, or the pool of blood expanding out from beneath my head. The tiny puddles that reflected a twinkling sliver of moonlight around me turned to blackness as I took one last breath. I couldn't feel any more raindrops pitter-pattering on my body. I only heard them, until everything turned to nothing.

***

One morning, as with every nightmare, my head jolted up from my pillow, drenched in sweat. After forcing myself to take several deep breaths through the discomfort of tightness in my chest, I turned my phone screen on next to me to check the time. This was the sixth nightmare, and the sixth time I'd woken up at exactly 5:04 in the morning. I let out an exasperated sigh and wiped my cold damp forehead with the sheet I'd just washed the night before.

I turned my bedside lamp on and looked into the mirror that hung on the wall to the right of my bed. Of course I was a mess. My roots were oily from sweat again. The dark circles under my eyes were even baggier than the night before, thanks to the exhaustion from adjusting to the recent changes in my life, and my interrupted sleep more nights than not. I pulled my hair up into a bun to cool off my neck.

I knew by now it would be impossible to get back to sleep no matter how hard I tried, so I decided to do the only two things I could think of in such an unsettled state- laundry and shower.

I slunk out of bed and threw my sheets together in a ball, reminding myself that it was all in my head. All the while, I ignored the reason why my nightmare was so aggressively repeating itself.

Nope.

I was stressed. And depressed.

And *nothing* else.

***

"Welcome home," my Aunt Olivia announced as she turned off the ignition of her new silver Acura.

I'd always imagined that the day I'd finally move to Newport would be a happy one to celebrate with my mom, but the reality was one of loneliness and grief. Any happiness I'd felt as the plane landed in Warwick that morning was buried under the heavy sense of emptiness I'd carried with me across the country all by myself. There was a twinge of relief as my aunt greeted me at baggage claim. As we drove across the Newport Pell Bridge at sunrise, I felt a level of safety in the familiarity of a place that held such a warm spot in my heart. We weaved through town on our way to the house and passed by several distinct colonial homes and old statues that were instantly recognizable to me from my childhood adventures of summers spent in Newport. This settled my anxiety a little bit deeper into my chest as I leaned back slowly into my seat, but it didn't leave. It never really would.

I stepped out of the car slowly in my hoodie and sweats, wiping my damp eyes with my sleeve and gazing up at the old home from the curb.

Charming and unassuming.

"Come on." Olivia smiled sympathetically, rubbing my back as she passed me. I watched as she weaved in front of me, her long, dark blonde hair in a high messy bun. The few grays she'd complained about in the car glimmered in the cloudy early morning light. She seemed to put the least amount of effort into her appearance, but somehow always looked more put together than anyone else. She killed the "no makeup" makeup look, and her minimalistic outfits were always presentable and clean. That morning she'd worn a navy and white striped button up with faded boyfriend jeans and tan loafers. When she threw clothes together she looked paparazzi-ready, but when I did it, I looked like I'd been living out in the wilderness for a decade.; Although, it was flattering for both of us whenever I was mistaken for her younger sister. In fact, everyone in our family had agreed that I looked much more like her than I did my own mom.

I stood admiring for a moment, then followed closely behind to the front steps of the house, sore and carsick.

Once I stood before the house and took a breath in, I was intimidated by the sheer size of it for just me alone. But I fell in love.

Olivia planted her boots in the ground, adjusted her tortoiseshell glasses, and crossed her arms. "Okay, what do you think?"

I quietly studied the structure for what felt like several long minutes. What *did* I think?

The house didn't stand out for any particular reason from the rest lined up along the street, but stood strong and established ahead of me. It didn't need to stand out in order to be unique from the rest; no hundred-year-old house in Newport was ever the same as another, unlike the newer homes where I'd come from. I was almost worried that with all of the money that Olivia had been putting in for renovations, the house would look way wealthier and higher-end than I deserved to live in. After all, her initial plan for the house before my life turned upside down was to rent it out as a vacation home online to tourists wishing to temporarily live the historically glamorous lifestyle that Newport was famous for.

The renovations were subtle, leaving room for the beauty of the original shell of the house to peek through. It didn't need to pretend to be fancier than it was, nor to paint a picture of a life it hadn't truly lived. It was sizable and confident in its foundations, yes, but humble. It wasn't one to flaunt to passers-by from the street, but I knew it had a story to tell to those who really cared.

Built on top of the red brick foundation was wooden siding that looked original, although there was a newer coat of light ivygreen paint on it. Along with that were clean white trim, shutters, and porch railings with four pillars holding up the porch awning. The pillars were basic, yet ornamented with simple, elegant, darker forest-green bracket moldings. The seven concrete steps that led up to the porch and front door were surrounded by blue hydrangeas on either side, and the railings along them were a beautiful black iron. The windows on both floors were clean, but without hiding the house's age; their borders and shutters were painted to match the white of the front door. This door had a window that would have allowed a peek into the entry of the home if it weren't for the cream lace curtain that hung from the inside. Below this intriguing little window was the number 31 in the same black iron as the porch step railing, and next to it, painted black to match, was a dainty mailbox attached to the house. Aunt Olivia and Uncle Ken had done such a wonderful job restoring the exterior of the home that I never would've guessed- if they hadn't told me- that it was purchased in a much more worn condition. Only the shingles on the roof showed wear and a tiny bit of damage, but it was unlikely that anyone would be inspecting it like I was. Not for a while, anyway.

I simply nodded and managed a small grin.

"Yeah?" Olivia laughed. "Built in 1900 *exactly*. Not too shabby for you?"

"No, I mean— I love it. I don't know how to thank you," I quietly reassured her, shaking my head and taking another step toward the house.

"By not thanking me anymore, Em. By just ... living and finding as much peace here as you can," Olivia explained, lightly patting my shoulder behind me. "Fair enough?"

I really tried to feel as much peace as I could about finally being in Newport for the foreseeable future, but guilt and grief kept me from fully experiencing it.

I cleared my throat. "Fair."

It wasn't fair, though.

We'd always wanted to move to Newport to be closer to Olivia, and because we felt such a strong attachment to it. My mom promised we'd make it out there together someday, but once she was diagnosed, all of the money we would've used to move was put toward medical bills and into my savings. My mom never had a chance, but there I was. On top of that, Aunt Olivia was now letting me live there for almost nothing- only three hundred dollars a month. That mere amount was being earned by working at Beach Brew Books, the used bookstore-slash-cafe that *she* owned. Olivia was paying herself, and we both knew that she understood that *very* well.

It was ridiculous, but we both knew that I desperately needed a fresh start closer to family. When she came to me with the idea I, of course, offered to pay her out of my personal savings I'd accumulated from my job back home and the money my mom had left for me. As expected, she adamantly refused and insisted that that money was to be saved for my own home and family someday. My uncle was a "fairly successful" —in his words, he was a humble man— realtor in addition to my aunt's two businesses. All that was left for me to pay for were pretty much groceries and my phone bill.

Oh, the perks of being a newly orphaned young woman.

"After all, I trust you a lot more in this house than I do several partying tourists every month." She opened her eyes wide and smiled. "Hey. Your uncle is gonna stop by every couple'a weekends to do the yards. I told him to just hire a gardener but I think he wants an excuse to see you."

"That's fine."

She smirked, then noticed my silence. "What's wrong?"

"Just wish she were here." I swallowed hard and walked up the steps to take my first look inside the house. There was a slight chill in my hand the moment I rested it on the iron railing.

Olivia followed me up the steps, and gently handed me the keys to the house. "I've told you this already, whether you believe it or not. She is."

***

Once I was out of the shower, I distracted myself with sudoku on my phone and a cup of coffee until my sheets dried. By eight o'clock, my bed was tidy again, and I headed down the stairs to the front door in my favorite navy blue Newport sweatshirt. It was loyal and cozy- warm enough for the crisp summer mornings that I rarely got to enjoy back in California, but not too thick that I'd be sweating on my lengthy walk.

As I went to grab my keys off the entry table, I noticed they weren't in the little clam shell dish I always left them in. They were lying on the floor right in front of the door like a dog antsy to go on a walk, as if my keys knew our routine.

Nope. No.

I swiped them up and swiftly slid out of the house, locking up behind me.

To Cliff Walk I went.

2.

FORTY STEPS

Brisk and overcast.

As I had every morning so far in Newport, I started out my day by walking down Bellevue Avenue to Cliff Walk, a walking path famous for picturesque views of the Atlantic ocean and the historic mansions that lined it. I held tightly onto the memories I shared with my mom in that place. It was sacred to me now. It was her favorite place in the world, so I felt I owed it to her to visit there every day. By that point, I wanted to avoid being in the house most of the day if I could because of the residual discomfort from my nightmares.

We'd visited Newport so often when I was a kid to visit Olivia and Ken, my mom's sister and brother-in-law, that I truly came to see it as my second home. The best summers of my childhood were spent there, and so many of the best memories of my mom were in Newport. She smiled the brightest there. Olivia's repeated offers to help us out financially in order to move out there were always appreciated, but mom felt she needed to earn that living on her own. Then she got her cancer prognosis and couldn't work anymore; shortly thereafter, she could hardly walk. She never got to open up the little gift shop and photo gallery she'd always dreamt of owning on Thames Street, which was considered "downtown" to the locals.

My route to Cliff Walk was the same every morning, with the same old lofi music playing through my earbuds, and as I'd started noticing, some of the same joggers and dog-walkers. Each day was an almost identical repeat of the one before, and I didn't think that needed to change.

As I turned the corner onto Narragansett Avenue, I relived the memory of picnics my mom and I had on the lawn of the Salve Regina University, which overlooked the ocean ahead of us. I was so deep into this daydream that I forgot to look up from the sidewalk. I hadn't noticed that someone else had also, in fact, forgotten to pay attention to their path. We collided at the corner and I was knocked to the cool sidewalk, clumsily landing on my butt.

"Oh, shit. I'm so sorry. I didn't even see you!" the stranger exclaimed. A couple of books she'd been carrying had fallen into my lap and onto the old cracked cement around me.

I quickly glanced around the intersection to make sure no one had seen our horrendously embarrassing meet-cute. Luckily it was still early and there was little traffic going up and down the long street.

"No, it's okay. I didn't see you either, so…" I picked up one of the books that she'd dropped and took a peek at it. I rolled my eyes as I read the cover aloud, *"Hauntings Within Newport's Dazzling Mansions."*

"Yeah, have you read it?" the stranger suddenly piped up and reached for the book in my hand. "I mean— I know that there's like … a ton of books like this, but Cain dives deep. I don't know how she finds so many people to share their experiences but they're so much better than the other basic —"

"I don't need to read it. My aunt's told me those stories a million times over," I mumbled and got back on my feet.

"Oh. So you guys are into it, too." She reached down to pick up her other book on herbs.

"Nooo, no. She's just the one who wrote it." I sighed.

"Seriously? That's fuckin' awesome."

"Mhm." I brushed my pants off. "A little muggy out for that jacket."

The young woman stayed bent down to fix her shoelace. "No, I gotta go to the library in style."

"I guess I'm always just too hot." I shrugged as I watched her recover.

She chuckled. "Ooh. We love the confidence. I'm Willow, by the way. It's nice to —"

The moment Willow stood back up and met eyes with me, she froze. I faced her, taking in her wavy shoulder-length dark auburn hair. The bright blue tips of her hair matched her eyes, which remained wide open. Her freckles stood out on her glowing light almond skin. To my surprise, she didn't move or even blink for close to five seconds.

A very long, awkward five seconds.

"Um."

Willow snapped back to reality and I wondered if she needed actual help or if she was just socially awkward. "Are you okay?"

Oh. She's starstruck by proxy.

"I'm fine," Willow replied robotically with one blink, and after a second of stillness, scrambled to get her stuff together.

"Can I do anything to — I mean—"

"No, sorry. I hafta go," Willow interrupted and rushed right past me. Her hair bounced against her neck and the collar of her yellow suede jacket as she fled off in the opposite direction of my path.

Was I rude?

Did I hurt her?

No, I was the one who fell. It's my ass that's sore.

...Am I okay?

I tried to push the last two uncomfortable minutes out of my head so I could focus on honoring my mom again.

After several yards of walking off that weird exchange with Willow, I reached Forty Steps on Cliff Walk and exhaled deeply. Luckily, no tourists were lined up to go down the steps that led closer to the crashing waves. It was still early, so very few people were out. Instead, it was quiet, and the steps greeted me alone.

Good morning.

I made my way down the slippery rock steps to reach the small viewing area at the bottom, and I stared off into the ocean waves below to revisit the memory of saying goodbye to my mom, as I did every day.

***

"Are you ready?" Aunt Olivia softly placed her hand on my shoulder. The day after I'd arrived to live in Newport, we'd decided to release some of my mom's ashes over the ocean at Forty Steps.

I couldn't find it in myself to hold my tears back, no matter how hard I tried. I'd been too exhausted since leaving my home in California to really let go and sob. But in this moment, the raw pain of losing her hit me almost just as strongly as it had the day she died. I clenched the little satin bag of ashes in my hand. Aunt Olivia had another in hers. Both of them were deep ocean blue, of course.

"I can't do it, Liv." I let out my broken words in between sniffles and tears.

"Yes, you can. She wanted this, you know. Part of her is always with you, too. This isn't all of her — it."

This isn't all of her. Such a disconcerting sentence to hear about your mother.

I glanced over at my aunt without moving my head. "You don't want to keep any?"

"Why would I keep that from you? It's yours, and it's special. She's your *mama.* She wanted to be with the two things she loved most in this world" — She reassured me —"*you* ... and here."

I stared deeply into the ocean below. I felt one with the waves that crashed rhythmically against the jagged rocks below. I tried to stay strong but waves of numbness alternated with intense emotional pain. It hit harder every time I thought of saying goodbye, every time I attempted to comprehend the fact that the woman who raised me was now reduced to a small amount of dust in a dainty little bag in my hand.

"It's hard."

"I know it is. But it isn't *really* goodbye."

I paused, staring out at the sea foam. "I made the right choice coming here. Just guilty."

"There's no need to feel that way." Liv sighed. "Easier said than done, but your mom would've loved this for you. She always wanted to come back and never *ever* leave. She just couldn't in this life. But now she's here, and you're here, and I am so *so* thankful that you are." We looked out at the horizon together for what seemed like hours packed into a couple moments.

"I'm gonna stay for a while, promise." With a sharp deep breath, I lifted my chin up and untied the bag, pouring the ashes gently over the stone barrier into the waves.

She deserved grace.

Aunt Liv watched me and then followed. Together we stood as the ashes dispersed into the breeze and over the water. Once the ashes were gone, I burst into tears and hid my face in Olivia's shoulder. She hugged me so tightly. I wanted to melt into her and disappear.

"I've got you."

I felt weak walking back up. We stayed there for over an hour that day, and she let me cry into her lap on a bench at the top of the steps. We both wore my mom's favorite rose perfume that day. All I could smell was her, so I pretended I was laying on her instead. I think Liv knew that. It was a different level of pain that I could never wish on anyone.

"You're home now, hun."

***

I stared blankly ahead at the crashing waves as they hit a lone rock further out in the ocean. While I was thinking back on that day, dark clouds had crawled overhead, the water a deeper murkier blue. It looked like it was going to start raining soon, and for the rest of the day, too. Right before I started back up the steps to let a couple have their turn visiting the small viewing space, I caught the scent of roses as I inhaled. It wasn't a simple generic rose, but mixed with an unmistakable comfort. A personal scent. I instantly thought of my mother's perfume, but explained it away as my memories mixing with the famous rose bushes down the way on Cliff Walk. It hurt too much to hold onto the hope that she was still with me.

On the walk back toward Bellevue it started to pour, just as I expected. I tried to pick up my pace as the clouds got closer, but I wasn't fast enough to beat it. I hadn't brought an umbrella, either, because that was just one more thing to hold. If I was rained on, I'd welcome it.

Once the rain started, I slowed back down and accepted that I was going to be soaked the rest of the way. I felt at peace focusing on the bittersweet comfort of being in one of my mom's final resting places. The rain was refreshing on my tired face, so I removed my hood and soaked in the moment- even if I got pneumonia from it.

This cleansing walk ended when a bright blue Prius drove down Bellevue, then made a U-turn to head in the same direction that I was walking in. It slowed beside me and I felt a ping in my chest.

It followed me as I walked faster, and I glanced back at the car every few seconds. The moment I started to jog, the driver of the Prius honked.

I wasn't sure whether to stop or run faster.

The car honked again more aggressively.

I froze as the car sped up a little to catch up to me.

I'm about to be kidnapped. On Bellevue.

I heard the driver halt and roll down the passenger side window next to me.

"Are you *really* running from the safety of a warm, dry car right now?"

At first, I only turned my eyes to glimpse at the car, but my vision was blocked by strands of wet hair.

"Emma!"

The voice sounded familiar. My heart skipped again once I finally placed it.

"Hey, remember me … from earlier?"

I hesitantly stopped and turned my body to face the car, relieved at the fact that I probably wasn't being abducted, but cringing that I was having another interaction with someone I now paired with embarrassment. "Yeah," I said over the sound of rain hitting the roof of the car.

Willow leaned and shouted over the passenger seat, "What the hell are you doing out here?"

"Walking."

"Where?"

"Home."

There was silence for a moment.

"You're soaked." Willow looked me up and down with a quiet chuckle.

"I know."

Silence followed yet again.

"You hungry?"

I squinted. "What?" I asked even more loudly over the rain, now pouring more aggressively than before.

"Are … you hungry!"

"I guess." I shrugged. It was a little early for lunch but I hadn't eaten anything that morning unless coffee counted as a meal.

"Get in!"

"I'm gonna get your seat wet."

Thunder sounded in the distance.

Willow tilted her head and raised a brow.

"Fine."

"I have a towel in the backseat," she added.

Of course I should've expected her to be prepared. After all, it seemed more unusual for someone not to have a pile of beach towels in their backseat during this time of year in Newport.

"You aren't kidnapping me, are you?" I was only half joking, but forced the slightest grin as an attempt to ease the awkwardness.

"Oh I *am*, all the way to the Creamery!" With a grunt, Willow reached over and opened the car door for me. She grabbed a large beach towel from the back to lay it over the passenger seat.

I stood for a second, a little anxiety still lingering in my throat and chest about getting in the car with a stranger- even someone who looked to be my age.

"Okay, okay! Now you're letting rain into my car. Are you getting in or not? Because I can just buy myself dinosaur chicken instead."

"*Dinosaur chicken?*" Willow needed to say no more. I rushed into the car despite the initial intimidation and plopped myself onto the folded up black and white polka dot beach towel.

"Welcome aboard."

3.

DINOSAUR CHICKEN, RAINBOW VANILLA, AND DEAD PEOPLE

The drive to Middletown— a small town on the same island — was short but made longer by the uncomfortable quiet. Once we arrived at the Newport Creamery it was already thundering more loudly frequently, which made me smile internally. Storms always balanced out my spirit, and oddly took the edge off of being in close quarters with a stranger. Willow swung into a parking spot right in front. We got out and slammed the doors shut in sync.

"Come on, come on!" Willow spat as she rushed to the entrance and held the door open for me.

As I reached the door, she shouted, "Wait!" and let the door to the restaurant slowly close behind her while she ran to the trunk of her car. She grabbed a balled up rainbow tie-dye sweatshirt out of it.

"Take this. You look ridiculous." Willow returned quickly and held it out to me.

"Thanks." I nodded subtly, took the sweatshirt, and opened the door for us to enter the dry, warm restaurant. I was immediately struck by the memories of coming here all the time with mom and Liv on summer evenings. I was amused by the vivid image, and by the fact that another grown adult seemed to enjoy dinosaur chicken just as much as I did.

One of the waitresses lazily looked up from her phone to greet us, pausing to look me up and down. "Two?" she asked, shoving her phone in her apron pocket to grab two menus from the counter in front of her. Business was slow, so we'd get a seat in no time.

"Yeah, but we don't need a menu," Willow declared.

"Well wait a sec. What if I wanted to …" I started.

The waitress raised a brow unenthusiastically and slowly blinked from Willow to me.

"Excuse her. She forgot an umbrella today." Willow smiled widely at the waitress and then turned to look seriously at me. "You need to go change. Looks like you missed the 'women and children first' memo on the Titanic."

"Kay, no menus." The waitress rolled her eyes and brushed her day-three brown hair behind her ear. "This way."

"Thank you" —Willow glanced at the name tag—"Autumn."

We followed the waitress back to a booth.

"Oh, good! There you go." Willow loosely gestured to the restroom door not far from our seats.

I shook my head and pushed the bathroom door open, looking back at my quirky lunch date before walking in.

Willow sat down in the booth and grinned brightly at the waitress, who didn't bother to return the gesture. She simply chomped her gum as she asked, "Okay so you *do* know what you want? Or …"

I entered the bathroom to pull myself together a little. I pulled my damp stringy hair into a messy bun, and quickly changed into the dry sweatshirt that was given to me. It was too bright and busy for me, and I wasn't a fan of tie-dye. At all. I dropped my arms at my sides and tilted my head. I blew a raspberry as I looked into the mirror. It didn't look *that* bad, and it *did* say "Newport" on it. On second thought, it was pretty comfy.

I debated kindly declining a meal and calling a ride. What was there to talk about? It was easy to assume that she was only hoping for a connection to one of her favorite authors.

But did I really want to go back to the house yet?

No.

I took a deep breath, reluctantly acknowledging the pull in my gut to go sit down. I spent a few more moments of quiet in the surprisingly tidy but dimly lit restroom. Whether it was hunger or actual curiosity about Willow's intentions, I decided to suck it up, ball up my wet clothes, and exit the bathroom to join Willow at the booth.

"Welcome back." Willow observed as she sipped on a glass of ice water. "That's a little better." She tilted her head and nodded once.

"Thanks." I slid into the seat. "It's not my style, but it's pretty comfy, so … I guess it'll work for now."

"Yep." Willow slid the straw out of her mouth.

My eyes scanned the restaurant, looking at anything other than Willow. She sat quietly, gazing down at her phone but never unlocking the screen. After a few minutes of alternating between looking down into my lap and at the other customers, I found a twinge of confidence, just enough to open up a conversation and break the silence. "So … what are you gonna order?"

With that, the waitress returned with two plates. I looked down in front of me after Autumn slid a plate my way. It was exactly what I'd ordered every time I came here as a kid: dinosaur chicken with onion rings instead of fries, and two cups of barbecue sauce on the side. I scoffed in disbelief. "Okay."

The waitress walked away briefly.

"What?" Willow asked in monotone.

"Funny, the only thing missing is—"

Autumn returned with a bowl. "Here." She set a dish of crazy rainbow vanilla ice cream down on the table and sauntered away.

"She deserves a raise for that personality." Willow rolled her eyes.

I gazed down at the bright blue, pink, and yellow swirls in my ice cream. When I was a kid, I'd always ask the waiter to scoop as much blue and pink as they could; yellow wasn't my thing back then, and therefore had no place in my dessert.

"Yum." Willow clapped. "Let's *eat* ! I'm starving."

I stared at her as she dove in for her fries, smothering them in ketchup before taking a bite. No, something was majorly off. I hadn't told Willow my order …

… *or* my name.

"How did you know to order this?" I shifted my gaze up from the food in front of me to Willow.

Had she cyber-stalked me? Had Liv revealed this very specific information in any of her books? There was no reason to; none of them were about her personal life. I'd never read them, though, so I couldn't know for sure.

There was a beat of silence. Willow shoved a fry in her mouth. "Lucky guess."

"Bullshit," I spat impulsively.

"I don't know. You told me in the car then, right?" Willow shrugged.

"Which one is it?" Almost nothing had been said in the car after I'd gotten in, and that was *way* too specific a guess. A medium cheeseburger meal was a guess.

We locked eyes, Willow still chewing. "Well, bon appetit." She chuckled nervously before popping a whole nugget into her mouth.

"How do you know my name? You don't look familiar to me, but you're acting like you know me. Do I know you from somewhere?"

"Earlier today."

"No— I mean— did we hang out when we were younger? Am I missing something?"

"Maybe." Willow nodded her head toward my plate. "Go ahead. Rex or Pterodactyl?" She began eating faster.

"Tell me how you knew that, though. Seriously," I finally bit into a piece of chicken. I didn't want to seem too comfortable, but I couldn't resist the hunger. Plus, it was the perfect meal. If I were on death row, I'd choose it as my final meal. Pathetic, but true.

Willow stopped chewing and swallowed slowly.

The first bite of dinosaur chicken was so good that I decided to extend a kind gesture. I clearly wasn't getting an answer, but I thought I might get more information if I took the friendlier route. "Look, I'm sorry to be rude but … this morning was awkward."

Willow sighed. "Well it's about to get a lot worse than that, so I'm glad you're enjoying your food," she announced.

"*Huh* ?"

"I weirded out on you this morning, I know. I'm sorry. But it was for a good reason." She chewed. "That's why I invited you here. I wanna talk about it." Willow leaned back against the booth.

"What is there to talk about?" I shrugged. "Is it because I'm your favorite author's niece?" I was only half joking.

"Um. No," Willow answered slowly and shook her head as she chewed. "She's a close third though."

"Okay." I waited for her to continue, focusing down on my food again instead of looking up at her.

"Alright, here we go. Please, just hold all your questions 'til the end, kay? Or I'll lose my train of thought."

I stared, and then nodded hesitantly with chicken in my mouth. I'd had enough with the anticipation. Regret about staying there slowly crept into my chest.

Willow leaned forward and took a deep breath. "I'm sensitive, too."

I couldn't help but to burst out laughing. "What?"

"C'mon. You know what I'm talking about."

I shifted in my seat. "No, I really don't." My chuckle died down.

"No bullshit. You know."

There was a pause as Willow shoved a fry into her mouth, followed by a long hard sip of water. After a quenched sigh she whispered, "I don't need to spell this out for you, do I?"

I was speechless, not because I didn't believe her. I just didn't want to deal with it. I didn't know how.

"We're here eating this delicious junk food because when we met this morning, it happened to me with you. Only, with you, I saw a lot more than usual."

"What happened?"

"Listen. Most of the time, it's just brief, quick, *gone*," she snapped. "But with you … with you, it was like a rapid fire slideshow of moments in your life. *That* … never happens."

I jutted my jaw out and furrowed my brow with the dreadful gut feeling about where this conversation was going. "So … what?"

"What do you mean 'so what'?'" She paused. "I don't take everyone I pick up on to lunch, dude. It wasn't just parts of your life. Some of the bits were shared. My life and your life combined."

"Are you hitting on me?" I scoffed.

Willow rolled her eyes. "Are you stupid? No."

"Just making sure … " I murmured.

"I mean— you wish." Willow yawned.

I looked up at Willow for the first time during the exchange. I had half a mind to walk right out. "What then? Is this you telling me you want to be my friend or something?"

"Drop it," she said.

"Drop what?"

"The denial."

"No."

Willow raised her brow and smirked. "Then you admit you're in denial?"

"What's your point?"

"We share a lot of memories— or I mean— we will." Willow nodded.

"I'm sorry but what? I just met you. Am I supposed to take what you're saying as gospel?" I inched closer to the edge of the booth.

"I don't think I said that."

"Can you get to your point, please?"

"Well, thank you for still sitting."

"Sure."

"But yeah, I'm basically saying we're going to be close friends."

My eyes closed slowly. "Can I go?"

"I'm your ride, but whatever." Willow shrugged.

"What else is there, then?"

"You're also wearing my sweatshirt."

I furrowed my brows and jutted my jaw forward.

"A lot, Emma. There's a lot else. Stop pretending like you don't know." Willow stared directly into my eyes as if she were studying my every muscular response. "And don't look at me like *I'm* crazy when you think *you're* just as crazy."

"I'm gonna go." I slid out of the booth.

"I'm sorry. It's not easy to just bring this up with someone I don't know." Willow brushed her dark auburn hair behind one ear.

"You're right. You don't know me." I shook my head defensively. "I'm done with … whatever this is." I waved my hands around. "Thank you for lunch, though. Really."

"Why are you leaving?" Willow scoffed.

"Stop, I don't wanna hear anything else." I grabbed my balled-up clothes in a rush.

"I know, but I wanna help you," Willow mustered with a mouth full of food.

"I don't need help." I gave Willow a pensive look before turning around toward the bathroom. "You can have your sweatshirt back. I'll go change."

"That's fine. I'll just go ahead and take care of the tip, too," Willow muttered.

I whipped around. "No, no. You can't *do* that. You can't *pull* that on me. It was really nice of you to offer lunch, but you can't just meet me and save me from the rain just to ... corner me and dump this shit on me and expect me to just—" I paused, shaking my head with a scoff. Deep down, I felt bad for leaving, but I wasn't ready to hear what Willow had to say about her "sensitivity" to anything. I never would be. "Forget it. I need to go."

"Fine, just keep the sweatshirt then. That one's old anyway," Willow spoke calmly.

I passed three booths on my way to the door before I heard her voice from behind me. "Ugh. I know you saw her the night of the memorial."

It felt like my heart stopped right there in that restaurant.

***

I sat alone on my bed four nights after my mom died, and two hours after her memorial. I let aunt Liv shower first because I didn't have the energy to yet. She and my uncle had flown out a couple weeks prior. The second they heard mom was getting extremely ill and very quickly, they were jumping on the next plane out to California. They wouldn't allow either of us to face the rest of this cancer alone once they knew she didn't have much longer. They helped plan the memorial, and stood next to me the entire time, along with a few other family members. Liv and Ken were the only ones I wanted staying the night, though. Uncle Ken was at the grocery store for us, and the other family members had either headed home or gotten a hotel. My few friends from school- who I'd distanced myself from during the escalation of my mom's cancer- had gone home right after the service. My grandparents had passed away years ago on both sides. My parents were separated before I was born, and my dad had died in a car accident right before I turned two. I couldn't remember him, and I had no siblings to share these losses with. Aside from Ken and Olivia, my life was pretty lonely to begin with, and painfully lonely after my mom died.

I stared directly down the dark hall from the edge of my bed, drained and easily lost in thought. I focused whatever energy I had left on my mother's bedroom door. It was closed, but I could see that, through the crack under the door, the light had turned on in the room. I sighed. I thought that Liv was showering in the bigger guest bathroom, but assumed that she had changed her mind and decided to shower in my mom's room instead as a way to feel closer to her sister.

The door began to open slowly, as if my aunt didn't want to disturb me. "Liv, you don't need to rush, it's okay." She'd only gone to shower less than ten minutes ago.

There was no response from her. Instead, the door continued to open smoothly and quietly. Once it was open completely, no one came out.

"Liv?" A single creak in the wood floor made my shoulders tense up, and after several seconds of silence, a figure walked out of the doorway.

My mom took two steps into the hallway and gazed at me vacantly. I was paralyzed with emotions once I made contact with her glazed over eyes. There was no expression on her face, yet I could feel her love and sadness. She appeared just as she had before she'd gotten sick. She looked full, healthy … except for her eyes. They were glossy and cloudy.

Her slightly graying golden hair rested on her shoulders, and she wore a beautiful handmade dress she'd bought in a small boutique in Newport one summer. It was turquoise and royal blue with a tan fringe on the bottom. She called it her "artsy beach time" dress. Her favorite.

She didn't move any closer to me, and I wasn't sure that I wanted her to. We gazed at each other, both motionless, until I could muster up a crushed, "Love you," that was met with the very slightest of smiles on her face.

I felt tears well up in my bottom eyelids, but couldn't find the strength to blink and release them.

Within a fraction of a second, the hallway light came on. It felt like being pummeled by a ton of bricks and before I could fully comprehend what I was seeing, she was gone. Liv came walking down the hall through the exact spot that my mother had been standing in just a second prior. When she died, we both knew what was coming, but this I hadn't foreseen. Not from her. I finally blinked, releasing a stream of tears down my cheek.

"Honey, I'm so sorry, did you call me a minute ago? I just got out." Olivia squeezed her light brown hair with a towel as she stood in my doorway.

I shook my head rigidly.

"Oh, honey." Olivia threw her towel over the door and rushed to me for a hug. "I'm so sorry. I'm glad I hurried. I didn't want you to be alone too long tonight — unless you want it, of course," she draped her arms around me. "I'm here with you."

I lost myself again, staring down the hall and half hoping mom would appear again for me. She never did.

"Em, I think tomorrow morning we should talk about where to go from here. I have an idea." My aunt rubbed my back and didn't say anything else. She'd already accepted that she wouldn't get a response that night.

***

I looked up and around at all the patrons and staff in the creamery. They all craned their heads toward us for a moment, aside from one man who wisely minded his own business. I was grateful for him, but glared at the rest of them after they went back to their own activities. I was worried what else Willow would throw out at me publicly if I continued to head out, so to save myself the embarrassment I turned around.

As I reapproached the booth and stood in front of her, Willow pursed her lips in between bites. I hoped that she could tell that she'd caused my head to pound and cheeks to flush red hot. "I'm sorry," Willow said after a silent stand-off.

I was still standing above her. "For what? For outing me just now? Or for conning me with lunch just to push your woo-woo shit on me?"

"My woo-woo shit, okay. Do you wanna sit back down?"

"No."

"Come on."

"Stop."

"Do you wanna take a seat?"

"*No.*"

"Okay but … do you believe me?"

I bit the inside of my cheek and glared at her. She remained calmly studying me. With a huff, I sat back down in my seat, slowly reaching for a dinosaur nugget. I chewed while spacing out on my brightly colored ice cream.

"So why don't you believe it about yourself?" Willow challenged.

Something back in the kitchen dinged.

"I don't … not believe it," I said with a nervous mouthful of food.

"Why do you refuse to acknowledge it then?" Willow paused to let out a sigh. "You're not alone. It's only what and how we see that's different. We carry the same burden, Emma."

"So you agree it's a burden?" I remarked.

"I mean, I know it's hard to swallow, and it's surely not easy to live with …"

"It's insane." I shook my head.

"You're not, though."

I swallowed.

"I'm not trying to sound pushy but you should really come to terms with it." Willow chomped into more fries. "There's nothing you or I can do to get rid of it or change it. I don't like seeing things that I have zero control over. A few weeks ago at Shaw's, I brushed hands with this cashier to get my change and I saw that she was gonna get in an accident in the same clothes she was wearing that day. Or this one time, I was sitting on a bench at the park and *knew* that the couple who sat on it before me were arguing bad and probably headed toward divorce. But I can't block it out, and if I ignored it, I'm positive I would be miserable, like you."

"I'm not miserable."

"If you say so. But you're using all of your energy trying to kill something that isn't gonna die and you've been doing that for a long time. Trust me, you can't block it out forever. Eventually it's gonna eat you up, or something's gonna happen that's gonna force you to confront it … So why haven't you just let it in?" Willow pleaded.

I stared blankly past Willow at the wall near the restroom. A painting of a cow in a bright green field stared back at me, almost as if it demanded an answer from me, too. I debated whether or not to contribute any further to the conversation. "Why do you care? I'm just trying to get by. I'm not involving myself in what I don't understand."

"You don't even wanna try?"

"Listen … I'm still grieving. I've been through enough. I'm just trying to start over. The last thing I need right now is to be pestered even more by the reminder that people die. It's scary, it's awful, and … I can't help them even if I wanted to."

"Why not?"

"I haven't been forced to confront it yet, and I don't see why I'd suddenly need to now just because you showed up."

"It barely has anything to do with *me*." Willow leaned against the back of the booth slowly and crossed her arms. There was quiet between us again as she scanned the restaurant and suddenly fixated on one spot by the front window near the entrance. "Emma, how many people are in here right now— not counting us?"

I scoffed. "Seriously?"

"Dead." Willow raised a brow.

Before scanning, I took a deep breath and matched Willow's posture.

There was Autumn the waitress, scowling as she wiped a table down.

Two cooks, one flipping a burger, and one pushing a plate onto the serving counter for another waitress, whose warm smile was much more worthy of a tip. Where was *she* when we walked in?

An active-looking and slightly disheveled young couple who seemed like they were taking a break from a jog to eat some salads.

A single older gentleman patiently waiting for his order to be taken.

A group of three elderly women who resembled the Golden Girls, quietly gossiping with their coffees.

"Ten," I answered matter-of-factly.

Willow smirked. "Are you sure?"

"I can count."

"So can I," Willow replied quickly.

I did as she challenged, only to pause and lose all of my confidence in the first answer I gave once I re-examined the single man across the dining area. He remained calmly waiting for his order to be taken. Come to think of it, he'd been waiting since we'd walked in. He had no menu, no drink, not even a set of silverware. The table was completely cleared off, and had been the entire time. He was a pale middle-aged man slumped idly in the booth, his eyes cloudy and glazed, much like my mother's were that night. The friendlier-looking waitress approached his booth with a broom, ignoring him as she swept.

"Waiting for an order that never was never will be taken," Willow said.

"You can see him?"

"No, but I brushed the booth as we walked back here. I can feel them sometimes, but I can't see them like you and Joel can. I just get glimpses in my head that stay kinda burned into my vision for a second. I feel energy. You probably would've known right away too if you'd paid any attention to him" —Willow pursed her lips— "Or your ability."

"Who's Joel?"

"Mmm, not yet." Willow cleared her throat.

"Huh?"

"Regret," she spat, looking toward the man's booth.

"What?" I asked, continuing to look at him, and tensing up as he slowly moved his head to meet my gaze. His sad empty eyes didn't blink or threaten me. Although I wanted to look away, I couldn't bring myself to.

"There's lots of regret sitting in that booth," Willow declared.

"Why is he here?" I whispered.

Willow focused on the booth for several moments. "Mm." She shrugged and took another bite. "I don't know. I can't force stuff to pop up. I just felt guilt and … stuckness."

"Stuckness," I repeated and nodded once.

"When I touched the seat earlier, I just saw him kinda fall over and grab his chest. My guess is that he probably came here a *whole* lot. I don't see why else he'd be here. I'd go to the White Horse if I had to choose a restaurant to haunt. I don't know." Willow let the words roll off her tongue.

I nodded slowly, noticing his gut slightly falling out from beneath his sweater. "You act like it's easy."

"Never easy. Just natural."

"Yeah but … you're just so nonchalant about it."

"It's all I know. Call me desensitized."

"How can you be so chill? What's the point?"

"In what?"

"Seeing them, in you doing what you do. If there's nothing we can do to change anything, what's the point? It just gets in the way of … everything. It gets in the way of living."

"Uh-uh. Wrong, friend," Willow shook her head as she chewed. "It *is* living."

"How?"

"We may not be able to change what's happened or what's gonna happen … to anyone — living *or* dead. But it doesn't mean we can't help them. Everything happens for a reason. I firmly believe that."

"Really?"

"Uh, yeah. Even if we can't understand why. We- you- were given these abilities for a reason. I can't prevent things from happening, but I can plant tiny seeds that will help them find peace. That poor woman I accidentally touched at the market … I saw the impact of that car crash. There was *no* way she was gonna survive that. Sooo … I told her that she had a beautiful smile and that she was doing an amazing job. I told her thank you and to drive safe that night in the rain. That's pretty much all I could do, but everything matters.

Even if it doesn't change a thing. If you accept it as a gift and *not* a burden, you can find peace within yourself. And you can help them find peace, too. You see those who we *assume* are gone. But they're here like us, just lacking a physical body. They're people too. They're only lonely because very few can or *will* acknowledge them. But you…" Her eyes widened.

I nodded softly at the man, and he gave one stiff nod back.

"Some are stuck, some stay by choice. But so often, there's pain and anger behind that choice. You have the gift of being able to guide them. *So* many people spend time trying to adopt a sensitivity to the other side, and a lot of people pretend they have it for the money and screen time. You … you're the real deal, and you should learn to own it."

I looked at Willow, then back to the man, who had vanished from his booth in a matter of seconds. I exhaled deeply.

"He's gone now, right? A lot of the time they need help or closure. Sometimes though, like that guy … I think they just want someone to know they're still here."

I gulped. "How do you know so much about it?"

"I really don't know too much more than you do. But I've had this ability all my life. And the ghost stuff, I have Joel. And books—the few that are written by people who actually care. Like Amy Bruni. Or … your aunt! She doesn't even *have* a gift. But you can tell she really cares about sharing their stories and honoring the history."

"Who's Amy Bru—"

"Ugh, what a shame. Whatever, it doesn't matter right now. What matters is that, like I said, you're not alone."

"Again, who's Joel?"

"My best friend, might as well be my brother. He's *exactly* like you, girl. We can help you accept it, or at least just support you. Few people have gifts as strong as ours."

"What does that mean?"

"I'll know when you know."

I finished my brightly-colored ice cream with one giant bite.

"Most people can only tap into it every now and then, and that's if they *really* try. We have it like that, times like … a hundred. And for a reason. I mean, I don't know what that reason is, but…"

I had no friends in Newport, but I hadn't yet felt like I needed any.

"You do need them, though." Willow touched the top of my hand briefly, seeming to effortlessly reply to my private thought. "Friends … No one should go through it all alone."

4.

THE DOOR IS ALWAYS OPEN

It was a quarter to three when we finally walked out of the creamery. We'd said little to each other the rest of the time we were there. We'd made an attempt at small talk, but it didn't seem to be too successful; It couldn't have been after such an intense conversation for two strangers. The rain had softened to a sprinkle, and it looked like Newport might've gotten a break from the deep gray clouds for a little while.

"I don't really think I need to ask, but you want a ride home, right?" Willow asked quietly once we reached the front of her car.

I looked up from the wet cement. "Actually, I think I'm fine. I like to walk, and I need space to … seriously some process things."

Willow gave a disappointed smile and nodded. "That's a long walk, but okay." She unlocked the car and opened her driver's side door. "I get it."

I was ready to be alone, but had one last question I needed to ask before turning away. "Was that all you saw this morning? Just the stuff we talked about?"

Willow furrowed her brows before giving a single nod. "Yeah, why?"

I nodded back, not entirely accepting that answer as it was delivered. "Just curious."

Willow gave a small smile and threw her bag in the passenger seat.

"Well, I'll see you around." I turned to start my trek across the parking lot to the sidewalk of the main road.

Willow stood outside her car for a moment, staring up at the clouds. "Kay," she whispered to herself after a deep exhale. I peeked back for a second to see her sitting in her car. She laid her forehead down on the steering wheel after turning on the ignition.

Halfway across the parking lot, I felt a peculiar growing pull to turn back. Although I wanted to go home and be alone for the entire rest of the day, I couldn't deny that feeling my gut. Was it curiosity? Guilt? Or an unfamiliar, undeniable sense of belonging?

Whatever it was, it was so strong that I just couldn't bring myself to take another step away.

No one should go through it all alone.

I patted the tops of my thighs, then clenched my fists.

"Dammit." I let out a breath and turned to face the Prius. I knew very well what I needed to do and I hated it. Just as I decided to step toward Willow's car, it began backing out of its spot. She didn't notice me as reached the parking lot exit.

I checked to make sure no one was watching and when the coast was clear, I jogged over to the passenger side door of the moving vehicle and knocked on it twice. "Wait." I waved a hand in front of the window to get her attention.

The car broke to a halt at the exit of the lot, and Willow looked up with a grin. The window rolled down. "Ride?"

"Yeah. I don't know what I was thinking. It'll be like an hour long walk."

Willow, once again, leaned over to open the door. "The door is always open for you."

I jumped in and clicked my seatbelt on. As we pulled out, Willow looked in the rearview mirror and cleared her throat. "And I changed my mind. I want my sweatshirt back."

***

Willow's car pulled into the front portion of the long driveway that extended to an old garage in the back of the property. The quiet ride back was only made less awkward by the soft pitter patter of rain against the windows.

Willow looked up through the windshield at the house. "So, this is it huh?"

"Yeah." I noticed that the front door was cracked open slightly and my heart leapt into my throat. There was no way. I'd locked it earlier that morning and made *sure* of it before I left. Maybe Aunt Liv had gone in for some reason, but she would've texted. Someone could've broken in. More importantly, was that better or worse than the alternative?

"It's beautiful," Willow remarked as we got out of the car.

"Very." I looked up and around at the house for any other signs of a disturbance, but there were none. "Um … Wanna come in for a few?"

Willow's eyes narrowed on me for a moment. "Yeah."

We made our way up the wet cement porch steps. Willow grazed her hand across the iron railing.

"Do you know anything about its history?"

"Not much. Liv hasn't told me anything really. Why?"

"Each house has a story. Especially in this town."

"She just bought it to turn into a vacation rental, but you've read her books. I'm sure she looked into it either before or after buying it. I can ask her sometime."

Willow studied the front exterior of the house until I pushed the door open completely. She shot her head toward it and leaned over to look inside as it creaked. "Nice wood." She chuckled while she inspected the entry door.

"It's sturdy. So I don't get why..." I trailed off, taking two steps into the small foyer.

I turned to see that Willow hadn't followed me inside, but was instead peering in hesitantly. "What?"

Willow straightened up. "Nothing. Just don't wanna intrude."

I jutted my head forward and gestured for her. "I invited you. You're fine."

Willow clicked the button on her key to lock the car and took a step in, making sure the door latched behind her.

I quickly made my way through the narrow foyer and further into the house to open all the curtains in the living room. The soft, dim outside light shone in through the old windows. The wood panels on the bottom half of the walls were from at least the 1970's, and the faded floral wallpaper was peeling in just a couple spots toward the corners of the ceiling. The tan carpet wasn't original, but was dated nonetheless. Liv and Ken had only gotten to the outside renovations so far, but I was in no position to be picky.

"It's a little ugly, right?" I chuckled, noticing Willow observing closely.

"Not if you're into the antique feel," she replied.

"I mean I am. But it's still kinda— I don't know. Maybe that's what makes it charming though. Sorry about the mess of boxes. I've been lazy about unpacking." I gritted my teeth.

"No, I love the boxes. Nice touch. Keep 'em there." Willow winked and brushed some of her hair behind her ear.

So far, the living room was lightly furnished with a gray L-shaped couch and the small round coffee table in front of it. I'd left my expert level word-search book and phone charger there. The end table against the wall next to the built-in bookshelf had just one small lamp on it. The only thing missing that would've made it warmer and cozier was a fireplace, but that was- oddly enough- in the dining room that I'd probably use once.

"It's a cute setup so far." Willow looked from the living room over to the staircase back in the foyer. She left the room and went to the base of the stairs, peeking up at the hall above. Although it was daytime, the hallway upstairs was always dark and looming. "It'll all come together."

"I should show you the backyard. It's gorgeous. I don't understand why my aunt is letting me live here for so cheap. I mean— I know why, but she's ripping herself off."

"What's your rent?"

I chuckled and headed down the small hallway beyond the living room that led to a short staircase down to the back door. "Three hundred."

"What?"

"Three hundred," I repeated and laughed gratefully as I opened the back door that led to the screened-in patio.

"Jesus. Her books must be doing well, then."

I chuckled. "No kidding. It's ridiculous."

Willow followed me out onto the covered patio out back. Through the windows in front of us was a large lawn, but further past the worn down, wooden backyard fencing was a forest behind the house. It was Newport, so a forest could only be *so* big, but it was a woods nonetheless.

"Kinda cool, huh?" I scratched my nose. "We don't get ... like ... bears or anything though, right? I don't wanna end up stumbling across any wild animals in the yard other than deer."

Willow looked over at me and paused before speaking. "*What* ?"

I peered cautiously at Willow and shrugged. "What?"

"Bears aren't your problem here." She followed that up with a short chortle and another pause. "You're funny. You'll be fine. But you should put a couple chairs and a fire pit out there. Make some s'mores! That'd be nice in the fall."

"Maybe. I don't really have anyone to share with aside from my aunt and uncle, so..."

"Well, I love s'mores so..." Willow murmured.

We walked out the patio door to the rest of the driveway in the back and gazed out into the small forest. I found momentary peace looking into the trees, but behind my attempts at humor and lightheartedness, I couldn't help but feel wary there on the back driveway. Willow's shoulders stiffened as she gazed out toward the trees. She seemed a bit guarded, unless I was just projecting.

"So where do you live?" I broke the quiet.

"Oh, we live down Van Zandt right before Washington Street. Near that park everybody goes to for fireworks every year." Willow nodded.

"We?" I followed up.

"Me and Joel."

"Ah."

"Yeah, but like I said, not like *that*. I tend to...roll the other way, you know?"

"Oh." I nodded. "Well, yeah. I remember where that is. Battery Park?"

"Mhm."

"When I visited here as a kid, we'd always go there for the Fourth with my aunt and uncle. All I could smell that whole night up until, like, two days after was mosquito repellent."

"That sucks, but that sounds about right. If you don't bring that stuff you'll be eaten alive out there."

We sat in silence, listening to the mourning doves coo from the forest as the clouds got darker up over the tops of the big old trees in the backyard.

"Thanks for hanging out, but I think I should call it a day."

"Yeah, we should probably go in. Looks like its gonna storm again soon."

"And I should finally start getting my crap together, too. I need to unpack the rest of those boxes, and all the stuff we talked about today, you know?"

Willow stretched her back. "No worries. I'll leave you to get acquainted with your new house some more." Willow turned to walk back inside, disappearing up the stairs and down the hall.

"What do you mean?" I followed behind. Back in the living room, I noticed Willow sitting on the couch, scribbling something onto the inside cover of my word-search book. She looked up when she was done writing and smiled gently. "Here." She stood and handed me the book.

I took it and noticed a huge star with a circle around it next to her phone number. "Thanks."

"No problem." She brushed her deep maroon hair behind her ear and placed the pen back on the table. Before she headed out the front door, she took one last look up the staircase.

"I'm a text away if you need anything."

"I think I'll be fine. Hopefully I won't drown in all the boxes tonight, but if I fall in I'll give you a call," I joked awkwardly as I plopped the puzzle book on a small white shelf beside the staircase. I took off the tie-dye hoodie before she could walk out the door. "Here. I didn't forget. Thanks."

"Stop thanking me, seriously. I fucked up your day, right? You should hate me." Willow snatched the sweatshirt playfully, smirked, and let herself out. She closed the door quietly behind her.

There I was, left in quiet solitude to process all that was said and done. Before anything, I rushed to the front door to lock the deadbolt *and* the top chain lock.

"*Fuck,*" I muttered to myself, staring down across the foyer and living room down to then back hallway stairs.

Creeeak.

"Hello?"

Ignore it. It's the house settling.

No, it isn't.

I heard one more quiet creak from the floor right above me as I gazed down at Willow's bubbly handwriting in my puzzle book, then decided to quickly add her to my contacts, just in case. I blew a raspberry as I scanned the house. *What first?*

***

I sat cross-legged on the bedroom floor surrounded by all of my desk supplies and stationery. I had somehow accumulated way too many pens, but not enough that I felt were too worn out to keep.

I looked at the time.

It's already nine?

I shook my head. My desk could've been organized earlier had I not taken a "quick break" to eat mac n' cheese; it had turned into three hours of watching videos on my phone. I'd at least praised myself for having gotten through all of the kitchen boxes and most of the living room that night. The pile of random boxes in my room, however, remained an untouched disaster. I really should've just kept any unopened boxes stored away in one of the other two bedrooms that I hadn't chosen to be my room. I'd picked the bigger room toward the back of the house with rose-colored wallpaper and two windows facing the woods beyond the property.

I sighed and got up to go to the bathroom, pausing Fleetwood Mac on my phone.

The rain continued outside and was all I could hear aside from my own footsteps on the creaky wood floor. I made my way down the hall and to the right to open the bathroom door. As I turned the light on, I heard something fall downstairs with a loud *thud.*

I gasped, jumping and grabbing my chest, my face flushed. I stood in the bathroom doorway until I worked up the courage to walk to the top of the stairs and peer down. I couldn't see much from my vantage-point, so I slowly made my way down and through the living room. Nothing initially seemed out of place, so I moved my investigation into the kitchen. Nothing was disturbed in there either, but as I turned to look back into the living room, I noticed that a small box of books that I'd forgotten about and left earlier on the built-in wall shelf had fallen to the floor. A deep sigh escaped me. I walked over to pick it back up, placing it in the center of the shelf instead. I kicked myself for having dumped everything so haphazardly while unpacking. It had simply toppled off.

Upon second thought, I decided that those books should probably go on the side table in my room instead, so I picked up the box and headed back upstairs. As I made my way up, I was hit with the unnerving feeling of a presence coming up behind me. I glanced back halfway up the stairs and found that I was still alone. I shook my head, annoyed that I'd become so paranoid, but hurriedly continued into my room anyway.

I plopped the box of books onto the center of the bed and bent down to pick up a mug that I made in college ceramics and then used as a pencil holder for the desk. The goal was to have my whole desk area perfectly organized by 9:30.

I'd only placed the mug of stationery and my laptop on my desk when Siri suddenly spoke up on my phone, which still sat alongside the box on my bed.

Boop boop. "Your name is Emma Reilly, but since we're friends, you've asked me to call you Emma."

I turned around to face the bed and blinked a few times. It was strange that my phone would pick anything up since I wasn't talking or playing any more music. I shook that one off as a glitch, and proceeded to place a framed photo of my mom and myself on the desk. I stared into my mom's glimmering eyes as she smiled next to Cinderella. I stood on the other side of the princess, with puffy, sparkling pink ears on my head, my arms reaching up with excitement toward the sky. My dream as a seven-year old had come true. My wish as I thought back on that memory was for life to be as simple as it was back then.

Boop boop. "I'm listening..."

Thoroughly spooked, I swung around and rushed to pick my phone up off the bed. I shoved the chatty AI in my sweatpants pocket and looked around the room.

"Hello?"

Behind me, I heard the same picture frame on the desk fall forward to hit the surface. Without hesitation, I grabbed my pillow to go sleep on the couch downstairs, leaving the mess of office supplies scattered on the floor. My plan for the night went right out the window, and I was fine with it.

***

Yet again, I found myself waking up from the same dreadful dream. Unlike the times before, my awareness of the nightmare hit and I forced my eyes open just before falling to the ground yet again,.

Once I woke up, however, I wished I hadn't.

A freezing cold chill focused on my forehead, as if someone was holding an ice cube to the center of it. There was a quick ping in my chest as my blurry vision quickly sharpened in shock to process the shadow of an arm extending across my chest up over my forehead. I opened my eyes wide to meet those of a child. Even in the darkness, I could see her pale and vacant, yet almost self-illuminating blue eyes and froze.

I gazed at her for what seemed like several minutes. I knew it in my gut; I'd experienced death through those same eyes. Coming to that realization, I caught a shallow breath. The girl's eyes widened and within the blink an eye, she was gone. I sprang up instantly and whipped my head around the room, listening in silence as my heart pounded in my chest. There were no noises coming from anywhere in the house to suggest that another presence was with me.

I tried my best to take at least three successful deep breaths before slowly creeping up off the couch to turn on every light on the first floor, making sure every single window and door was locked.

It's sleep paralysis.

I'm tired and stressed.
I'm jarred from meeting Willow.
I'm just tired.
I hate this.
No, no, no.

After ensuring there were at least no other *warm* bodies in the house, I quickly made my way upstairs and into my room at the end of the hall. I closed that door and locked it too. I jumped up onto my bed and backed up against the headboard. I remembered that my phone was still right there in my pocket so I pulled it out and gazed at Willow's name in my contacts. For a lengthy minute, I debated whether or not I should reach out to her. It was only five o'clock in the morning anyway, and I probably wouldn't get a response for hours.

I can handle this on my own…
But Willow definitely wouldn't judge, though…right?
Ugh.

Hey it's Emma.

My fingers hovered over the keyboard before quickly typing:

**R u up? I had another nightmare and just saw
a little girl and now I can't sleep.**

Instantly and unexpectedly, my phone vibrated with a text notification.

**Cute…try to get some sleep and we'll talk
later in the morning…ur fine :)**

Cute?

I didn't *feel* fine, not one bit, but I needed something that would calm me enough to allow me to sleep for a couple more hours until I could explain everything to Willow.

With an ounce of trust in my unbothered new acquaintance, I climbed into my sheets and forced my eyes shut after putting on a random true crime podcast for background noise. By some miracle, I fell asleep within twenty minutes, even with all the lights on.

43

5.

TAKE THIS PINEAPPLE

I woke up at around 8:30 in the morning to stillness, quiet. As I stretched my arms and back, the smell of coffee wafted around the room. I furrowed my brows, not having remembered making coffee the night before. Maybe I had, though. It could've been when I came down with the assumption that I wouldn't be able to sleep on the couch or when I'd turned all the lights on in the kitchen.

I looked around my room and quickly noticed that before me, my desk was arranged tidily. The mess of pens, notebooks, and random trinkets on the floor was cleared off and set carefully on the desk.

I hadn't done *that* the night before. It wasn't how I would've arranged things either, but it was still nicely done.

Creepy nonetheless.

The image of the little girl flashed in my head like a photograph negative. I jerked my head to the bedroom door and saw that it was unlocked and open again, so I crawled out of bed to shuffle across the hall and downstairs. I was immediately met with the sight of a fresh cup of coffee resting right on the bookshelf against the staircase. I made my way to it and stared it down for several seconds. The steam flowed softly above the mug and dissipated into the air. Just like her.

"Was that you?" I whispered. There was no way. A tiny impressed smile snuck across my face as I picked up the hot mug. "Thank you."

Could she hear me?

Suddenly, a shuffle sounded from back in the kitchen.

"You're welcome."

"*Shit* !" I jolted, burning my lip and spilling some coffee over the rim.

Willow emerged from the kitchen doorway and sauntered across the living room into the entry. "I warned you that you'd be forced to confront it someday." She shook her head and stood with one of my Disneyland mugs in hand. *The audacity.*

"What the *hell?*" I exclaimed. "You broke in?" I cringed at my own cracking voice.

"Um, no. Someone here has a habit of leaving doors unlocked." Willow cleared her throat. "I take it that person isn't you."

"That doesn't mean you can just *waltz* right in!"

"That's an overstatement. I definitely walked right in."

"And you said we'd talk later this morning!"

"It is later."

"It's eight in the morning and you're in my house." I stood in the same spot by the base of the stairs without taking another sip of coffee or even wiping up the spill dribbling down the side of the cup.

"You're the one who texted me that you needed help so I'm here to help … Do you like pineapple?"

I blinked slowly and jutted my head forward. "I— what? Yeah," I mumbled.

"Well here. I brought you one." Willow gestured to the coffee table. "Please take it. For a flourishing friendship. It's also a symbol of welcoming."

"Well. You clearly felt welcome enough to just *come* right in and make yourself at home," I spat.

Oof. Justified but bitter...like this coffee.

"Woah, woah. I went to knock on the door and it kinda just opened. I came in to see if you were okay … which you obviously were. I didn't want to disturb you."

"So you thought to clean my *desk* … in my *room* …while I was sleeping?"

Willow grimaced. "I didn't touch your desk. I'm your barista, not your housekeeper."

There was a beat of silence between us as we stared at each other.

I scoffed. "Well thanks, I guess." I sighed.

"You're very welcome." She smiled brightly. "So …what happened last night— or this morning or whatever?"

"Well, I was—" I started.

"No wait! I have a better idea!" She ran to set her mug down next to the pineapple and held a finger up to me as she texted with her other hand. I waited quietly, just trying to catch up mentally. It was too early for this. "Kay. I texted Joel to meet us at Beach Brew. Your aunt owns it, right?"

"Yeah, but why?" I shook my head.

"I want a scone and I want you to meet Joel." She gazed back down at her phone when it chimed. "*Noice*, he's down to meet us there. I thought he'd still be asleep … Good for him." She nodded subtly with raised brows.

"Well *I* just woke up." I squinted. "I literally just rolled out of bed. I'm not even close to ready."

"It's fine. I'll wait for you. As long as you look better than you did at lunch yesterday."

I thought it best not to respond to that.

"Lighten up, geez. I'm kidding."

I rolled my eyes and took one last sip of coffee before going upstairs to shower. I needed a few minutes alone to wake up. I didn't even have the energy to tell her to wait outside.

"Are you gonna finish your coffee?" Willow asked as I made my way up the stairs.

"No."

"I'll finish it for you," she reassured loudly as I reached the second floor.

I closed the bathroom door behind me just as noisily.

***

By the time the two of us had walked into Beach Brew Books, it was close to ten o'clock. The bells on the door knob let out a welcoming jingle into the quaint downtown cafe. The whole place smelled of old books, rich coffee, warm butter, and fresh blueberries. I'd once told Liv that she should sell a signature Beach Brew candle in the shop with those core scents combined, which was purely selfish of me. She told me I was brilliant but never followed through.

Willow took a deep breath and nodded. "Mm. Mhm. That's what I needed."

"We can sit over there. That's my usual spot." I made my way past a wall on the left lined with dark wood bookshelves; the cafe doubled as a quaint used-book store. I sat down at the back table situated by a large window facing the bobbing yachts and sailboats on the wharf. I let out an eased sigh. In such a familiar safe place, I felt more comfortable recalling my experience from the night before.

"Do you want me to go order for you? Joel should be here in a few," Willow explained.

At the same time, I made eye contact from across the coffee bar with Thompson, an elderly man who had worked loyally for Liv for close to a decade. He grinned at me and held up a hand to let me know he'd be right with us.

"No, it's fine," I replied softly to Willow and smiled warmly back at him with a wave. I adored Thompson as if he were a grandparent or a great uncle. I'd grown up visiting him, too. With Beach Brew came Thompson.

He slowly made his way over to our table and cleared his throat. "You always hafta sit the furthest away. I may need all this exercise, but I don't want it, you know." He shook his head and laughed gruffly. "How you doin, honey?" He bent over to kiss the top of my head.

"I'm good, Thomps. You don't have to come all the way over here every time, either, you know." I patted his shoulder softly.

"Oh well, I like the view from this table, too. You're not the only one." He smiled and cleared his throat again. "What can I get you kids?"

"Just my usual."

"Well if it ain't broke, we won't try to fix it. And for- who are you, dear? Believe I've seen you here, too. At least a couple'a times." He turned his attention to Willow.

"You have, I'm sure. It's Willow, and I desperately need a blueberry scone and a dark roast. *Please.*"

"I think I can do that for ya." He nodded with a wink.

"It's on me." I offered.

"No, no. It's on *me* today," Thomps corrected, then looked back over to me, "When do you start? Your aunt told me she's puttin' ya to work soon."

"Next week. Just need a few more days to settle in, I think." I glimpsed back to Willow again and swallowed hard.

"Oh well." He paused. "You'll be makin' tips in no time. Just don't spend it all on the books." He nodded and walked off slowly.

"What a cutie. I love him." Willow chuckled, noticing the door bells jingle at the entrance. "There he is. Man of the hour."

I followed Willow's gaze and met Joel's briefly but instantly. He made his way to the back, waving shyly at us. He was pretty thin, and very handsome. His curly chestnut hair peeked out from beneath a light knit beanie, his hands tucked into his dark brown chino shorts.

"Hey, Wills." He pulled up a chair from another table and swung it around to sit with us.

"You're late." Willow clicked her tongue.

"Can't be late if you never gave me a time." He settled in casually, giving me a shy nod. "Hey."

"Hi." I waved nervously. His deep green eyes took me by surprise and I racked my brain for a response.

Oh my god, just say something.

"This is Emma." Willow introduced me quickly.

Idiot.

"Well, very nice to meet you, Miss Emma. She wouldn't shut up about you last night." He nodded toward Willow. "Demanded we meet." He smirked.

"Well, here I am." I shrugged, doing my best to recover from my embarrassment.

"Okay. Now that we're all here … go ahead and continue with your story." Willow prompted me.

"Um." I looked at Joel and back to her.

"It's fine. I know already." He reassured me softly. "No judgment."

"Okay." I swallowed. "So last night I woke up from this nightmare I've been having since I moved into the house. I'm always this little girl running from someone in the woods, and then I hide in a big twisted looking tree. The person I'm running from goes away, and then I try to climb down but I slip and hit my head on a rock. I feel myself dying, and then I fade off and wake up.

"But last night for some reason, I caught myself dreaming and woke up before the fall. So I opened my eyes and saw this little girl standing over me touching my forehead. I panicked and froze and then she was just … gone. I don't know. It happened so fast and I was so out of it that I didn't see much of her, except for her eyes. I *knew* those eyes.

"I know it sounds stupid but … I know I've seen through them. Like, I *felt* her eyes." I caught my breath after reeling off the story.

Neither of them responded. Joel picked at the skin around his fingernails and gazed out the window. Willow looked directly into my eyes but then darted to Thompson bringing over our food.

"Your sea salt caramel mocha and pistachio muffin, Emma. Not sure those two go so well together, but there ya go. And your very important blueberry scone for you, Miss Willow." He chuckled gruffly as he slid the plates onto the table, "Anything for you, sir?" He peered over at Joel.

"Oh, no. I'm okay, thank you." He looked up quickly and shook his head.

"Alright, then. I'll getcha some water." He patted his apron.

"Thanks, Thomps." I smiled at him as he waddled his way back behind the counter to take another customer's order.

"You're not stupid." Joel spoke up, studying my leg shaking under the table.

"She wants you to understand what she went through," Willow added. "Right, Joel?"

"Mhm. I mean— I'm not an expert but that's what I first thought."

I chewed the inside of my cheek. "Why? That was the first time I saw her, and she hasn't tried to communicate with me before in any other way."

"Maybe she's just feeling you out. She could be more scared of you than you are of her, especially if she can sense your ability. Maybe she's trying to see if you're friendly or not," Joel explained.

"I felt her energy immediately when I walked in yesterday. It's strong, but harmless. There *is* a lot of negativity in that house, though … sorry," Willow apologized.

"She can probably feel that you're safe by now, but she might still be nervous if no one's ever communicated with her before. She's just a kid and you're a stranger who just moved into her home … probably. I don't know." Joel shrugged. "I'm sure Willow already told you. I see them too."

I nodded.

"Well, I'm glad you're talking about it. Willow said you didn't like the idea of even acknowledging it, but trust me." He paused to look into my eyes. "You made the right choice letting it in— letting *us* in— even a little. I know we just met, but you're the first person I've talked to who's sensitive, too. I mean— Willow is— but that's a different kind. Anyway, what I'm saying is … I'm here to support you. Any friend of Willow is a friend of mine." He smiled.

"Aw," Willow joked as she took a big bite. "No, but seriously, she was showing you what happened to her because she's lonely and lost. She's probably not *trying* to traumatize you." She spoke with a mouthful of scone.

"Okay, so … what next?" I asked. "I don't have a manual for this. Do I just keep letting her do it? I mean— Do I try to talk to her?"

"I think you should," Willow stated confidently.

Joel nodded. "Even if it's just into an empty room. We can't always see them when they're hanging around. From what I understand, we see them when they want us to."

"How?"

"I think it takes a shit ton of energy to manifest and communicate. When you don't see them, they're either not around, too weak, or they're choosing to kind of … sink back into an in-between. Does that make sense?" Willow took a sip of her dark roast. "I don't know. Just what I've read."

"I'm not exactly sure how it all works either, but that seems to make sense to me, too." Joel agreed. "If you talk to her, she may feel more inclined to show herself to you outside of just those nightmares."

I sighed. "What if I don't want her to, though?"

"Mmm, but do you want better sleep, though?" Willow presented a valid point.

Joel bit the inside of his mouth. "You don't *have* to do anything. But if she's shown you that same vision of her death several times already, I don't see why she'd stop now. Clearly she needs something else."

"Unless you scared her away by waking up in the middle of it," Willow added.

"Mm." Joel briefly considered that. "You'll probably keep experiencing her. Especially if that was her house. In her eyes, you may just be a stranger in her home. It may put your mind at ease if you just talk into the air— however ridiculous it may sound— and let it be known that you're aware that you're sharing a space, and that you aren't a threat."

"Mhm." Willow asserted her approval on the matter.

"I don't know. There's just one thing that really confuses me about it." I furrowed my brow and gazed out at the ocean's horizon line outside the window.

"What?" Joel asked.

Willow suddenly tensed up and stopped chewing, "Who was she running from, right?" She looked down into her lap.

Joel spoke softly, "I wish I had an answer for you. But that could also be why she's showing you. Maybe she wants someone to know what happened if there was never closure. It's all just theories right now. There's really nothing to do but continue being cautious in the house and make sure she knows you're friendly."

"Yeah." Willow cleared her throat and got up to throw away her napkin and paper plate.

I sipped my mocha in disappointment. "I wanted a more solid solution than this."

Joel cocked his head and studied my face. "Sometimes it takes a little … time to figure things out."

"Well, let's bookmark this conversation. Who wants to go for a walk downtown? I'm ready to get movin'." Willow stood up and tapped her fingers on the back of the chair.

"Go ahead. We'll be right out." Joel didn't break from me.

"Kay, hurry up." Willow spun around and walked out the door.

Joel rolled his eyes and took a deep breath in. "I know how awkward this must be."

"Yeah."

"I just wanted to tell you that you're gonna be okay. If I were you right now, I wouldn't be handling it nearly as well as you are. I've had this thing since … always, I guess … and I still don't know all the rules. If there are any. When a spirit comes to me, I just try to help the best way I can. I've never *lived* in a haunted house, though, so…" He trailed off.

"I didn't ask for this."

"I know you didn't. Neither did I." He gulped. "The earliest ghost I can remember … kept coming to me in my sleep, too. The first one I could actually recognize as … like … not a normal person. "

"Yeah?"

"Yeah. Imagine being, like, six, and seeing a guy with a messed up head, caved in chest and dislocated arms by your bed."

"Ew. God."

"Yeah. It was pretty fuckin' terrifying. Until he started telling me he had a little boy around my age, and that he wanted me to tell his son that he loved him."

"Wow."

"He was *so* scary looking. But he made it easy for me, believe it or not. Really nice guy. Long story short, I told my mom. Turned out, he was just a man who had died two years prior in a hit and run a couple'a few blocks down. He probably spent so much energy searching for someone who would listen and see him for what he was."

"Your mom knows?"

"Yeah. My parents get spooked so we don't talk about it a lot. But they know it's just a part of me. I came to them with *so* many stories as a kid."

"What happened to him?"

"Well, the kid was a little older than me, but he went to my school. So one night, I told him that I'd seen his son at recess and that he seemed happy. At that age, I didn't know how to start a conversation with a bigger kid to get any info out of him without creeping him out, right? I couldn't just come out and tell him that his dead dad told me to tell *him* that he loves him, you know?"

"Yeah, that's … tricky."

"But in the end, I think just hearing that his son was okay was enough. He was lost in my neighborhood and couldn't find his house. I told him that I'd be his son's friend at school and make sure he wasn't lonely. That's all I could do back then, and I think he knew that. His name was Tony. He thanked me and left, and I never saw him again."

"Do you think he moved on?"

"Maybe. I hope so, if that's what he wanted. But he made ghosts not seem *as* scary anymore." He winked at me.

"Hm." I gazed out the window at the light reflecting off the ripples in the water.

"Do you remember your first ghost?" He leaned his cheek against his fist.

I pursed my lips and watched a seagull land on the roof of a small restaurant nearby. "No."

When I looked back to him, he was studying my face intensely. He nodded. "It's okay if you don't wanna talk about it."

"Yeah," I felt tears well up in my bottom eyelids.

"Anyway, all that is to say … I'm here for you. I know it's a lot, and it makes … *very* little sense. I also know the gravity of our gift, but I also know that Willow can be a bit much sometimes, a little overwhelming. So if you ever just need someone who will just shut up and listen, I'm your guy." He smiled empathetically. "Or if you want to hear any more of my thrilling tales, I'd be happy to tell them."

"Thank you."

"Now, let's go take a walk and not talk about any of this for a bit, yeah? I'll even buy you some kick-ass fudge down the street. Whatever you want. Just as part of the welcome package." He warmly offered me a treat.

I managed to return the smile. "It sounds better than the pineapple Willow gave me."

"Ooh, hold on. Don't knock the pineapple. She's never given *me* a pineapple before. That's a big deal. I think she likes you." He chuckled.

I think I actually like you guys, too.

Thomps approached the table again right as we were gathering our things to go. "Here ya go, kiddo." Thomps coughed gruffly as he set three bags with cinnamon strudel muffins in them on the table next to me.

"We're about to leave," I replied.

"Yeah I know." He raised his thick white eyebrows. "So what? It's yesterday's batch. She's not losing any money by me givin' em to you. Take em to-go. And don't come back around here, understand?" He chuckled.

"Nice to meet you, Thomps." Joel nodded.

"You too, son. Welp, have a swell day, folks."

6.

THAT'S A PRETTY NAME

Willow dropped me off at home later in the afternoon after I'd spent the whole day downtown with my two new companions. Joel had followed through on his offer to buy me a very large chunk of cookie dough fudge at the Newport Fudgery. The three of us walked all the way downtown past the tourist strip toward the quieter shops, then all the way back up Thames Street to have a late lunch at Brick Alley Pub, a popular downtown haunt. Willow introduced me to their lobster nachos, which you had to special order since they weren't anywhere on the menu, and were therefore considered by Willow to be a "secret item." Once we were all properly full, we headed back to Washington Square where we'd all parked earlier that morning. We'd spent a solid hour on a bench at that park just … hanging out. Talking about normal things, parts of life I'd forgotten to care about. For a while, I'd forgotten what my hobbies were, because all of my time was spent caring for my mom. For the first time in months, I was reminded that I was my own person. While Willow and Joel got to know little parts about me, I got a chance to relearn myself.

I'd also been so wrapped up in thinking about my mom on my morning walks that I'd forgotten to truly see what surrounded me. That afternoon, though, we spent time talking about how nice the breeze and soft sunlight in the trees were after so much rain. The light reflecting off the ocean provided a subtle sparkle to our view of the coast from the hill.

I smiled as I hopped out of Willow's cobalt blue Prius in front of my house. "Thanks for today."

"Why? *I* didn't buy you anything." She shrugged.

"You didn't have to." For the first time in weeks, I didn't feel alone.

"Relax tonight. Try not to worry about things until there's a reason to, kay?" She reassured while patting my shoulder softly.

I nodded and looked down at the sidewalk after having been reminded of my uncomfortable situation. "I'll try."

"'Atta girl." Willow winked as I closed the car door. Before backing out into the street again, she waved and then took off.

I was alone once again.

I dragged my feet up the front steps between the bright hydrangeas that glowed in the warm light of the sunset. I was relieved to see that the front door had remained closed this time while I was gone. I stopped mid-way up the steps to take a good look up at the house. There was a slight breeze in the trees lining the street, but aside from that, everything was calm and quiet outside. I really hoped things would stay that way once I went in. With a deep breath, I finished my trek up the steps and into the house. *Huh*, the door had remained *locked*, too.

So far, so good.

The second I stepped in, I flicked the entry light on even though there was still the summer afternoon light coming in through the windows. It just made me feel better about being in that big old house by myself.

I remembered Willow and Joel's advice to try communicating with the little girl in the house. Although the thought truly terrified me, I felt compelled to get it over with so I could move on with my evening instead of risking the same thing happening again that night without a warning. I cleared my throat, and felt the silent stillness in the house, wondering if anyone would really hear me.

I sighed. "Um."

This is ridiculous.

I was talking into the air. What if I was being dramatic and it *was* just sleep paralysis?

"If there's anyone in here" —my voice cracked and I cringed — "I don't mean to— I'm not gonna— shit. If there's anyone here, I'm not gonna try to scare you away or hurt you or anything…okay?"

Why was that more nerve-wracking than my college theatre class performance?

Because you know in your gut you have a whole different kind of audience.

I paused, waiting for a response, then shook my head. "Kay. I'm gonna do my own thing now. I hope you do, too." I cleared the lump in my throat, feeling foolish.

Crickets.

I didn't get a single response after an hour, to my relief. So I kept my word and did my own thing, making some quick bean and cheese burritos for dinner with a glass of wine.

Because I could.

***

Around nine o'clock that night, I sat upstairs on my bed, playing some word scramble puzzle on my phone. I'd finally finished unpacking by some miracle. The alcohol had settled into my system gracefully, which calmed me down enough to go without the background music that usually kept any unwanted noises from my attention. A soothing distraction.

I sat in silence, watching as a confetti effect came across my screen for completing another level.

Just as I hovered my finger over the "new puzzle" button, I heard a small creak just outside the bedroom doorway. I craned my head up to notice that the second door down the hall on the left was cracked open and swaying, just barely. While I found this slightly unnerving, I considered the possibility that the cause was the night breeze coming through my cracked-open windows. I glanced out the window and studied the dark quiet mass that was the backwoods beyond the property.

As soon as I nodded proudly to myself for not jumping to spooked conclusions, I heard the same wooden door creak further back, left halfway open. I jumped and froze with my eyes fixed on the door. I sat on my bed across the hall from the sight, blinking several times to make sure I was seeing correctly. The light in the spare bedroom remained off, as it had since I moved in. I didn't have enough furniture to fill it yet, and had left it empty until I decided what I wanted to do with it. I was leaning toward turning it into an office once I could find a way to purchase at least two new book cases and a cute little reading chair to accompany my desk. Without a car, I couldn't do any of that yet so I kept the little desk in my room with me, and that spare room was left empty.

Or so I thought.

I felt stupid for talking into the empty house earlier, but felt compelled to try again.

Just to see.

I didn't move an inch off my bed, but spoke quietly. "Is anyone there?"

No response.

"If there is, I don't want to intrude on your space. So let's just…" I paused and took a deep breath. "I don't know.."

Still, nothing more came from the room nor anywhere else in the house.

The image of the small girl in the shadows watching over me flashed before my eyes. "But could you just … make the nightmares stop? I won't bother you if you don't bother me." I sat still, in that moment so tired that I was willing to try anything to get a better night's sleep. "Plea—"

A lump formed in my throat instantly. My eyes focused on a small pale hand suddenly reaching around from behind the spare bedroom door to grip the side of it. First the hand, then a head peeked out, followed by a torso that wrapped around the door, holding onto it like it was a security blanket. From the darkness and into the dim light that poured into the hall from my room, emerged a petite figure hunching over shyly.

I'd forgotten to breathe as the girl slowly shuffled down the hall toward me. She planted both feet on the wooden floor near my doorway with her head pointed down at her dirty white mary-janes. I could feel dry-mouth setting in as I studied her. Her frilly socks were disheveled, one scrunched down to her ankle, the other pulled up and unfolded onto her shin. Her knees were scraped, and a familiar light dress was torn in a few places on the skirt. I could never see the color of it in my dreams, but it resembled that of a fresh lemon. In her condition, though, it looked like the lemon had dropped from its tree into the dirt and was then stepped on by a muddy shoe. A button was missing on the front of it at the chest, and the lace trim along the collar and the edges of the puffy short sleeves was dingy. The girl's bronze bangs sat messily on her forehead, with the rest of her hair a matted, damp, and curly mess. Upon closer inspection, the right side of her head was not only mangled but mixed with dark clotted blood near the crown.

I sat paralyzed waiting for the girl to make some kind of movement. After several beats of eerie silence, the girl slowly looked up. I braced myself for contact.

We locked eyes instantly. I was *positive* that they were the same ones I'd seen and felt a life end through. They were cloudy and sunken in, unblinking. Her mouth was plump with a small cut on the bottom lip. There was no trace of warmth on her face; her cheeks weren't a cheery rose like a little girl's should be. In fact, she was blueish, almost translucent.

I gave my best effort to swallow the lump in my throat, but couldn't get it down to speak. Even if I could, I hadn't the slightest idea what to say.

"I'm sorry." She spoke unexpectedly, the cut on her lip cracked and chapped. "I don't mean to frighten you."

I inhaled sharply at the girl's gentle voice. It didn't at all match the terrifying exterior; I'd expected something distorted and frog-like, more similar to the horrors in *Evil Dead*.

"I've scared you, haven't I?" She frowned all the while keeping direct eye contact with me.

My eyes widened and I gave a stiff nod. I wanted to reach for my phone, but couldn't find the strength or coordination. I was temporarily disabled.

The girl's eyes softened as she took a step closer, now standing in the door frame of my room. "Is your name Emma?"

"Ohhh God." A chill ran up my spine.

She tilted her head inquisitively.

"Yes," I squeaked.

"Hello, Emma." She smiled slightly, "that's a pretty name."

I had no words. Words did not compute from my brain to my mouth.

"My name is Lynette."

"Okay," I muttered hesitantly in response, still frozen in place from when I first saw the door move.

"It's nice to meet you." She gazed down at the phone in my hand. "I like your music box."

I held it up slightly in front of me. "This? Oh, no. It's … my phone."

"That's a *telephone*?"

"Yeah. I mean— they're probably different from when you—"

"Wow," she interrupted in awe.

I nodded slowly. What else was there to say? *Why are you forcing images into my head while I sleep?*

"Is this your house?" I asked instead.

"Yes." Lynette gazed down at the wood floor.

"For how long?"

"I'm not sure. A long time."

I took a deep breath. "And you know that you're…" I trailed off, feeling guilty for asking a child if she knew she was-

"Dead." Her eyes shifted from the floor and straight to mine. They were empty, yet I could feel the sadness in the clouds that glossed over them.

I gulped. "Is that why you—"

"Yes."

"You *were* trying to show me."

"I'm sorry."

"Why?"

"No one knew the truth. My big sister thought she knew but she didn't and— well I tried to show her too, but she was just so sad that I couldn't get through. She couldn't ever see me, and then one day she didn't come home. Do you know where she went?"

The poor girl didn't understand why her family would ever move on.

…You can find peace within yourself. And you can help them find peace, too.

"What's your sister's name?"

"Gwen," she whispered. "Can you find her?"

"I— I'll do my best, but—" I bit the inside of my cheek. If Lynette died a long time ago, her sister may have already died, too. Then how was I supposed to help?

"What year is it for you? I mean, when did you …die?"

The little girl stared off into the corner of the room for several moments, as if frozen in thought, "1949," she said.

"And you … *need* her to know the truth?"

"She needs to know it wasn't her fault."

I nodded hesitantly. "Okay. I'll try to help you."

"Thank you, Emma." I watched as a tiny smile formed on her pale lips. I tried to force a smile back through my fear. A little dead girl with a bloody head in my bedroom should've been enough to make me pee my pants and flee, but I wasn't *too* afraid of her, oddly enough. They always say in horror movies not to trust the spirits of the children; they're certainly demons trying to gain access to you. We're always warned about ghostly deception, but I felt her death. It was real, and I was touched by her innocence and heartbreak. I trusted it.

"Who were you running from?" I blurted.

Lynette let out a quiet gasp and with it, she vanished within the blink of an eye from where she stood. Just like the man in the restaurant, just like my mother. There, and gone.

Dammit.

Once she was gone, I leaned forward and rubbed my eyes with the palm of my hand. One short encounter had drained me, and I'd gotten very few answers. As I sat on my bed with my face buried in my hands, wondering if the nightmares would finally stop, I felt the unmistakable discomfort of being watched. The floor creaked from the side of the bed, and something felt wrong. I remembered Willow mentioning negativity in the house. Maybe that was it, but I didn't look. I refused to acknowledge *any* presence for the rest of the night-whether it was Lynette or not.

7.

ON PAPER

The next morning, I summoned Willow and Joel to the house to inform them that we would be partaking in a research party that day. I wasn't going to wait until Lynette felt like opening up to me more. I needed answers immediately- not only to help Lynette find whatever closure she needed to move on, but to uncover the story behind the house for myself. Once all of this was over, I could carry on with reconstructing my life. First, I needed solid facts.

Oh God. I'm turning into Liv.

In fact, *she* probably knew somehow that there was some shady history to the house. She may have even bought it to market as "haunted" once it hit the rental site- not to be scammy or gimmicky, but because owning a haunted home and sharing it with others eager to experience it excited her. It was just funny that she had conveniently forgotten to mention that bit to me before I moved in.

I would deal with her later.

Once my new friends arrived, I didn't give either of them time to walk any further into the house than the foyer before explaining to them what happened the night before. Willow wasn't surprised. Joel kept quiet for the most part, simply nodding along with my recount and offering supportive words.

It was Willow who asserted herself and took on the responsibility of assigning jobs for the day. I was to go with Joel to the Newport Historical Society to look for property records while Willow headed to her favorite place in the world— except for the crystal shop down on Thames— the Newport Public Library. She was dying to dig through old *Newport Times* articles like a "little treasure hunt." At least *she* thought this was entertaining.

I suggested going around to the neighbors to ask if they knew anything about the house's history or previous tenants, but Joel made the perfect point that I may not want to bring attention to the house, especially if Liv didn't actually know anything, and if I didn't *want* her to yet. Once she found out, she'd be delighted and jump at the opportunity to write a book about owning her own haunted home … and *then* market it as such online.

"We'll meet at Beach Brew at three, okay? That should be long enough to at least get an idea of whether or not we'll have any luck at all." Willow nodded as she dropped us off the Historical Society main building at 11:00 am. "Have fun, kids."

Willow split up from Joel and me with a wink, and we all urgently got to work with our figurative detective hats on.

***

3:00 pm sharp.

Joel and I had finished early and decided we'd just walk to our meeting spot to wait for Willow. Since she hadn't arrived early, we'd assumed she'd either found a plethora of information, or had gotten lost under piles of archives looking desperately for *anything* to share with us. We watched as she burst into the coffee shop, seemingly energized from being surrounded by old books for hours. I expected Thomps to shoot her a glare; he hated when people slammed the door because he worried about his antique bells on the doorknob breaking. Usually he worked until closing, but he wasn't there at all that afternoon. I was disappointed. I could've used his warm old smile to break the tension of this entire situation.

"I brought serious notes," Willow declared as she abruptly slammed her butt into a chair and thrashed her bag open to pull out a composition book.

I looked at her with wide eyes. "You took notes?"

"You *didn't* ?"

"We did." Joel rolled his eyes.

"Well then what's with the look?" She paused with her notebook still in her hand.

"I just … didn't expect you to go so hard on this. That's all," I muttered.

"Well I wasn't gonna be lazy and take pictures. The font was too small to zoom in on and it's against library rules, so…" She pursed her lips with attitude.

"No, no. Thanks for caring enough to do that." I sniffled, cupping my lavender tea. I needed its calming properties to prepare myself for what I may discover.

"Purely selfish. I enjoy the hunt." She winked and continued to throw the book on the table.

"Well, what did you find on your hunt? Because we didn't get too much on ours." Joel shrugged.

Willow smirked and skimmed her notes. "Then I win. *Newport Times*, September 5, 1949. I wrote the whole thing down word-for-word."

"Impressive."

"Mm, not really."

"Your detective efforts are appreciated either way." I shrugged.

She took a sip of the tea we had ready for her. "Mm. Thanks, boo. But there's not much to it. Like this tea. I should've asked you to order me a citrus mint wellness brew instead. This is too mild." She sighed.

"You told me to order whatever I got," I replied plainly. "It's lavender, Willow. It's not mild." She stared at me for several seconds, clicking her tongue to taste the tea again.

"Well." She looked back down at her notes. "Shoulda gotten the citrus mint wellness blend."

"Wills. Read." Joel reminded her of the task at hand.

"*Ahem.*" Willow cleared her throat dramatically. "Okay, so … September 5th, 1949…

"In the early morning hours of September 4th, the body of eleven-year-old Lynette Salley was discovered in the woods behind her family home on Chandler Street. Salley was reported missing when her father and older sister were unable to locate her in the home around 2:00 am. Officers responded to the home and searched the nearby areas. The location of the body was discovered during the search at approximately 5:00 am, and the crime scene was then secured for investigation. The body was discovered by Dr. Salley's eldest and now only surviving daughter, Gwendolyn Salley and was identified and confirmed by the Newport County Sheriff's Office the same day.

"The cause of death has been determined as impact trauma to the head, the manner of death subsequently confirmed to have been accidental. After investigation of the scene, it was quickly reported by the Sheriff that the child had fallen from a tree in the woods while climbing it, likely during the storm on Saturday night. Although it is unknown why Salley would have been out in such conditions, both family members gave a statement that the home was secured and safe prior to the disappearance, but that the back patio door was left open upon discovering Salley's absence from the home. The area is still under investigation to uncover any further details regarding the child's death.

"Lynette Salley was the youngest daughter of Newport doctor, Clyde Salley. The family is grieving their loss and politely asks for privacy during this time.

"…that's what we got on that." Willow concluded her report.

I sank further back in my chair and swallowed, trying to rid my throat of the large lump I felt.

"You really wrote all that?" Joel stared down at her notebook.

"Yup." Willow tapped the paper, pursing her lips and looking between the two of us with raised brows.

"Okay, well … that's confirmation of what you've been dreaming. Right, Emma?" Joel gazed at me sympathetically.

"It's right there on paper," Willow attested. "At least we aren't all crazy."

I nodded. "It's so sad."

"It is." He agreed.

"It *is*, but it still doesn't explain who was running after her." Willow raised a brow. "There's definitely more to the story, but nothing that was ever reported publicly. What did you guys find?"

"Just property records, mostly." Joel and I looked at each other while he spoke calmly. "Clyde Salley owned the home from 1943 up until 1952 when he sold it."

"That's not long but it makes sense with what else I found." Willow bit the inside of her cheek.

"What?" I asked meekly.

"Uh, Gwen Salley died not long after Lynette. She was found dead in '51. I found her death certificate and a small newspaper blurb after I did a little more digging." She inhaled. "Sorry, Emma."

My chest sank. "How? I knew there was a good chance she was dead, but it's still disappointing."

"Apparent suicide. So, I guess that's a dead end." She took a sip and noticed Joel's glare. "Shit. No pun intended."

"Makes sense. Clyde must've sold because there was nothing left for him here but pain. So much death in one family … I'm sure the town was talking. Where did she die? In the house, too?" Joel interrogated her.

Willow shook her head. "Unknown exactly. Just said 'body recovered on shore, presumed suicide by drowning'." She shrugged.

"Well, this sucks." I rubbed my forehead. "We don't really have anything new that's helpful to me. Now I gotta tell that poor girl that her sister is dead and she'll never see her again. How does *that* provide closure?"

"I mean, maybe if she knows that, she'll cross over hoping to —"

Joel stopped talking once Willow grabbed his arm and quietly squealed. I followed her gaze and saw Liv appear from the back office to grab something from the register area.

"I've never seen her here before." Willow awed in my aunt's presence.

"Well, she chose the wrong day to come in." I shook my head and got up without hesitation.

I marched over to the front counter and leaned onto it with both arms, staring at my aunt. Seeing her in that moment, I didn't care about whether or not she knew about the house.

She quickly noticed me out of the corner of her eye and smiled, holding up one finger while she was on the phone. "Mm, right

… Yeah … Okay. Well I can have it over to you by Friday instead for a proof … Okay sounds good … You take care, Saundra … Buh-bye." She hung up to greet me cheerfully. "Heyyy, kiddo! My agent is super excited about my newest book. Have I told you about it yet? I think it may be one of my most favorite yet," she prattled.

"Does it happen to be about the *house* you set me up in without providing a backstory?" I blurted.

Her glee instantly morphed into shock as she raised both brows and clicked her tongue. "Come again?"

"You conveniently forgot?"

"Em, what are you talking about? What's going on with you?" She grimaced and handed me a muffin over the counter. "Eat something."

"*No.*" I took it, anyway. It was pistachio. She knew I couldn't resist.

"What's your deal?"

"What's *yours*? You know exactly what I'm talking about. Don't pretend. I know why you bought the house." I could hear Willow whisper something to Joel from our table, but when I looked over they were both staring straight at us.

Aunt Liv's eyes followed mine. "Are those friends?"

"Uh-uh. No. Tell me why you bought the house." I pushed in a hushed tone, leaning over the counter closer to her.

"Tell me why you're so heated first." She challenged me.

Luckily, most of the coffee shop patrons were seated outside or busy doing their own work. "Because you bought a haunted house and decided to keep it from me," I said through my teeth.

Liv straightened up and tilted her head to one side with her arms crossed.

"You put me in a *haunted … house*, Liv." My voice cracked.

"What happened? Have you seen something?"

I scoffed. "No, but I've heard rumors around the neighborhood."

"From *who*?"

"I don't know. People. I've just heard stuff."

Liv relaxed her shoulders. "Honey, so has every other person about every other house on Aquidneck Island. Do you know how many supposedly 'haunted' houses there are here? Just because it's old and someone died there doesn't automatically make it haunted." She sighed.

"So you *did* know."

She took a deep breath and glanced over at the front door. No new customers had come in.

"I feel like that's something you might've wanted to tell me before I moved in." I rolled my eyes and stormed away from the counter back to my two-person audience. "Thanks a lot."

"Damn." Willow gripped the corner of her composition book.

"Stop." Joel nudged her.

I stood in front of them and watched Willow's eyes widen.

"Yeah, I knew." Liv explained, "I'd heard some buzz when it went up for sale again, and since I was in the market, it piqued my interest. There's rumors here and there, but nothing solid. Okay? No one died on the property, by the way. There was a girl—"

"I know already. I did all my own research." I cut her off.

"*I* actually did most of that research." Willow corrected me. "Willow Graham." she extended her arm across the table to shake Liv's hand. "I'm a regular here, and I've read several of your books. Fantastic work."

I cringed as Liv returned the gesture. "Nice to meet you, Willow. And?" She shifted her eyes.

"Joel … uh, Quinn." He nodded with a friendly wave.

Liv redirected her attention to me. "Honey, I'm sorry I didn't tell you. You don't buy into that woo-woo so I didn't think you'd care. But you're right. I should've told you, especially since we are both in a … sensitive place right now." She rubbed my shoulder gently.

No kidding.

"It was a long time ago that that girl died, and I've never had anything happen to me at the house, okay? We spent hours there every day. And you can trust that, because if something had, I'd be all over it and you know that. If I'm not writing you shouldn't be worrying," she explained.

Exactly why I won't be telling you.

I'd gotten my frustrations out and needed this conversation to wrap up before she started thinking any more about the house. The last thing I needed was for my life to become a spectacle. There would be no James Wan movie made about my home.

"Of course." Willow stepped in for me. "It's just jolting to find out something like that, I think. But now that Emma knows the facts from the fiction, she can settle in a little and get used to the house as it is." She smiled brightly at me. "Right, Em?"

"Yes! It's a beautiful house, hun. We can't change the past, but we can try to make a better future. That's what you should be focusing on." Liv grinned warmly and brushed her hair behind her ear. "Well, I should get going. This was just a pit-stop on my day full of nothing but boring errands." She paused and grabbed my hand. "Try to move on. I love you."

I can't move on if Lynette doesn't.

"Love you, too," I muttered.

"*But*— if anything does come up, lemme know. Kay? Bye guys." She waved to my friends as she hastily headed out the door with her black Kate Spade crossbody bag on her shoulder and her phone in hand. The bells jingled as the door closed behind her. I zoned out on the shelf of books along the wall as the bells quieted down gently.

No one spoke for several seconds. Finally, Willow interrupted the soft jazz over the speakers. "Well. It's not true what they say … 'don't meet your heroes' … I think she's delightful."

I shot her a heated glare.

"I think that went better than it could've," she added, pursing her lips.

I turned to face our table. "I'm gonna walk home. See you guys later." I grabbed my small canvas tote.

"Hey, it's okay. Please don't go." Joel hung his head.

"I'll text you." I pushed in my chair. "I'm just … over this right now."

"Aren't we gonna talk about our next steps?" Willow asked quickly.

I looked at her and ground my teeth. "Nope." I headed outside the cafe and back up the wharf for a partly-cloudy, humid afternoon walk.

There were no next steps, and nothing left to discuss. I knew what my only option was.

8.

GO GET IT

I truly did have every intention of telling Lynette. I just needed a glass of wine under a cozy blanket first. I sank into the couch alone that night sipping my cheap cabernet and waiting for her to show herself again.

You…are going to tell the little dead girl in your house that her big sister is also dead. You're gonna do it and then she'll move on and it'll be over and you can…do whatever you were gonna do with your life. Which was…what?

I took another sip from my one and only wine glass. It was gifted to me by Liv from the White Horse Tavern- a true staple of Newport's rich history- for my twenty-first birthday a few years back; she'd sent it in the mail since we couldn't go visit that year. I thought back on the memory of a time one summer when Liv, Ken, mom, and I went to dinner there.

***

I was excited to eat there, even as a teenager. I loved the feel of historical landmarks, and even more-so colonial ones. At the beginning, I was loving the atmosphere, but during dinner, I'd seen a man in colonial garb standing by one of the fireplaces in the restaurant. I tried my best to focus on my dinner and ignore him but he wouldn't leave. He'd slowly turned his head from the flames to briefly glance at me in his long, loose, front-laced shirt under an open vest that looked like canvas. The top was tucked into dingy light amber trousers. Both his face and short ponytail were damp with sweat that glistened slightly in the light of the flames. His contribution

71

to the colonial theme was immersive yet unappetizing, his energy overwhelmingly disconcerting. It seemed I was the only one affected by it, though, as everyone else continued dining gleefully. He didn't interact with anyone but me.

"You okay, honey?" my mom asked as I stared at the fireplace, my empty fork hovering over my plate.

"Nothing," I responded automatically, glancing from the man to my mom. Our candlelit table gave a off warm dim glow.

"Didja see a ghost?" Aunt Liv flashed her eyes wide as she leaned over her lobster dinner. "You know, this *is* America's oldest tavern. 1673. I wouldn't be surprised." She wooed half-jokingly.

"Liv, stop teasing." My uncle chuckled.

"Oh Ken, come on." Liv playfully shoved him.

"She's kidding, babe." My mom reassured me. "What's wrong?"

I looked down at my own plate of pasta and shook my head. "Just a headache," I added, closing my eyes and rubbing my temples to sell the act. I thought maybe the tighter I squeezed my eyes shut, the more likely my problem would resolve itself.

Please go.

I opened my eyes to take a peek. To my relief, the man was gone, and no one in the rest of the dining room was fazed.

Why am I the only one?

"I'm gonna go to the bathroom really quick."

"Do you need some Tylenol? You got any in your purse, Liv?" Uncle Ken wiped his mouth as he watched me quickly shoot up toward the entrance area.

Luckily, I didn't see anything else out of the ordinary that night. I tried my hardest to forget him and eventually the memory faded to the back of my mind, but never disappeared. Their food was far too good for me to vow never to return, and I did eat there a couple times after that. I just made sure to avoid each and every fireplace in the tavern. My eyes would be directly on my plate or whoever was talking to me.

Unless they were dead.

***

I blinked back to the present moment and stared out the window across the room. From my place on my couch, I was met with my reflection against the darkness outside. I finished the last few sips of wine in my glass, and went to exchange it for my phone on the end table.

Wait— what the— what? Where is it?

I could've sworn I'd left it right next to me, but maybe the cabernet was taking the edge off a little too much. I got up to look for it in the kitchen, which led me into the dining room. I walked into the front living area, and back around to the foyer. A complete circle, and no phone.

I hadn't gone upstairs, though. I scratched my head and stood in the doorway between the foyer and the family room where I'd just been sitting. As I squinted at the floor near the couch, I heard faint music playing upstairs. Soft keys of a piano, smooth brass…

Had I gone upstairs?

My eyes narrowed. Even if I had, I wouldn't have left my music on.

I groaned, mainly because I had to venture up the stairs while buzzed, and because I dreaded what I'd find up there. I knew in my gut that I'd had my phone right next to me on the couch.

The upstairs hall light was still on from that morning. *Whoops.* While it was relieving, it only increased my comfort level about five percent.

I took each step one at a time, which seemed to take forever. Once my feet reached the wood floor upstairs, I exhaled deeply.

The music was clearer now. If I'd left it anywhere upstairs, it would've been my room since that was the only place I ever went into up there other than the bathroom. My light at the far left end of the hall was off, but I noticed simultaneously that the music wasn't even coming from that direction. Instead, the spare bedroom door across from me- which I always kept shut- was cracked open. The music was coming from there, clear as day.

You can still book it out of here.

I took a creaky step forward and made it to the door to lean over and peer into the thin open crack. Not only had I spotted my phone, but I'd found the thief.

Naturally, I was terrified at the sight of the little dead girl dancing alone to jazz music on my phone in an empty old room, but there was an odd comforting energy surrounding it. I peeked over a little bit further to see more through the crack, but my weight shifting made the floor creak louder. I cringed.

Lynette froze in a distorted twirl, her neck craned and arms posed in mid-air, as if someone had just pushed pause on her. She slowly rotated her head to investigate on the sound.

How much did I drink?

Our eyes met and she gasped, breaking her pose and straightening up like a little toy soldier. I gasped right back and jumped out of view, leaning against the hallway wall to take a few mindful breaths to assess the situation. She seemed just as scared of me, and almost embarrassed.

Just like a normal kid…How human.

"Hello?" I asked into the chilly air.

Moments passed with no response, so I peeked back into the room, now empty and silent. The dim ceiling light was still on in the room.

I pushed the door open halfway. "Lynette?"

She was completely gone. *I* had scared the ghost away. What a turn of events.

I ventured into the center of the room, slowly inching my way to the other side to snatch my phone off the windowsill.

I turned around and went to my contacts to text Willow and Joel before leaving the room, but a familiar soft voice interrupted my thought process.

"Are you mad?" Lynette reappeared in the doorway.

I looked up slowly. "Uh…freaked out, yeah." I kept my thumb hovering over the send button just in case this encounter went south.

"I'm sorry." Lynette took a step closer.

I felt a ping in my chest. "It's okay. I— uh— just really need this on me" —I shook the phone nervously in my hand— "like all the time."

"Is that *really* a telephone?" She peered over to get a another look at it.

As she studied my phone, I exhaled slowly. "Yeah."

"I'm sorry I took it." She shook her head modestly.

"It's okay…"

There was a pause. We stared at each other blankly until Lynette took another step forward and tilted her head. "I tried to leave you alone so I wouldn't scare you again."

"Swiping my phone and running off with it didn't really help that." I slid my phone in my pocket.

She sighed. "I just miss music so much."

"What were you dancing to?"

"One of my favorite songs. It's Benny Goodman. Do you know of him?"

"Of course I do. I love him." I cleared my throat. "How did you figure out how to play music on this?"

"Is that lady always on the phone to help you?"

"No, it's just something in the phone."

"So someone works *inside* the phone." She sneered. "I suppose a lot *has* changed."

"No, it's like the phone's nickname."

"Why does it have a name?"

"It's just like a— it's called AI. It's new tech."

"But I've heard you call it Siri."

"You know what— it doesn't matter."

"It's not a real person you're talking to, then?"

"No, it's a robot. AI is a kind of robot, I guess."

"Woah." Her mouth gaped idly.

"Yep."

"You talk to it a lot. And it listens. Like magic," she whispered.

"Eh, I guess."

She gave a small, shy grin and looked up from her shoes. "You're nice." Lynette nodded in approval. I watched as she continued to stare at my pocket. Her eyes sagged as she started turning around to vanish down the hall.

I noticed the bloody wound on her head and had to look away to the floor. "Wait."

Lynette froze, then retreated from the hall toward me again until she was only about three feet from me. I sucked in a breath. Her skin and blue eyes were so sad and tired.

"You can ... hold onto it for a little longer." I tried to stop shaking as I slowly took my phone out and extended my hand toward her.

Oh my god, what am I doing?

She looked from my face to the phone in my hand. "Really?" Her eyes widened. "I used to dance with Gwen all the time."

"Take it. I'll come get it in ... like ... an hour ... okay?" I shook my head slightly.

I'm really sharing my phone and striking up a deal with a ghost right now?

"Alright." She smiled up at me.

"Siri, play Benny Goodman." I spoke as clearly as I could and gently slipped the phone into her freezing hand. "See? Magic."

"Thank you."

"You're welcome." I sighed.

Lynette walked past me toward the window, and I felt a cold breeze cross the left side of my body. She set the phone back gently on the wide windowsill facing the street and looked at me. "I won't break it, I promise."

"I believe you." I gazed at her, feeling unsettlingly comfortable. A morbid sense of intrigue and familiarity made me hesitant to look away. Her tender charm was puzzling against the grisly, uncanny visual projection of her energy.

Lynette didn't move again while we looked at each other, and it took me a second to realize why. "Oh, do you want me to go?"

She looked down and nodded bashfully.

"Oh— okay."

I blinked incredulously and made my way out.

I tried not to look back at Lynette before I quietly closed the door behind me. I was giving privacy to a spirit.

To dance.

To music on *my* phone.

As I left her alone in the room, the soft jazz music became muffled. I didn't know what to do with myself. I leaned against the wall in the hallway and held my face in my hands.

What … is this? I'm not even alone when I'm alone.

At that moment, I wished I could talk to my mom about all of this. She'd always let me unload and vent about everything that overwhelmed me. She was a very talented listener, always helping me slow down to dissect each worry, each issue, so I could make sense of them and figure out the best solution. She was probably the one person I could've talked to about this beside Willow and Joel. Everyone else would've been convinced that I'd lost my mind. Aunt Liv probably would've believed me. But I wasn't telling her any of this if I didn't have to.

For the next hour, I'd have to sit and stew until I could text the group chat.

I brushed my fingers through my hair and decided to go read on my bed, but I ended up only reading a few pages because I couldn't stop looking up into the hall. It was hard to focus when I could see the spare bedroom door and the light peeking out from under it.

When I looked at the little antique clock on my desk across from me, it'd only been twenty five minutes since I'd left Lynette. The music was still playing, so I took a deep breath, closing my book and my eyes.

Just a couple minutes later, the music suddenly stopped. I opened one eye, breaking from my mini meditation. I sat up and peered at the closed door ahead.

That doesn't sound right.

"You done?" I called hesitantly from my bed and was met with no response. The door creaked open slowly until it was halfway open.

The light in the room shut off immediately after I asked. but I still got no reply. I watched as my phone slowly inched out of the darkness, then slid out of the room and midway into the hall.

Was that a yes?

I gulped, not expecting that to be the way Lynette would return my phone. It was profoundly creepy, even if it was unintentional.

I didn't move, but wondered whether or not she would walk out of the room. I was so tempted to go grab my phone and text my new friends, but I didn't want to get up and go into the hall just yet.

Something's not right.

I slid my legs off the side of the bed. I was prepared to venture cautiously into the hall, but then the bathroom and hallway light turned off, too. The entire floor was pitch black now aside from my small desk lamp.

"Hey, not okay. You're scaring me now."

My mind wandered back to Willow's claim that she'd picked up on a strong negative energy in the house as well. I'd momentarily forgotten about it because Lynette's vibrations were so gentle. Once I remembered, a spike of fear penetrated my chest and I felt a pressure fill the room.

I stared at my phone for what felt like minutes, until a deep whisper in my left ear chilled me to the core.

"Go get it."

The cold sharp voice sent a chill rushing down my spine, my eyes widened almost enough to pop right out of my head. Petrified, I exhaled shallowly, unable to even blink.

The second my phone lit up with the ringtone at full volume, I instinctively jumped off the bed and darted into the hall, scooping up my phone and almost slipping. I sped down the stairs at what felt like light-speed, misstepping twice. Luckily I was able to catch myself both times and in a matter of seconds, I was at the bottom and out the front door. I made my way down the porch steps with haste and found temporary safety on the sidewalk.

I heaved, shakily holding my phone.

Willow was calling.

I scurried to hit the green button before it sent her to voicemail, "He— helluh— hello?"

"Are you okay?" Willow shouted into the phone.

I knelt down on the cement without turning my back on the house. The lights were still on downstairs and I realized that in my panic, I left the front door wide open. "I don't know. I'm outside, I heard a voice in—" I sniffled. "I— I ran," I mustered out in an attempt to catch my breath.

"We're coming. I need you to breathe and tell us what happened, okay?"

As I stared up into my house searching for the words to express the itching, bouncing fear in my chest, a tall male figure walked into plain view and leaned casually against the front doorframe. My heart dropped all the way down to my bladder. I couldn't see much detail on him with the light inside the house coming from behind him. He wasn't much more than a silhouette himself, facing the darkness out on the street.

I didn't need minutiae to recognize him. It was the man that taunted and chased through the trees in Lynette's memory and in my nightmares. It was that cocky, dapper silhouette.

What I could manage to take in before I looked away and balled myself up in self-preservation on the sidewalk was what seemed like business casual clothing and slick hair that glistened subtly from the light of the street lamps. His abnormally large and twisted smile let his teeth gleam, standing out against his dark form. His eyes glowed as if bright moonlight were reflecting off of them but that wasn't possible; the moon was shrouded behind clouds above and behind the roof. Something inside me knew it had no worldly light source; it was a fiery evil illuminating from within, a wicked jack-o-lantern placed confidently on my doorstep.

"Emma? You there?"

I couldn't reply to Willow, nor could I move. I struggled to catch my breath.

I glanced up once to see him stand up tall and straight as a board, wave, and slowly turn around to close the front door behind him as if he'd owned the place. Once I heard the door latch, I felt my chest cave in and a wave of heat hit my face. My hands began to sweat and shake. I couldn't explain the mixture of anger, heartbreak, fear, and anxiety that permeated my body. Maybe it was the fact that I'd already encountered him in my sleep, or the change from the past few months catching up to me. Everything had been building, and then everything came crashing down with the sight of him.

"Hello? *Hey*. We're on our way. You're out of the house, right? Hello?"

I trusted that Willow would arrive quickly but I couldn't speak. My heart pounded as I hung up the phone and squeezed my eyes shut, melting into a seat on the curb. Fear of his return turned into the frantic compulsion to keep opening my eyes and looking at the front door, only to quickly hide away in my crossed arms. The last time I looked at the house, the lights were on, and one of the front living room curtains billowed slightly. Other than that, there was no activity from within the house— nothing I could see, anyway.

When I finally heard the Prius screech into the driveway. my eyes were open but buried between my knees and glued to the sidewalk beneath me.

9.

ALWAYS YOURS

I wasn't keeping track of time, but it couldn't have taken long for my support crew to pull up into the driveway and jump out of the car. By that time, my breathing was a bit steadier.

"What happened? What are you doing out here?" Willow planted her feet in front of me, blocking my view of the house and breaking my daze.

"I saw him," I replied dryly.

Joel knelt down next to me and rubbed my shoulder. "Hey, it's okay. Where did you see him?"

"I was with Lynette, and then she wanted— she had my phone and then I went to take rest so she could keep— so she could dance but—"

"*Huh?* " Willow knelt down next to me, more-so like a coach giving a pep-talk than a friend providing comfort. "Emma, listen. I need you start taking deeper breaths right now so you can explain to us what just went down. Let's get you inside."

"*No!* Are you crazy?" I shook my head. "I'm not going back in there."

I locked eyes with Willow. She studied my face intensely as crickets chirped from the surrounding hydrangea bushes in front of the house. The light blue flowers gave off a warm, dim, purplish glow, like little orbs floating in the night.

"Hey." Joel spoke softly. "We'll all go in together, but it's late and you probably don't want anyone seeing you like this, right? Let's go inside, okay? No one's gonna hurt you."

I looked into each of his emerald eyes.

"I promise," he added.

I watched as Willow's eyes shifted to him, then back to me. She quietly stood up and reached her hand out. "Let's go, girl."

I held her hand tightly and brushed myself up off the sidewalk. She squeezed my hand back, then broke her grip on me to head up the front steps before us. Joel sighed and chivalrously gestured for me to follow her. "We got you," he said reassuringly.

I could've refused to go inside. I could've begged them to take me to their place. But if I wasn't there, it meant Lynette was there alone with him. I didn't want that, although she probably didn't need my protection. I also knew that I would have to go back in regardless, and it was better to go in with friends than later by myself. That was my new home, even if there was a monster in it.

Maybe we *were* crazy.

Willow wiped her black boots on the welcome mat and stepped through the doorway. "Well, he didn't lock the door, but he could've. So he must want you to come back in." she observed. "He's territorial, just maybe not over the house."

I didn't walk into the entryway yet. My foot hovered over the threshold.

"What? Are you waiting for an 'all clear'? Joel, get in here." Willow jutted her head forward.

He gently brushed past me to look around the downstairs briefly. After a second, he turned to us and nodded his head. "I don't see anybody. I think we're okay for now." He smiled sympathetically at me.

With that, I stepped in but hesitated to close the door behind us. "Couldn't he still be watching?"

"I guess. But I'm feeling a heavy pull downstairs," she stated confidently. "That usually means that's where the energy is coming from."

"In the basement?"

"Mm. He's basic." Willow took a moment to smirk at herself, then walked into the family room to join Joel, who had curiously ventured further into the house. "I'm guessing he just wanted to take a moment out of his busy schedule to introduce himself to you." She scoffed.

Why do they always hide in the basement?

I closed the door and followed my companions.

The three of us huddled together on the couch. After I calmed down a bit and gave my account of the night's events, we all sat in contemplation.

"He didn't hurt me," I mumbled, staring straight out the window into the darkness.

"I've felt his energy. I feel like if he wanted to hurt you tonight, he would've been more aggressive," Willow reassured.

"I think he *was* pretty aggressive." I stared at the floor.

"Okay well I think he would've at least tried."

"Remember, Emma. I've never been hurt by a spirit. Not even the angry ones. Okay?"

"Mm." Willow pursed her lips.

"What?" Joel craned his neck over to her. I insisted on being situated in the middle under a big cozy blanket for my protection. I leaned my head back so they could talk across me.

"I just— I think he may be ... different from ones you've dealt with. Just because he didn't hurt you tonight doesn't mean he's good news. Not to undermine your portfolio, Joel. I just don't think he's that easy."

"Easy?" Joel yawned.

"I think it's safe to assume he was the one chasing Lynette in your dream but we still don't know who the hell he is and why he's here." Willow reminded us.

"*Obviously*. Did you think I'd forgotten that?" I snapped back.

She raised her brows at me. "Um, *nooo*. I'm saying that it's possible he may just be ... malicious, in life *and* death. Not just lost—"

"You're right. *But* maybe we're missing a piece and shouldn't be making assumptions. There could be a misunderstanding somewhere and that's why he's angry. He may *not* be malicious," Joel explained.

Willow nodded slowly. "I appreciate your never-ending optimism, Joel."

I mustered a hopeful half-smile at him.

"But I know what I felt, and you're wrong." she finished her thought.

Go get it.

"He taunted me. He toyed with me. He must've scared Lynette away, too. I'm sorry Joel, but I don't think there's any misunderstanding here." I spoke to Joel but locked eyes with Willow, who nodded slowly again.

"It doesn't change that he hasn't hurt you." Joel circled back to his previous point.

"Maybe he likes to play with his food first," Willow joked dryly, then probably realized how terrifying that thought actually was for *all* of us. "Kidding." She gulped. "Just kidding."

There was silence in the room for some time, which was finally broken by Joel. "Did you tell Lynette about her sister?"

"No." I bit the inside of my lip.

"We need to find out the connection between this guy and Lynette. There isn't much to do about this until then," Willow responded.

"We'll stay here with you tonight. Okay?" Joel volunteered.

"Yeah … what time is it?" I asked, peering into the kitchen to see the clock on the microwave. It was already eleven o'clock.

"We're happy to stay. But I need to stretch out, so…" Willow trailed off, grabbing another blanket from the back of the couch and one of my throw pillows. She plopped down on the floor in front of us and got herself cozy before opening up a YouTube video on her phone. "If anything happens, wake me up. Night, guys." She yawned and popped her earbuds in.

Joel and I were left in quiet. I stared over at the steps that led down from the family room. At the bottom, the back patio was on the right and the basement steps were on the left. Before the top of the short stairway was a wooden door. I wondered why he would stay lurking down in the basement, and if I should get up to close the door. It seemed pointless. It would hardly keep him out.

As if he'd read my mind, Joel lightly nudged my shoulder. "Would it make you feel better if I closed it?"

I nodded immediately. "Just because— sorry. I know it's dumb."

As he leapt over Willow, whose eyes were already closed, he spoke softly. "It's dumb to apologize for wanting to feel safe."

"Thanks."

He shut the door and dead-bolted it, then headed back over to the couch. "Do you mind?" He pointed down at the blanket I was using.

"Yeah— no. Go ahead," I stammered.

He settled in under the blanket, pulling his knees into his chest. "Are you sure you didn't want to go sleep in your own bed? We'll stay down here and keep an eye out. Maybe an ear, too."

"No, I'm sure. I'd rather just be with you guys. I'm still shaky from what he said to me up there."

"I mean— understandably." He chuckled quietly. His face lightened up for a moment before returning to an empathetic gaze. "You know…"

I watched as he took a deep breath and looked off into the kitchen doorway beside us. He sighed. "She really just wants to help. I know she seems … snappy," We both looked down at Willow, who was already fast asleep on the floor, one fallen earbud resting on her cheek. The video kept playing on her phone. "But it's because she's protective. I guess what I'm saying is … I'm sorry if she comes off as intimidating. I know I probably wouldn't appreciate the pushiness if I were just now coming into my ability."

"No, it's okay." I hadn't thought about it much until then. "I think I actually needed it. Otherwise, I would've kept pretending it didn't exist." I nodded to myself. "Then I'd feel more alone than *ever* tonight."

We both heard a creak from above us. "That's from up in my room."

"Do you want me to go check it out?" He offered his protection as he looked at the ceiling.

I shook my head, too exhausted to take in any more excitement for one night.

"She talks about you a lot."

"How do you mean?" I wondered.

"Just about how she felt when you met. She said she could feel a whole friendship. There's something different about you."

"That's weird," I whispered.

He simply chuckled again, and leaned his head back against the couch. "Yeah, she felt like a creep about it all. Said it was worth it, though."

"I just mean— not to be rude but … I've only known you guys for a couple of days. The circumstances are just … wild, though. They've kinda made it feel like I've known you for longer."

"It's funny how quickly you form a bond with people when they're the *only* ones who can even begin to understand what's on your shoulders. I'm lucky I have her."

"Yeah." I nodded.

"And now you. There's a real kinship in sharing the same weight on your shoulders. Especially between the two of us, you know?"

"Yeah." I paused, crossing my arms under the blanket I shared with Joel. "She said it shouldn't be seen as a burden but a gift."

"She's full of shit." He laughed quietly. "Sure it's a gift. It feels … really rewarding actually … to help someone move past their pain. But obviously there's more to it than that. I mean— you're dealing with death. There's darkness by default. It's okay to accept it as both. Burdens *can* be a gift and I try to remember that. I don't think we'd have such a sensitivity to it if we weren't worthy."

"That's quite the hero's speech."

"Psh." He shook his head humbly. "I'm just trying to help you stay realistic without losing sight of the positive." He yawned again and closed his eyes, "Cause there's always some there."

"Well, thank you for that." I caught the contagious yawn and tried to get comfortable enough to rest my eyes. Both of us needed sleep, but I was positive I wouldn't be able to. However, I realized not long after we stopped talking just *how* much my fear had drained me once the adrenaline slowed down. The second my eyes closed, they stayed that way.

***

Emma.
My eyelids fluttered open, then heavily closed again.
Emma.

"Hm?" In my sleep, the distant voice didn't phase me.

"Emma," a voice whispered directly into my ear.

My neck jolted off the back of the couch. I looked around the room. Joel and Willow were still fast asleep, but when I shifted to my right I saw Lynette standing next to the arm of the couch, looking right into my eyes. She still appeared mostly vacant, but I could sense worry in her. Even though I trusted my intuition that she didn't pose a threat to me, the unexpected sight jolted me fully awake with unease.

I whispered, "Lyn— what—"

"He's been watching ... around the house."

"What's his name?"

"Emma?" Joel mumbled beside me. He turned over onto his right side to face me, then he settled back to sleep.

Lynette looked down at Joel, then me. "Who's he?"

"Lynette, what's his name? Who is he?" I whispered, brushing off her inquiries. I needed to know, but I didn't want to wake Joel.

"Who are you talking to?" Joel squinted sleepily. After one hard blink, he opened his eyes and had the same reaction I did to seeing a bloody-headed little girl watching us sleep. "Oh shhhi—"

"Shhh." I laid a hand on his arm quickly to calm him, "Friends." I tried to reassure both of them.

"Jack," Lynette whimpered.

"Huh?" Joel asked.

"That's his name. Jack," she muttered.

"Jack who? I want a full name."

"Carlson," she whispered.

"Okay, well ... I'm not gonna let him hurt you." I reassured her, but realized that the truth was ... I didn't think there *was* anything he could do to her at that point. I wasn't going to remind her of that, though.

She shook her head slowly.

"What's wrong?" I asked, instinctively reaching for her hand. We only touched for half a second, but it felt like a freezing electric current had zipped up my arm from her fingers. I pulled away sharply.

"He's scary but he can't hurt me anymore. He's been watching you." I didn't break from her gaze until we heard two loud bangs from behind the door that led to the patio and basement. Lynette gasped and vanished in front of us.

I jumped, but kept staring blankly at the spot where Lynette was standing.

"Hey, it's okay. Don't freak." Joel put his hand on the back of my shoulder.

"What the hell was *that*?" Willow woke up visibly upset, and rubbed her eyes aggressively. I couldn't tell if she was scared or angry.

"I don't know, but I'm gonna go check. Stay here," Joel announced as he got up to investigate.

He made it to the door and unlocked it, flipping on the light switch to illuminate the old linoleum steps down to the ground level. I saw light hit the wall that I was zoned out on.

I heard Joel take a few steps down the stairs, and then pace back into the family room. "Come look."

I glanced over but didn't move up off the couch.

"Emma." Willow tried to snap me out of my gaze.

"Seriously, look," Joel called. He made his way back over to the couch and stood in front of me. "Have you seen this before?"

I gazed up to see him holding an old black and white photo of a couple standing outside the house. One of them was obviously Carlson. I knew that arrogant smile and those piercing eyes. He wore a button up dress shirt and slacks with a hand shoved in one pocket. The young woman seemed full of life, with wavy dark hair down to her shoulders and a smile like summer sunshine. Her light dress seemed to billow in the breeze by the way the skirt swished to her right in the picture. Even in monochrome, she sparkled like labradorite catching the light at the perfect moment and angle. While she looked straight up at him on her left, his focus was off to the right at something out of view.

"Who is it?" Joel wondered.

"I can take a guess." I took the photo, faded and stained over time. "It's her sister."

As Joel studied it with me, he noticed something on the backside. "Hold on." he flipped it over in my hand. There was a note written in cursive: *Always yours Jack.*

"That's him." I felt a piece of the puzzle click into place.

"Well, someone wanted us to see this, and if it wasn't Lynette, it must've been him. Why would he want us to see this?" Joel mulled it over.

"Well, it's something." My eyes were glued to the photo. He looked familiar, of course, but so did she. Like with Carlson, it was the eyes and smile that stood out, but in a very different way.

I realized Willow had remained uncharacteristically quiet, so I looked over at her to find that she was sitting hunched over the pillow.

"Wills? Thoughts?" Joel invited her two cents, but she stayed motionless, her eyes fixated down on the dark abyss that was the basement entry.

"Wills?"

I didn't have to know Willow long to instantly recognize the look that had washed over her. It was the same one she'd had on her face when we first met, when she'd apparently seen so much about me. The same shock and overwhelm, yes. This time however, it was joined by an unmistakable sense of fear in her eyes, but whether it was fear of the unknown or *known* was uncertain.

"You okay?" I asked gently, stepping toward her.

She gazed for a moment more, then blinked and looked up slowly. Her expression changed then as she became aware of her audience. "Yeah. I'm fine, just tired. The knocking freaked me out, just— it was super loud." She swallowed. "I'm going back to bed, or floor … whatever," Willow muttered and positioned herself back to the way she was laying before.

A feeling gnawed at me that she was keeping something from us. My instinct was confirmed by the concerned glare Joel shot toward her after she laid down to rest. Neither of us pushed, but exchanged a skeptical look before trying to fall asleep again, at least until the sun came up.

Joel and I plopped back down in our spots on the couch. He turned on his left side facing me and rested his face in his palm against the back of the couch. "Emma."

I turned to him, pulling my blanket up to my shoulders. "Do you think he'd hurt me?"

"Like I said, nothing's *ever* hurt me. Never even tried. I wish I could promise you that he won't, but I don't know who we're dealing with. All I know is that you're not alone. Maybe Lynette's just worried for you because … maybe he tried to hurt her before … but we don't know for sure until we hear it from her. Just rest for now and we'll come back to all this later, okay?"

"Okay." I shifted my eyes to Willow on the floor. "Is she keeping something from us?"

"I don't know. Her face usually says it all, but I've never really seen *that* look before." He sighed.

I had no idea what else to say about the situation. I needed rest so I could think it through in the morning with a semi-refreshed mind. I closed my eyes and tried to take deep belly breaths— in through my nose, out through my mouth— just like my mom had taught me. A few minutes into my meditation, I felt myself start to drift off. I also felt a brief, soft brush against my cheek.

"Good job. It's gonna be okay." I heard a faint whisper from Joel next to me.

I tried my best to believe him, but one uncomfortable thought echoed in my mind while I slept, making it hard to truly accept his reassurance.

Jack Carlson, why were you out there that night?

10.

YOU COULD BE HAPPY HERE

I woke up to shuffling in the room, and immediately worried it was another visit from one of our resident ghosts. I fluttered my eyes open and saw a blurry Willow folding up her blanket and forcing her feet into her boots. I slowly raised my head off of...

...Joel's chest?

I scrambled to sit up straight.

"Where are you going?" I whispered as I quickly readjusted myself on the couch, crossing my fingers that Joel hadn't noticed I'd ended up on him. "You aren't gonna comment on that ... make fun of me?"

"No. I'm going out," she replied, clearly not worried about keeping her voice down. I rubbed my eyes and saw her clearly. She ran her fingers through her red-velvety hair to tie it up in a ponytail that glistened in the rays of morning sun. The silky bright blue ends stood out in the light that shone through the blinds. She rushed to tidy up her campsite from the night before, as if something urgent needed her attention.

"Out where?" Now I pushed for answers. Just from the time I'd spent with her so far, I could tell she was being especially vague, removed.

"Library." she tossed her pillow onto my lap.

"For what?"

"More research."

"About the house?"

"And about what's-his-name." Willow nodded once and laid the folded blanket on the coffee table. She reached for her jacket that hung from a hook near the kitchen door.

"Jack Carlson."

"Yeah, him."

"Well then I'm coming." I volunteered instantly. This was my home's history to figure out. If we were in any danger at all, it was my fault for getting them involved.

"No, you're not. I need some space. Just to think. But I'll let you know what I find … okay?

"Yeah, but—"

"No, I'm not mad at you."

"I didn't think you were," I replied dryly.

"Good." She put on her mustard suede jacket and brushed her hair behind her shoulder.

"Are you okay?" I pried.

"I'm dandy." She tilted her head and dropped her shoulders, "I'm overwhelmed and I want answers. For all of us."

I scoffed. "So do I."

"That's awesome. We'll get some."

"So let me come with you and do my own search. We'll compare." I suggested eagerly.

"How about you just chill with Joel and do something that doesn't involve worrying about any of this shit?" Willow spoke quickly, maintaining her position.

"I could ask you to do the same thing. It's my house. I don't get it."

She simply shrugged.

"Fine."

"I'll see you guys soon." Willow turned around. I followed her to the foyer before she waltzed out the front door. Through the window I watched as she flew down the steps and quickly jumped into her car. She peeled out of the driveway like she was late for something, and was gone in a matter of seconds. I blinked and turned back to Joel, who was unbothered and still asleep on the couch. As if he'd sensed being watched, though, he fussed for a moment and then stretched his arms and back as he opened his eyes. He looked around the room for a second and his eyes made their way to the foyer arch. "Whatcha doin in there?"

"Walking Willow out, I guess." I sighed and returned to the family room.

He tossed his hands up. "She was my ride."

"I don't know. She was all frantic. Said she was going back to the library. I told her to wait for me but she definitely just dissed me. She said she 'needed space to think'."

"That's not a great sign." Joel cringed.

"What if she knows something?"

"There's probably a good reason she's keeping it to herself, then. She'll tell us eventually. I trust her." He nodded. "Until then, you wanna go grab some breakfast? On me." He grinned and yawned. "I could go for Ma's." He licked his lips.

"Me too." I gritted my teeth. "But as much as I *do* want an apple dutch crumb … no car." I pouted sympathetically.

"*Damn.* You're right. Raincheck." He winked. "I guess we'll walk somewhere. Let's head toward Broadway. I know a couple places."

"So do I." I smiled.

Despite Willow's bizarre departure, it felt good not being alone so early in the morning, in addition to the fact that I hadn't had another nightmare that night.

***

Later that afternoon, I stood in my kitchen sipping my third cup of coffee for the day. The first two were enjoyed with Joel and some thick waffles at a corner cafe on Broadway. I was worried at first that a long walk and breakfast alone with him would be awkward, but his calm and easy-going energy proved me wrong so much so that it was difficult to part with him after. He took an interest in me, particularly my summer adventures in Newport. I recounted several memories, and we laughed together when I told him about the time I stepped on a crab at Third Beach. It pinched my little ten-year-old toe so hard that it was still attached when my mom yanked me out of the water. I'd screamed bloody murder so loud that my mom thought there could've been a shark in the water.

I chuckled to myself, looking out the kitchen window toward the trees behind the house. That breakfast was a glimmer of hope for a content life here.

"Did you like the little memento I left you?" a voice behind me asked.

My heart pinged as I jumped at the unexpected presence. I should've known I was never *really* home alone. I knew the voice, and had dreaded this moment.

I just wanted to enjoy my coffee.

I stared out at the driveway to gather myself before turning to face the intruder.

He smiled sinisterly, leaning against the doorway to the dining room. The light of the afternoon sun revealed a deep stain originating in the center of his button-up shirt, spreading outward on the fabric like a macabre painting of a single maroon bloom. There were other smaller bursts of red in several other spots on his torso that accompanied it.

"The picture back there?"

He simply grinned and nodded his head slowly, raising his thick yet well-groomed eyebrows in satisfaction.

Although I was terrified, I couldn't help but be thoroughly disgusted. Arrogance was never impressive. "Gimmicky."

As he took a step forward, I set my mug down on the counter behind me.

"How are you finding your new home, Emma?" he prowled.

"It's fine." I sniffled.

He paused with a smirk. "You know, this is my home, too."

"Okay." I hoped that Joel or Willow would come barging in early. Joel was too polite, but it was a possibility for Willow.

"I see you and Lynette have reintroduced yourselves. Very touching." He looked down to the ground and back up at me slowly.

"Why are you still here?"

He scoffed, picking at one of his fingers. "Well that's not the warm welcome I'd hoped for."

"She was your girlfriend, right? Gwen."

"Oh, she was much more than that."

"She's dead."

"Mm." He sauntered over to me, standing only a foot or two away. "That's disappointing."

"She has been ... for decades," I clarified. His proximity to me sent shivers down my spine.

"But is she really *gone* ?" He leaned in closer and whispered into my ear like he had the night before.

I froze staring straight ahead at the empty dining room. "She's not here. It's just you and Lynette. Whatever you did to" —I stammered— "I don't know what happened to you, but Gwen's gone and you need to leave Lynette alone. There's nothing left for you here." I kept a decently tough façade but still couldn't move, paralyzed by his freezing cold energy.

"Is she *not* in this house?" he whispered.

"Who? Gwen? No, I just said that—"

"Look me in the eye ... and tell me you didn't miss me," he admitted slowly.

"*What* ?" I blurted, yanking myself backward into the counter.

"We both know very well *what*." He teased.

"Is that what the photo was about? Do you think— I don't even *look* like her."

"You may not want to admit it, but you know deep down ... that fate brought you back here." He smiled. "And you know exactly why."

I glared at him. "No, I don't."

His smile disappeared, leaving him stone-faced with an ever so slightly furrowed brow. "I've been watching you ... admiring from afar. You're so soft with her. The way your hand floats above the stair railing. The way your eyes soften onto the pages of the books you read. The way you kiss the cup when you sip your coffee like—"

"Stop." I clenched my fist.

"It's just like her. I see it. You seem innocent enough, and you may have a beautiful new set of eyes, but behind them I still see that same anger." He looked back and forth between each of my eyes, so close to me now. Only inches from my face, he caused a chill to crawl up my spine like a brown recluse.

"I'm not angry."

"You're not a good liar either, darlin'." He scoffed.

"You need to go." I spoke through a clenched jaw.

"Why *are* you so angry?" He paused. I couldn't break from his eyes. "Is it because death follows you? No matter how hard you try to run from it—" he whispered into my ear again, and slid his icy hand halfway up my thigh— "it's always gonna be right behind you." I felt the same tingling of electricity that I'd felt when I'd barely touched Lynette's hand, but it felt so wrong now, venomous.

"I—"

"And you can't be mad at me about Lynette. You know I didn't do it." He shook his head.

"Get … *off* me," I growled, and lunged myself forward through him. Shaken, I took several steps backward into the dining room.

Carlson raised a brow and tilted his head robotically. "You're getting a bit emotional."

"My name is Emma. That's my *only* name. I'm not your girlfriend, not in any way. She's dead, and so are you. Whatever happened before your life ended doesn't matter anymore."

"*Oh*, it matters."

"You need to move on. Lynette, the house, me…you need to leave it all alone," I demanded with as much gumption as I could muster.

He strolled past me into the living room at the front of the house. He moved with an effortless self-importance, clearly throwing my request out the window. "You don't remember *all* the nights we'd get to drinking and take our dancing into your father's study? Right here?" He pointed stiffly to the carpet in the center of the room, revealing a twinge of desperation and bitterness.

"No. I don't. It's not my memory." I eyed the front door, hoping one of my friends would waltz through.

He slowly reapproached to stroke my cheek, studying my face with his pale glassy eyes. "He wasn't ever home enough for you. You needed a man here to take care of you … Mm, hair's almost the same color, too."

My lip quivered as I felt the sting of tears rushing to the inner corners of my eyes.

"I hear you're having nightmares."

I sucked in a breath. "Yeah."

"Well, that's no fun."

"Why were you out there with her?"

"Mm, I don't need to answer that, do I? You seemed to know exactly what happened that night. But you were wrong. And you know it. You're no better than me. You can deny that 'til the cows come home, but like I said, it's in your eyes."

"I don't—"

"Shhh— you want me to move on so we will. Regardless of what happened that night, you were brought back to me. *Always yours, Jack.* It's in *your* handwriting. So let's talk about what comes next."

I scoffed quietly at a loss for words.

"You seem confused, so let me help you understand. We … are going to finish what we started, and not make this any harder than it needs to be." His icy hand rested on my cheek. It was what I imagined frostbite to feel like. "*Always yours.* Just say it. That's the least you can do for me."

I felt pressure building up in my chest. Cold air surrounded my hand as his slithered toward it. "No."

"We can be together. All three of us, a family. Wasn't that your dream?"

"I'm not—" I repeated, shaking my head as his face moved in.

"You could be happy here. But you know what needs to happen for you to make this right … with me, with her … with God." He smirked. "You should've known better than to think leaving like *that* would get you into heaven. That's a sin, Gwenny."

I shook my head stiffly.

He licked his lip. "You really don't want to drag this out. Do you really want to see what this situation looks like drawn out?"

"I told you. I'm *not*—"

"Don't make this difficult."

"I don't even *know* you," I snapped.

Just then, I heard the front door swing open as Willow stepped in with a look of concern.

"Emma?"

Carlson looked toward the door, and took two paces back. "We're not done with this discussion."

He and the gashes in his clothing were gone in a matter of seconds. Only a creeping cold cloud and an foreign sense of violation lingered.

"Is that him? Oh my god, it is. Are you okay?" she blurted as she darted into the living room. "It's fucking freezing in here."

I stood still, staring out the wide front window onto the street. The summer sun was setting. It should've felt refreshing, warm, and radiant on my skin, but instead resembled the light of a distant wildfire pouring into the room.

"Is he gone?"

I felt pressure built up in my chest. There was, of course, fear in me, but pure abhorrence joined it for a man convinced he knew me better than I knew myself. I'd been introduced to a liar who seemed to refuse any accountability in Lynette's death, insistent that a poor young woman owed him her affection even in death. But he was mistaken; neither of us belonged to anyone.

"He's just left," I muttered with a single exasperated nod. I looked over to my friend, who for once appeared unaware of what was going on, "He" —I tried to return my breath to a calm, resting rate— "thinks I'm Gwen."

"What?" Willow looked just as confused as I felt. She took a glimpse around the room and then spoke hesitantly, "I mean- does he have eyes? I—"

"You're later than I'd hoped." I exhaled as I felt the chill dissipate.

She dropped her arms to her side. "I do my best."

As if gently guided, my eyes found their way to the fireplace mantle. There was nothing in the dining room at all so far, and after such a hostile encounter with Carlson, I never wanted to step foot back in there. But as I studied the dusty mantle, a realization washed over me. Something very important to me hadn't yet been unpacked. I didn't quite know what to do with it; nowhere had felt sacred enough to display it. Then, I knew its place. It would protect this room.

"We gotta sage the shit out of this room, Em," Willow said with clear intent.

"Yeah, that too."

11.

CANDY

I spent that night in the house alone, despite the repeated offers from Willow. There was something important I had to do by myself. As she'd vowed, Willow had saged not only the dining room, but the entire house not long after arriving. As luck would have it, she carried a smudge stick and a matchbox in her purse, prepared at all times to remove negative energy from any given space.

Not all heroes wear capes.

I'd be the first to admit, I was skeptical of the sage, even after Willow explained the supposed science of it to me. After she left though, I did feel some relief. Whether the sage actually did hold spiritual properties or not, aromatherapy was highly effective.

Breathing more easily than earlier, I'd carried one particular box into the dining room and carefully sliced the tape open. I softly shooed away the packing popcorn, and gently cradled the urn as I removed it from the box. I ran my hand down the elegant blue marbled glaze, right over a spot in the design that happened to resemble wings. I didn't think it was intentional, but it was a testament to how angelic she was by nature. I dusted the mantle and laid the urn gently on the wood, backing up a couple steps to admire it in its new home.

***

Beep. Beep beep beep. Beeeeep.
Ding. Ding. Ding.

I stared up at the white ceiling. The various chimes from all of the machines attached to my mother only added to the discomfort I felt on my barely cushioned "bed" in our small hospital room.

At least it was private.

"Em," my mom called from her bed, clearing her throat and letting out a painful groan with it.

"Yeah." I sat up immediately, letting out a pained grunt from my sore back.

"C'mere, babe," she spoke softly from a few feet away.

I stood up and made my way to the chair next to the bed. I plopped down. "Do you want some water?"

The television mounted to the wall was the only light illuminating the room, aside from the bright green and blue buttons that glowed on the big bulky machines from the other side of my mom. It was easy to lose time in a hospital, but I was informed by the news on tv that it was nine o'clock already. The nurse would be returning in the next half hour for more blood work.

"Where's Liv?"

"She went downstairs to grab us some dinner. Mama, do you want some water?"

"No, honey."

"Okay, well. You need some, so…" I swallowed and held the styrofoam cup up to her, bending the straw to meet her pale lips. The crushed ice shifted to the front of the cup with a crunch.

She took a couple small sips, and then nodded stiffly for me to move the cup away. I wanted her to drink more, but I wasn't going to push. That wouldn't do anything at this point.

"Baby." she closed her eyes.

"Yeah."

"You know, they're probably going to ask if we want to move to hospice care."

"Stop."

"No."

Beep. Beep beep beep. Beeeeep.

Ding. Ding. Ding.

"You and I" —she coughed— "both know … that no matter how many pokes or pills they give me … it isn't gonna … make this body any better." The amount of pauses she had to take made my eyes well up with tears. Her voice broke. My heart broke.

"Mom." I scoffed, feigning simple annoyance with her comment. I brushed the teardrop aside before it could hit my cheek, before my mom could see it.

"Wiping it away doesn't … hide it. I know you're— I'm sorry. I know that you're …. struggling."

"So are you."

"Don't pretend to be fine just to … make me feel less guilty." She let out a shallow sigh.

"I need to be strong for you. I have to be able to handle all of this."

"That's an awfully big … burden to put on yourself, Em."

Beep. Beep beep beep. Beeeeep.

Ding. Ding. Ding.

"So?"

"So, enough." She grabbed my hand and squeezed it with whatever strength she could muster. She gently tapped the padding on her bed with our interlocked hands a few times. "I'm gonna tell you what's gonna happen. Step…by step." She cleared her throat again. "They are gonna come in tonight … or tomorrow … and tell me this is … it. And that's that. We'll … figure out a hospice situation and … deal."

I searched my mind for a response, but had none. I stared at the bedside heart monitor screen.

"I'm sick of being poked." She let out a long, tired sigh. "At least now we know the answer."

"I'm scared, mom."

"Don't be. I'm not," she responded without hesitation.

"What am I gonna do?"

"Whatever you want."

"I want to stay with you."

"Well, *that's* not gonna be very fun."

Beep. Beep beep beep. Beeeeep.

Ding. Ding. Ding.

"Go to Newport." My mom smiled weakly and gently shook my hand in hers. "Go be with them."

"That's too far from home, mom." I let out a whimper as I spoke, "It's too far from you."

"We can ... sort out the details later. But either way ... I'll go where you go. It shouldn't be the other way around. You need to go out and ... live your life, girl." She chuckled.

"How can you laugh right now?"

"How can I *not* ?"

I sat there in tears, sniffling and wiping my snot with my sweatshirt sleeve like a toddler. The news anchors blabbed on in the background about yet another mass shooting.

"It may be good for you ... a fresh start over there. It's what I'd do ... It's what I might do." She winked.

"Why?"

"Because if I can't do it in this life, I'll go do it on the other side. You can ... come with me or not."

"Mom." I cocked my head.

"Why *not*, honey? It's Newport. You'll have some money. I don't know ... just think about it."

"Mom."

"At least think about it, for me. It'll do you good after all this. You may feel more at home ... *away* from home."

"After all this? Why are we talking about it like they've already told—"

"*You* brought it up." She shrugged stiffly. "Fine. We'll ... come back to it late—"

As if on cue, a gentle knocking on the door was followed by a short blonde nurse with a high ponytail entering the room with a small shy smile. "Hi there, hope I'm not interrupting. I'm Sarah, I'm gonna be your nurse for the night, okay? Just wanted to pop in and introduce myself."

"Not interrupting at all, thank you ... so much." My mom waved subtly at her with the hand that had an IV in it.

"Oookayyy. Let's see here..." Sarah beamed down at my mom with care as she pulled a stool up to the computer and several other assorted monitors.

I stopped listening after that. I stayed next to her all night. I even slept in that awful chair. I passed out thinking about the next steps, the inevitable that was all but confirmed by the doctor.

They broke the news to her the next day.

She died at home two weeks later.

***

I took a deep breath as I gazed down at my mom's smile in a picture on my phone. She'd urged me every day until she died to consider going with Liv to Rhode Island. I hadn't agreed to it until after she'd passed, and I felt guilty for never having given my mom that peace before she left us. I decided quietly to myself to move to Newport not long after the night I saw my mother's spirit in the hallway. I believe that was her final attempt to nudge me.

Did I make the wrong decision?

I pressed play on one of the songs Lynette was dancing to the night before. I quietly waited a few seconds to see if the music alone would bring her out. "Lynette?" I grew impatient quickly and called from the middle of the floor into the -as far as I knew- empty house.

I swayed with the sound of the piano and the snazzy saxophone, tempted to get up and dance myself. I closed my eyes and listened, taking deep breaths. Right as I began to open my mouth to call for Lynette a second time, I heard creaking on the floorboards and opened my eyes.

Surprised by how happy I was to see her again, I smiled. "Hi."

"Hi, Emma." She took a step forward. "You're listening to my music!" She gasped excitedly, forming a bright smile on her otherwise pale lifeless face. For the first time, I saw a glimmer of happiness in her eyes like one small speck of glitter on a dull gray office carpet. I could almost picture how cute she would've been smiling with rosy cheeks and vivid blue eyes in life.

"*Your* music, huh?" I challenged her, pushing my hands back behind me against the wood to lean back.

"My favorite, anyway." Lynette's shoulders drooped, then she looked down at me. "Have you found her?"

I felt my face flush. I wasn't ready to crush her heart. "Lynette" —I inhaled— "I..."

She nodded slowly. "You didn't."

I ran my tongue along my bottom gums, feeling the ping of guilt in my chest. "I didn't, no. I'm sorry."

"Is she dead?" Her eyes froze onto mine.

A lump settled into my throat.

She didn't break away from my eyes. "How did you find out?"

"We found her death certificate" —I paused— "at the library. She's been gone for a long time."

"How?"

I shook my head. "It just said natural causes."

The small but stoic girl finally broke eye contact with me to move her head steadily toward the fireplace mantle. "I think deep down I knew … Did you lose someone, too?" she asked.

"I did."

"Who?"

"My mom."

"Me too. She got really sick. I don't remember her much because I was little … just seeing her cough up blood. It was scary, but then … she stopped hurting."

"Mine got sick, too. But I remember because it wasn't long ago." I recalled taking care of my mom around the clock for the last few weeks. "Liver cancer."

"I'm sorry." She gazed at the ground.

"Me too." I sighed.

Lynette seemingly glided from the fireplace to the wide window across from it. The music played softly on my phone. "Gwen and I used to dance together all the time."

I nodded, feeling a lump form in my throat. Guilt. None of it was my fault, but I wished Gwendolyn was still alive for her. How could I help her *now*?

"Will you dance with me?"

" Oh, I'm not a great dancer," I admitted.

"You don't have to be." Lynette turned around and smiled softly. As she approached me, I noticed that she actually had a reflection in the dining room window. She stopped about two feet from me, and reached down for my hand. Without thinking and by pure intuition I grabbed it, and like the last time, I winced when we touched. It didn't feel like a hand, of course, as there was no skin to touch. All there was was the initial surge of electricity up my arm, then coldness, as if I were laying my hand on a block of ice. It felt really uncomfortable at first, so I let go and sat up straighter, shaking off the numbness.

"I'm sorry." Lynette looked at her hand.

I stood up clumsily, and left my phone on the mantle. "It's okay. Just not used to this … kind of dancing…" and by that I meant with the dead. I extended a hand to her again nonetheless. "Here, take it."

She placed her hand in mine once more and I tried to hold back my response to the initial odd tingling by deeply inhaling. I didn't want to make her self-conscious, because it was clear now that she was capable of feeling so.

The music continued to play in that empty room lit by a small old chandelier. I shifted my weight onto one foot and heard the floorboards squeak under me. After about a minute, Lynette had gone from awkwardly swaying to doing a few spins, letting out tiny giggles here and there. It was cute, if I ignored the blood on her head and dress. I think she enjoyed having a dance partner for the first time in a long time.

I gazed out the window and past the mirrored image of us, I saw the night sky illuminated by the moon. Dark clouds drifted in front of it gracefully. I wished there was a curtain to hide the fact that perhaps, to passersby, I was attempting a very basic swing dance by myself. They'd assume their new neighbor was a complete oddball. If I could see her reflection, did that also mean they would see her there with me? In *her* condition, it would be much better if they'd caught me alone.

I looked around the room one more time to make sure no one was watching from outside- or inside- the house.

"It's just us right now." Lynette swayed in place.

Underneath the gruesome tragedy, she was so pretty and pure. She never had a chance, and now, all she had at that moment was Benny Goodman and me. If I could bring her *some* kind of happiness and companionship in the afterlife, I wanted to. Crossing her over didn't have to be of the utmost concern, did it? Not right away, anyway.

Lynette held onto me as if she were clinging to the memories of her childhood, her sister, her livelihood. Was this still her childhood? Dancing with her felt like jumping into an unheated pool for the first time in the summer. It was terrifying, exhilarating when you first hit the water. Once you kept swimming for a few minutes with your teeth chattering, the shock went away. Then it just felt refreshing.

We needed each other that night. As we danced and twirled to one song after another, I realized that both of us were daydreaming of happier, simpler times before neither of us understood why things were happening the way they were. Each time we made eye contact, the more I felt her. When I looked into her pale, vacant blue eyes, I could feel her confusion; why was her chance at life taken so early? I felt her disappointment in never being able to do the things she'd imagined accomplishing in life.

"What did you want to be when you grew up?" I asked.

"A candy maker."

"Excellent choice." I nodded encouragingly.

"Or a doctor like my daddy" —she continued— "so I could make people feel better."

"Now *that's* wonderful."

She looked up into my eyes, flashing her snowy light blue orbs at me again. "Did a doctor try to help your mom feel better?"

"They tried, of course. No one could fix the sick. But you know what always cheered her up?"

Lynette cocked her head slightly.

"Candy." I winked.

She smiled shyly, her damp curls swaying slightly.

"You'd probably love today's candy. There's way too much of it. It's awful."

Lynette nodded.

Our entire interaction tasted like Sour Patch Kids; it was pungent with an uncomfortable bite, but much, much sweeter if you stuck it out. Easier to take in again, and again. Eventually, the sugar just made your mouth sort of raw, but you focused more on the flavor than the soreness. In fact, experiencing her soft energy was almost addictive, like the blue and red gummies. Contagious, even. The worst thing that could possibly happen to someone had happened to her, at such a young age, too. Yet, she moved to the beat of the music with an otherworldly grace.

We danced for at least half an hour, barely speaking to each other after that exchange. We didn't need to. Accepting and appreciating each other's presence was enough. Just the two of us there.

There *was* one moment while we were dancing, however, that I could've sworn I'd felt someone else watching from the archway between the front living room and the foyer. The heaviness pulled my attention away from the little oasis we'd created. Lynette never mentioned him, and I didn't see anyone when I glanced over my shoulder, nor when I spun around airily to the beat of big band drums, saxophones, and trumpets.

Was he there, hiding behind a veil I couldn't understand?

12.

THAT MUST BE ILLEGAL

I'd gone to sleep comfortably in my bed after our little dancing escape from reality, and opened my eyes to the same rainy forest that I'd experienced several times before. But this wasn't the same starting point, or the same nightmare.

My pace was hurried, but not quite a run. I felt the short heels of my shoes sinking into the mud every time I took a step. Looking down, I saw a beautifully flattering light dress. I was heavily disappointed that the rain and mud were ruining it, but I had no choice. What was back here that was worth ruining such nice clothes?

I made my way through the woods until I reached the same clearing as before. I knew this because I instantly found Lynette's body lying against the rock that cracked her skull. It was even more heartbreaking to see her from a different perspective. My hands shook and I cried out bone-chillingly, *"My baby!"*

It wasn't my voice, but it was gut-wrenching.

I approached her body and met her empty and half-open eyes. My housemate and dance partner. I panted as my chest tightened, convulsing and reaching down to grasp onto the lifeless little girl. I gripped her tangled hair in my fingers and rocked her back and forth in my lap.

"No. No, no, no. No, *no.*"

Between deep sobs, "Baby girl," escaped my mouth repeatedly as I tasted blood on my lips. I wiped it off frantically, realizing it wasn't mine but Lynette's, from her hair resting against my chin.

For what felt like years, I rocked there on the muddy ground with my sister.

Then like a jump cut, my view abruptly changed to that of walking slowly but shakily through the trees. Between wiping salty tears off of my cheeks and eyes, a dark figure emerged in front of me. I followed it through the trees until I got closer. A tensed man wandered the woods with his back facing me.

"Jack?" My voice cracked. "Jack."

The figure stopped in his tracks.

"*Jack!*" I shrieked again.

He turned around to face me in the rain, subtle moonlight creating a dull glow on his chiseled face. With tears blurring my vision, I panted, "What did you do—"

"Gwen, I—" he tittered nervously.

"What happened to her, Jack? Wha— what did you do to her?" My eyes shifted down to see a knife in his left hand and my heart jumped in fear and anger. It was too dark for him to notice that I'd seen it glimmer in the moonlight.

A spotlight on his guilt.

"What did you *do!*"

Rain pattered down onto the leaves and mushy forest floor beneath us.

"You were supposed to take care of her," I whispered shakily.

"I didn't hurt her, Gwen, I swear I" —he dropped the knife to the ground— "Come here."

I trembled uncontrollably, all throughout my body. My knees felt weak. I wanted to collapse to the ground.

I took two steps towards him, breathing more heavily with each foot forward. I fell to the ground in front of him, sobbing and hiding my face in my hands.

"I— I came out here to find her, Gwen. She ran from the house. *She* ran away." he bent down slowly to touch the middle of my back. It sent shivers up my spine.

No.

"Don't *touch* me." I lifted one hand away from my face as he comforted me, and slid it toward the knife on the ground. He was too busy defending himself to me to notice.

"I didn't *hurt* her." He paused to inhale deeply. "Is she— is she okay?"

"*No,* Jack! She's *dead-*"

He clapped a hand over my mouth from behind me. "Gwen baby, I need you to shut your mouth and listen to me. Calm…down. I came here to bring her back the house, but *she* ran off. Whatever happened between now— God*damn* it. If she's dead, it wasn't me. Now be quiet before someone hears both of us out here," he spat.

No. I gripped the handle of the knife so tightly my hand cramped up quickly.

"You wouldn't want the police coming now, would you?"

"Would *you?*" I struggled to speak through my sobs and his callous hold on me.

"*Shhh.* I already told you. I didn't come out here to *kill* her, Gwen."

"Then why do you have a *knife, Jack?*" I questioned through clenched teeth and weak breaths.

Before he could respond, I ripped his hand off of my mouth and thrust the knife into his side with as much strength as I could gather. He groaned loudly and toppled over to the ground. I quickly stood over him, one of my heels sticking in the mud and slipping off of my foot.

Jack Carlson's dapper top and dress pants were quickly soaked and bloodied along the side. His face was hidden from me now, only his eyes lit by the moon. "Gwen—"

With tears flowing down my face, I stepped over him and swung the knife into his chest again before he could fight back.

I stabbed him again, into his stomach.

Slash.

Again, into his side.

Into his heart.

Slash, squelch.

I wanted him to hurt as much as I did. As much as Lynette did. I wanted to see terror in his eyes.

"No!" He gurgled with each stab plunged into him. "Fuck … I — I…" he managed out of his mouth as blood gushed out of it. "You can't…"

Warm blood hit my face. He kept groaning, so I fought the wave of queasiness and kept driving the knife into him until there was no movement, no gurgling, no pleading. Sobbing and in shock, I dropped the knife into the mud and felt something dark leave me as realization hit me…

What have I done?

I dizzily turned back from the scene and knelt over to vomit into the mud. The taste of soured vanilla and acidic coffee filled my throat and mouth as I purged out the demon that had entered me just moments before.

My chest rose and sank heavily as I stood up over my dead lover. His shredded body was splayed out beneath me. His eyes stared back at me, frozen in horror. His lips slowly twisted upward, resembling a grin, yet his body was emptying, draining.

I felt empty, too.

Survival mode kicked in and rivaled my panic. I snatched the knife back up and before I woke up, one thought flashed to mind.

Nancy. I need Nancy.

***

"I cried for a while after I woke up." I sighed, summing up the events of the past day. We sat outside in the sun eating at a locally famous restaurant, Flo's Clam Shack.

"He's convinced that *you're* Gwen … reincarnated? That's … new. I don't understand why." Joel bit the inside of his top lip.

"I don't know, either. He just said that he can … tell. My eyes, the way I dance with Lynette—"

"You still need to explain *that* whole event to me," Willow reminded me as she took a big bite of a clam cake dipped in ketchup.

I rolled my eyes. "Down to the way I sip my coffee. It's ridiculous."

"He's gotta go." Joel shook his head.

"Yeah. He's psycho. I'm definitely *not* her…"

Willow narrowed her gaze on me with an eyebrow raised.

"What?" I sneered and looked down at my shrimp.

"Your first nightmare, you experienced Lynette's death. That's because she wanted you to see what happened to her, right?"

"Yeah, why?"

"Okay. Second nightmare, you're in Gwen's position. Carlson's death, but Gwen's POV. And *her* ghost isn't around to give you visions so—"

"Uh-uh." I shook my head as I chewed. "Stop."

"So either Carlson gave you *that* vision somehow, or-"

"No, hold on." Joel joined in. "How do we know Gwen isn't around *at all?*"

'Because she's ... not," Willow replied simply.

"Maybe not when you're around. We can't rule it out."

"Fine, whatever. But I have *never* sensed an adult woman's energy in that house, other than Em, obvi. I think by now I would've picked up on it."

"Also, why would Carlson give you that dream from Gwen's point of view? Why wouldn't he just show you from his? Wouldn't that be more jarring, anyway ... if he was trying to intimidate you?"

"*Or* ... he's giving it from Gwen's perspective to convince Em that she's reliving a past life," Willow argued. "Like a regression."

"How could he access a perspective that isn't his?"

"How do ghosts walk through *walls*, Joel?" she challenged. "Maybe he's just making it up based on what he experienced to manipulate her. Unreliable narrator."

"He wouldn't need to manipulate her if she really was Gwen." Joel was quick to disagree.

"If she doesn't remember, then *yeah*. He would." Willow paused. "I'm not saying she is, I'm just saying ... Remember the show with the little boy who claimed he was a World War II pilot?"

"Okay, this is getting too complicated too fast. Guys—"

"Listen, I'm not putting money on the table yet, but I'm just saying ... there's a table."

"Who the hell cares?" I snapped. "This whole Gwen topic isn't even important. For all we know, he senses that we're a threat to his control over the house and he's using all this Gwen bullshit as a distraction, which is *clearly* working."

Our table got quiet, but the tension was broken for a second by Counting Crows' "Big Yellow Taxi" playing on the patio speakers.

"It doesn't matter. Either way, I want him gone." I took a long sip of my pineapple hard cider.

Willow and Joel exchanged a look, "Well" —Joel started— "you could convince him to move on like it was his own idea, but I don't really see that happening right now." He gave me a sympathetic look.

"Or you could force him out," Willow said.

"What do you mean? You don't think your *sage* did the trick?" I cocked my head to the side and pursed my lips.

"*Hey.* I never claimed it would. I said it would help purify the energy in the house, but that's not gonna force him out." She glared at me for a second, obviously offended, but then softened her eyes. She fixated on the ocean across the street in thought. "We could burn it."

"*The house?*" I blurted.

Willow grimaced at me. "*What?* No, what the fuck?" She shook her head with a disappointed sigh. "The body."

"*What?*"

"We salt and burn it, purifying and releasing the spirit from its energetic attachment to the physical realm," Willow elaborated.

"Did you just steal that from *Supernatural*?" Joel raised a brow.

"No, loser. Lots of cultures believe in it." She justified her idea. "And I got it from *Supernatural*, too."

"Woah, wait. We don't even know what Gwen did with the body. I didn't get that far."

"She probably didn't either, babe," Willow clicked her tongue. "Let's find that body!"

"Shhh! No way. That *must* be illegal," I whispered.

"Probably." She shrugged. "But how badly do you want him gone?" Willow shot back.

"Does that work though?" Joel weighed.

"Better safe than sorry. Worth trying."

"Is it?"

"Maybe you'll have another dream," Joel suggested. "Wills is right. She probably couldn't have gotten far at all on her own, and in the woods, there's plenty of space to bury a body."

"The last thought I had before I woke up was that I needed *Nancy*. I don't know who that is, but maybe she was a friend of hers. Maybe she helped get rid of him. His body could be nowhere *near* here," I hypothesized.

"Maybe. But we don't wanna wait around for you to have another dream, and we have no leads with this Nancy chick. Maybe if we just go out there…" she trailed off.

"Are you thinking you'll pick up on whether or not he's still out there?" Joel followed her thought process.

"*Or … maybe Emma will have another vision.*"

"I don't have visions. I have nightmares. There's a difference." I shook my head and corrected her. "I'm never awake for them. I'm not like you."

"Mm. Maybe you're still just too closed off to receive them when you're awake." Willow went on unbothered.

No one spoke.

There was a moment where Willow looked directly into my eyes for several seconds, and I couldn't tear away. I watched Joel out of the corner of my eye as he looked back and forth between the two of us.

After a few moments, Joel interjected, pulling Willow out of her gaze. "Wills?"

I'd won this staring contest.

"Were you having a moment?" I asked.

"I just really think we should go out there. I think we should start looking for answers the best and most available ways we can, as soon as we can." Willow cleared her throat and patted her wallet in her jean pocket.

"It *could* be worth a try." Joel swallowed a bite of his fries and gave me a sympathetic smile, "We aren't hurting anyone by walking around in the woods."

"We're talking about finding and burning an old, dead, *murdered* body. You both realize that, right? Doesn't that make us accomplices?"

"Mmmm … does it? I feel like that's a gray area." Willow raised a brow.

"Willow, I'm extremely concerned by how eager and willing you are to do this so quickly, but … to keep you safe and comfortable in your home, Em, I say we might as well try to figure out where he is." Joel smiled and started to reach his arm toward me, but he stopped himself and took a sip of his soda instead. I noticed, though.

"Just think about it for a couple days, or until something else happens with Carlson. Because it will." Willow balled up a napkin and tossed it in her red food basket. She caught the attention of our server with an enthusiastic wave. "Hi there, check, please!"

AUGUST

13.

FOR NOW

Weeks had gone by, and I still had no answer for Willow. She pressed me all the time, but by some miracle, Carlson hadn't shown his face again, so that had been my excuse for putting off the search for a dead body.

We'd expected his presence to become stronger over time, but even Willow hadn't had any visions related to him or his energy in the house. It was a topic at every sit down at Beach Brew. Even if it was just, "Anything new?" or "Still nothing?" My answer was always no, and that was fine at first. But the longer I went without seeing him, the more uneasy I felt, like the calm before the storm. It was sunny, but we could see the clouds rolling in from the distance, and we could smell the rain. There was that faint, subtle breeze that fluttered past our wind chimes to remind us that something was on its way. We all knew he was hiding somewhere.

But I *could* try to ignore the idea of his return until I had no choice but to confront him again. I could pretend I'd never seen him so close to my face, never heard him taunting in my ear or brushing my leg without consent. I could pretend that it was just Lynette and myself sharing our home. There was nothing else to do.

That didn't mean I couldn't be prepared, just in case. Sometimes, on nights when Lynette and I would sit by the fireplace reading— our new favorite activity together— and I'd try to get information out of her. I'd ask open-ended questions that might have led to more about Carlson. She would always either give me a vague answer, keeping to the book she borrowed from me, or disappear quietly and completely for the night. Because of my failed attempts and the fact that Lynette was very quiet most of the time anyway, my questioning slowly died down each night until I eventually decided to simply enjoy my time with her and not push. It must've been something that really bothered her, but that just made my curiosity and disgust for him grow.

Joel and I tried to find information on him elsewhere, too, to no avail. There was no mention of any Jack Carlson in the local records. It seemed so far like we weren't going to find anything else out unless it came from one of our ghosts.

"And that's fine. Maybe your sage *is* working after all, Wills." I chuckled in the backyard one sunny, late summer afternoon. The breeze blew through our bare feet.

"Told you." Willow sipped her iced oolong tea in the hammock we'd just bought at Christmas Tree Shop. Yes, that was the name. I'd never understood why, since they were open year-round. I'd never been there when they had their Christmas trees out, but assumed they must've been some *really* nice trees if they'd named the whole store after them.

"Whatever," I chuckled. "We'll see. It's only been a few weeks." I shrugged.

"What? You *want* him to show up again?" Willow raised an eyebrow.

"No, *god*, not that. I just don't want to get too comfortable telling myself that it's smooth sailing from here until I know it's permanent. I don't know how spirits work. Maybe they go on vacation," I joked dryly. "Who knows if they even have a sense of time?"

"The spirit world is unpredictable." Willow cleared her throat. "Which is why I still think we should just burn the body in the meantime."

I responded sullenly, as usual, "Still don't know what body you're so certain is out there."

"Anyway, how's your babysitting gig going?"

"She's as fine as she can be." I felt a tiny smile creep up on me. "She horrified me, you know? But it's funny. Now one of my closest friends is a dead kid. I don't even notice the blood half the time now. Is that weird?"

Willow slowly turned her head to me and grimaced subtly with her blue-tinted aviators on.

I quickly followed up, "No, I know it is. This whole thing is. I'm slowly … accepting that." I sipped my watermelon mint lemonade.

"Closest friends?" Willow seemed surprised. "Hm. Look at you."

"Well, I mean— yeah. She lives in my house. I see her almost every day, whenever she can work up the energy. We don't even talk much. But I really do like having her around, Wills. I don't even think I *need* to understand why. It doesn't make sense. Nothing does. Nothing *has* since I met you … asshole." I laughed and reached to pat her shoulder as we swung gently in the late summer breeze.

She shook her head. "Don't blame me. It was gonna happen either way." She sighed and looked down at her glass.

"Well regardless, life got messy really fast."

Willow harrumphed.

I sensed a shift in the tone of our conversation. "What's up?"

"Nothing, just weird how life works. Everything happens for a reason, but also no reason at all. Maybe we should all just stop questioning everything so much."

***

Later that night, I sat on my couch with Joel after a short shift at Beach Brew. Willow had gone home to do yoga. I'd promised I'd get around to letting her teach me some, but I didn't feel like leaving the house that night.

"Elle said you gave her a free donut today. How nice of you." Joel winked.

I melted a little, but slapped a cool and collected response of my emotions. "I told her not to tell anyone. Don't snitch. I'll lose my job." I feigned an overly worried face, then winked back. I'd met Joel's sister Elliot a few days ago in crossing. She was quite a few years younger than us, and feisty. I admired her for that.

"Is Thomps back yet?" Joel inquired.

I exhaled. "Oh, yeah. But he really shouldn't be. Liv said he insists on working, though."

Joel shook his head. "Damn. I wouldn't wanna work at all, let alone food service, after a stroke."

"I don't know. Liv thought about laying him off just so he'd stay home and rest, but he says it was very mild and that he's 'over the damn thing'."

"What a legend." He chuckled nervously. "Hey, I actually stopped by to tell you something."

"And here I thought you actually wanted to hang out."

He shifted in his seat. "It's not a big deal. Just finally found something on Carlson."

"Kind of a big deal, but okay." I narrowed my eyes to focus on his information.

"So there was a tiny little blurb in the … like …gossip column of a newspaper about Gwen's death. One 'source' reported that Gwen spoke of her boyfriend running off for another woman not long after Lynette died. It was later corroborated by a note Clyde Salley found in Gwen's room from 'Carlson.' They theorized that perhaps she killed herself at sea because she was heartbroken by the second loss in such a short time."

"Well, that's BS." I sighed.

"Yeah, but it means Gwen covered up his death, probably successfully. I still can't find anything on his death or even an investigation into his disappearance."

"Well good for her." I sniffled.

"I mean, she still killed herself," Joel whispered.

I shrugged sadly.

Out of nowhere, my phone started playing a Bix Beiderbecke playlist. I turned to face the other side of the room. "Hi Lynette," I spoke into the air, fearing she'd heard our conversation.

She appeared from the foyer. "Hi," she cheeped, "What are you doing?"

Crisis averted.

"Just talkin'."

"Hi, Lynette." Joel greeted her with kindness.

"Hello, Joel." She smiled. "Would you like to dance?"

"Oh, I don't think I want to dance right now. I'm tired from work." I scrunched up my nose, feeling guilty for refusing her. "Sorry, sweetie."

"Please!" She shifted her gaze to Joel and teetered on her heels. "Not with me," she sang.

I chuckled and looked at Joel, who blushed. "Why do you want me to dance with Joel?"

"Because we always dance, and I wanna watch *other* people dance. Like a show!"

"Ahhhh, not tonight."

"Please ... *please*," she whispered.

"Aw, come on, Em. Don't let her down like that." He nudged my arm and stood up to hold out his hand. "May I?"

I widened my eyes at Lynette and she giggled softly.

"Oh, *God.*" I cringed, my face flushed with cherry red embarrassment.

Lynette jumped onto the couch next to me and beamed brightly. It warmed my heart, but her bloodied head was right in my face. I grimaced but tried to hide it again so she wouldn't feel bad, "Okay." I sighed and took Joel's hand, which was warm and comforting, not freezing like my usual dance partner's.

As he led me in our simple steps, I asked, "Did you take classes or something?"

"Are you kidding me? Hell no, I have no idea what I'm doing." he laughed and shot his eyes into mine shyly for a second.

After a couple dances around the room, we noticed that Lynette was gone. But we kept swaying for probably three more songs. Our excuse was that Lynette may still be watching from somewhere unbeknownst to us. We wouldn't want to disappoint her.

At one point before we stopped, I laid my head on his shoulder briefly. He reminded me quietly, "I told you everything would be okay, and it still will be." He leaned his head softly on top of mine for a second and I breathed deeply, appreciating the fact that I was allowing myself to enjoy this moment despite the darkness and confusion surrounding it. Whether I understood it or not, life was okay.

For now.

I'd take what I could get.

14.

THANKFUL

"Does he scare you?" Lynette appeared without warning by the side of the couch one evening while I was playing another word game on my phone.

I jolted, "Who?"

She looked into my eyes and paused.

"Oh, right. Carlson?" I whispered.

She nodded.

That was out of left field.

I glanced around to make sure I couldn't see him, then shook my head remembering that that didn't mean he wasn't watching. "A little."

She nodded and looked down at the floor in disappointment. "Are you gonna try to make him leave?"

I bit the inside of my cheek as I turned off my phone screen,. "We're gonna try."

Lynette nodded again. She walked over to the window and left her back facing me.

"Lyn, you know you can tell me what happened with him, okay?"

I waited for several moments, expecting her to vanish or change the topic like she had during my previous attempts but she didn't move. She watched out the window at the trees swaying in the night. The light cool breeze was our first sign of fall approaching. I felt bad again for pushing such a little girl to talk about something so traumatic. This was wrong.

"Lynette, I'm sorry. I just want to—"

"He tried to hurt me. So I ran … really fast," she whispered with the soft airy sound of leaves rustling outside.

Surprised, I slowly put my book down, got up, and walked toward her cautiously as if she were a wounded wild animal. When I got to her, I sat my knees on the floor and looked up at her. "How did he try to hurt you?"

She kept gazing outside at single corner street lamp down the way. "Gwen went to book club with her friends one night. Jack was supposed to watch me until she got back."

I was alarmed, but didn't want to scare her off by asking too much. "I wanna help you. We're gonna try to get him out of here. I just wish I knew what happened so I could help you better," I whispered.

"I tried to be brave. I tried to find somewhere safe, somewhere he wouldn't find me."

"I bet you did." I reached out to comfort her.

Lynette took my hand, and suddenly the sight of her hand in mine turned into that of playing with a doll on the living room floor.

"Lynette! Come on down here. I got somethin' for you downtown today," a male voice piped up joyfully from down in the basement.

"Coming!" I stood up in my little pretty dress, and skipped down the steps and onto the top of the basement stairs. I peered in. "Yes?"

"I bought you a gift today while I was out. Do you want it?" Jack Carlson faced me at the bottom of the basement stairs. Although initially hesitant, I bounced down to meet him and followed him into a smaller room. He towered over me in this trance, and smiled with one hand behind his back.

"What is it?" I replied anxiously in Lynette's sweet voice.

"Come look."

"Okay."

"Well, go ahead and close the door behind you, now. It's a surprise and I don't want anyone to see it before you do, and if Gwen gets home early I don't want to ruin the surprise for her. I want *you* to show her when she gets home," he whispered and winked at me.

"No one's home, but alright." I spun around and slowly closed the door to the stuffy basement room, suddenly feeling something wrong in my gut. The sinking feeling was instinct telling me to leave. I felt the dress skirt flow down back onto my legs as I turned around to face Carlson. If Gwen could trust him, so could I.

"Good girl. Ready?" He spoke softly.

I nodded and watched as Jack pulled his arm out from behind him. It was a small tan box with a blue label on the top. I knew what it was right away. It was a sweet little baby doll.

"A Kewpie! Thank you, Jack! I've wanted one ever since I saw it in the shop the other day!" I exclaimed and moved closer to take the box and open it.

"I know. Now hold your horses. Do you know *why* I got this for you?" he playfully pulled the box back toward his chest.

"Because Gwen told you I wanted it?"

"*Nooo*," he sang. "Because I saw it and it reminded me of you. Look at those rosy cheeks. Big bright eyes, sweet innocent smile…" He trailed off, his gaze moving from the doll to me.

I shifted my weight in Lynette's little body. "May I see it out of the box?"

"Don't you want to match your new doll?" Carlson whispered and looked from me to the door, and back. I looked at the box; the doll came naked.

"What?"

He stood, quietly surveying my reaction.

"I think I'll go back to playing in the sitting—" I inched backward.

"Lynette." his eyes stared like daggers into mine as he gestured to my dress, "Take your clothes off, darlin'."

My heart pounded. "No, I don't-"

Carlson set the doll box on the metal work table behind him and slowly approached me, placing his palm on my cheek to rub it. I'd felt that before from him, and hated it. Lynette shouldn't have had to experience it, too. My heart dropped.

"It's okay." He bent down and leaned in close to my ear. The strong scent of tobacco hit me, which had before been a pleasant smell that I associated with my grandfather. That was ruined now.

"I'm not gonna hurtcha. But I've got a secret for you. Can't tell anybody."

I froze.

Without letting me respond, Carlson inhaled deeply and exhaled his breath onto my ear. "I…have always thought you were so pretty," he touched my hair and swept it behind my ear with gentle aggression.

"I think I'd like to go back and play now," I squeaked.

"You're not going to thank me for your new doll?"

"Thank you … for my doll," I whispered, staring straight ahead at the box on the table behind him.

"You're welcome," he continued to whisper into my ear. The warmth of his breath felt sticky and venomous. "But I want you to show me that you're thankful. Then I'll give you the doll."

I shook my head slowly. "I did … It's okay. No thank you, I've changed my mind. I don't think I want it yet. I'll wait 'til Gwen gets home. Can I please go, Jack?"

He shushed me and kissed my ear with force. I felt a sharp sting in my chest and bolted to my right, slipping away from him. I tried to open the door but he got in front of me. "You ungrateful little — All the things I do for you girls, all the money I've spent … for you to be so disobedient…" He paused, then took a step toward me.

"I'm going upstairs now."

"If you want Gwen to be happy, you'll take off that little dress. You wouldn't want me to be sad and leave. That would make Gwen cry. You don't want that, do you?"

I gulped. "Jack stop, please. I don't like this, and when I tell Gwen and daddy that—"

His eyes narrowed and his face turned red. He lunged at me and tightly gripped my arms, pushing me to the ground. The hardwood floor hurt my tailbone, as did the pressure of his knees on me while he tried to tear my dress off. As he pulled at the neckline, the fabric rubbed harshly against the back of my neck, but it didn't work. He started moving one of his hands up the skirt of my dress while the other was gripping my shoulder. "Ungrateful little girls like you stay little forever."

I kicked and kicked my legs as hard as I possibly could with his weight on me. Once he lifted his body to lean forward toward my face, I was able move just enough to knee him in a spot that I knew would hurt, and I shoved his head back. He writhed in pain and fell to the side on his back to hold himself.

My vision was blurry with fear and my face was hot and throbbing. I rushed to my feet with all my strength and kicked him between the legs again, although scared that he would grab my foot.

I turned and rushed to the door to fling it open and—

"Then I just ran," Lynette said softly as I dizzily came back to the present, and watched as Lynette continued to stare out the open window, unblinking.

"Out to the woods…" I finished shakily. "I'm … so sorry." I couldn't believe what I'd just heard and seen, and all at once. Finally, I knew Jack Carlson.

Rage built up in my chest and for a moment, I almost hoped that he'd show himself, but there was nothing I could do to him if he had.

"I miss my sister, Emma. And my daddy. After it happened, I could see them, but they couldn't see me anymore. Time went by, and I didn't grow. I saw Gwen cry all the time, but Jack was never there to help her. I didn't see him again for quite some time … not until right before Gwen left. But eventually he ended up here, too. Then I could tell he was like me…"

"He's not like you, Lyn … Gwen killed him. That's why he's here. She found you that night. She thought he'd killed you," I explained.

He might as well have.

She shook her head, not once looking away from the dark silhouettes of the trees outside. "I'm thankful that she tried to protect me, and proud of her for being able to protect herself from him. He won't try to hurt any other little girls now, but he hurt her. I saw the pain in her eyes every day after, and there was nothing I could do to help her."

"We're going to make him go away, okay?"

"How? He still tries to find me but I always hide away to my safe place. I don't come back until he's gone."

"Where's your safe place?"

"I'm not sure. Further back, I suppose."

I shook my head. "I wish I knew what you meant."

"No, I don't want you to…"

I looked down at the ground, confused. "We're gonna try something, soon," I reassured her, looking up and deep into her eyes.

She finally looked back into my mine. "He doesn't deserve to live here anymore."

"He never did, and he won't for much longer. I'll figure it out," I promised softly. "Thank you for trusting me. I'm so glad you told me."

With that, she faded away. I was alone by the open window. Tears welled up in my eyes as soon as she left my sight, and I felt helpless. For her, for me. Utterly violated. There was nothing I could do to help Lynette, except find a way to bring her peace by getting rid of Carlson. I wanted to bring her family back to her. I wanted to go back and save her. But the worst had already happened to her and I couldn't do anything about it. I didn't know if I would even be able to get rid of Carlson. Knowing what he'd tried to do to Lynette, and what he'd done and said to me, I was scared for my own life in that moment.

I shifted my eyes around the entire downstairs to make sure he wasn't watching me or enjoying my frustration, my disgust. Discouraged, I stared down the steps to the patio and basement. Despite the pit in my stomach, I quickly reminded myself of what he did to her, and what he continued to do in my family's house.

I texted Willow immediately that night to let her know I was ready to go find him.

***

Knock, knock, knock.

"Hey, kiddo." Uncle Ken grinned and extended his arms immediately after I opened the door to him the next morning.

"Hey, kiddo right back." I returned the hug and patted his back.

"How's it goin?"

"It's goin," I simplified. "You here to mow my lawn?" I gestured toward the backyard.

"Ho-*ho*, I'm here to mow *my* lawn."

Should I tell them?

Ken made his way back down the porch steps and around the house. Before he disappeared behind the side, he stopped by the dining room bay window and beckoned nonchalantly. "You comin'?"

I didn't have shoes on, but decided I didn't need them. I could use some grounding. Before I could catch up to him, he headed to the garage at the back end of the driveway and opened the rickety door. As I watched him haul the lawn mower out, I felt the cool cement kiss my bare feet. I crossed my arms in my sweater and let a small smile creep across my lips. The early autumn breeze moseyed past my cheeks as I looked up at the big pine tree that stood in the middle of the luscious green backyard.

"Thanks for coming to do this. You wanna come in for some coffee after?"

"Does shit stink?" He laughed.

"Okay, I'll go make some. I have muffins from Shaw's, too, if you want one."

"Why don't you add that to my tab? Gimme maybe twenty minutes. I'll be right up … I'll be gross, but I'll be up there." he started the mower and slid his sunglasses down from his forehead. His "Life is Good" shirt also had a little guy mowing a lawn on it, and his sneakers had green grass stains on them. He was definitely on theme, except that his faded baseball cap just said "Newport" on it. That was Uncle Ken, though. He didn't go anywhere without it on the weekends.

As I turned away from admiring my uncle, I looked up into my bedroom window. In the window stood a confident Carlson, waving delicately and tauntingly down at me from next to my bed. While I wanted to get Ken's attention, I knew he most likely wouldn't see it or hear me; he was at the very back of the large yard. I stood still on the driveway making eerie, direct eye contact with him before cocking my head sharply and walking into my house through the screened-in patio door. I let the door slam behind me and headed up to make myself and my uncle a nice, peaceful brunch.

He could watch me if he wanted, but I was going to enjoy my visit. He had no idea that I was ready to try and find him wherever he was out there. He deserved to die twice, and I wanted him to burn this time.

15.

WE DID IT

"Hi," I greeted Willow at the front door the next evening. "Remind me why we have to do this at night."

"It's not even that dark yet." Willow took a moment to gaze up at the overcast sky, the sunset peeking through the clouds. She blew a raspberry and strolled inside.

"It's going to be." I would openly admit to being scared of doing this. I wasn't only worried about what we might find, but of anyone shady we might come across hanging out back there at night.

"It's not a huge forest, Em. Breathe."

"That doesn't mean it's safe."

"I never said it was, but come on. Why are you acting like this is the Blair Witch?"

"It might be. There could be a dead body out there."

"Don't be so dramatic. It's bones."

"Does that matter? How are you even expecting to *find* the grave, again?"

"The same way I expect to find out anything about anything." She paused. "I told you. Intuition... and I stumble upon it. Plus, I'm counting on you to pull your weight, too."

"I'm not in charge of that."

"Mm, you don't know that." She paused again after winking at me, and cocked her head. "Are you okay?"

"After the other night, no. I just want to find him and—"

"He'll pay for what he did to them," she said as a creaking sound from the top of the stairs interrupted our conversation. "Let's go."

I made it a point to grab my phone and slip it in my back pocket just in case we needed a flashlight, or 911.

I followed Willow out the back patio door and across the lawn. Most of the trees back there and beyond the tall fence were just beginning to turn for the season. Many of them were witness to what happened that night, and one of them was involved.

Willow trekked into the woods without hesitation. I took a look back at my house before entering the maze of trees. The house looked so innocent from a distance.

My friend stopped to turn around at me. "Comin'?"

I nodded and followed right behind her. Twigs, leaves, and even some acorns crunched and snapped under my shoes.

She stopped after about thirty seconds of walking. "Do you feel anything yet? See anything?"

"Not really."

"Me neither. Do you recognize anything from your dream?" Willow took a look around. It was almost silent where we stood.

"No, it was really dark … and like, decades ago. Nothing's gonna look exactly the same. I—" I felt my focus slightly shift and sharpen. "Maybe just keep going straight."

"Ooookay," Willow noticed the change in my tone and gestured for me to walk ahead of her.

I tried not to think so hard and just let myself step where my feet decided to fall. I hadn't ventured back there before and couldn't remember much from my dreams, but I felt like I had shifted to autopilot. An invisible pull on my chest came from directly ahead. After a few moments, I realized that I *did* know where to go after all.

The clearing.

There it was.

Willow caught up from a few steps behind and stood beside me, brushing her shoulder with mine. It was okay, though. She didn't break my focus, and her closeness was comforting. I noticed out of the corner of my eye that Willow had glimpsed at me and given a sly smile, but she didn't say a word.

My eyes scanned the area, zeroing in on a large, lonely rock situated comfortably below a full, twisted tree. It stood in front of us, slightly to our right, and I knew that was it. My vision alternated rapidly between my current view in front of me, and that of the rock dripping with blood alongside the dead body of a sweet little girl. That had never happened to me before. I stumbled back a couple steps, caught off guard, and shook my head to get the image out. I wasn't going to relive that death again. I couldn't. That wasn't where Carlson was, anyway.

"Left," I blurted without thinking.

Willow nodded and continued on with me out of the clearing. Left for a ways, then a sharp right to go several steps further. I stopped and saw a flash in my vision again. I stared down as I caught a glimpse of Carlson spread out below me, his bloody mouth gurgling, "This," I whispered, "He died here."

"Good. Trust it, Em."

I felt a pull to my right and then another left, even deeper into the woods. I followed it, Willow close behind but giving me space to work.

"Stop, stop. Gwen dragged him here on her own, but…" I started, but within an instant felt like I was slowly fainting back into a fog, disoriented and dizzy. Then I felt myself jolt as if waking up from one of those half-asleep dreams of tripping on the sidewalk or falling off a cliff. Around me, it was dark and rainy. Willow was gone, replaced with another slender young woman with short dark waves and a worried look on her face. She gazed down below my feet and shrieked. "*Oh* my—"

"*Shhh*, please. *Please*, help me," I pleaded with a whimper.

The lady looked back into my eyes, moonlight reflecting off of them and the droplets on her face. "You've *killed* him, Gwen," she whispered sharply. "A thousand times over! How do you think *I* can help?"

My knees buckled. "I *had* to! She's *dead* ! He *hurt* her, Nan!" My whisper almost reached a scream. "He *hurt* her and I let it happen! I was supposed to protect—"

Nancy reached across Carlson's body and clapped her hand over my mouth. Unlike Carlson, she was gentle, "Not a soul can ever find out we were out here. *No one…* can *ever* hear a single noise from us."

I sniffled and nodded frantically, softly removing her hand from my face.

"Do you want to … move Lyn?"

Tears streamed down my face in the light rain, "I— I can't go —I can't go back there."

"You don't want to move her out of the rain?"

"I can't go touch her, Nan. I can't touch her. They— they need to be able find her. They need to know what happened, right? They need to see that she was— that she was— I can't see her like that again, Nancy. I can't—"

"Okay, okay … Shhh…"

"I can't do it, Nancy."

"Shhh… Yes, you're right. Okay."

I nodded frantically and whimpered in between my sobs, "Okay."

The young woman gaped down at Carlson's body again. She used the back of her hand to brush a few wet strands of hair off of her cheek. Finally, after several breaths, looked back up to face me. "What are we going to do with him?"

I shook uncontrollably.

"Let me think a moment." She approached me and gripped my shoulders tightly. "I love you," she whispered.

"I love you too," I replied in a hushed cry. But that compassion wasn't nearly enough to fill the raw gash in my heart.

Nancy nodded and exhaled deeply as rain continued to pour on us, soaking her navy party dress. "Take his legs. I'll hold his shoulders. We're going deeper into the forest and we'll bury him there, alright?"

"What if we reach the other end of the forest? It'll be close enough to another entrance. No one can see us!"

"No one will. Come, take his legs."

I nodded, internally thanking her profusely and giving my best attempt to quiet my weeping. Nancy gripped the metal shovel that I forced her to take with us from her house several doors down. "Now I see why we needed this, Gwendolyn."

We hauled Jack's body through the trees as the shovel, which Nancy held under her arm, trailed the mud.

We felt Jack's dead weight on our drenched bodies and plunked him to the ground. "This has to be far enough." Nancy grunted. With haste, Nancy plunged the shovel into the mud and began digging with all the strength she had. I wasted no time, either, pulling up gobs of mud and foliage from the ground with my bare hands, desperate to get Jack's body hidden before anyone stumbled upon us. I threw the chunks behind me.

We gasped for breath as quietly as we could, pawing at the site for what felt like eons. We lost ourselves in desperation, in the background music of our panting and the raindrops on our heads. "Just … another two feet maybe and we'll be cooking." Nancy nodded and inhaled sharply. Although I was thankful for the rain in that it would deter others from wandering out our way, the mud began to slip back down into the hole at a while.

"I can't do it!" I panicked, feeling my wrists tighten and cramp up.

"No, no." She shook her head, "This has to be deep enough. It's deep enough. Hurry," she whispered and gestured her head toward Jack.

With a simultaneous deep breath, we braced ourselves as we lifted Jack and tossed him into the grave. A deep sloshy thud permeated the ground as his body landed limply into the hole. I looked into Jack's empty eyes as he gazed endlessly at one of the four soil walls around him. I had done that to the man I'd planned to marry. I was burying my future.

"Come on." Nancy gripped my shoulder and rushed to cover the pit. I watched as a large clump of mud hit the left side of his face and covered his eyes.

I'd done this.

I'd killed a man in cold revenge.

I frenzied to the ground and stabbed my fingernails into the mud again, shoving and throwing it violently into the grave.

He'd done this.

He'd ruined what could have been a happy, stable life. A successful marriage, a family.

He'd killed my girl.

His heartless, lifeless body was disappearing into the cold mud. His body was torn, gashed, covered in red.

I did this. I let him into my life. My family.

She's dead because of me.

I let him in.

By some miracle, with any luck it was God's forgiveness, Jack's body was finally completely covered by a fresh mound. Hopefully, we would remember where it was in order to make sure it was never disturbed. I looked for a landmark around us, and settled for a tree that was notably thinner than those surrounding it that had a decently sized tree hollow high up on the trunk. He deserved no other marker.

"We did it." Nancy panted heavily from above, her dark blue dress soaked. My weak hands hit the cold mud and I hung my head in my knees. "Gwen. No one will ever know."

I looked up exhaustedly at my friend. "I'm so sorry, Nancy. I'm so sorry."

She's dead because of me.

"No one will find out what happened here, Gwen."

I sobbed.

"Shhh, come here. We did it. It's over."

"We did it," I whined weakly.

"Serves him right … in all honestly." Nancy bent down to embrace me, dropping the shovel in the mud. We both trembled.

A sinking feeling hit my stomach. *What do I do with the box?*

"We did it," I repeated aloud as my vision flashed to a brighter woods, my closest confidante standing right in front of me. I stood up from down on my knees in the patchy grass, noticing that the same skinny tree still stood exactly where Gwen and Nancy left it.

Willow's mouth gaped. "What did you see?"

"This is it. This is where we buried him." I gulped, short of breath. "It's right where you're standing."

She stared back at me with wide eyes. "…We?"

"How long was I gone?"

"Like a few minutes … Are you okay?" She blinked and took a step toward me. Her eyes were wide and her mouth was open slightly.

She held an arm and palm out with her fingers spread open as if I were a spooked horse.

"I'm fine," I muttered, slowly coming back to awareness of my present surroundings.

"You were crying." Willow tilted her head and squeezed her fingernails into her palms. "Like …. I thought you were about to have a panic attack."

"Yeah."

"Are you good?"

"Yeah."

"I almost called Joel."

I exhaled. "Why didn't you?"

"I trusted that you could handle it on your own."

I nodded heavily and brushed my cheek with my finger. My face was cold and damp.

"Okay, then." Willow sighed, patting her sides with a sad baffled expression on her face.

I simply nodded and bit the inside of my cheek. After a few beats of quiet in the trees, I looked back to Willow, then down at the ground below my feet. I knew his body was down there. "So we'll dig here."

"You sure?"

I shrugged with a lump in my throat. "Yeah, unless you have any new ideas."

She shook her head. "Nope."

"Okay."

My friend nodded back at me slowly. "Okay. Well, let's tell Joel." She took out a medium-sized clear quartz crystal from her jacket pocket and set it down in the spot I'd guided her to.

"He shouldn't get a marker."

"It's for us, not him…very temporary." Willow spoke slowly to me. "Try to relax, okay?"

I took a deep breath. Everything about this felt surreal, but everything in that vision was all *too* real.

How did I do that?

We headed back to the house just as the sun disappeared beneath the horizon and behind the woods.

"We'll tell him tomorrow." Willow cleared her throat as I walked her out the front door later that evening. "I'm just tired, and you should really get some rest after what happened back there." She seemed uneasy. "I'll try to come up with a plan of how and when to do this," she turned around to her car.

Something felt off. Did my vision scare her? I couldn't understand why it would, but then again, I had no idea what I'd looked like from her point of view. I may have looked bizarre, maybe even possessed…or maybe she was just as overwhelmed as I was by how quickly the situation had escalated.

She stopped in her tracks as if she could sense my concern. "Em, try not to overthink this. Everything's gonna be good. I'm glad you came around. You're truly gifted." She gave a small empathetic grin, hit the button on her keys to unlock her Prius, and drove off down the street. I watched, leaning against the front doorframe and wondering how it would really feel to watch flames dance over a grave.

16.

NOTHING IMPORTANT

The next morning, we delivered the news to Joel via our group text that we'd found Carlson's unmarked gravesite. When we told him how I'd figured it out, he was both impressed and disturbed by how vivid my vision was. I reminded them that I could still be wrong since we had no proof until we dug up actually human remains. I knew in my gut that I was right, but that fact alone scared me. Not only did that mean that we *were* going through with our idea to uncover a dead body, but that I'd tapped into another ability I didn't know what to do with.

On the other hand, I worried that I was unraveling, overthinking; was I actually just losing my mind? I alternated between a concerned trust in my gut and complete self-doubt while my friends remained confident in me.

I sat on the couch drinking coffee before my shift at Beach Brew. I hadn't seen Lynette or Carlson that day, but my guard was up. What if he knew what we were planning? How much, and how far could he see or hear? Could he travel if he wanted to, or was his spirit also tethered to this house?

As if Lynette could pick up on when I was thinking about her, she appeared next to me at the arm of the couch. "Hi, Emma."

I glanced up and smiled. "Good morning."

"Are you going to work today?"

"Mhm." I didn't know what to talk about with her after our last exchange, so I decided to follow her lead.

"Will you bring me a new book today?" she whispered and stared at me wide-eyed as I took a sip.

"Of course." I nodded, smiling warmly at her request. "What kind?"

She didn't break from me for a few seconds. "Well, I think I'd enjoy another adventure …   I liked *Harry Potter* but I think I want to read something more real life this time…" She suddenly showed a sparkle of life in her eyes. "Maybe something closer to Huckleberry Finn."

"I'll see what I can find for you." I was happy to see she was still able to find some semblance of joy in the small things. She was just a child, after all. She always would be.

***

After my shift, I walked into the house and was instantly greeted by Lynette skipping up to me quietly, almost floating. She looked at me with her arms behind her back and her shoulders squeezing up to her little ears in anticipation.

I closed the door behind me softly and rifled through my bag to pull out a copy of *Catcher in the Rye*. "Here. I thought you might like this one. It's a classic, but it'll be new to you since it was written a little bit after you … Anyway, it's a little bit more mature. I didn't have to read it until my junior year of high school, but I think you'll be able to handle it." I flashed excited eyes at her and held out the book. "Mm. I love the smell of old used books."

She looked up at me and gently took the book out of my hand. "Thank you. I'm sure I'll love it." She paused for a moment before walking away with her new project, and stepped forward to hug me. Her cold arms wrapped around my waist and I felt my body tingle with light discomfort, similar to the feeling of your foot falling asleep. It was a safe, but not particularly pleasant numbness.

She let go of me and calmly made her way up the stairs with her book. She moved like a cloud, disappearing around the corner of the hallway at the top of the stairs. To people who couldn't see them like we could, was that just the image of a book floating up the stairs?

I meandered into the kitchen, where the clock above the stove said it was a quarter to seven.

Dinnertime.

After having been on my feet for a couple hours, nothing sounded better than preparing myself a lovely frozen pizza. As I cut open the plastic wrapping around the food, I suddenly sensed a presence with me. I stopped my activity immediately and darted my eyes to the fireplace in the dining room behind me. I must've fixed on it for a couple of minutes— thinking back on the first time I'd ever faced Carlson— because the oven beeped loudly to let me know it was done preheating. I jumped with a short gasp.

Wow. Relax.

I finally turned away from the fireplace to focus on "cooking" my supreme triple meat pizza or whatever it was. But after I slid the pizza onto the rack in the oven, I felt pulled to look back into the dining room again.

"Hello?" I closed the oven door and stared into the empty room. "Lyn?" I slipped my oven-mitt off and laid it on the counter.

I waited motionlessly, expecting someone to appear in the room. With an increasing heaviness around me, I felt a dense invisible fog filling the entire downstairs. My heart pounded as I glanced away and back to the stove timer.

Am I even hungry now?

I tried my best to disregard the energy in the room, even if it was Carlson's doing. He'd have to try harder than that now.

I noticed that the photo of Gwen and Carlson that I'd left on the shelf in the living room was now sitting on the counter next to the knife I used to open my pizza. I scoffed and shook my head. "Nope," I muttered under my breath, whether he could hear me or not.

My whole body jolted as I heard a huge *shatter* in the dining room. My body froze the second I realized what it had come from without even having to turn around and look.

My mother's urn was broken into several pieces on the wood floor at the base of the fireplace. The actual bag of ashes was torn open in a single spot, leaving a mess spilling out on the ground.

My heart descended into my stomach like a broken elevator shaft.

I rushed over and fell limply, crumbling over the sight. I didn't want to disturb it any further, but I had to clean it up as soon as possible. I had to fix it. I burst into tears and hovered my shaking hand over the bag.

"Oh my god, oh my *god.*"

Through my tears, I could see a blurry Lynette quickly appear and disappear ahead of me in the front living area. I heard a breath above me, but it wasn't her. As I glimpsed up toward it, I found Carlson leaning his elbow against the mantle, "My mistake, darlin. Must've just…" He mimed pushing something over with one finger. "Hope that wasn't anything important." Then he vanished.

Lacking the capacity to fight him back, I melted into a ball on the floor and sobbed, growling through my cries.

Out of the corner of my wet eyes, I could see Lynette slowly approach me from the bay window but I didn't acknowledge her. She stood in front of me, clasping her hands together silently. I closed my eyes and bowed my head in defeat. My chest was tight, my face throbbing. My stomach was in knots.

In an instant, I went numb, freezing in the warm summer sunset that came through the windows. A gasp for breath escaped me as I realized that the electric chill was Lynette bending down to hug me. I briefly opened my eyes to look at her and was greeted with bloody hair in my face. I would've jolted back at the sight, but had come to understand by now from my time with her that it wasn't blood. It didn't feel like blood, didn't smell like blood. It wasn't rot and gore; it was a projection of suffering engrained into the energy of a pure soul. It was an wide-open spiritual scar much stronger than any physical wound, an illusion caused by fear, heartbreak, and an inability to move on. But the pulpy red mess on her head was also proof that death wasn't the end of it all. For better or worse, it was a continuation, and a whole new world of comfort for me.

She stayed there with me as my eyelids grew irresistibly heavy. The sides of my head and the back of my neck relaxed. After a few minutes, all I could hear were distant sounds coming from the kitchen, but I couldn't get up. My consciousness drifted from a heartbroken blur to the relief of nothingness.

***

"Hi, honey." My mom knocked on the half-open door of my bedroom.

"Hey." I sat drawing in a notebook on my new bright blue comforter.

"How ya feelin'?"

"Shitty."

"I'll let that one slide given the circumstances…"

"Sorry," I said and focused down on my sketch of a big weeping willow tree. I sniffled and tilted my head, criticizing my work.

My mom approached and sat down on the bed with me. "Has Marc texted you at all?"

"No … I don't … I don't want him to." I sniffled and wiped my nose with the neck of my sweater.

"What do you want for dinner?"

"Nothing."

"Okay…" My mom sighed, "Burritos it is."

"I'm not hungry."

"Well, you need to eat something. You didn't even have your waffles this morning, either. *Waffles*, Em."

"I'll heat 'em up later."

"What— You think I saved those? They're gone, girl."

I looked at my phone and found that I had no missed calls, no new texts. It was the same empty wallpaper that was there two minutes ago. I squeezed my eyes shut, threw my head back toward the ceiling, and groaned pathetically.

"I'm sorry, honey. I know you're feeling really … sad."

"We were fine, mom. There was literally *nothing* wrong after school on Friday. I don't *get* it."

"I know." She put her hand on my back and blew a raspberry. "It happens. It happened to me, and I *know* there's nothing else I can say to make it better."

"I really, really liked him. It hurts so bad, mom. I don't … I don't know what happened. He just wants to be friends? Since when? Yesterday?" I wiped a tear from my eyes. "How am I supposed to go to school tomorrow?"

"Well, you're going," my mother stated matter-of-factly.

I sniffle-cried while hiding my puffy face in my shirt. I felt the messy bun on the top of my head flop forward.

"And guess what."

I shook my head and stared down the inside of my crewneck toward my thighs. My shorts were giving me a wedgie as I leaned forward but I was too depressed to move and fix it.

"You … are going to show up in class. With class. And you're gonna go about your day whether he talks to you or not. You're gonna keep your chin up whether or not there are tears running down it and then … you're gonna come home. And we're gonna eat Ben & Jerry's," my mother said smoothly. I looked up out of my warm stuffy shirt and leaned back against her. My head was pounding from crying all day.

"What if people look at me?"

"People are always gonna look at you. *I'm* looking at you."

"What if they make fun of me? What if they know what happened?"

"If they make fun of you, then I hope they're dumped next." My mom scoffed.

"I have to see him in second period. It's gonna be so awkward."

"Yeah." She nodded, gazing down the hallway.

"What am I gonna do?" I tried to take a deep breath.

"You're gonna be awkward, honey. Break-ups are awkward. And that's ohhhkay. Heartbreak is heartbreak. It's never fun. It's never beautiful. Trust me. Heartbreak of *any* kind is going to absolutely destroy you. This may be your first, but it won't be your last. So, I'm gonna tell you this now. When someone breaks you, watch yourself fall apart. Let it happen. But then … after you've accepted that you've crumbled like a little cookie … get some glitter glue, really look at the pieces, and start rebuilding yourself one piece at a time. You like puzzles. You'll be just fine."

"That was all very" —I shook my head— "Lifetime of you."

"Thank you."

"I just feel like I have to look like I'm over him already, and I can't just pretend to do that right now. I don't even feel like I can put make-up on tomorrow, mom."

"Em, I said to glue them together one piece at a time. Don't force pieces together if they don't click back into place. Then you're gonna end up with your whole puzzle messed up later on and you'll have to start over. Be smart, and be patient with yourself. Then once you've rebuilt yourself, you'll feel stronger because of how crazy a puzzle you finished. And then you've conquered that heartbreak. But every heartbreak turns you into a whole new puzzle. So you'll always be challenged and you'll never be bored in life."

"That doesn't sound fun."

"It is, too! I'm trying to be inspirational, honey." My mom chuckled at me. "It *is* fun. Because you get stronger after each one if you solve it mindfully. And then that's growth. And seeing how far you've come is really rewarding. *That* … is fun."

"Damn," I whimpered.

"Go ahead and feel like it's the end of the world for now, because the coolest thing about it, is that it's not. Go into this hurt knowing that you're gonna dust yourself off after the helpless feeling fades off. Be all kinds of heartbroken. But don't ever mistake it for being irreparable."

"Love you." I smiled sadly as I stared out my bedroom door into the living room at the end of the hall.

My mom kissed my forehead. "Love you." I sat up to grab my water bottle; I'd forgotten to drink any that day. She stood up and made her way to the front of my doorway. "So I'm gonna go start those *burritos.*"

"Thanks."

"Also, he had kinda goofy hair, anyway," my mom said and shrugged loosely, then walked back down the hall.

Once she'd vanished into the kitchen, my vision got blurry as if I were under water, and in the distance I heard her call out softly and sweetly, "Wake up, Em!"

***

When I opened my eyes, I was still on the wood floor by the fireplace, with a blanket draped over me and a couch pillow nudged halfway under my head. The smell of cheap, burnt pizza hit my nose

146

and I looked up in panic. I was met by Lynette's eyes looking right back at me.

"I took care of your supper," she whispered, sitting next to me.

I nodded blankly and took a shallow breath, remembering what had just happened to my mom's urn.

"I wanted to stop him but I wasn't strong enough to-," she placed a cold hand on my head and ran it admiringly over my hair. The chill was refreshing.

"No. Don't go near him."

She nodded obediently.

"Did I pass out?"

She shook her head shyly, "I helped you. You needed to rest."

I shifted uncomfortably on my side, but didn't get up.

"I took some of your energy. Just enough for you to sleep. That way, I could also clean up for you," she gave one simple nod toward the kitchen. A thin black disk sat on top of the stove.

"Thank you. I'm so grateful that the house didn't burn down, but—"

"I couldn't put it back together, but I saved as much as I could," a small moving box rested next to me with the salvageable pieces inside, the mess on the floor gone.

I blinked long and hard. "You did all that?" I asked exhaustedly.

"Did you rest well?" the little girl asked.

"How long was I out?" I couldn't see the clock in the kitchen and I didn't have my phone.

"Quite a while. It's getting just past midnight," she whispered.

"Oh," I stared forward at Lynette, and then slowly laid my head back down on the pillow.

"Maybe your friends can fix it."

I swallowed and nodded weakly, letting out a weepy sniffle.

"Please don't cry. Would you like to go to bed?"

I shook my head. I didn't want to move or think.

"It's okay, Emma. Sleep," she placed her hand on my damp cheek and I quickly drifted away again while gazing at the cover of *Catcher in the Rye*. My deep anger was masked momentarily by sadness, defeat, and exhaustion. But in my sleep, I dreamt about gluing myself back together ... just enough to get rid of Carlson.

17.

PLANS

Days went by, yet again with no sign of Carlson but that didn't comfort us enough to stop our planning to getting rid of him. In fact, there wasn't much to plan at all other than to actually pull the trigger— or dig the shovel in.

"Honest to God…" I started.

"Which one?"

"Huh?"

Willow chuckled. "Nothin, nothin … Go ahead."

"Do you think it'll actually work?" I asked Willow one day as we sat looking out at the sea in light sweatshirts sipping our tea under a blanket. We'd unofficially adopted an old wooden bench along Ocean Drive as our own, and visited it often.

"Trial and error, babe. Aside from getting a priest involved." She scoffed. "I think this is the best thing to try … for now. It's his bodily attachment to the physical. We'll burn sage with it and then pour salt over whatever's left. We'll do all the things. He's all bones by now anyway so it won't all be gone after, but we'll burn what we can. His clothes … hair … stuff … Hopefully it'll weaken the bond enough to release him from here."

"And then we cleanse the house again," I watched the waves crash up against the rocks below and ahead of us.

"Yep. Salt and sage, baby. Those two have always helped purify our house and just make the air feel fresher. Been doin it for years. I don't know for a fact that it'll get rid of such strong negativity, but it's worth a try. Unless you're changing your mind and wanna stop by a church … I don't."

"*No.* I wanna keep quiet as long as we can…"

"You really don't want word getting around? Not even to Liv?"

"No. I just want peace, not attention. I feel like life hasn't stopped since my mom died and I can't catch a break to make a new plan for my future yet. I was uprooted across the country— not that being here itself is a bad thing— and then all *this* with us …. It was a huge change, too much in such a short time. I just want to be done and move on. I don't want to be the crazy exorcism story of Newport."

Waves crashed ahead of us and clouds rolled in.

"*Well,* no one mentioned anything about possession. Calm down."

I sniffled and shook my head, craning my head up to look at the overcast sky above. "Whatever."

"What do you want to do after all of this goes away?"

"I mean— it won't, though. I have this … for life. I guess I'll have to learn to coexist with that world."

"Okay yeah but … what do you want for *yourself,* Em? Outside of dead people." She sipped her tea and stared out at the ocean with me. A soft breeze brought a hint of sea salt to the taste of peach tea and honey.

I licked my lips and sighed. "I wanna help people who've felt the same pain I do. Maybe grief counseling. I'd have to go back to school, though. All I have is my bachelor's." I rolled my eyes. "But if Liv is gonna let me live this cheap for a while, it wouldn't be too much of a problem to save up. She may even help me."

"Have you talked to her lately?"

"Yeah."

"And?"

"We're fine, I guess."

"Does she know you're miserable in your new house yet?"

"No, she'd just want me to leave. And then she'd want me to stay with them and I don't wanna intrude because— just, no."

"She have a big house?"

"Yeah," I replied.

"So I'm not sure I'm really seeing a problem."

I lowered my head and glared at her. "Stop. I can't. Lynette shouldn't be on her own with him. She doesn't deserve that if I can help it. She just wants the same thing I do. We're both alone."

"You're not."

"It's a different kind of lonely."

Willow nodded. "I guess I can't understand that kind yet, then. I haven't lost anyone before. It just felt like it when my parents split because I knew they were getting a divorce before they did and I was just a kid. I was mourning our family's demise before it happened … but … it's not comparable to what you went through."

"I'm sorry." I took in a breath of fresh air and thought about the couple of very fuzzy memories I had of my dad. All I had were stories and pictures.

"Don't be. They're better off now. It's still kinda … you know … but they're friendly."

"Yeah."

"They'd like you." Willow smiled as the waves crashed.

"The sad thing is … we know they're somewhere out there in some form, right? Gwen, my mom, my dad … If he and Lynette are still here, they could be, too." I sighed. "So why aren't they?"

The sound of the ocean echoed the rhythm of our breaths. It was becoming a chilly east coast autumn. Unlike California, the seasons actually changed here, and distinctly. I shivered a little, but I was never really bothered by the cold.

"I wish I could tell ya, babes." She frowned.

I glimpsed over at my friend. "What about you?"

"What about me? I'm boring."

"Come on. What's *your* future look like?"

Willow gazed from the sea-foam down to her cup of tea and let out a single chuckle. "I … haven't seen a damn thing. Not what you'd expect, huh?"

"Well, what do you want, then?"

She stared blankly at her travel mug. "I guess my plan was to write. I went to school for creative writing, so…" She trailed off.

"Oh, nice. What would you write?"

"No idea." She squinted up at a seagull flying overhead. "Honestly, I wanted to be a female Stephen King."

"Why not, then?"

"Because I tried so hard but then realized that I'm just Willow."

"What's that supposed to mean? You can still write. I think Willow Graham is a great author name."

She pursed her lips. "Mm. Willow *F.* Graham."

"F is for what?"

"Fern."

"Your parents really went hard with the plant names, huh?"

"Ah, shit. Yeah, they for *sure* had a theme. But it's also my grandma's name."

"Fern," I repeated with laughter.

"*Shut* up." Willow gave a wicked side-eye. "Yours probably sucks, too."

"Lorraine."

"That's definitely a grandma name too, dude."

"It *was.*" I giggled. "She died when I was a kid."

"Why are you laughing about that?" She playfully whacked my shoulder. "Honor your elders, bitch."

I howled and threw my head back to gaze up at the blue-gray sky. "No, no. I don't mean it like that. I just laughed because—"

"See? You're no better than me." Willow smirked.

I took a second to collect myself and yawned before asking, "Well, is that still the plan though?"

She looked me in the eyes and smiled softly. "Sure."

"Sure?"

"I mean, yeah. I'll do it here and there when inspiration strikes. I'm not a fan of planning *too* far ahead, though. If I set too many goals and don't get to everything, I know I'll be too disappointed in myself. So … I'll just go wherever the wind carries me, you know?"

"Yeah." I nodded.

We spent the next few minutes in silence, as we often did during our hang-outs, just to think and enjoy each other's company. There were never awkward silences between us anymore. We'd grown far past that day at the creamery, and in such a short time.

I finally spoke up with another thought. "Do you think I really could be…"

"I don't know. Are you? We've hashed this out before and we can do it again if you need to, but we're not gonna get anywhere new. Do you really, in your *gut*, think you are?"

"I'm torn."

"What is there to be torn about?"

"It's such a weird thing to wrap my head around. I never had visions about her before I moved here, no past life … whatever you call it."

"Regressions?"

"Whatever. I don't know much about her, either. But my last couple visions seemed so real, and I care about Lynette so intensely. It was so much easier than I thought to *not* be terrified of her."

"Does that *have* to mean you're Gwen?"

"Carlson's convinced I am."

"Okay. So? Where are his credentials?"

"I guess … Maybe he's just getting in my head."

"Girl, he already is."

"Damn," I blew a light raspberry.

"Stop worrying about whether or not you're some other chick reincarnated, okay? There's no way to know. What difference would it make to who you are now, anyway? Even if you *were* her in some past life, you aren't the same person today whether you slap a new name on your soul or not. You aren't the same Emma you were a year ago or when your mom passed. You're not even the same Emma I met last *month*. We change into new versions of ourselves every single day and I don't know Gwen Salley, but I know you." She leaned back and stretched her legs out in front of her.

Her feet shook in her thick socks as she gathered her thoughts. She'd bought us matching pairs at a gift shop downtown. They were fuzzy enough to be comfy, but thin enough to let the refreshing breeze through to our feet. They had pineapples on them and were our official "fuzzy-tea-time-outside socks."

I exhaled, "Yeah."

"You wanna know who you are?"

I shrugged, expecting an obnoxious quip like she usually gave in an attempt to ease the tension of deep, emotional conversations.

"For starters, you're Emma Reilly, a girl who nearly gave me a concussion one day on a walk—"

"Not fair." I scoffed. "And actually not even close to true."

"Shhh! I'm not *done!*" She closed her eyes tightly to focus. "You are Emma, in *this* life. Maybe the only one you've ever had or ever *will*. This one, on this day, on this bench. You're brave—"

"I have anxiety all the time."

"You're *brave* … even if you get so sucked into it sometimes, but that doesn't define you. It's a whole different being than you. You're just learning your relationship with it, just like you're learning how to handle your ability. A lot of sensitive people have anxiety because they're absorbing so much energy around them and not always recognizing it. It's not inherently *you* that's the problem.

"Also, do you think I would've done the same thing as you and accompanied a stranger to lunch? Hell no, well— probably not. If some crazy chick I'd just met tried to tell me that she was psychic and that *I* could see dead people, I probably would've noped right out of there and taken my food with me. But you, however … freaked out or skeptical … stayed and gave me a chance to talk. Sure, I confronted you and proved it to you right there, but you chose to believe me. You could've just stayed in denial and left and never talked to me again. You're way more intuitive than you've allowed yourself to believe and after everything you've been through, you still have *so much* to give.

"You let a dead little girl borrow your phone just so she could listen to music. You buy her *books*. And can we talk about how you live in a house with not one, but two ghosts? One of them is a complete prick and anyone else would've bounced after the first encounter and never come back. But you stay because you worry for *her* safety. You've let it in. Joel and me … You've helped us just as much as we've helped you."

"Oh, stop." I rolled my eyes and hid my blushing cheeks with my sweatshirt sleeve.

"No. You've become the third link in our chain in no time because what we share is *real*. We're bonded by an understanding of each other that no one will ever know unless they deal with it, too. We understand that no one actually understands *anything*. That's scary, but it's good to have other people around you who also know that."

I gulped.

"I'm talking too much. But I saw it that day in the creamery. You're powerful and you're going to help people. That's who you are. Regardless of whether or not you've lived before. Don't forget that. Everything happens for a reason, and we met for a good one." Willow nodded to herself and became silent, staring again into the waves.

I waited to see if she would add onto her speech, because she usually didn't just stop talking. But that was it. She said nothing else until we finished our tea.

We put on our shoes and packed up our blanket and mugs shortly after as it started to get chillier with the incoming clouds. Before we got in the car, Willow stood up straight with her hand on the driver's side door handle. She stared out at the ocean and then turned to me with a sigh.

"What's up?" I stopped before hopping in, whooshing my messy wind-blown hair out of my face as I looked to her.

"Can I … give you a hug?"

I winced. "I— yeah. Are you okay?"

She quietly walked over to my side of the car and took me in a friendly embrace. I stared out at the waves across from the parking lot, gently patting her back.

Willow never answered me, but before letting go of our first ever hug, she mumbled into my ear, "God, I really hope this shit works the first time."

SEPTEMBER

158

18.

BLACKBIRD

The bell tolled three in the afternoon at Trinity Church. I sat alone on an iron bench, finalizing my plan notes for the body-burning festivities we had set for that night. I'd made a list of supplies we might need, and Googled some prayers or affirmations to add in for extra protection. Knowing myself, I'd get embarrassed and not actually say any of it.

I just wanted it to be over and done with.

September brought beautiful, vivid, warm colors to the leaves on the trees in Queen Anne Square, and volunteers for the church were setting up their pumpkin displays for their annual fall fundraiser. I could smell the seasons changing, the earthy musk of the crisp leaves mixing with the cool bite along the wharf. Even the daylight was inexplicably different. A bright gilded veil had drifted down over us as another shimmering summer floated away with the few sailboats on the water ahead. A breeze billowed through the square and blew my hair in my face as I texted Willow about backpacks. I sniffled and brushed my hair behind my ear, clearing my vision enough to see a short, wide shadow approaching me on the cobblestone. I looked up from my phone and smiled.

"Hey, kiddo." Thompson cleared his throat and grinned. "Mind if I sit with ya?"

"Hi, Thomps," I said softly and patted the cool iron next to me, "Whatcha doin today?"

He grunted as he sat, and patted the khaki material on his thighs. He let a few seconds pass before responding, "Ohhh, nothin much … nice day today."

I nodded, looking down the hill of the square out at the wharf ahead. The yachts bobbed on the water alongside the seafood grills and gift shops.

"I don't see you as much as I want to. But *gah*, your aunt just doesn't shut up about you. She's real proud. So I wanted to ask you myself … how the hell are ya?"

I chuckled, glimpsing into his old eyes and back toward a couple of sailboats drifting past the downtown strip. "I'm okay. Hangin' in there."

He scrunched up his nose, as he always had done when he was thinking really deeply. "Ah. Well that's about what you'd expect from someone dealing with as much as you are. Your mom would be proud of you, too…"

I pursed my lips and nodded.

"Anyways, you've got a cross-country move under your belt now. New friends, too, by the looks of it. Good ones. You keep 'em close."

"I will." I squinted, people-watching from my perch as tourists and residents alike made their way down the cobblestone sidewalk of Thames Street.

"Well" —he slapped his knee— "I feel like takin' a walk. Comin'?" He stood up, stretching lightly with his hands resting at the bottom of his back.

"Shouldn't you be at home resting when you're not working?" I narrowed my brows.

"Oh, I got plenty of rest. Plenty of time. But I wanna go take a peek at those pumpkins." He gestured to a side door of the chapel. The steps leading up to it were lined with a gorgeous variety: perfectly round orange, bumpy warty green and white, and short fat yellow. Autumn in New England was my favorite cozy cardigan.

"Sure." I accepted.

We strolled along the path up the square back toward Trinity and its centuries-old graveyard, where most stones were so worn from passing time that no one could even make out whose resting place it marked. Some gravestones were broken in two or three pieces nestled behind a rusted picket fence. At the church, we took a right and walked along the little garden behind the clergy house. I'd never really been back there before, and had never noticed the darling little water fountain situated there.

"So…" Thompson said over the soft trickling of the water. "What's weighin' on ya?"

"Hm?"

"There's somethin'."

"Oh, it's just" —I bit a piece of loose skin on my lip— "Everything."

"Go on."

"It's nothing."

"Is it nothing or everything? It can't be both, kid."

"There's just someone in the neighborhood who comes around sometimes starting problems."

"Who?" He frowned.

"No one you know." I shook my head. "But he's manipulative, threatening. And there's this little girl who's … pretty scared of him, but he won't leave us alone."

"In *your* neighborhood?"

"Yeah…"

"Hm." He harrumphed.

"I just want him to go back to wherever the heck he came from."

He stopped in his tracks. "He doesn't even belong there?"

"No, he used to live there, but not anymore. Not for a long time. He comes around trying to keep control over what was his, I guess … I don't know."

"Should the cops be involved?" He furrowed his brow.

"*No,*" I spat quickly.

To that, his eyes widened. "Well, okay. If you insist. I trust your judgment. But do you think you've got this under control on your own?"

"I'm not on my own."

He nodded once with a confident grunt.

"Anyway, we have to get him to stop coming around," I summarized.

"It seems to me … that this guy is making you all feel pretty unsafe in your own home, huh?"

I nodded.

Thomps tugged at the collar of his baby blue and navy plaid flannel shirt, "So … are you just gonna let him?"

"No," I grumbled under my breath.

"Ohhh now, you didn't ask but I'm gonna give my shiny two cents on this. However he spent his time there was his choice. But his time is up, now. He can go gracefully, or he can stir up problems. And he's chosen the latter. Well, I've never been one for violence or fighting. I prefer to talk things out with people like grown civilized humans. It seems to me, though, that you've given him that chance to leave with dignity and he didn't take too kindly, at all."

I sighed, gazing down at the coins that flashed brightly from the bottom of the fountain whenever a breeze moved the shade of the trees aside.

"When people can't be ignored or reasoned with, we unfortunately have to confront them with a healthy and mindful level of aggression. But don't you stoop to their level, Emma. No matter how upset you are," he warned. He stopped on the walkway and put his hands on my shoulders. "Don't you let anyone push you around. I don't care how old or scary they are. His time is up there. *You* are not to be pushed around."

He looked beyond me to the chapel building again. "Got way too much life left to live than to let someone blow out your flame or fuel it too much that it gets out of hand. You stay steady."

"I'll try. Thank you for the advice … But hey, don't tell-"

"Your aunt tells me everything about you, but I'm not tellin' her a thing. That's your business. I just value that you chose to share it with me." he winked warmly. "Well, I'd better get going. I've got a whole damn list of errands and people to go see today."

"I thought you said you had nothin' going on today."

"Well, it's both." He gently pulled my shoulders into him and hugged me tightly. "I've watched you grow up all of these summers into this … marvelously strong young woman you are now. You're reinventing yourself here and you don't have time to go takin' on any more or less than what you can handle … only what is gonna nurture your soul. This asshat is hindering your growth." In my ear, he whispered, "That's *your* home, not his."

As he spoke to me, I gazed into the window of one of the old clergy offices beside us. I felt his warm hug turn to a familiar cold numbness at the same time I realized that, in the reflection of us in the window, I was by myself.

Shit.

"Thomps—"

"Be good, kiddo."

A cold painful chill ran up my back and a rush of tears in my eyes. I didn't need to look away from the window to confirm that he was gone.

David Leo Thompson had an infectious laugh. He took life seriously by not doing so at all. He was unoffendable, and so kind that he could transform the most miserable into warmer, better people-even if just for a moment. That moment always mattered. Of all the summers I'd spent visiting him at Beach Brew, I'd never seen him angry. The more angry he was with someone, the more kindly he treated them.

He'd bring coffee and donuts to work for us almost every morning, even though we were already at a coffee house. He was loyal to Ma's. We'd joke that he'd chosen the wrong employer. To that, he'd just shove a maple cruller into his mouth and shoo us away.

When he'd come over for dinner at Liv's, he'd be the goofiest drunk we'd ever seen without *ever* taking a sip of alcohol. We'd watch cartoons together in her living room before eating, and he'd chuckle at them like a kid. The couple times we'd stopped by his house to say hello during visits to Newport, we'd catch him watching golf, always in a silly pair of socks. Sometimes, he would to play acoustic guitar at Beach Brew when I was much younger- not for tips, just for fun. I could vividly remember him playing "Blackbird," his favorite song.

He was wise enough to know exactly what he and I both needed before he moved on, and he was kind enough to make me one of his last stops. He helped me by letting me help him.

And it was an honor.

19.

NOTHING BUT OLD BONES

It was on a Sunday evening that we packed up our shovels, flashlights, and a backpack full of goodies: salt, gasoline, matches, and sage. We wore all black and moved stealthily into the woods right before sundown as if we were breaking into an art museum to steal a Van Gogh.

It wasn't an issue finding the quartz marker for our dig-site. I knew exactly where to go, and led the group through the trees without hesitation.

Once I stopped and looked down at the crystal, I suddenly felt guilty, and Willow could sense it.

"What?"

"It's just harsh."

"*What* ?"

"This." I dropped my shovel.

"Burning a dead body?" Willow shrugged. "We're doing everyone a favor here. I wouldn't feel too bad about it."

"Wills," Joel started.

She scoffed, "Em, there's no shame in protecting your home. This guy … is *bad*. And it's not like we're killing him. He's already— I mean—" She gestured to the ground before us.

"We're destroying a spirit," I whispered.

"We don't know that," Joel said reassuringly, still gripping the handle of our tool bag.

"Energy can't be created *or* destroyed. Only transferred. We don't know where he'll go or what he'll become, but hopefully he won't be here," Willow added.

Joel nodded. "He had a choice."

"*Amen*. He dug his own grave." She smirked in the dim warm light of the sunset in the trees. With that, she removed the crystal from its spot in the dirt and leaves and put it in her pocket. I watched as she took the backpack from Joel, unzipped it, and took out a large zipper bag of pink Himalayan salt. She cleared her throat, "This is also pink halite. It's not just salt. It's pure and edible and has been used for protection for centuries. It's known for creating healthy boundaries, releasing attachments, and promoting self-love and a sense of purpose. In other words, it means saying 'no' to this prick and evicting him. We're gonna sprinkle this in a circle around where we're gonna dig. Oh! And then in a cute little circle over ... there. So we can be protected but also away from the fire while it's burning. Hopefully, it'll keep him out if he senses that his body is being disturbed. That is, if he can get this far out here."

"Well he died out here, so I'm assuming he can."

She pursed her lips at me and tilted her head with wide eyes, "Well. That's why we have this."

"Do you really think this is going to keep a ghost who's strong enough to break my mom's—"

"To be completely honest with you, Em, I haven't tried this before, but we're gonna find out." Willow began sprinkling salt around the site, large enough to give us room to dig without ruining the circle. The sun began to creep down further under the treetops. I noticed a sullen expression on Willow's face as she focused intently on making the circle as steady and perfect as possible. Luckily for us, there wasn't much of a breeze that evening to disperse any of the salt. She took a deep breath as she closed the circle. "Blessed be," she said under her breath.

"Okay ... ready?" Joel asked her.

Willow simply nodded, stepped over the salt ring, picked up a shovel, and plunged it into the dirt with one strong push. She furrowed her brows and sighed. "Come on, let's go."

With that, both Joel and I followed her lead, digging from the center of the salt ring where the crystal had marked Carlson's supposed grave. While we occasionally kept an eye on the outside of our protective circle, our focus remained on locating his body, and getting the job done as swiftly as possible.

As it got darker, we whipped out our flashlights, our senses of urgency heightened in the looming trees. I wiped my forehead and heard Joel gasp quietly. We all paused for a second, panting heavily.

"Guys," Joel whispered shakily, kneeling down to shine his light closer into our hole, about five feet deep. "*Guys!*"

"Is it——" Willow started.

"It's bones," he interrupted, out of breath. His eyes widened.

"Holy shit." Willow took a shallow breath.

We knew what we were there to find, but actually hitting it affected us differently than we all expected. "Okay. Are you sure it's not … like … an animal or——"

Willow bent down to quickly brush the dirt off of the hard yellow mound, just enough to see an eye socket and nasal bone. She looked up straight into my eyes. "It's a human skull. See, right there you can see the——"

"I don't need to see it." I turned away and gripped my shovel tightly. A couple tears dribbled down my cheek not because I felt any sorrow for the life lost and thrown into the dirt, but because of the profound realization that hit me. I held enough power to locate a dead body, and that below me were the remains of the man who'd harassed me in my own house.

Look at him.

I gazed down at the skull peeking out from the dirt. To my surprised, it didn't radiate the same menacing energy that was present whenever he entered the room. The entity who'd towered over my heartbroken panic wasn't the real man at all. He was a glorified projection, a spectral illusion of aggression. His intimidation was self-preservation. He had nothing, he *was* nothing … without someone to torment or keep his memory alive. His threats toward me were a cheap peeling band-aid, and Gwen was the deep purple bruise on his rotting ego. He'd let two targets slip through his fingertips and then he'd been bested by one of them, a woman he thought he could disrespect.

He was nothing but old bones.

And that made me smile.

"Well, I'm honestly super surprised that it stayed buried this long." Willow cocked her head to the side briefly.

"Yeah." Joel stared down at the skull.

There was a moment of silence while we all processed the discovery.

"Okay." Willow straightened back up. "Let's uncover the rest and light it up."

I wanted to sleep in peace that night, so I held my shovel and dug it back into the ground to move the dirt around the skeleton. Out of sheer adrenaline, I was able to speed up my pace to get the rest of the bones up, but remained mindful of not disturbing the salt as I threw dirt back. My shoulders and arms cramped up, but after about five more minutes, the body was exposed.

We all bent over to study the grave.

"Damn, how did the two of them do this on their own?" Willow dropped her shovel.

Joel simply shook his head incredulously.

There it was. Jack Carlson wore the same light gray button-up and black tweed trousers I'd seen him wearing each time I ran into him. The same outfit from my nightmares was tattered and dirty, deflated over the bones as the body decomposed. There were shredded holes in the fabric from the multiple stab wounds left by Gwen, and the many bugs that had likely explored his corpse over the decades he'd been hidden back there in the woods.

Gwen had once stood exactly where I was then, our heaving chests full of guilt and defeat. We'd both stared down at this spot with such hatred, with hearts full of resentment and loss.

Were we the same?

A breeze flowed past us, serving as a reminder that the clock was ticking.

"You're sure it's him?" Joel asked.

"Positive." I confirmed without an ounce of doubt or hesitation.

"Who *else* could it be?" Willow jutted her head forward and gave Joel a dirty look in the dim illumination of our flashlights. She seemed rushed but for some reason, her urgency came with aggression.

Without questioning her attitude, we stood up. Willow took out the sage, gasoline, and matches. She carefully poured the entire canister of gas she'd filled up earlier that day into the hole, making sure it covered every inch of him. She sprinkled sage over the grave, and threw a few branches off the ground into the hole. Then she handed me the pack of matches.

"Why?" I asked.

"This is your job, Em." She spoke intently and held the pack between my hand and hers.

His time is up. I heard Thompson's voice echo in my mind. *You are not to be pushed around.*

"Here," Willow took a match out and lit it. She passed it to me, and held my hand tightly as we stood together in front of the grave.

"Joel, back up and cross your fingers," she ordered, turning to me, "We don't let Joel around fire. I'll tell you later."

Joel shook his head in annoyance.

I didn't respond, too invested in the moment. I held the match in my right hand and watched the flame flicker down to the wood. When it did, I took a deep breath and dropped the match over the grave. In an instant it lit up into a fiery pit, but I felt a cold hard sheet of air slap me across my face. Willow and I both jumped back. I crouched down, rubbing my cheek and watching the flames rise.

Now he was where he belonged. His own little Hell.

While the fire raged, we backed up and outside of the salt circle. We huddled together and sat in the dirt surrounded by a smaller salt ring Willow made around us as an after-thought. I prayed silently that the fire wouldn't get high or bright enough to be seen by anyone through the trees at night.

No one said a word.

At one point, briefly, I saw what appeared to be a deep black shadow standing across from us on the other side of the fire, watching. I told myself that it was all in my head, that it was my eyes playing tricks on me with the light of the flames against the dark silhouettes of the trees.

After a while, the fire went down just enough that we could approach the hole and check on what was left, then we watched up close as the fire slowly went out. We got impatient toward the end, and just dumped some damp dirt over what small flame remained, then let the extinguished site cool off in silence.

In the very likely case that the bones didn't burn completely— and they hadn't— we had a plan, and as if we could all communicate telepathically, we knew when the time came to bag up the bones. We used gloves, of course, and black trash bags. I felt like a serial killer, and even more so when we destroyed any evidence of our presence there by mixing the dirt and salt together with our shoes. Then we closed the hole back up into a new mound of dirt, even placing leaves and twigs over it to be extra convincing. After that, we packed up, hurried back to the house to lock up. We immediately jumped into Willow's Prius for a nighttime drive down Ocean Avenue to King's Beach, a small fishing spot with some rocks overlooking the waves. While Willow drove cautiously, Joel and I kept our gloves on and nervously held onto the two doubled-layered, Carlson-filled trash bags. We all kept quiet. We knew why we needed to do this, but it felt icky, dishonest … And we were probably breaking some kind of law.

When we arrived, we parked and tried to act as nonchalantly as possible as we carried our bags out to the beach. We rushed to fill them with rocks and sand and scurried up the small hill from the shore to a cliff that overlooked the tame waves. They were an odd in-between that mimicked my level of confidence in what we had just done *and* what we were doing there. I felt a sinking pit in my stomach right before we got rid of him. I was carrying *real* human bones, a body left behind from a homicide. Then I thought of Carlson watching me from my bedroom window, and toppling over my beautiful mother's urn. I thought back to the vision of his sweaty hand roughly clasping over Gwen's mouth, and the way it slid up my thigh, ice cold.

Without any further consideration, I tossed my bag as far as I could into the ocean with an angry grunt. Joel followed with the second bag of bones and rock. We watched as they bobbed in water, all of us hoping that they'd sink quickly or be carried far out to sea— or ideally, both. We held our breath as they disappeared from view beneath the surface of the dark foamy water, then let out a relieved sigh in unison.

We stood there on the cliff even after the bags had gone, all wondering if we'd made the right choice in dumping them. At the sound of my shoe shifting in the sandy pebbles on the cliff, Willow nodded slowly, "Come on," she whispered. "Let's go home."

As we walked back to the car across the street, Joel brushed his hand against mine, "I have to trust that we did the right thing." He reassured me quietly.

I bit the inside of my cheek and nodded.

On the short ride home, I dozed on Joel's shoulder in the backseat with my gloves still on. He lightly nudged me when we got back to the house, "Hey, we're back."

"Please stay with me tonight," I muttered in exhaustion.

"Are you kidding me? I'm using your shower and going to bed." Willow got out and hastily headed up to the front steps.

"We'll stay. Don't worry," Joel whispered as he helped me out of the car. It locked with a beep that seemed much louder in the middle of the night.

Once the three of us had made it through the front door, Lynette appeared at the top of the staircase. She took a few shy steps down and studied us from head to toe. Our clothes were covered in dirt and ash. Our faces were dirty, our hair disheveled from the wind on the coastline. We all needed a hot shower and a full-night's sleep.

"Why are you so dirty?" Lynette asked.

"We look ... *disgusting*." Willow cringed into the mirror by the front door.

"Hi." I mustered.

"Did you make him leave?" she squeaked.

I swallowed. It was quiet in the house.

Willow looked away from herself and followed my eyes up at the stairs, "What did she say?"

"We tried something," I replied softly.

"Are we safe now?" Lynette's eyes drooped.

"Maybe ... I hope so."

"We'll see," Joel added quietly.

Willow dumped her keys on the entry table, locked the front door behind us, and walked directly toward the stairs, "I'm out. Behave yourselves." She made her way up slowly. "Can I borrow some pajamas? Eh, I find 'em. Also … I'm sleeping in bed with you, Em. Love you guys. Goodnight." She stopped halfway up. "Excuse me, Lynette. I'm probably gonna walk through you if you don't move, so … sorry," she rambled.

The little girl vanished silently right before Willow could reach her.

"We did it," Joel put his hand on my shoulder. "What do you wanna do while she showers?"

"I need water," I said plainly and made my way through the dining room to the kitchen.

"I'm proud of you, Em."

I stopped and turned to face my friend, "Why?"

He scratched his upper arm, still standing in the foyer. "Because you're a badass."

I simply nodded at him.

"Can I have some?" Joel asked.

I blinked, "No, Joel. You're not allowed," I joked dryly, but couldn't help but smile exhaustedly as I walked away to get us each a glass of ice water.

20.

IT'S HARD

Five days after our little bonfire in the forest, Liv approached us as we quietly ate our breakfast together. It was a slow morning at Beach Brew, aside from patrons- past and present- coming and going to buy a large snickerdoodle latte on a five-dollar special to honor Thomps. She was donating all of the proceeds from it to chip in for his memorial. It was his favorite drink there; he'd even come up with the idea of sprinkling cookie crumbles on top of the whipped cream. I zoned out on the customers as they left flowers out front to pay their respects to their favorite employee.

My aunt stood watching me as I spied another visitor gently placing some freshly cut hydrangeas outside one of the long front windows of the shop. She sighed. "Service is at 5:30. You kids going?"

"Wouldn't miss it." I nodded. I hadn't told anyone, much less my aunt, that I'd been blessed with one last conversation with Thomps. In fact, I acted shocked when Olivia called to tell me the news a few days before. I felt I'd already gotten all the closure I needed about his passing directly *from* him, but was still going to the service to give my thoughts and support to the family. Because the old man was quite the local celebrity, his daughter decided to make it a more public viewing at the church. Anyone who cared about him was welcome to come say goodbye- or in my case, to say goodbye again.

"Yeah, we'll be there." Willow gave a sympathetic smile. She had dark circles under her eyes and spoke slowly.

"Good, that's good." Aunt Liv nodded with her hand on her chin in contemplation. "Dinner at Brick Alley is on me tonight, okay?"

"Wow. Thank you, Mrs.-"

"Again, Joel … just call me Liv. Today, we're all family here." she patted his shoulder and walked off behind the counter.

Joel shrugged. "We'll try to make the best out of this day. That's what he would've wanted from us, right?"

I nodded, fixated on Willow. She'd been abnormally quiet and mellow that morning. She'd even sipped her tea looking down at her phone. She'd normally be chatting up a storm because she took tea seriously. That was her designated shit-shooting time. Joel caught on and cleared his throat. I gazed over at him, then back and forth between my friends. He shrugged.

"Wills—" He started.

"You okay?" I put my hand on hers.

She looked up from her phone and stared directly into my eyes blankly for a moment. Once she realized how transparent she was being, she perked up instantly. "Why wouldn't I be?"

I stammered, "I … I don't know. You've been a little absent this morning."

"Really tired." She swallowed. "I'm fine. It's a great day to go to a funeral." She stood up and pushed her chair in. "I'm actually gonna go get ready now, or I'll end up forgetting and showing up looking the way I do now. And that'd be *most* disrespectful." She flashed her eyes sarcastically.

"Okay." Joel shook his head slightly. "See you at home, then."

"Yup." She snatched her black leather bag off the back of the chair and flew out the door.

" 'It's a great day to go to a funeral?' *Really*?" I leaned back in my seat.

"I don't know. Your guess is as good as mine." Joel watched her turn the corner and out of sight. "Yeah. She's very … not herself today. That doesn't happen too often."

He stared at a younger man docking his boat outside right near our window. "I mean, we're all a mess after last weekend, right? It was a lot. Maybe she's just drained. Maybe she saw some things during all of it that we didn't."

"Maybe." I sighed. "I'm not gonna push."

***

Later that afternoon, we sat toward the back of the full church. The three of us were, of course, joined by my aunt and uncle during the whole service. It was beautiful seeing so many people come to honor Thomps, but I wasn't expecting it to be an open casket. I could see some of his pale face peeking out from the opening, and was debating whether or not I wanted to approach it at the end of the service.

I tried my best to pay full attention to the people speaking, and not the fact that another person I loved was lying dead in front of me. With everything that had happened recently, however, I found myself frequently zoning out on the back of the pew in front of me. Thompson's daughter Linda allowed anyone who wanted to speak to come up to the podium before closing out the service, so there were many people taking their turn on-stage.

As the current speaker walked down from the front, Linda stepped back up and spoke into the microphone, "Thank you for such kind, beautiful, words, Jim." She patted her tissue under her eyes and cleared her throat. "Alright, would anyone else like to come up and say a few words, or was Jim's speech too wonderful to follow?" The audience chuckled softly.

There was no way I was going up there. I shrank back in my seat and glanced around the church, expecting the service to wind down from that point.

"Wills," Joel whispered from beside to me. I turned to look at my friends, and saw that Willow had already stood up and started making her way across the people between us and the aisle.

I met eyes with Joel, furrowed my brows, and cocked my head to the side. He simply shrugged and whipped his head around to watch Willow walk down the aisle to the front. Before she took her place behind the podium, she stopped in front of Thompson's casket and bowed her head. Linda smiled sadly and gently handed her the microphone.

Before speaking, Willow looked directly at Joel and me, and then straight down the aisle toward the church entrance. "Hellooo." She paused, grinning awkwardly into the audience and gripping the microphone. "I'm sure almost none of you know me. In fact, Thomps — that's what my friends and I called him— didn't know me very well either. I knew him a little better after my friend formally introduced us at Beach Brew. I'd only ever known him from there, as many of us did … He was never without a warm smile on his face, and although I didn't know him as well as many of you did, I think that smile told me everything I needed to know about him." She sighed and looked down.

"I try to take lessons from every single person I cross paths with, and Thomps taught me a few without even trying. His love for life was clear, and while his body got older, his spirit seemed younger every time I ran into him. That told me that he wasted no time, no words … He was a reminder not to overlook any experience, good or bad. He seemed to take things as they came. He touched everyone, and he did his job here. He made it all count.

"Um … I don't know how much longer I have here either, and I don't know if I'll have as … fabulous … and impactful a reputation as Thomps did. But I know that after I leave here today, I'll do my best … Thank you."

With that, Willow took a deep breath and passed the microphone back to Linda on her way off-stage. She made her way back toward us, but instead of returning to her seat next to Joel, she headed straight out of the open church doors.

I pursed my lips tightly with my wide glued on Linda. "Thank you, sweetie." The poor woman cleared her throat. "I know we all—" She choked up. "I know this isn't easy for anyone who knew my dad. In any capacity. I'm so glad he made a difference to you. So" —she nodded shyly— "if there isn't anyone else who'd like to share…"

As her words trailed off, her eyes searched the room looking for raised hands or voices speaking up. "Okay, well then … with that, I want to thank you all for coming to honor dad's memory today. Even in grief, it warms our hearts to know that he was so loved. If you'd like to join us for some refreshments in the next room, you're more than welcome to." Linda gazed out the door, seemingly searching for the mysterious young lady who had given such a speech. She wiped her eyes with her free hand. "Be safe getting home, and God bless you."

She stepped down and into the group of immediate family for support. They all hugged each other at the front of the pews.

I wished I'd had that much family around me.

I shook off my inappropriate jealousy and stood up with the rest of the congregation. As I began to make my way past the people in our row, Joel grabbed my hand, "Em," he gave me a look of concern.

"I'm gonna go talk to her, Ken." I heard Liv mutter solemnly as I passed her.

I gently weaved through the crowd and apologized to anyone that I accidentally bumped into while exiting the church. Once outside, I wasn't able to see Willow anywhere. I did see a sign with an arrow that directed toward a small garden to my left and around the side of the building. I followed it.

In a small shaded courtyard surrounded by flowers, I found my friend. She was pacing alone in her black body-con dress and cardigan in the center of the garden, with her hand on her cheek. Her matching combat boots shuffled quietly in the grass.

"Willow," I called softly, looking back at the crowd to see if anyone was headed our way. Luckily, everyone stood out front mingling. My gaze returned to her. Joel and I both knew that it was best to give her space.

Not this time, though.

I took several steps toward her, "What was all that back there?"

She looked up and scowled at me. I shook my head in response, waiting for an answer. She scoffed.

"Drop it, Wills," I asserted.

She stopped and turned her whole body to face me, "Drop *what*?"

"Come on," I took another step, "*This*. The tough-ass thing. Let it down and just talk to me."

"I know you spoke to him." She tried to divert attention from my request.

"To *who*?" I entertained her, anyway.

"Thomps."

"So?"

"Why didn't you tell me?"

"I didn't know I had to."

"Well you didn't but—"

"Why does that bother you?"

"I don't *know.*"

I recoiled, squinting in confusion.

"Just wish you would've told me. He *just* died."

"No, stop. I don't know what you're trying to get at here, but we're talking about you right now. You went up there. You stormed out. Don't turn this around on me. What's going on? You haven't been yourself all day. All week."

"Maybe it's because we burned some dude's remains, dumped them in the ocean, and then went to a funeral a few days later!" she started raising her voice at me.

"I knew it."

"Oh, really? Was it obvious?" She snapped at me.

I went right up to her. "Why are you *angry* right now? Stop talking to me like I did something wrong to you."

She jutted her head forward, crossed her arms against her chest, and rolled her eyes.

"*What?*"

"If I hadn't met you—"

"If you hadn't met *me?*" I repeated in disbelief.

"Now there's all this dead people shit I have to deal with and I'm just—"

"What? Was there not already? How is this my fault? Whatever you're *dealing* with, we're all just trying our best. Don't take it out on me. We're all dealing with this same—"

"*That's* fucking wrong."

"How am I supposed to know if you don't tell me? I'm not psychic!"

"Seriously?" Willow glared.

"Well— if there's something else, come to us. If you're struggling, *come* to us. How can we help you if—"

"You can't."

"Stop acting like you know everything."

Willow shook her head and chuckled angrily.

"Willow … don't shut me out. Don't make me your enemy right now when—"

She gritted her teeth. A tear escaped down her cheek quickly, "I'm … *sorry*! Okay? I'm sorry. It's hard! I'm tired. It's hard seeing nice people die! It's hard dealing with negative energy, life and death being thrown in your face constantly. And there's no 'off' switch for this, either. There's no *medication*. I don't wanna know all this shit! I hate knowing that there's nothing I can do … or say to stop-"

I hugged her before she could finish. She sobbed into my shoulder for a minute without either of us saying anything. "But you know there's more to this."

She responded muffled between sobs, "That doesn't make it easy. And after this, it's not the same. There's *one* life like this, and then it all shifts and then I don't know what else there is," she blurted into my shoulder, "I don't want to know what happens next but I also do because—" She sniffled.

"Because what?" I stroked her hair.

"It's just a lot to hold in all the time," she cried, "It's hard."

"I didn't know his passing would affect you like this…" I mumbled into her hair. There must've been a lot festering inside of her— more than she'd told us— for this to break her. She always held it together so well. She always had it under control.

I felt a hand on my other shoulder and then another warm addition to the hug. Joel didn't need to say anything once he'd caught up to us. He knew there weren't many words for this moment. We didn't need them. We just needed each other.

It *was* hard.

While the three of us embraced, another cool hand patted my back twice. There he was, comforting us at his own funeral.

***

The next day, Lynette and I sat on the screened in back patio in two white wicker chairs from Aunt Liv. The fresh autumn breeze entered through the windows gracefully.

Lynette giggled as she dropped an eight card down on the pile in the middle of the fold-out table between us.

"No! Seriously? Again? I only had *one* left!" I slapped my cheek with my last card.

She glared at me playfully and confidently said, "Clubs."

Mourning doves cooed as I pursed my lips, "*Weasel,*" I snapped and reached over to pull several cards from the draw pile. Finally I found a nine of clubs and slammed it down exhaustedly, "Goodness gracious, child."

"You could still win," Lynette taunted, studying the huge spread of cards in my hand.

"There's no way. You only have two left."

She dropped another card. Three of clubs.

I drew again until I found a three of diamonds, "Ha!"

Lynette frowned, reaching for the draw pile. Very quickly, though, she changed her expression and pulled her hand back from the draw pile to delicately place a three of hearts down with a cute smirk. "I win."

I narrowed my eyes on her, "How?"

She shrugged stiffly. "Gwen taught me."

"Yeah … well. I'll get you next time."

"Wanna go again?"

"*Again?*" We'd just finished our fourth game of Crazy-8. She'd won three.

"Yes. I promise this time I won't win. I'll let you win."

"I don't *want* you to let me win. I want to beat you on my-"
Click click.

The two of us paused at the quiet but out of place sound. I looked out the window to the backyard to see if there were any animals around. As I scanned the tree near the porch door, I noticed the light above the basement steps flickering out of the corner of my eye.

"Lyn." I gestured behind her toward the basement door. I stood up to stand in the porch doorway, looking down the steps to the cellar. No one was there. The light turned off, and didn't turn back on again for the minute or so we spent silently watching it, "It's probably just the bulb." I swallowed and looked back to my little friend. "It's old."

Lynette's eyes were fixed on the light.

"It's okay." I hushed softly.

"I don't think I wanna play anymore," she murmured.

"Are you sure? We can go play up—"

Before I could finish, she and the joy of her victory had vanished.

181

OCTOBER

21.

FOR THE BIRTHDAY GIRL

The most amazing birthday gift was waking up on the morning of October eleventh on my own time rather than being jolted awake by a nightmare or a whisper in my ear.

The second best gift was the realization that it was yet another twenty-four hours without any sign of Jack Carlson, marking one month exactly since we'd carried out "Operation Burn Baby Burn."

The third most delightful gift was getting a text in our group chat from Willow:

Dinner at 7!!! White Horse... ;) Dress like you come from money.

A second text came through right after:

Also happy birthday! Love you!

Joel responded:

Happy Birthday, Em. :) Sounds great.

This time around, I felt more confident that I could handle any spirits that interrupted my dinner at the old tavern.

I sat sipping my coffee in the living room with the soft warmth of morning sunlight streaming through the windows.

"Happy Birthday," a soft voice cheeped from the kitchen. I turned around to see Lynette playfully bounce out from behind the kitchen wall into the doorway.

"Thank you." I smiled at what would've otherwise been a jump-scare. But that weight was lifted, as I'd seemingly only had one roommate recently, despite Willow's constant visits. I was growing accustomed to Lynette popping in without warning.

"What will you be doing today?" She sat next to me rather cheerfully.

I chuckled. "Well, this." I raised my arms to gesture around the room and then plopped them back in my lap. "And Willow and Joel are taking me to the White Horse Tavern."

"Gee, that sounds fancy."

"It is." I smirked. "Wanna help me get ready a little later?"

"Yes!"

"Help me pick an outfit?"

"A dress!" Lynette exclaimed.

"Well there's a limited selection of those, but sure."

"You have time to go shopping."

"You're right. I do," I replied.

Lynette smiled shyly and then whispered, "You hafta wear something pretty for Joel."

"Oh my ... stop." I rolled my eyes playfully.

"Pink." Lynette asserted her recommendation confidently.

"Ehhh, well ... we'll see. I'd hate to disappoint you."

"I wish I could come with you." She sighed.

I took in a gentle breath. "So do I."

There was a small beat of silence. "There's a surprise for you in the dining room," Lynette declared, holding one of her small arms out to guide me.

I took her hand and stood up. "What could you have possibly done for me?"

"You have to close your eyes," she added quickly as we turned the corner into the kitchen. I held onto the ice cold tingling. I trusted it.

I felt the floor change from tile to wood as we went through the kitchen doorway into the dining room. After a few steps, she stopped us "Okay. Open."

I faced the fireplace. On it was my mother's urn, its cracks and shards neatly glued together. Not every piece was perfect, and some small gaps and holes served as a reminder of Carlson's intent to tear me down. It wasn't pristine, but it was the same special urn while also being a brand-new one. The blue was still blue, and the love was still there. "Oh my God…"

"Um, it was a bit of a group project."

"What?" My voiced cracked. I felt the light sting of tears rushing to my eyes. I blinked several times to try and clear it.

"Well, it was my idea, but Willow and Joel fixed it."

"When?"

She simply shrugged and let out a quiet giggle. "It's a secret."

"Lyn, I—"

"Oh no. Are you upset?"

I sighed. "Not at all. Thank you." I let the tears drip down with a small grateful grin.

Lynette approached me, and timidly hugged me around my waist. Goosebumps spread down my arms. I stood stiffly for a moment before taking a deep breath and relaxing into the chilly embrace.

"I'm sorry he did that to you. I'm sorry I can't fix it all the way," Lynette whispered.

"I'm sorry, too," I muttered, staring at the damaged vessel.

"Willow told me to tell you not to mention this at dinner because it will ruin the … 'lit vibes.' I'm not sure what that means."

"It's okay, I do. Thank you, sweet girl."

***

My friends and I sat in a full dining room that night. We'd all ordered the lobster mac and cheese because it was agreed that that was, without a doubt, the best dish on the menu. A waitress returned to our table with a second glass of cabernet for me. "For the birthday girl," she sang smoothly as she slid the glass over to me.

"Why thank you," I'd begun to loosen up more than usual, of course.

"Of course." Our waitress with big black curly hair, and bold eyeliner winked at me. Her subtle gold glitter eyeshadow twinkled in the dim warm light of the dining room.

"Damn. She's hot." Willow watched as she sauntered away, and pulled a gift bag out from under our table. I hadn't seen it yet because I'd arrived after them as instructed. "Happy day-of-your -birth." She cleared her throat.

Joel smiled, "It's from both of us."

"Jeez, Joel. Did you really think I was gonna take full credit?" She sneered.

"Yes." He nodded confidently.

I chortled. "You guys didn't need to get me anything."

"Yeah, well … oops." Willow shrugged and took a bite of her food. "Open it," she said with a mouthful of food.

I dug into the bag and rifled through the tissue paper, grabbing onto my soft gift to pull it out. I immediately understood it once I saw it. It was a Newport sweatshirt, very similar to the one Willow had let me borrow the day we met and went to the Creamery. But this one was unlike hers in color; rather than bright orange, purple and green tie-dye, this one was a mix of pastel pink, blue, and yellow.

"Like—"

"Like your rainbow vanilla," she nodded triumphantly.

Willow and I both knew it was a half-gag, but also incredibly sentimental. "Thank you, *both*."

"You're welcome, Em." Joel smiled.

"Except … I was expecting pint of it, too."

"I'll get you a goddamn gallon, bitch." Willow laughed.

"*Wills*," Joel snapped quietly.

"Nah, nah. She knows I love her." She winked at me. "Glad you like it."

"I *love* it," I responded passionately.

"Good, because that's it for your gifts other than dinner. But I'm only covering one more glass of wine after that one. I gotta draw the line somewhere," she announced and shook her head.

I laughed and took a long sip. As I swallowed, I felt the warm pleasant burn of wine flowing down my throat.

"How's the new job?" I asked her.

"It's good. Simple. Just managing social media, mostly. But I think I may end up doing more writing for their website, too, though."

"That's great!"

"I'm so glad you went for it. I told you you'd get it." Joel nodded as he swallowed his food. "Debt forgiveness, too."

Willow sighed. "Eventually. I'm just psyched about paid government holidays. You don't get *that* in retail."

I glanced up with a deep relaxed sigh, only to spot a familiar figure standing by the fireplace. I felt my smile vanish with the realization of what I was seeing.

Joel must've noticed my quick change in mood. He followed my gaze and saw what I was staring at. "Em?"

"What?" Willow asked. "Wine hit too hard?"

I shook my head. "I wish. I'll be right back."

I stood up from my seat and approached a painting on the wall next to the fireplace. Then I held my phone up to my ear so I didn't look insane. I glanced over at the colonial-era man to my right.
"I've seen you before," I asserted.

"And I you," he responded matter-of-factly with a single nod of acknowledgment.

"You remember me?"

"Would I be able to simply forget one who saw me so clearly?"

"I wasn't aware that you noticed … Years ago, too."

"I notice everything here, ma'am," he looked out at the dining room. His garb hadn't changed one bit.

"When did you die?"

"1720," he responded stoically.

"How?"

"I fell ill. It took me with haste." He turned back around and stared into the flames in the fireplace.

"I'm sorry," I whispered. I noticed what looked like a few open sores on his face. Maybe that was why his hair was so wet; his fever must've been fierce. "Why do you stay?"

"I never got my liberty in life. But I do enjoy the company of those who have."

"You've been here a long time."

He nodded slowly. "And I will remain until I know in my soul that it's time to return to God. Until then, this is my liberty."

I gave a sympathetic smile, noticing the small rash around his mouth and chin. "What's your name?"

"Benjamin Warren." He made eye contact with me briefly. "Might I have yours?" He quickly grinned before looking back to the fire.

"Emma. It's nice to meet you." I sniffled.

"The pleasure is all mine."

"How old are you?"

"22."

"You were so young."

"What brings you to the tavern tonight?"

"I turned 25 today."

"I wish you a joyous life."

"Thank you. I'll do my best." Willow and Joel were looking over at me. I gestured at them to shoo their curious eyes away. "Are you happy here, Ben?"

"As happy as a dead man could *possibly* be," he spoke dutifully with an old English accent. "Will you return?"

"Eh" —I shrugged playfully— "for you, of course." I smiled.

"Then, Miss Emma, tonight you have given me life." He chuckled stiffly and disappeared.

I pretended to hang up my phone and put it back in my pocket as I returned to my entourage.

"Your new friend died upstairs." Willow cringed. "Smallpox."

"I'll be sure to tell him that next time." I sighed. "Very nice gentleman ... Weird, though."

"What?" Joel wondered.

"The guy?" Willow sipped her drink.

"No. Making friends with a three-hundred year-old man." I smiled bashfully.

"Don't tell me you have a crush, Em," Willow raised her eyebrows a few times flirtatiously, "You like older men, huh?"

Joel cleared his throat. I noticed his cheeks flush red in the candlelight.

"Shut up. He's younger than me." I shook my head and took another giant bite of my lobster Mac.

"Oh. Right. A cougar, then."

We laughed together.

***

"Hey Em." Joel cleared his throat. We waited outside while Willow bought a souvenir shirt from the very small gift shop counter in the lobby of the tavern.

"Yeah?" I held onto both my leftovers and Willow's.

"Do you like the sweatshirt?"

I tried to suppress the giggle I felt making its way up from my belly. "Did Willow not tell you?"

"Tell me what?" a concerned expression washed over his face.

"I'm not a fan of tie-dye," I confessed.

He gasped. "*What?* Why did she tell me you'd love it then?"

"Because I do. It's more a symbol of our friendship at this point. Kind of an inside joke." I chuckled and glanced to the entrance to see if Willow was done yet.

"Well, shit. I'm sorry." He kicked a pebble on the ground.

"Don't be, I—"

"I'm glad I got you something myself, then." He swallowed and gently pulled a small box out of his pocket.

My eyes widened and I felt my face get hot. Luckily it was dark out and the lights outside weren't enough to expose my blushing. "Joel, you didn't have to do that!"

"I wanted to, though. It's nothing big, but— well here." He stammered and took the to-go boxes for me so I could open it.

It was a simple white box with the elegant green logo for the Newport Mansions Store on it. I furrowed my brows inquisitively as I opened the box, and inside found a charming golden bangle bracelet with a delicate pineapple charm on it. My heart rose up into my throat. "*Joel*," I cracked. A small yellow gem shimmered from the middle of the golden charm.

"You know, the whole thing with the pineapple… friendship, warmth, all that. I know it's probably touristy, but…"

"No, no," I reassured him as I slid it onto my wrist in awe. "It's beautiful."

Our eyes met for a brief moment. As I took the boxes of food back from him, my fingers brushed across the top of his hand. Maybe by accident, maybe not.

"Well, that's pretty." Willow marched up to us with her new black souvenir t-shirt rolled up in her hand, and eyed my wrist. "Thanks for letting me in on *that*, Joel."

"You don't need to know everything before it happens, Wills."

"Yeah, well … I still like the intel."

I smiled, twirling the little pineapple between my fingers.

"Gotta keep some things a surprise, eh?" He chuckled nervously.

Willow raised a brow and pulled the car keys out of her pocket. "Let's get you home, birthday girl."

I looked down at my phone and realized that it was a quarter to nine. Time flew by with the two of them.

As we walked into the compact side parking lot, Willow gasped. "We need to figure out our Halloween plans, people! We only have three weeks."

"Then we've got three whole weeks." I rolled my eyes as I pulled the Prius door open for my carriage ride home with great, great company.

22.

S'MORE

A few days before Halloween, our trio sat on the back patio around a fire pit we'd bought at the Christmas Tree Shop. The sky was pink, the marshmallows were toasted, and the pumpkins were carved.

Joel slid a crisp jumbo mallow off of his stick and stuffed the entire thing into his mouth.

"Oh my *god!*" Willow laughed as she toasted her third.

Joel's face lit up in alarm and his mouth gaped open as he fanned his tongue. "Iiiiiz too haw!"

Willow shrieked. "Of course it is, dumbass! Give it a minute."

I laughed, my eyes darting between the two of them. Willow slapped the knee of her ripped black jeans.

Joel spit the gooey blob of sugar out on the grass.

"Ew." I chuckled, not wanting to express too much entertainment by his misfortune.

"It was *way* too hot." He gulped a sparkling water.

"Slow down with puffs, bro." Willow shook her head. "Or at least use the rest of the s'mores stuff, too. I bought a shit ton of graham crackers specifically for this. Not mad, just disappointed." She chuckled.

There was a quiet moment while Joel and Willow recovered. I simply sat gazing at the evening sky. This month had been the perfect New England October I'd dreamt of living for years. The deep red and blue clouds drifted by smoothly, much like I had since Carlson had disappeared.

"Where's Lynette?" Joel asked after recuperating from his marshmallow injuries.

I snapped back to reality to process his question. "Oh, she's been pretty quiet lately. Not sad or anything, just a little quiet." I remembered our last real conversation on my birthday. Since then, we hadn't spoken too much aside from playing cards and reading together here and there. "Nothing major."

"Are you still gonna help her?" Willow asked.

"I don't know how. I think she still wants closure about Gwen. But…"

"Tell her Gwen is on the other side waiting for her." Willow took a sip of hard cider.

"I don't want to say that if I don't know that for a fact." I immediately rejected the idea. "That's just a lie."

"Well, have you *told* her how her sister died?"

I shook my head.

"We'll figure it out, Em." Joel grinned sympathetically and reached over to place a hand on my shoulder.

"I don't think I want her to leave." I bit the inside of my cheek. "And I don't know if she wants to, either. Actually, I think I *am* helping her just by being here. I like how everything is right now. If things could just stay this way, that'd be great."

Willow nodded slowly. She finished another cider and patted her thighs. "Anyone want more?" She gestured to her empty bottle.

"I'm good."

"Grab me another one I guess." I yawned. "You're a bad influence."

"No, no. I can handle my liquor. Don't be blamin' me." She disappeared inside.

Joel and I met each other's eyes as the mourning doves cooed goodnight and the fire crackled.

"You're wearing your pineapple today." He added a new marshmallow to his skewer.

I raised a brow at him. "I wear it *every* day."

"I'm really glad you do." He beamed.

No more words were exchanged between us until Willow returned. We enjoyed the quiet calm we shared; no small talk was necessary for us, either.

Willow came back with a whole new six-pack of cider, letting the door of the screened-in patio slam behind her. "Let the drunking *commence!*"

"Drunking?" I repeated.

"Oh, *absolutely* drunking." She stood with confidence.

"I thought you said you could handle your liquor."

"I can. I'm just handling a *lot* of it right now. Come on." She slapped our shoulders. "Let's party as hard as three psychic loners can! *Woo!*"

I leaned over to Joel. "How many has she had?" I whispered.

"I'm pretty sure four." His eyes widened.

"Oh Jesus." I smirked.

"*Yesss.* Thank you Jesus and Hecate and Brigid and …everyone … for this amazing night and this amazing cider. And yes, you both, too. I love you both so, so much. Like *so* much. And *that* is why I bought you that sweatshirt, my love," She blabbed on. "I show my love through sweatshirts."

"I don't have any from you." Joel pursed his lips.

"*Shit!*" Willow exclaimed. "Kay, tomorrow I'll get you one … 'cuz it's starting to get chilly and you need a new one, Joel." She spoke quickly.

"Okay, Wills." He nodded.

"I *promise,* Joel."

"Oookay." He humored her.

"God, I freakin' love you guys!" Willow plopped back into her folding chair and dug into a bag of candy corn pumpkins we'd bought that day.

***

Later that night, Joel and I were making our way back from the kitchen down to the backyard. We'd gone up to grab some water bottles and chips. Willow had insisted on getting them herself, but I didn't think it was wise to let her walk up any amount of steps with the amount of alcohol she had in her system. Joel had offered to come help.

Our hands were full, but Joel stopped us at the top of the steps leading down to the back patio and basement.

"Wait." He interrupted our walking and set the bags of chips he was holding on the floor.

"What's up?"

He leaned toward me and whispered, "Willow is totally out of it."

I stood between Joel and the wall. "Yeah. Should we cut her off and lay her down in here?"

He laughed quietly. "Probably."

"What is she even doing?" I gestured to the bottom of the steps.

We leaned back to see her outside through a window from where we were standing. "She's toasting ten marshmallows on one stick."

"I thought we ran out."

"She must've hoarded them."

"And she was telling *you* to pace yourself on the mallows." I giggled.

"Aaand she just slid four of them into her mouth." Joel observed. "Honestly, I'm kinda impressed."

I pursed my lips and closed my eyes. "Wow. Is she *okay?*"

"She's fine." He took a step toward me, and gently held my wrist in his hand. "Looks happy as can be."

"What's up?" I asked again. That's all I could come up with as my heart pounded. I gulped nervously; his touch didn't feel just friendly that time.

"I really am glad you love your bracelet," he whispered. "You wanna know a fun fact about it?"

"Sure." My voice shook but I cleared my throat to try and hide it.

"I didn't just get it for you because it was your birthday."

"No?"

"No." He smiled, his sharp yet gentle eyes studying my face.

"Really?"

"Really," he repeated with a shyly, slightly adjusting the burgundy beanie on his head.

My breathing became shallow and I tried to deepen it. "Was … it on clearance?" I attempted to joke.

"You're worth *way* more than clearance, Emma." He laced his fingers together with mine. "And I doubt that the Mansions Store even does clearance." He chuckled, looking away and down the stairs.

"Hey." My chest pounded.

He looked back over at me and leaned in even closer.

I eased back flush against the wall. "Thank you, Joel."

"You handle our ability better than I've ever been able to." He softly brushed my hair behind my ear, and kept his hand resting against it. I closed my eyes as he spoke. "I don't think I've ever—"

"*Woahhh*," a voice oohed.

My eyes shot open, and my back leapt away from the wall instantly. Both of us snapped our heads toward the bottom of the stairs to see Willow teetering at the base.

"*Finally.*" She lifted her arms and then tossed them down loosely at her sides.

We froze, my face flushed red hot.

"You guys" —she shook her head in pure disappointment— "that took *way* too long."

Our eyes shifted to each other and back to her.

"I wanted my chips like forty-five minutes ago." She slurred.

"Wills, it's been five minutes since we left you," Joel explained with a straight face.

"That's about—" she wobbled as she looked down at her wrist to examine her nonexistent watch— "five minutes too late." She shook a finger at us.

"You should go lay down," I suggested.

"I'm capping you. You're done." Joel glimpsed from me to her. "Come upstairs so I can help you lay down."

"You can have my bed." I offered. "Just go rest it off."

Willow rolled her eyes. "Whatever. I'll listen this time because your bed is super comfy. Isn't it like that mega memory foam?"

"Mm, nope."

"Oh."

We both stared at our friend with small, entertained grins on our faces.

"Willow, you're busted," I hooted.

"Fine but next time I'm calling your manager … and I know you guys just want me gone so you can make out but that's okay 'cuz I knew it was gonna happen all along anyways." She sauntered up the stairs, leaning against the wall a few times. "I'm a muh-fuckin' psychic."

"Oookay. Come on." Joel held her hand and assisted her past us and all the way through the house to the stairs.

"I love you guys literally *so* much." She grunted as she walked messily up the first couple steps. "Emma, I love you!" She whined loudly as she disappeared with Joel upstairs.

I fixed my gaze down the steps toward the patio.

She knew "all along"… what else did she know?

"Is she okay?" Lynette squeaked from behind me.

I turned and cleared my throat. "Yeah, she's fine."

"Just checking." She smiled.

"Do you know what alcohol is?"

"Yes, he drank it all the time," she whispered.

Of course he did.

"Well, yeah. Willow drank a lot of it tonight."

"Oh."

"Mhm."

Lynette sweetly but mischievously looked up at me. "I saw you and Joel." She smirked. There was a glimmer in her eye.

Joel reappeared at the base of the stairs. I straightened up quickly, shushing my little friend. "We will discuss later," I said through my teeth.

She giggled and vanished into the kitchen from the top of the stairs.

"What's going on with *her* ?" Joel raised a brow.

"Which one?"

His head gestured toward the kitchen.

"Oh. She was just checking on Willow." I shook my head.

He nodded. "She's fine. I dumped her on your bed and tossed her shoes off. She didn't budge. She's down for the count." He clicked his tongue. "I didn't tuck her in or anything."

There was silence as we stood across from each other, teetering back and forth on our heels like two kids on the playground with crushes on each other. "Well, should we—"

"Yeah. I'll go clean up everything out there. You stay in here and relax, okay?" Joel decided for us.

"I guess you guys are staying over, then?"

"Yep. If we put her in the car, she'll destroy the interior." He chuckled. "Don't worry. I'll take the floor again, like a gentleman. *You* can have the couch, m'lady." He winked playfully and made his way outside.

Nothing else happened that night with Joel. We stayed up for a while talking about little things, but our conversation from earlier that night was never picked back up.

23.

DON'T GO

I sat in a white wicker chair on the front porch looking out at the street. The trees along it were blooming white and pink. Fluffy white clouds filled the bright blue sky above us. "Would you like some more?" I asked, extending my arm toward a porcelain teapot sitting on the table between us.

"Oh please." Nancy leaned forward for a refill of tea. "Go on. You've spent enough time prattling on about your garden. I know that's not why you invited me over."

I took a deep breath and set my cup down after a sip of the light floral tea. I flattened out the skirt of my dress on my lap repeatedly, "Oh well ... now I'm not sure when Jack will be home."

"Why does that matter?" Nancy raised a brow and stared directly at me. "I suppose you'd better get to talking."

I sighed. "Nancy, you can't tell anyone."

Nancy blinked once, her face going from intrigued suspicion to stone. "What did he do, Gwen?"

I shushed her softly, leaning forward across the table next to me. A tiny bit of steam escaped from the teapot's spout. "Nan, please. Try to be understanding. I think ... I think there may have been a misunderstanding the other night between us and ... maybe I wasn't clear enough about not being in the mood to fool around."

"*Gwendolyn.*"

"Shhh."

"Did you—"

"We've never had sex before. I thought we were going to wait until marriage but" —I shook my head— "Maybe I gave him the wrong impression."

"Just say it."

"Maybe I did something that could have been interpreted as changing my mind and wanting to—"

"Gwen, did you have sex?"

I froze and looked down into my lap as I processed the question. I swallowed hard.

"*Gwen.*"

"Yes." I gulped.

"And is that a problem?"

"It's not what I'd imagined it to be."

"How? I know you're holding back."

"Like I said, he must've mistaken something I said for— I mean … there must've been some kind of signal I … I just— it took me by surprise."

"I know you … far better than to accept that this happened with your consent."

I shook my head, taking a small sip with a shaky hand. Tears rushed to my eyes as I set the dainty cup down on its dish.

Nancy exhaled deeply as she put everything down to place her hand on her forehead. "I told you."

"Nancy—"

"I told you I didn't like him."

"I don't want you to think—"

"Are you hurt?"

"Well, I'm inexperience, so I wasn't quite sure what to expect. Maybe I wasn't positioned comfortably or—"

Nancy reached across the table and grabbed my hand with both of hers. She stared into my eyes. In our silence, I heard birds chirping around us, mourning doves in the trees.

"I will not tell a *soul*, Gwen. But I need you to be honest with me … Are you hurt? Yes, or no?" I saw that her eyes were now glassy, as well.

I shifted my gaze toward the house across the street. A neighbor came by walking with a stroller. Moving my attention back to my best friend, I inhaled deeply and shook my head to move my hair off of my face. I nodded subtly.

"Leave him."

"I can't." Gwen lowered her head, then to save face, lifted her chin up in false confidence.

"*Leave* him."

Gwen's lip quivered. "He's done ... so much for us. He's helped around the house while my father's gone. He cares for Lynette, and ... he wants to get married someday, Nancy. Maybe someday soon."

"So do a thousand other men in Rhode Island," Nancy's short brown bob jiggled as she laughed incredulously. I could see the disgust for Carlson on her bright red lips, "I don't even think you *need* a man, let alone him. You could focus your time on your drawing, your art. I haven't seen you paint since he started coming around."

"Well, he enjoys drawing, as well."

"Why don't you do it together?"

"He prefers to work alone."

"Even then, why doesn't be encourage you to do it more often?"

"Well, I think he must've forgotten. He's quite busy."

Nancy nodded slowly, deep in thought with her eyes narrowed on Gwen. "Doing what?"

"Nevermind that. He wants a child. With *me*. A sweet little rosy, plump baby. And he's told me how good of a moth—"

"You can't be a good mother if you allow your child to be raised around an abusive father. We won't be women who let that fall to the wayside. We won't be the quiet ones. He's abused you—"

"Shh!" Gwen hissed quickly. "Simmer down."

"No. You simmer *up*. What makes you think he won't harm a child?"

"He wouldn't."

Nancy's eyes pierced me for several seconds.

Gwen shook her head to dismiss the thought, "He makes good money."

"So does your father, and so could you. And he makes good money ... doing *what?* He's never given an answer that makes any sense."

"He's a businessman."

"In the business of lying..."

"He came out here to get into advertising. He's done some illustrations for—"

"Blah, blah. All of his stories sound like phooey and quite frankly, I don't know how you can read into it. You're blinded by infatuation, Gwen, but he's a crumb. Sure he's a charmer, and probably objectively good looking" —she sighed— "but this is no longer a honeymoon phase, that much is clear. Do you think his respect for you will *grow* over time? As you age? No, it won't. You'll get the wedding and the family but you'll be miserable. And I'll have to sit and watch it happen. End this before it gets out of hand. Please ... Once is enough, if what you're saying is true."

"It *was* once."

"Well then we'd better keep it that way."

"I'm sure it was a mistake. It won't happen again. There's an explanation for it ... I'm sure he didn't mean to hurt me. I mean, he said he wants to marry—"

"No more."

"He loves me, Nan. God brought him to me for a reason, I'm sure of it."

"Then why bother telling me this today?"

"Because you're my best friend."

Nancy took one last sip of tea and looked out at the house across the street. She shook her head without looking back to me. "I've heard enough of your defending him." Nancy scratched behind her ear and exhaled audibly. "You're gonna need my help one day," Nancy nodded assuredly, yet with genuine concern washed over her face. Her green eyes sparkled with conviction.

"Will you?" Gwen asked sadly.

"Always."

***

"Emma." A whisper in my ear made my head shoot up from my pillow on the couch. I found my hand dangling off the side, loosely holding Joel's.

I slid my hand out of his and looked at my phone for the time. It was close to five o'clock in the morning. I looked around to see who'd called me. There was no one in the dark living room, but there was a dim light coming from the stairway down to the basement.

Instantly I feared that a drunken Willow had stumbled down there and gotten into trouble. I got up and— despite my uneasiness— stepped over Joel to make my way down. The stairs were a short cement curve that led to the cold space below the house. The old light above the steps had been turned on; the string still dangled under the bulb.

"Willow?" I whispered into the large abyss as my feet reached the bottom. I realized that I really should've woken Joel before coming down, just in case. The space was long and narrow, with a couple small side rooms. I'd never seen a larger basement in my life. Then again residential basements were few and far between in California.

I cleared my throat. "Wills?"

One of the side rooms to my left caught my attention. The worn wooden door was cracked open, and another dim rusty light had been turned on in the room.

"Shit," I spat out as I recognized the room looming across from me, the same one from the vision of what led up to Lynette's death.

I took a few hesitant shuffles into the room. It was musty and empty, with the exception of a vintage looking shoebox sticking out from a small open nook in the wall. There were a few broken wooden planks beside it with loose nails thrown about as if someone had pried the planks off the wall. I hadn't been in here yet because it creeped me out and I saw no purpose in exploring it.

"Wills?" I asked into the stuffy air a third time even though she was nowhere in sight and there were no sounds down there.

The lid was just barely popped open, providing a peek into it. Grim curiosity pulled me to open it. I'd hoped to find a rat skeleton and some old postcards or newspaper, but my intuition said there was more.

I slowly approached the box and knelt down in the dust, dirt, and cement powder. My heart began to pound as I brushed off the lid.

In faded print was a blue rectangle with the name *Roblee* scrolled across it in what must've been white font before but were a dull yellow now. Once I lifted the lid off, my heart dropped.

Tied together neatly in a pale pink ribbon were several strands of light blonde curly hair. Aside from how old it probably was, it seemed nicely brushed. It was about the length of my pinky, and the ribbon was lightly stained in a couple spots. My heart raced as I dropped it. My eyes stumbled upon a piece of paper folded in half. It too had yellowed with age so I picked it up gently and unfolded it.

To my horror, there was a charcoal drawing of an unfamiliar little girl strewn across a cushioned chair. She couldn't have been any older than twelve. Her long dark hair was swept over one shoulder, revealing her neck on the other side. The artist was talented enough that I could easily make out dark marks around her neck, as if they'd paid extra attention to that area to get the details just right. Her eyes were eerily detailed as well, staring straight at me from the page. The expression in her eyes— or rather, lack thereof— was instantly familiar.

Empty, lost.

Dead.

I gasped with sympathy for the child, wishing I could pull her out of the picture and call for help. As I placed the drawing down shakily, I noticed a name and year written in the bottom right corner.

Betty, 1945.

"What the *hell* ?" I whispered under my breath.

Under the drawing was a photograph. It didn't match the little stranger girl from the drawing. I recognized this face immediately. It was Lynette. She stood in front of a bush holding out a big full flower. She had the same shy smile I'd been lucky enough to see a few times before. This Lynette had big bright eyes and a clean flowy dress. It was different from the one she'd died in, and wore now. This dress was similar in style, knee-length with puffy sleeves, but this one was checkered with no frilly lace detail. Or blood stains.

The back of the photo had something written on it, too.

Lynette 1949. Sweet sister, you are so loved.

I tilted my head in confusion, comparing the handwriting on both the drawing and photograph. They weren't the same at all.

The final object in the box was a *very* familiar Kewpie doll, but I didn't reach out to examine it any further.

My heart pounded in my chest, unsure of whether or not to touch anything else again or to even to put the items back in the box. I studied it with my eyes darting between the objects. "Wills," I squeaked.

"She isn't down here," a deep voice spoke smoothly from behind me.

I instantly felt nauseas. Tears escaped my eyes as I turned to face him. He stood leaning casually against the doorframe, arms crossed, "Funny how attached you get to little trinkets like that … more-so, even, than your own flesh and bones." He paused. "Where's your friend, Emma? It's pretty chilly out this evening. It'd be a shame if she'd wandered and caught a cold," Carlson fake-pouted, but quickly followed it up with a small smirk.

Without a second thought, I rushed past Carlson's freezing presence and sprinted up the basement steps to find the patio door open in front of me, letting in a cold breeze. I hadn't even noticed it before because I'd been distracted by the basement light.

"Em?" Joel groaned from the top of the steps in a sleepy daze. He rubbed his eyes. "What were you doing down there?"

Lynette appeared behind him as I stood panting.

"Hey, hey … what's wrong?"

"Emma, I— I don't think you should go out there," Lynette muttered softly.

I shook my head frantically at her and bolted through the covered patio out the back door to the yard. I heard Joel shout my name but I ignored it as I rushed across the lawn to the backwoods. I let my thumping heart and sinking gut guide me.

I pushed through trees in the dark fog of the early morning. Joel followed behind, calling for me. Lynette appeared next to me, but I raced past her.

"Emma, go back and dial emergency services."

No.

Lynette stopped me again right before the opening to the clearing. She stood in front of me, pain in her eyes, "Emma, please. Don't go. Please go home."

"Em!" Joel's voice cracked in the cold air.

"Don't go," she whispered.

No. No.

Without hesitation I ran straight through the little girl, not allowing her energy to affect me this time. I entered the clearing, and it took me no time at all to find Willow. I immediately melted to my knees.

As I hit the damp, cool ground, a shriek so chilling to my core escaped me. It didn't even sound like me. Guttural, yet shrill. It was an impossible sound made real only by immense horror and shock. It was haunting. Another quiet high pitched cry followed it. It was the moment in a nightmare when you tried to scream for help, but nothing ever came out. Nothing was ever loud enough for anyone to hear or save you. It only ever jolted you awake.

This terror was our reality.

Joel hastened past me and closer to the tree. He looked up, dumbstruck, and collapsed. Deep sobs echoed through clearing. He needed to see it clearly, but I'd seen enough to know.

Willow hung from the looming branches of the oak tree that had already claimed her. Her arms were limp beside her, her head dangling down from a rope tied around her neck. She wore her black jeans and oversized gray sweatshirt. Her dark red hair laid softly on her shoulders, kissing the back of her neck. There was usually a beautiful shine to it, but every strand was dull now. The electric cyan tips had been fading the last few weeks. She was drained of any color. Though almost closed, a sliver of her vacant glossy eyes peaked out. Her body didn't move, didn't even sway. There was no movement, not a single twitch or groan. She was pale and still. There was nothing at all to suggest there was any life left in her. She was an empty vessel, her bright flame extinguished in the frigid air.

And we were too late.

I knelt down weakly in the damp dirt. Joel scrambled to take his phone out of his back pocket. I watched idly as he quickly dialed

911 and cried into the speaker. I felt the shock settle in; I didn't even shed a tear.

"Please, please! Oh my god she's hanging! Please help, oh my God! Oh my god … No, no! Not in the house she's— she's— we're out in the woods behind the house! Please … Oh my *god*. Hurry, please! I don't know if she's breathing! I don't think she's breathing! She's just hanging there! Oh God! Oh god … okay. Yes, okay. We're at 31…"

He continued to sob fragmented sentences into the phone, but it faded from my perception as I watched my best friend hang from a tree that had now ended two lives. I let the warm fog of shock envelope me, clouding my vision. Joel scampered over to me and held me tightly as he hyperventilated on the phone with the dispatcher. I barely felt him, barely heard the screaming, or the sobbing … or the sirens as they arrived at the house.

I didn't know how long had gone by before paramedics, fire, and police found us back there. But at some point, they stormed into the clearing to meet us at the scene.

Emma dear, close your eyes.

NOVEMBER

24.

SORRY FOR YOUR LOSS

"Did she ever mention self-harm?"
"No."

"Did she mention making any plans for the near future?"
"We had plans for Halloween. We were gonna go to a festival at Fort Adams."

"How much had she had to drink that night?"
"She had a lot. She was definitely drunk. That's why she stayed over at my house. We knew there was no way she'd make it home without puking."

"Was she coherent when you saw her last?"
"Yeah. I'd say she was still coherent, but really…goofy. She mostly made sense but you could tell she was drunk."

"So she never mentioned hurting herself?"
"Not to us, no. There was one conversation where she seemed overwhelmed in general, but never … suicidal. We never thought she'd ever do that. She didn't let on that she was that…sad. I guess she didn't want us to worry. I don't … I don't know…"

***

Dear everyone,

I'm so sorry I gave you no warning. I didn't have much of one either, but I also had as much warning as someone CAN have. I've known for some time that this would be the way I go. I didn't know exactly how, or when, or even why. But I knew this was coming. I guess I feel better just keeping this note on me, instead of making whoever finds me have to investigate and turn my room upside down looking for a note. I wanted to save you some time, so…you're welcome.

To my family, of course I love you. That much is obvious, at least it should be. But it still needs to be said. Please don't think you did anything wrong raising me, or that you could've prevented this from happening. Because you couldn't. I couldn't, either. I just hope you can be there for each other now and take care of yourselves. I'll be fine. Thank you for everything you ever did for me. Except for not allowing me to go see Fleetwood Mac on tour in middle school. I'm still really bent out of shape from that…

To my two minions, you knew me the absolute best in the end. I'm sorry I didn't tell you about this. Emma, you've experienced so much loss already and I'm sorry to become another. Joel, you're my brother and I love you so much. There wasn't much left unsaid between us except for this. I knew you especially would try to stop this from happening, and I didn't want to deal with the arguing. Be strong for Elliot. She may not act like it, but she needs someone to look up to who isn't old like our parents. Now that I can't be there to do that, it's your job. I expect you to watch over her even more now. But Elliot, for God's sake, tone it down with the cussing and the attitude. Respect others, and respect yourself. I love you, chosen little sister. Back to you, Joel…I expect you to take care of Emma and if you don't, I'll do something about it. I don't know what exactly. But I'll figure it out. Don't let this strain your friendship. Please. It's just the two of you left in our weird little trio now, and I don't know how you'll keep the show going without me, but I have faith that you will.

Emma, there is probably so much I didn't get a chance to tell you, surprisingly. That's okay. We'll catch up someday. You have such a gift, and such a strong spirit. I know this seems like the end of the world right now (not because I'm so important but because you've already been through so much) but it isn't. You're going to come back from all of your grieving stronger than ever. I know that for a fact. I do need to confess something to you, though. Ever since the day I laid eyes on you, I've known that this was the way my life would end. Please don't feel like it's your fault…because it isn't. I take back what I said at the church that day.

Everything that happens in life was going to happen all along. There's no changing it. Like I've told you from day one, all we can do is try to help others accept what life has for us. I didn't know you long at all, but so much can happen in a short amount of time to bond two people together. Please know I love you, Em. More than you know. Whenever you need me…that bench on Ocean Drive. Go there. That's our place, always.

This may seem harsh, but I need you both to accept that I'm dead. We all die eventually. I just got on the train earlier than most I guess. I hope I wasn't too scared, and I hope it didn't hurt. But if I was and if it did, just know that I'm okay now. This needed to happen.

I will explain everything once I know it all I know, I acted like I already did. Plot twist, I didn't.

I love you, and I'll see you soon. I promise.

-Wills

Ps. Please bury me at Heron Point Cemetery in Providence. It's really pretty, and I think I'd be happy resting there. Thank you.

***

The funeral was held at Heron Point Cemetery— as per her request— a week after we found her.

The first days were an absolute nightmare. A blur. We were questioned by detectives a couple times, but after the note was confirmed to be her handwriting and the autopsy found her cause of death to be constriction of the neck by ligature, the manner of death was confidently declared a suicide. Case closed, seemingly still with no answers.

Joel and I were left heartbroken and baffled.

Mind-blown. Stunned.

Everyone was.

She was buried on a small hill near the back of the cemetery. She would've loved that she wasn't very far from a cool old gazebo, and that she was on Coastal Avenue right across from Willow Avenue. She would've been pissed that she wasn't *on* Willow Avenue though, and would've half-jokingly demanded that someone else's grave be moved to make room for hers.

Everyone she knew and loved gathered up on that little hill together that day.

Her parents, who were divorced but both very kind, held each other's hands. She would've loved to see that. Her dad came from Boston and her mother from Pennsylvania. We'd met them days before the burial for coffee to talk about how wonderful a friend she was to us. There seemed to be some awkwardness between them, but tragedy had placed that in the background. They seemed to show only love for each other the second they learned they'd lost their only child. She'd told them about us, of course, and said we were the closest thing she'd ever had to siblings. We knew that already, but it warmed us to hear it from someone else.

Her aunts, uncles, and cousins had joined from all around the country since she had several. Most of her cousins were around our age, but a couple were in their thirties with children of their own. A few people she and Joel had gone to school with came to show their support, even though they were no longer close to either of them. It was all appreciated. Joel's parents and sister Elliot were, of course, in attendance. I'd met them briefly once or twice before, but since he and Willow lived together, we never really hung out at his folk's. They were absolutely devastated, and standing beside the Grahams. Then there were Aunt Liv and Uncle Ken on one side of me; Willow would've been twistedly tickled to know that one of her favorite authors was there to mourn. On the other side of me was Joel, holding my hand tightly and sobbing.

I *wanted* to sob with everyone else throughout the burial, but I couldn't. I felt so much that I felt nothing, and I simply stared ahead at Willow's shiny ebony wood coffin. It sprinkled off and on that whole day. Of course, the weather would be gloomy and dramatic for her funeral. We were all just grateful it hadn't snowed yet that season.

It was a closed casket service. The pain was already gut-wrenching enough for all of us. The last thing we wanted to see was someone who was once so fiery, so witty, so ready to tackle what life had to throw at her…empty. It wouldn't have looked "just like she was sleeping" like they say, either. Willow would've called bullshit on that because she looked like a hot mess when she was asleep. An open casket would've made her look too peaceful, too pretty. But she wasn't peaceful or pretty when she died. I couldn't see her like that again.

I felt so absent for most of the gathering that I didn't even take in much of what the minister said during the eulogy. It's awful to admit, but nothing they said would change that she was dead so I didn't care to hear it. It was the same feeling that hit me at my mom's memorial: anger, confusion, hurt, anguish … all mixed together to form nothingness. This void wasn't just another rerun for me, but an entirely new season.

Liv, in tears, kept her hand resting on my shoulder. Not only was Willow a dear friend of her niece, but a loyal fan and far too young and brilliant to die.

Joel and I hadn't said much to each other before the funeral. We were both just trying our best to process and be present. We drove separately with each of our families, but the moment he saw me up on that hill, he ran to me and sank into my arms. Willow told him to take care of me, but I needed to take care of him, too. And that was how it had to be. We would take care of each other because we were alone, a tenacious trio reduced to a despairing duo.

Elliot, who was nine years younger than us with a sassy, tough-ass exterior most of the time, bursted into tears behind Joel toward the end. She'd known Willow for pretty much most of her life, and had grown to see her as a chosen older sister. Joel reached his free hand back to grip hers, and although she normally would have worried about looking ridiculous and pathetic, she knew no one there gave a damn.

Willow knew the whole time.

Quotes from her note echoed in my mind throughout every day since her parents had shown it to us. It was the hardest thing to ever have to read, but we needed to know exactly what it said. Unfortunately, it didn't explain much about why she'd done this to herself.

This needed to happen.
Why?
I'll see you soon. I promise.
When?

We hadn't seen her once. Realizing this, I shot my head up and out of my brain fog momentarily to glimpse around the graves surrounding Willow's. Nothing. No sign of her.

Once the burial was concluded, Willow's family members all congregated to share condolences. Before joining the rest of her family, her parents hugged both of us, her mother kissed our cheeks lightly. "You were exactly the friends she needed. Thank you for that. *Please* keep in touch. You're family … I *mean* that, Joel."

Joel didn't respond, but nodded his puffy tear-soaked head.

"Thank you, Mrs. Graham." I muttered.

"Please, call me Elaine." She grabbed my hand and rubbed the top of it with her thumb before breaking away. "It was a blessing to finally meet you, Emma. You meant an awful lot to her. I can see why."

As Elaine walked away with Mr. Graham, someone unfamiliar approached Joel and me.

"Hey, Joel." The man gulped and scratched the back of his neck.

"Yusuf, man…" Joel gave his best attempt to hold back more crying. "Thanks for coming. It's nice to see you again."

"No problem … Willow was super cool, man. She, uh" —he paused— "she told off this kid in PE once. That guy Roderick. I don't know if you remember him. He caught my dad coming out of the rehab building one evening. Was giving me a hard time about him in class … Willow stepped in and called Roderick out on the fact that his dad was seen drunk around town all the time. She told him not to make enemies of people who could be his only true friends … people who would actually understand. I don't remember what else she said but she made Roderick cry. She was a badass, and she deserved better than this. I'm so sorry, man."

Joel nodded. "Yeah, I remember that day. She was— she was pissed."

Yusuf gave a sympathetic smile and made eye contact with me. "Hey."

I nodded unenthusiastically. "Hi."

"I'm Yusuf … we went to school together."

"Got it."

"Did you go there, too? I don't remember seeing you."

"Nope."

"Anyway" —he swallowed again and held out his arm to Joel for a handshake— "I'd better get home. I'm … so sorry for your loss."

Joel returned the gesture and sniffled.

Yusuf headed toward Willow Avenue and the parking lot a ways down.

"That was nice of him." Joel began crying again.

"It's all bullshit!" Elliot exclaimed and stomped over to us in tears. "That's all they have to say … everyone! 'Sorry for your loss, sorry for your loss!' It's just autopilot but they don't fucking *get* it! They don't even know."

"Ell—" Joel started.

"No! Don't even say anything, Joel! You *know* they don't understand what it's like to lose someone like this!"

"You don't know that," I inserted.

"I don't care! Anyone who *has* lost someone like this knows that 'sorry for your loss' doesn't mean *shit*!" She sobbed. "And you know who *should* be 'sorry for our loss'? *Her!* "

"El, you need to stop," I warned as calmly as I could.

"She just goes and decides to fucking *off* herself like that! At your house, too?! She had to go and be poetic as hell about it. And for what? She had no reason! She had people who *loved* her! Clearly she didn't feel the same because she just left! With no answers. Just a stupid ass letter! With jokes! She couldn't even take a fucking *suicide note* seriously."

"We don't know what happened, Ell." Joel tried to deescalate her by putting a hand on her shoulder.

"You're making a scene. We're asking you nicely to stop. *Please*," I spat.

"Why? We know what exactly happened! She knew you guys would find her there so what the *fuck* kind of friend is—"

"Elliot *stop!*" Joel shrieked.

The distraught teen melted toward the ground and collapsed on the grass. Joel looked at me with glossy red eyes and held himself over her in a tight hug. They cried together, Joel burying his face in her dark caramel. hair. Their parents rushed over once they heard the commotion.

Figuring it best I leave them to handle that matter as a family, I slowly backed away. They deserved privacy.

I made my way down the quiet Willow Avenue, walking past tombstone after tombstone. There were so many lives that ended with this as their final resting place. It felt wrong that Willow was just another stone among hundreds, maybe thousands, now. They all eventually blended among each other into obscurity to the world … except for one that jumped straight out to me along the walkway and made me stop in my tracks to do a double-take. A beautifully elegant yet simple stone that tapered up and into a smooth dome shape at the top rested next to me. It wasn't the stone itself that caught my attention. It was the name on it.

DR. CLYDE J. SALLEY
1905-1969
LOVING FATHER
MAY HE FIND REST WITH HIS ANGELS

Below it were three smaller graves.

ELIZA MAY SALLEY
1908-1947
BELOVED WIFE & MOTHER
SENT FROM HEAVEN, BLESSED ANGEL RETURNED

GWENDOLYN PRUDENCE SALLEY
1926-1951
BELOVED DAUGHTER OF GOD
BLESSED SOUL FORGIVEN

I knew the last of the family of tombstones before I read it, and it broke me into smaller pieces than I already was.

LYNETTE ADELINE SALLEY
1938-1949
PRECIOUS CHILD
FOREVER PURE WITH THE LORD

"Are you a member of the family?" A voice cracked behind me.

I looked back to see an elderly woman, shakily holding her cane. She had a face that seemed familiar but I couldn't quite place it. I wasn't sure who I would've known in Providence, anyway. She was with a younger middle-aged man.

"No."

"Mm…" She nodded slowly.

"Are you?" I asked hesitantly.

The frail woman looked down at the cement and tried to clear her throat. "Oh, no. Not for many, many years."

She got winded and took a seat on a bench nearby with the help of the man accompanying her.

"She was a good friend of one of the daughters," he explained.

My eyes darted to the woman. "You knew Gwen."

Both of them looked at me in confusion. The man seemed stand-offish once I asked.

"No, no, I" —I stammered in overwhelm— "I know bits and pieces of the history— I live in their old hou—"

"In Newport?" The woman barely had time to rest before she shot back up with surprising speed for her age.

I nodded.

"I come here every month to honor my dear friend. She's long gone now, but" —she shimmied over to me— "it's too deep of a routine these days to skip it."

My curiosity only grew as I studied her emerald green eyes.

The woman took a shallow breath and chuckled. "There was a time we went back to her place and poked fun at one of our hoity-toity friends, Judy. We had a book club … yes. Always at *her* house … Judy … Always with 'the best wine in the neighborhood' and her fancy-schmancy tea cakes. We'd go" —she snickered— "we'd go back to her house after book club sometimes and drink wine that *didn't* taste like overpriced dirt … *That's* why I come here. To remember the small bits … some better than others … of my *one* honest-to-God real friendship in my whole life."

"Do you need help, Gran?" the man asked.

She shushed him. "So much history in that home…" She took a deep breath and glimpsed over at me.

"I know."

"Do you? Are you mourning them, dear?"

"No."

"Who, then?" Her eyes looked heavy with empathy.

"My best friend."

"Mm, too young … just too young. My condolences." She studied Gwen's grave. "I *do* hope you didn't lose your her the same way I lost mine." She shook her head slowly.

"I did."

She narrowed her gaze on me and took a couple step forward. "Well, *how* would you know that?"

"Are you Nancy?" My voice shook.

"Who's asking?"

"My name's Emma Reilly."

"Emma…" She took my hands in hers. "Yes, Nancy Wilcox. How in God's green Earth do you know who I am?"

I sighed and studied the man, who seemed puzzled yet intrigued by this meeting. "Would I be able to … speak with you sometime, if that's possible?"

"Why?" The man interjected.

I debated whether or not to answer honestly. "I'm a friend of Lynette's."

"Come *on*, Gran. Let's go."

"Hush now, Todd."

"Seriously, Gran. This is a joke."

"I said *hush*," Nancy repeated. "*Is* this … a joke?"

I shook my head earnestly. "I need help." I cracked. "I'm desperate."

"I thought we'd buried that story a long time ago."

"Not deep enough. I'm sorry to bother you, really. But would it be possible to get together sometime? I might be grasping at straws but—" I pleaded with whatever energy I could muster.

"Certainly," Nancy responded without hesitation.

25.

GO THERE

I hadn't spent a night in the house since we'd found Willow. I'd refused. Instead, I'd been staying with my aunt and uncle in their guest bedroom. They took a couple days off to stay with me, but after that, they had to go back to working. It was just as lonely there as it would've been in my own room. My first night back, I begged Joel to stay with me, and although he wasn't ready, he did it for me. I needed him there. He was the only one who truly knew what we were dealing with.

No one else had shown their face around the house- not Lynette, nor Carlson … nor Willow. We had no idea where she was, or if she even had any control over whether or not she kept her promise to us.

We sat quietly in the living room that first night back. I picked at my nails and zoned out at the wall while Joel played games on his Switch.

I piped up. "I'm gonna go to bed."

At the same time, he spoke. "Are you sure you want to meet with Nancy?"

I stood up and glared down at him. "*Yeah*. Why?"

"I just— I don't know, Em. Maybe we should just leave it all alone. Maybe you should consider asking your aunt and uncle if you can move in with them."

I shook my head and scoffed.

"I just don't know what information you're gonna get from her that'll change anything."

"I don't know either. But I'd rather get whatever answers I can instead of doing nothing."

"Em" —he sighed— "We tried. Look what happened. The last thing we need is—"

"I don't care."

"I just don't think we should be risking our mental health on this."

"My mental health is at rock bottom already. A pizza date isn't going to make any of it better or worse."

"I just don't want you to hurt yourself looking for whatever answers you think we need. It's not worth it."

"If there is even *one* more thing … one small thing we can just try to—"

"Like what?" He stared.

"I don't know yet."

"So what makes you think Nancy will?"

"She knew them."

"So do you."

"I—"

"It's not in our control anymore."

"You don't know that," I pleaded.

"Em."

"Why are we even arguing?" I blurted.

"Exactly, Emma. Why?" He stood up. "I just want us safe. I want *you* safe. And I find it odd that we found Wills right after Carlson shows back—"

"Don't say his name right now, please."

"Then you agree. It's weird."

I shook my head, not wanting to entertain the idea, but it itched in the back of my mind, "I want us safe. But Lynette matters too."

He sighed and ran his hand through his hair. "Yeah, she does. But—"

"What?"

"But" —he paused— "but she's already dead, Em." He lowered his voice.

"So is Willow." Tears filled my eyes but I was used to the sting. "*She* matters."

Joel didn't respond.

"What if *she's* stuck here? Do you still think we should just leave *then*?"

"We can tell Liv. We can trust her. We can take care of the house, and come clean to her … and still not *be* in it, putting ourselves in danger."

"I can't think straight … I'm trying to do my best right now to function … This conversation's achieving nothing."

"Maybe doing your best means not being here for a while."

"I wanna keep my distance from everyone."

"Why?"

"I don't want anyone else hurt."

Joel cocked his head to the side. "Hurt?"

"Willow said she knew she was going to die that way since the day we met."

He paused, then took a step toward me. "You don't know what that means."

"Means it's my fault." My voice cracked in the quiet room.

He teetered.

"I want to see her, Joel."

"I do, too. But my priority right now is you, and keeping *you* in a safe environment."

"I hate it here. But I just … can't leave. Nowhere feels safe right now, anyway."

"I'll get us a room somewhere. Let's just … go."

"I need to stay. I don't know why, but I can't go yet."

"Emma, why? *Why*? I don't get it," he tossed his Switch on the cushion next to him. There were several seconds of silence as we stared at each other in tired frustration.

"You don't have to be here. We all grieve differently and if you want to grieve by arguing with me when I'm just trying to help everyone, that's fine … Just go back to your games. Or go home. But I want to find answers to things that matter. I at least want to try." I stormed out of the room.

"I go where you go," he said clearly after I started up the stairs. "Damn it," he whispered sharply into the stale air.

I laid in bed that night, staring up at the blank ceiling and thinking about Willow's note.

... that bench on Ocean Drive. Go there. That's our place, always.

***

There we sat again on that bench, often to look straight out at the waves crashing against the rocks right below us. We didn't even talk a lot of the time we spent there, but it was nice to have someone to space out with. We both needed beautiful quiet alone time to think, but we wanted to be alone together.

The weather was particularly overcast and windy. It *really* started to feel like fall was rolling in, but that didn't keep us from bundling up in our sweatshirts like we always did to drink coffee or tea in the salty air by the ocean. That day, I wore my brand new "rainbow vanilla birthday sweatshirt" that I actually adored so much.

I heard Willow sigh next to me.

I leaned over to nudge her shoulder with mine.

"You know" —she started— "all things considered, life is pretty good."

"What makes you say that?"

A cold gust of wind met our faces, blowing our hair back. "I mean, all the loss you've endured— not to bring up a touchy subject —"

"It's fine," I reassured.

"All the loss, all the change you've been through ... and here you are, still toughing it out. Still able to breathe and enjoy the little things. If I were you, I'd have abandoned all hope by now, but you ... you're special."

"Gee, thanks." I rolled my eyes. I got the sentiment, though.

"And me ... I'm just glad I get to be here with you today."

I looked over at her. She squinted out at the Atlantic, inhaling the sea breeze. "Stop it." I chuckled.

"What?" She craned her neck at me. "It's true. I love Joel. But it's not often you find a friend in adulthood that you connect with so quickly."

I smirked. "I guess I wouldn't know."

"See? Exactly. You get my humor." She laughed.

"Yeah … but our friendship started under very … unique circumstances."

"So? Circumstances that were always meant to happen."

"Can we really compare ourselves to normal friendships, though?"

"We don't have a normal friendship, is what I'm saying. In my humble opinion, we happened for a greater purpose. And I think that's pretty cool." She nodded confidently and took a sip of tea. "I don't know. You're just … different. Somethin about that spirit of yours."

"Are you coming onto me again?" I chuckled.

She tilted her chin down and furrowed her brows.

"Well, thank you. *You're* pretty different too." I nudged her shoulder.

It started to sprinkle, so we headed back to her car across the street. She asked if I could drive so I did. She spent the entire trip back down Ocean Drive toward Bellevue with the window rolled down completely. She laid her head on the window panel and let the cold air and soft droplets of rain kiss her face. Her wavy dark hair was a mess immediately but she didn't care. At one point I looked over at her and in the side rear-view mirror, I saw her look up at the clouds and smile to herself. A genuine smile. She wasn't busy trying to solve any problems or make anyone laugh. It was just a raw smile accompanied by a single tear that ran down her cheek. Whether it was emotion, or just the wind making her eye water, she looked truly moved by life that day.

"You okay?" I asked just to make sure.

"Just grateful," she replied simply.

I left her alone to enjoy herself for the rest of our drive. She didn't move the entire way home to my house. She looked out at every tree, every seagull, every mansion we passed that day with a smile.

That was the day before she died.

***

I woke up from the bittersweet memory, lifting my head up from my pillow. I was hoping to see her standing by my bed, or sitting on the floor doodling on my sudoku book. She wasn't. There was nothing but darkness and a snoring Joel on the floor beside my bed. I couldn't go back to sleep that night. I thought hard about the questions I wanted to ask Nancy when I saw her.

The questions mounted, but one question repeated like a scrolling message on the bottom of the tv when the news was on. Sadly, it wasn't one that Nancy would answer for me, and it would probably keep scrolling through my mind for a long time.

How could Willow leave us like that?

26.

TRY

"You ready?" Joel came down the stairs as I fixed my hair in the mirror by the front door. He wore nice dark jeans and a heavy leather jacket. It was snowing lightly for the first time that season.

"Yep." I sighed. It was the first time I'd worn makeup since Willow's funeral.

"Got the keys?"

"Yep."

"Address?"

"Yeah."

"Okay, cool. Let's go." Joel opened the front door for us and gestured me out the door politely. "After you."

Willow would've joked that our relationship had escalated way too quickly, that we needed to slow down before Joel moved in with me. The truth wasn't nearly as exciting. Joel had realized he'd preferred to stay at my place instead of being in the apartment they'd shared for a couple years. We weren't together. In fact, we were both incredibly lonely. He'd been sleeping on the couch or on the floor next to my bed for several nights, but we hadn't talked much. We didn't have the energy to, and there wasn't anything to talk about, anyway. Nothing was fun, and nothing was new. We weren't out exploring or creating new memories; it wasn't fair to go out and even try have a nice time when our friend was six feet under. I wasn't working. I just existed. I read. I watched tv, or slept. He spent his time blocking out reality and escaping to his video games. He would go to his family's house when I would go visit my aunt and uncle, but we didn't go anywhere else. Neither of us wanted to be out in public in the case that we ran into someone who knew about what had happened to Willow. There were whispers around town, and we couldn't handle the hushed buzz.

The only thing that was worth talking about between the two of us *was* Willow, but it hurt too much. When we did brave the topic, we were only bonded by trauma. It ended in hugging and crying. That was it. We left each conversation feeling closer, yet even further apart than before. Any relationship that may have been blossoming before her death was also buried. There was nothing between us beside the necessity to provide some sort of security in familiarity. We were each other's quiet support, the closest approximation to true empathy. We were static, as if we'd both fallen into a deep, dark, murky void the moment we laid eyes on Willow that morning. Everything moved too quickly, too slowly, and not at all, simultaneously. Joel and I still had a very new friendship, but it had also gone terribly stale since her death.

She would've been extremely disappointed.

Joel put on a beanie as he waited for me to lock the door behind us. "Careful down the steps. It's slippery," he warned.

"I know."

We were going to meet Nancy Wilcox and her grandson Todd at a small Italian restaurant in Providence, where she'd lived since the 80's. *Rocco's Italian.*

Once we were situated in the car with the heat on, Joel backed out of the driveway in Willow's old blue Prius that had been gifted to him by her parents. At first he hadn't wanted to accept it; it was a whole car. They'd reassured him that it was paid off and that she would've wanted him to have it, anyway.

It still had her beach towels in the backseat.

"Alright. Let's hit the road." He took a deep breath. He still didn't see the point, but knew I needed something from it- even if I wasn't entirely sure what that something was, either. I told him I could go alone if he would just let me borrow the car, but he told me I wasn't driving alone to Providence with the coming snow. He still wanted to be there for me, fulfilling his new duty as my care-taker, I guess.

"Hey," Joel spoke up before turning off my street. "You okay?" The blinker's red arrow flashed on the dashboard.

Click, clack. Click, clack. Click, clack.

"No," I responded honestly, making it clear by my lack of eye contact that I wouldn't be providing any more details. I swallowed our argument from the other night and tried to force it all the way back in my mind. My heart still ached from the tension.

"Em, do you wanna talk?"

"No."

We didn't speak until after we'd crossed the Pell Bridge, but even then they were short exchanges about navigation. He didn't ask me any questions. He just let me handle things, however I needed to.

***

"Emma, good to see y'again." Todd shook our hands firmly after we found them at the table inside the restaurant. It was a hole in the wall that they swore by, and I wasn't going to question Nancy's word.

"Thank you for meeting with us." I spoke shakily. Joel brushed his hand against mine briefly. I yanked away nervously.

Todd's eyes shifted to Joel.

"Joel."

"Oh. Good to meet you." Todd cleared his throat and gestured toward the tables for us to go ahead and join them.

Joel nodded over the classic rock hits radio playing. "You as well … Thanks."

I made eye-contact with Nancy, who sat at a table in the middle of the dining area, smiling warmly over at us. Her short gray hair was frizzy but curled, similar to how it was cut and styled in my visions. She still chose a bright red lip.

"Sorry dear. Once I'm down, I don't get up for a while." She shook my hand over the table.

"No worries at all." I swallowed and took a seat across from her.

Joel sat beside me and grabbed a menu. Nancy was kind enough to offer to buy us lunch, so Joel and I just bought a medium pizza to share. There was only small talk about the winter weather coming in and some local seasonal festivities until a teenage employee brought us our order with an incredibly impressive wait-time.

Todd bit into his steaming calzone and nodded. "Not too shabby, uh?"

"Oh yeah," Joel agreed as he chewed a slice of our pesto mozzarella and tomato. "It's great."

Nancy made eye contact with me again as she took a sip of her iced tea, "So" —she cleared her throat frequently— "not to abruptly change the subject, but I'm too old to beat around the bush. So I'll cut to the chase and ask you again. How do you know who I am?"

After a moment of contemplation, I responded, "How open-minded are you?"

"I'm a spry ninety years old. I have seen a lot of bat-shit crazy things, especially in my second marriage ... but that's not what we came here to discuss. Yes, I consider myself to be particularly open-minded." She smirked.

Joel's eyes widened as he chewed.

"I'm having visions." I put it all out there.

Todd wiped the corner of his mouth with the back of his hand. He chuckled and shook his head over his plate. "You gotta be kidding me."

"Mm..." She nodded. "Of what?"

"Wait, wait. I mean— all due respect to you kids but *Gran*, you don't actually—"

"Goddamn it, Todd. We talked about this right before they got here. *Let* ... her talk." She placed a hand on his shoulder.

"I ... um ... I know what happened the night Lynette died." I leaned forward and lowered my voice. "I know you helped her." I remained stone-faced.

She took a deep breath. "Alright."

"Do you believe me?"

"I'll *tell* you if I don't, honey. Go on."

I shot my eyes between everyone at the table. "Are you sure? In front of ... ?" I pointed my head in Todd's direction.

"What's going on?" her grandson asked.

"He's a big boy. He can handle it." she didn't break away from me.

I bit the inside of my cheek, suddenly not hungry at all. "She came to you … at some point that night. She begged you to help. You moved him, and you buried him in the woods behind the house. I saw it in dreams, and then we found him … We dug him up, we burnt it … and we dumped what was left."

Todd leaned back in his chair, taking a moment to rest his calzone-filled gut. His brows furrowed intensely as he held his hands up in confusion. "What da *fuck*, Gran? What is this about? Who the hell are you talkin' about?"

"Why did you do all that?" She leaned in toward me.

"He's been … harassing us … in my home." I swallowed, watching as she nodded.

"Hm," she set her napkin down on the table gently, "I see the tears in your eyes." She blinked slowly. "I'm not surprised that death hasn't kept him away … I *never* liked him. *Ever.* I warned her, too."

"I know you did, but he's still there. With Lynette, too. We tried to get rid of him, and we failed."

"You have the sight, don't you?"

"Something like that." I sighed. "Both of us." I glimpsed over at Joel.

He pursed his lips shyly. "Yeah. We see them."

"The friend you lost…" Nancy started. "Is it all related?"

"I don't know," I whispered weakly.

Nancy handed me a tissue from her purse. "Here, dear. Don't use these napkins. It'll tear at your under-eye skin. You don't need micro-abrasions and wrinkles at your age." She shook her head. "He's responsible for killing that poor child— her *and* the Remington girl."

"He didn't kill Lynette, though. She really did fall out of the tree. But she died trying to hide from him."

"So he *is* responsible."

"Yes, but he never had the chance to hurt her like he hurt…" I tried to remember the name of the little girl I saw in the drawing from the basement. "I think her name was Betty."

"Betty Remington. Gwen found the drawing of her in a box when she got home that night."

"I found it out in the basement, too. The night we found…"

"It's okay, Em," Joel put his hand on my thigh for a moment and then lifted it to continue eating.

"She stumbled upon it while she was looking for the two of them. Betty was found dead in a park in Portsmouth when I was in high school. Gwendolyn had just finished school that spring. It was *all* over the papers. But the case went cold. Gwendolyn met Jack about a year later. Gwen discovered the drawing of poor Betty … and then, well, she found sweet Lynette and we knew … 'Course, we couldn't tell the authorities that he killed Betty, given we'd taken care of the murderer ourselves. We didn't want an investigation opened up. We claimed that Jack had left Gwen for some tourist gal and moved out of town with her. That was our story, and we stuck with it. No one ever reported him missing, I suppose, and we let it all go to rest … or so I thought. Gwen and I *knew* he had to have been involved in Lynette's death but the police were adamant that she'd fallen. We were so confused. We kept quiet … and then one day I got the news about Gwen…" She gazed out the restaurant window to the street.

"You're telling me" —Todd leaned back in and hissed quietly — "you helped dispose of a body of someone she *killed* ?"

"That is exactly what I am saying to you." She looked her grandchild square in the face and spoke clearly. "He was a child killer. Of at least one child … But I consider it to be two. Did you really find all of this out in visions?"

I bit the inside of my cheek. "Some."

"Some?" Nancy posed.

"Lynette told me herself what he tried to do to her." I looked down at my plate.

Nancy tilted her head and cleared her throat again. "Before she died, Gwen said she thought she was going crazy. Seeing him in the house. Having nightmares about Lynette. I'm sure it pushed her to do what she did."

"May I ask how she killed herself, exactly?" I shifted in my seat.

The music played overhead while Nancy remained silent.

"I'm sorry, I shouldn't have—"

"No. She'd been missing for a couple days. I was very worried. We all were. She hadn't mentioned anything to me about leaving town. She would've. But she did say God was making her pay for what she did and that she was going batty. She said it wouldn't stop. They found her two days after Mr. Salley filed the missing persons report. She'd washed up along the rocks near— uh, let's see … oh— what is now Brenton Point."

"*Brenton Point*?"

"I'll spare you the gruesome details that were sensationalized by the news, but she was found in very … poor condition. She'd drowned herself in the ocean. And that was it … Simply left a note apologizing. That's all."

"I'm sorry." I ran my tongue across my front teeth, as if by doing so I'd come across the right words to say in response. "Truly."

"It's been a long, long time."

Todd nodded along with thick furrowed brows, trying his best to follow the conversation.

"And don't you say a goddamned word about it, Todd," Nancy ordered, then took another deep breath. "Why did we meet here, Emma? How can anything I say help you?"

I zoned out on my plate, realizing I couldn't handle another bite. *What was the point in this? I can't fix anything.* "I…"

Joel wiped his mouth with a napkin. "I think Emma just wanted to see if there were any other missing pieces to the history of the house that may help get rid of Carlson or help Lynette cross—"

"I'm sorry, dear. I'm afraid I'm not much help, unfortunately." Nancy's hands trembled slightly as she placed her napkin on her plate and sat up as straight as she could, "Gwen and I hid that box behind bricks in the basement wall. The box with that drawing of Betty Remington. We hoped no one would ever find it. We should've known better."

"I didn't really find it." I sighed. "It was laying out on the floor the night we found Willow. It's like it was pulled out to be found. Like he wanted me to see it so he could throw it in my face. He's proud of it. It's his work. He probably stole the photo of Lynette from Gwen, too. It was all of his trophies, and he was planning to add to it the night they died. It's unfinished, so he's still attached."

"We burned the body, but he doesn't care about that anymore. That box is like, his legacy. We burn that and maybe…"

I nodded.

"I won't ask any more questions about what you two are dealing with. I trust that would take more time to explain than the time we all have today."

"Yeah." I nodded, trying to sort out the thoughts in my head. "Thank you for believing us."

"I have no reason not to."

"You don't think we're crazy?"

"You both seem very sane. Plus, I have no room to judge." She raised a brow and tapped her nose.

"Thank you."

"Get that little girl some peace and rest if you can. She was a *doll.*"

"I'll try my best." I closed my eyes.

My best won't be enough.

"I couldn't bring myself back to that home. Too much time has passed. I can't relive that part of my life too much or I'll give myself a heart attack. I can only keep the Salleys' memory alive by honoring them. But I don't know how much longer I'll be able to. I could drop dead tomorrow."

"Gran stop," Todd inserted.

"Visit them for me … when you visit your friend. Give them my love." She inhaled weakly. "You know, you're quite like her, yourself." She chuckled.

Joel took a deep nervous breath in.

"Gwen?" I bit the inside of my cheek again and felt a pit in the bottom of my stomach.

"Always looking out for others first." She stared into my watery eyes. "Underestimating yourselves."

"Nancy, I— Carlson thinks *I am* Gwen. Reincarnated or something. He's convinced that I came back because I belong in that house with him after what Gwen did."

"Well, are you?"

"No I— I don't think so."

"Well, then there's your answer." She blinked.

"But what if I am Gwen?"

"Well then, what if?"

"That's exactly what Willow said." I sniffled.

"Willow seemed smart, then."

I felt Todd and Joel anxiously watching our exchange.

"I want Lynette to be able to move on. But she wanted to see Gwen again and I can't bring her that because she's gone."

"You two seem very gifted. Now that you know what happened to Gwen, you could go try to find her where she … passed … and see if she'll come to you. She was very lost right before she died, and she probably is still. Try and see if you can guide her home and if you can't, you can at least see if there is something she knows now that will help you get rid of that bastard. Maybe you can somehow prove to him that you aren't her … if you are, in fact, not her." She winked, shakily taking a sip of her tea. "It's all a crap-shoot but you've got to try something."

I narrowed my gaze on her.

"She died in the ocean. She wouldn't be where they found her, right?" Joel shook his head.

"I don't know. Are the rules clear cut?"

Neither of us responded.

"There was a high tide and rough waters around the time of her death. The police always told us they didn't think her body had gotten very far. Just go try to communicate with her." Her tired but sharp green eyes stared into mine. "Brenton Point. Just … *try*. Who could it hurt? If there's even the smallest chance that you could still send him straight to Hell, *try*…"

***

"Good luck, and good *lord*. At least today you're given me hope that *this* isn't all life is. Because wherever we go next, I'm surely headed there." Nancy nodded to me as we walked out of our meeting that day. She had her cane in one hand but held onto my palm with the other. Before she started walking away with her grandson, she let our hands slip from each other. "Please keep in touch and let me know if I can help in any other way. Take care of yourself, kids." After she turned and started making her way down the street, she stopped and added, "And if you ever *do* … get the chance to speak to Gwendolyn, please tell her I … well, please tell her I love her."

27.

NO ONE THERE

Everything we'd discussed with Nancy had meant nothing. I'd searched up and down Ocean Drive and Brenton Point every day for over a week, waiting for a washed-up looking phantom woman to approach me with the solution I needed. I'd sat on the shore of every small, secluded beach along the drive.

Nothing.

I'd sat for hours daily at Willow's and my bench.

Nothing.

Not a sign from Gwendolyn Salley, or my best friend. There was no one there.

I'd torched the entire box that I'd found in the basement that night. All of his trophies had gone up in flames, but there was no way of knowing for sure if his spirit had gone with them. I'd hoped some angel with good news would come down and congratulate me for banishing the beast. On the other hand, I'd even half-expected Carlson to show up laughing in my face to tell me that I'd done nothing to force him out, but there was no one.

Joel and I hadn't spoken much more than a "hey" to each other. There was nothing to do anymore. Joel was right. There were no answers from meeting with Nancy. I'd wasted our time.

I wanted someone to watch a movie with at night so I didn't feel so alone, but Joel wasn't emotionally available to me anymore. Lynette hadn't shown herself since she'd warned me not to go any further into the clearing. Maybe she was just as mortified to find Willow dead as we were. Her poor soul had experienced enough darkness already. I'd call out to her from time to time, but she'd never shown up. The book she'd been reading hadn't budged from its spot on my coffee table.

Willow was nowhere to be seen, or even felt. It was torture not knowing what had happened to her. She'd made a promise, but there was no way of knowing if she had any control over that. My heart broke every time I thought of the possibility of never seeing her again. I'd never felt such a natural connection with someone in a friendship sense before, not even with my longest lasting pals back in California. To have it stolen from me when it was one of the few good things I had left in my new upside-down world was gut-wrenching. She wasn't there anymore to bust my chops, or talk way too much about something I didn't care about— but that she was an "expert" on— to distract me from my anxiety. I wanted that back. I, at the very least, wanted to know *why* she decided to leave us without it in our lives. I tried so hard every day to figure out what had happened to her. There had to have been something else we were missing. She gave us no warning. Nothing.

She was fine, and then she wasn't. She was right there with us. And then she was under a gravestone.

She used to sit next to me on that bench, and now when I went, I was alone. I used to sit on the left side, but now there was plenty of room for me to sit in the middle if I wanted to. But I didn't.

Beside me used to be her goofy smirk, her fiery jokes, the smell of her herbal tea … Then, just like that, there was no one there.

28.

SOMEONE THERE

I tried so hard to shove all of the nagging, miserable thoughts, and the never-ending loop of unanswered questions deep down and out of my mind. One evening, I stood focusing on the hot water hitting my back in the steam of the shower. I let my tears blend in with the stream pouring down my face and closed my eyes tight for at least twenty minutes. This was a new ritual.

Be still.

The shower is warm. It sounds nice, it sounds like rain.

Breathe. Just breathe.

Just focus on the hot water.

This is what comfort has to be right now.

"Well."

I felt my body turn quickly and hit the wall of the shower. My back slammed against the cool tile. My eyes shot open as I felt a hand grip my neck. Through the water hitting my eyes and blurring my vision, I saw him, and my heart leapt against my ribs.

"Joel," I crackled out for help.

"No, no, no, no. You listen to me."

"Stop." The water pelted against my face as I gasped for air.

"*You*" —he squeezed— "thought burning a pile of *bones* would get me to just pack up" —he used his other hand to run his hand through his slick messy hair incredulously—"and leave? I admire your determination but that's not quite how that works, doll." His hand brushed the dripping strands of hair out of my face. The water didn't phase him.

I felt sharp electric zaps going off throughout my entire body.

"Why shouldn't I just kill you right now?"

The shower sounds like rain.
The water's warm.
His presence made the warm water feel ice cold.
Breathe.
I couldn't.

"Mm, no." He leaned in toward me and spoke almost in a whisper, straight to my face. "Here's what we're gonna do. I … am gonna give you one more chance" —he held my face in his free hand and tightened his grip with the other. His thumb stroked my cheek, his eyes pierced into mine— "to do what you need to do."

Breathe.

"Just because I'd love to see the shame in your eyes … when you do it. One more chance. After that … I think I might have to help you."

I felt myself fading. His hauntingly bright eyes stabbed into me, his crazed smile was like a sharp edge plunging into my soul. His jawline alone probably could've sliced my arm open. "You have such pretty eyes…"

"Joel," I wheezed with what strength I had.

He ran his icy hand up my abdomen and pushed it violently into my bare chest. "Sh, shh, shhh. Stop. He can't hear you." He shook his head stiffly. "So, we've got one more day … or the next person that walks into this house … is in trouble. Mkay?"

The lump in my throat grew.

"And I'm going to watch you beg *me* this time … to stop. And I won't. And it'll happen again, and again. Until it's just you and me."

My eyelids started to flutter.

"I won't lose you this time. So make a decision, and make it fast" —he gently patted my cheek— "or I'll make it for you."

He gave my neck one last freezing, burning squeeze and with a smile, pushed off of me. I immediately crumbled down to the shower floor. "Go get some clothes on," he snarled as he vanished.

I stared blankly at the water rushing through the drain. I wanted to go down with it. Petrified, limp, I grasped at my neck as if to keep it from falling off my shoulders.

Be still.
Shower sounds like rain.

Within the blink of an eye, the water below me was saturated red. Thick coagulated clumps of blood, and chunks of mud plopped off of my body and onto the shower floor.

Focus…hot water.

Breathe.

The strong smell of rust and musty iron permeated the sticky, steamy hot air as my vision alternated between flashes of the present and the bloody bathtub.

Hot water.

Thick lines of dirt and deep maroon suddenly and briefly appeared underneath my fingernails. I quickly gripped my arms and dug my fingernails into my skin as I watched blood rush down the drain. In another flash, I noticed that I was wearing a familiar filthy lavender dress. It was soaked and clinging to my body.

I finally rubbed my eyes aggressively and caught my breath enough to let out a shriek— not unlike the one that escaped me when I found Willow's dead body hanging— as I collapsed into myself.

"Emma?" a voice squeaked. Lynette cautiously peaked with one eye from behind the shower curtain.

I sobbed into my arm.

"Did he hurt you?"

"Go!" I snapped, whipping my head toward her.

She let out a small gasp. "I'm sorry." She was barely audible over the shower and my state of shock. She held her little hand out to me through the side of the curtain. "Go!"

"But I wanna help."

"*Get out!* " I screeched.

She said nothing else, and her hand quickly slipped away.

I sobbed deeply, curled into a ball. I inhaled sharply and let every wail out of my body until I couldn't breathe again. I started choking, coughing, gagging, hyperventilating. My throat felt like sandpaper. I wasn't even naked on the shower floor anymore; I was somewhere else entirely.

Violated.

"*Em!*" Joel burst into the room and slashed the curtain open; the bathroom light illuminated the shower but I squeezed my eyes shut to blocked out any more stimulation.

The loud *boom* of the faucet echoed as he slammed the the water off and quickly draped a towel over me. I shivered under it as I sobbed, trembling uncontrollably. As the harsh chill from Carlson still ran through me. I felt pressure on my back as he wrapped me up tightly and held me from above. He was careful of where he touched me over the damp towel. My instinct was to push him right off of me after what had just unfolded, but his weight provided grounding back to my immediately surroundings.

"It's okay, it's okay," he lied into my ear as he tried to rock me in the small bathtub. His voice was safety.

"No! No, no, no,…" I couldn't think straight enough to formulate words together in a sentence that made any sense so I just kept repeating, "No, no, no…"

"I know," he replied sadly.

I kept my eyes taut in darkness, desperately attempting to erase the last few weeks, months…

He nuzzled his face into my hair, "I know. I'm so sorry."

***

That night, it was a culmination.

I sat criss-crossed on the edge of my bed, finally calmed down enough from my melt-down to breathe. The last two and a half hours had become a blurred storm of furious painful tears. I lost control of my body, overcome by the assault I'd just experienced, and the guilt I felt about Joel having to intervene. He shouldn't have had to see me that way. None of it was his responsibility. None of it was his fault.

It was all me.

If I hadn't moved to Newport, hadn't gone walking that day, hadn't met Willow and Joel, none of this would have become his burden. Willow would be alive. Joel would be happy, not sleeping on an uncomfortable couch downstairs that night in a dangerously haunted home. He wanted to sleep with me in my room, but I wanted to be alone. He just wanted to protect me, but there was nothing he could really do to a dead man who was capable to strangling me. I told him to go home where he'd be safe. He said that he was either leaving with me or not at all.

And he was right. Days before, he was right. And I hadn't listened. We should've left when he'd suggested we did. I hadn't listened.

There I was in bed with a headache and bruises on my knees from hitting the shower floor. Strangely enough there were no marks on my neck, but I still felt it. The pressure, the desperation in my chest to breathe. It was my own fault. But I didn't have the strength to leave. I didn't have the strength to get up and get water. All I had the strength for was bed.

I sat up against my pillow, staring down the dimly lit hallway.

"Lynette?" My voice was fractured, my throat dry and raw.

There wasn't a single creak in the wood floor, or a whisper in her old bedroom. The door to her room didn't move open an inch down the hall. I'd contributed to her feeling unsafe in her own home. I'd scared her off.

I sat in silence, weighing my options. In the deep fog of pain, shame, and emptiness, one outweighed the couple others I had. A sudden pull gave me the energy to slide off the bed slowly and close the door quietly so it didn't echo or wake Joel downstairs.

I got on my knees and looked at my desk, at my deep bottom drawer I used for art supplies. They were in there. I'd saved some of my tools from my college drawing class; there were expensive charcoal pencils, Bristol Board, and kneaded erasers. It was a bunch of stuff I never used anymore but kept because of the sheer amount money I spent on it. I pushed aside the junk. I wasn't looking for any of that. But when I found the dozen or so razor blades left in a double zip-locked bag at the bottom of the drawer, I inhaled as deeply as I could in such numb overwhelm. I used to have to sharpen my charcoal pencils with them over a trash can. But I wasn't drawing anything that night.

I sat on the floor against the side of my desk and carefully pulled a blade out of the bag. It shined, unused, in the dim light of my rock salt lamp.

I was so, so tired.

I'm sorry, I thought to whoever may have been listening to my thoughts. God? My mom? Willow? I wasn't sure. Maybe all of them. Maybe none.

I held the small razor in my hand. Trembling, I went to kiss the sharp corner of it to my forearm. There was an initial sharp ping of the blade pressing into my skin. I shook my head as tears dripped down my face. It wasn't enough. The sting wasn't strong enough to quiet down the guilty thoughts and rapid "what-ifs" that sped through my mind. Images of him ambushing me in the shower flashed in my head like a painful scattered slideshow.

I lifted the blade and positioned it to my inner forearm. It gently cut into the skin, and I felt the ripping burn as I pulled it across my arm. I inhaled sharply as the pain increased and then settled back as I removed the blade from the thin, straight trail of blood that appeared on me. I exhaled deeply, watching as the red line get darker and wider. The blood rushed to the surface, a harmful temporary distraction from my inner turmoil.

I immediately wasn't proud of it. I knew it was wrong. No one should enjoy this, ever. No one should feel so low, so powerless that they arrive there at such a sad, sad sense of relief. But in that moment, I understood why so many do. It was just too much for my mind to take at once. I understood that, perhaps, the physical manifestation of pain was a simpler, easier toll on the soul than the mounting emotional agony. It was visible, it was a universally understood wound. It was easier to accept then. The blood acted as a blinding barrier, keeping out any more mental stimulation. As I stared down at the deep maroon stream, I felt my surroundings fade around me into a white void. In that waking nothingness, I found the delusion of safety.

I felt the building urge to place the blade back onto my skin at a new starting point. My thoughts were now an eerie whisper, but that made them even stronger than before.

Again.

I brought the blade back for a second time. How many would it take to make the thoughts quiet down? I just wanted all of the thought to stop.

"Hey!"

A familiar voice shot across the room and straight into my ear. I gasped and dropped the blade on the ground next to me. My head jolted up, bumping back against the desk. The razor flew from its spot on the wood floor into the abyss under my bed.

"What the *fuck*!"

I closed my eyes and held the back of my neck.

"*Hey*!" I felt a breeze blow my t-shirt slightly and a freezing cold cloud of air in front of me. "What are you *thinking*?"

That voice.

"Oh, my bad. You're *not* thinking!"

I slowly opened my eyes. Through the blurred vision of my tears and very close to my face, there were the familiar eyes that I knew before as bright piercing sky blue. They were now a duller shade of blue-gray, but still accompanied by the attitude of a single raised eyebrow.

I blinked several times to clear my vision. I heard my bedroom door burst open.

There was silence as the realization hit us both.

"Wills?" Joel stood dumbfounded in the doorway, gripping the knob so the door didn't bounce back and hit him.

Willow slowly and stiffly leaned away from my face. She ignored Joel, staring straight into my eyes. She was even paler than she was in life. Her hair was still beautiful, her blue tips still present but faded. Only a few sections showed deflating curls. She appeared almost just as she had that night in the backyard making s'mores. She wore her same ripped black jeans and gray heather hoodie that she wore when she died.

She didn't blink. Her eyes never broke from mine, much like the day I met her on Bellevue. She stared blankly. at me like she had during her visions. She rose steadily, backing away from me to stand beside my spot on the creaky wood floor.

Joel's eyes widened further when he caught sight of my arm. His chest rose and fell heavily, "Em," he whispered, "Why" —he rushed over to me and held my arm up to inspect it— "did you do this?" His eyes drooped as he brushed his hand across my cheek. "Why didn't you come get me?"

"I'm sorry," I mustered.

He looked deeply into my eyes and shook his head. He left the room with a loud sigh, rubbing the back of his neck as he stomped into the bathroom to grab a wad of toilet paper. He returned to me and patted my arm carefully. The paper stuck to the clotting blood.

"We need a warm washcloth." He sighed again and looked up at our sudden company. "And you…"

"How long has it been?"

"Bout a month," Joel responded simply.

"What day is it?"

"November 30th."

"Shit." She spoke with far less enthusiasm now than in life. "I missed Halloween."

"We didn't celebrate."

"What about Thanksgiving?"

He shook his head.

I pressed the toilet paper ball against my arm, feeling the sting as I pushed. "You left us."

"Em—" Willow started.

"*No*," I growled. "You told us *nothing*, but you left a fucking note in your pocket?"

"Emma." Joel held my arm.

"I'm sorry."

"*You're sorry?*" I snapped, tears flowing down my face.

"It wasn't like that." Willow gazed down at us.

Joel looked up at her and shook his head. "What, then?" He quickly stood up and went to the bathroom again. I didn't say another word to Willow. I simply stared down at my fresh wound. Joel returned to my side with a warm damp washcloth and some Neosporin.

"Found some." He waved the tube of ointment in his hand. He inspected my cut again. "It doesn't look too deep, thank God," he whispered and dabbed the cloth gently on my arm. "Why, Em?"

There was silence as he made sure my cut was clean, then rubbed the thick balm on it. "I didn't see any band-aids in there but there's some at my parents. Or I can run to Stop and Shop … No, they're probably not open. Umm…"

"Joel, I'm fine," I stuttered.

"I think Walgreens might be open."

"It stopped bleeding."

"I don't care." Joel shot his eyes onto mine and they stayed there. "I don't care."

I felt Joel let go of the washcloth; the pressure of it on my arm lightened as he held my hand.

"Are you guys a … thing … now?" Willow asked.

Our eye contact broke as our attention was directed up to her. "No," we said in unison. I cleared my throat and wiped the couple tears that welled up under my eyes.

"Everything is the same, Wills. Since you died, we're…" —he trailed off and let go of my hand gently— "the same. We're stuck."

"I'm sorry."

"And … I just can't wrap my mind around why you did this to us. I don't get it. You could've told me. You could've come to us." He worked himself up into a light pant. "I mean— if you *knew* long enough ahead to write that whole letter and carry it with you…"

"What pushed you?" I asked.

Willow stared blankly into the space on the floor between Joel and myself. She didn't breathe, obviously, and she didn't blink. She didn't move. She was completely paused.

"You don't have any explanation for us? Not even an, 'I was drunk, I don't remember' … if you don't wanna go into it? I mean…" Joel tried to pull something out of her.

"*Hello?*" I snapped.

There was no response.

Then it hit me. "*That* tree, too," I hissed, my face throbbing with anger. "You had to pick *that* tree? What kind of message was that supposed to send—"

Within less than a second, Willow bolted toward me in a thick haze from her idle stance by my bed to kneel next to us. It felt like a bag of ice against me when she gripped both of my hands tightly.

I knew what was coming.

29.

PUT ME DOWN

My point of view changed abruptly within a bright flash. I'd gone from my place on the floor to a sprawled out position on my bed. Groggy wooziness hit me like a ton of bricks.

Crickets chirped in the distance from outside my bedroom windows on either side of my bed. It was chilly.

"Willow."

"Mmm?" I groaned and rolled over onto my stomach to slide off the side of the bed. My feet hit the cool floor but my socks kept them warm. "Hellooo?" I singsonged.

I was watching that night through her eyes. I wasn't ready to experience this vision but I couldn't pull myself out.

"Ch-ch-ch … Ah-ah-ah…" Willow laughed drowsily, mocking the classic background chanting used in horror films. She took wobbly steps out the door into the hallway. "Guys I feel sooo *not* good right now." She yawned, rubbing her forehead once she stopped in the middle of the hallway.

"Willow," a voice called from the bottom of the stairs.

"What?" She replied in a loud whisper, unsteadily following the call down the staircase.

"You left your phone out back." The voice guided her in her ear.

"Ah *shit,*" she whined, then chuckled at herself.

As cautiously and considerately as she could, Willow made her way through the foyer and into the living room. As she passed through, she tip-toed cartoonishly and looked to her right. There we were. Joel and I were passed out, myself on the couch, Joel on the floor. It was unsettling to see myself, even in a vision. I felt displaced, out-of-body.

She saw me before she died. She could've woken me up. I could've woken up, could've kept her safe. I felt a pull toward the couch, wishing I could grab myself by my shoulders and change the course of that night. Instead, Willow smiled and let out a whispered, "Aww," then continued sneakily down the stairwell to both the back patio and basement. She was too intoxicated to realize that the only two people who would've called out to her were out like a light. It never even dawned on her.

She stood on the landing and teetered in place, sniffling as she studied the darkness outside. Crickets chirped out back as the breeze blew the tree branches in front of the window. As she went to reach for the door to the back screened in patio, she heard a soft *cling* from behind her. The light above the basement steps was on and the chain to it was swaying gently.

Bloop.

"Aw, man." Willow groaned after hearing her phone alert from in the basement. She headed down the slightly twisting, cold cement steps. She hadn't remembered going down there that night, but hadn't put it past her drunken self, either. She sighed as she sloppily placed both feet on the basement floor. She rubbed her eyes, "Damn. Creee-pyyy."

Willow saw another small light on in a room off to the side of the main basement walkway. She figured that must've been where she left her phone at some point. Entering the room, a chill filled the stale air, and she took in the musty odor of the old bricks and stones lining the walls. Then it caught her eye; her phone was lying on the ground next to a dusty old box. Maybe she dropped it while on the hunt for more alcohol earlier. She could've gone down there for a number of reasons with how drunk she was. She shrugged and bent down to reach for her phone. At a glimpse her home screen only showed a couple texts from her mom and notifications she didn't care about from her email.

A shuffle behind her caused her to jump. She shoved her phone into her pocket and spun around loosely to stand. "Hey I— I wasn't trying to wake you up I just realized I guess I left my—"

A low voice whispered sharply and closely into her ear, accompanied by a freezing cold chill on the back of her neck and shoulders. "Disappointing, isn't it?"

Willow was instantly petrified. She felt an electric ping deep in her chest. It stung like dry ice stabbing through her.

Everything went black as Willow's eyes closed, her eyelids fluttering rapidly for a few seconds. When they opened back up, her consciousness felt distant, yet my point of view remained the same. Not only did I feel out of control of this vision, but Willow did now, too. She was a small, weak, panic in the back of her own mind with the rest of her body following someone else's lead.

Willow and I watched behind a curtain of possession as she took a deep triumphant breath and headed back up the cold basement steps. Slowly, she turned to head out the patio door and toward the dark mass of trees behind the house.

Stop. I don't want to go out there.

A pull from deep down tried to turn away, like an audience member cringing and yanking their body back in their seat to urge a character in a horror movie not to go toward the killer. No matter how much you shook your head or waved at the screen, they did it anyway and ended up butchered thirty seconds later. Steadily, Willow's legs moved further into the woods, despite her desperate but aggressively hushed thoughts to run.

Why are you doing this?

You tried. You really thought you'd done something.

We were protecting ourselves.

For a dame with such insight, I'm surprised you were fat-headed enough to let your guard down. In this house, too. Alcohol isn't good for you. Did no one teach you that?

Where are we going?

You're pretty far gone. You need some rest.

No I don't.

I heard these thoughts fire back and forth at each other as Willow weaved intently through the trees. She stopped in a very familiar place to all three of us.

Why?

Because you couldn't leave well enough alone.

They deserve a peaceful home.

So do I.

What you want isn't peace for anyone. It's control.

Willow's body slowly approached the black oak tree with all of its contorted branches, and gazed down to find something lying on the ground.

What is that?

You should've known better.

Willow bent down to grab the rope that rested at the base of the tree. Then she stood up, her hand grabbed onto the lowest branch and, with impeccable coordination and strength, climbed the tree one branch at a time, as if she were a skilled climber and completely sober.

Willow reached a thicker branch that must've been at least ten feet off the ground, and looked down.

Put me down.

Of course.

Put me down. On the ground.

You know, we're very similar. You pretended to have it all together, to have all the answers. You saw it all, you knew it all. And you wanted so badly for it to work … for everything to be peaches and cream … but you knew. Even when you dumped me in the ocean, you knew deep down … it wouldn't do anything. But you gave your friends false hope. You lied. You're no better than me.

Crickets chirped, hiding in the bushes below. The air gave a gentle breeze that otherwise would have been soothing and cozy. This night, it was an eerie whisper cautioning Willow to keep her balance, but she wasn't in any position to control that.

I didn't want to be a husband. I didn't want to settle down. But marrying Gwen, that would've given me respect … normalcy.

What you did wasn't normal.

Exactly. Normal isn't in our blood, Willow.

We're aren't the same. You're sick. You're a predator.

Shut up, the deep voice in her head growled. *People like us … with all these secrets … we don't get a normal life, a normal death. And you don't get to burn me and get away with it.*

Willow tossed the rope over one thick branch and began fashioning it into a noose as if she'd had sufficient practice. After it was finished, Willow let go and let it hang in front of her, swinging gently.

Do you like it?

How did you get that?

People leave a lot of little treasures in basements.

Why are you doing this?

Willow's arm reached up again to pet the noose.

Getting me out of your way won't make things easier for you.

Both of Willow's arms grabbed the rope and put the loop around her neck. Willow's body stood unnaturally straight, still, and perfectly balanced on the hefty horizontal branch despite the breeze. The noose greeted her with rough rubbing across the back of her neck.

I want her weak.

Carlson's angry, disgusting lust sent a chill up the spine.

You have a history of underestimating women.

Uh-oh. I think you're out of gas.

Willow's foot shimmied to the point where her feet were hanging halfway off the branch.

I've heard enough from you. This conversation is over.

Willow tried— in the split second before her feet lost contact with the branch— to catch herself, but it was simply too late. She felt the dark presence escape her body swiftly after taking one fateful step off the branch, and within the blink of an eye, Willow was hanging, gurgling, struggling to pull at the rope around her neck. Gravity tightened its hold on her.

Even once she was in control of herself again, she had no power. She wasn't lucky enough to have broken her neck immediately, either. She gasped and choked for what felt like an eternal nightmare. Her wheezing was the first to go, turning to silence. The crickets sang goodbye to her as her view of the clearing blurred. She spent her last moments alive wondering if anyone would have known to come look for her. In her final thoughts, she worried for us because it was no use to worry about herself anymore. Willow's consciousness drifted from fear to devastated acceptance. Although she normally came off as quite confident and at times brash, her final thoughts were humble and selfless.

I'm so sorry I couldn't protect you. I'm sorry. I'm so sorry. I love you. I'm so sorry. I'm so…

Eventually the sad, guilty, repetitive thoughts were muted, and Willow's mind went blank. Her body went limp, and swayed slightly with the wind. After that one soft breeze against her, I felt nothing except for a light floating sensation before everything was nothing.

30.

MORAL OF THE STORY

I caught my breath. "Wills," I squeaked.

Joel saw my lip quivering and furrowed his brows, "What? What did you see? What did she show you?"

I shook my head, looking at Willow. It was her story to tell.

"Why did you show her?" Joel barked.

Willow shifted to look at him.

"Show me, Wills."

"No." She stared blankly.

"Why not?"

"You wouldn't be able handle it." She didn't hesitate.

"What the hell? And Emma *can*?" He gestured to my arm. I bit the inside of my cheek and cried quietly.

"She needed a wake-up call," Willow stated.

"I think you showing up was enough of one."

"You don't need to see how your childhood best friend died," she explained briefly.

"Neither did she."

"She's experienced a death vision before."

"Not yours."

"A child's."

He shook his head and scoffed. "I need to know."

"And you can … without experiencing it. I'm not showing you," she responded quickly.

"Then why didn't you just tell her too? That's *fucked*, Willow," Joel snapped, his face flushing red.

"Joel."

"No, that's not okay!"

"Joel, Emma needed to see it because she needed to know exactly what Carlson said to me."

"Joel, I'm fine," I cut in.

"Clearly, you're not. Look at you." He paused. "You had *no* good reason to show her what happened, especially after finding her like … like this." He took a deep breath. "Someone needs to tell me what happened. Right now."

The room went silent. Crickets from outside caught my attention, and my mind flashed straight back to the vision. Those chirps would never sound the same to me again. "It was him," I muttered.

He gulped audibly and his voice cracked as he pronouncedly blinked once. "What?"

"He lured me to the basement that night and I guess … for lack of a better term he … possessed me," Willow recalled, her head drooping. "I let my guard down."

Joel and I stared at our friend, who'd never looked so defeated.

"I usually did breathing exercises and all that …visualization stuff every night before bed to protect my energy. Calm myself. But I was wasted. And I forgot. I always believed your body was a form of protection for your soul, and that if you didn't take care of it and shield it, it could endanger your spirit … make you susceptible to energetic threats. I guess I was right. I know it sounds really hippy dippy. We just don't understand how it all works, I still don't. But there's obviously truth to it."

"Why didn't he just take me?" I asked.

Joel bit the inside of his cheek.

"That's an easy win for him. He wants you to submit to him. He's better at holding a grudge than me."

"That seems like more work for him than just killing me. I've been weak since I moved here. He could've done it at any time."

"I don't know." Willow shook her head. "Maybe he wasn't strong enough. Maybe he needed to hide out after we pissed him off to reserve energy. Also he's just psycho."

"He's territorial and obviously controlling over women. To him, 'Gwen' probably just means any woman who fights back." Joel stared at my arm.

"Either way" —Willow stood— "I'm dead, and he's still here. So ... the moral of this story is, don't get extremely drunk in a extremely haunted house." She remained stone-faced.

Joel sucked in his breath before speaking. "How often will we see you?"

"Honestly, now that I'm here, I mean— in my humble opinion, people with psychic gifts like us probably have stronger spirits and energy in the first place. So I feel pretty good for a ghost..." The words were phrased as if she were joking, but her face was completely humorless. "I'll be around as often as I can be. Unless I don't want to."

"I'm ... so overwhelmed," Joel understated.

"Then why did it take you so long to show up?" I looked down at the bloody wadded up cloth. The site still stung but had been pushed to the back of my mind during most of the conversation.

Willow glared down at my arm. "Yeah, I haven't forgotten about that. What were you thinking?"

"Answer my question first."

She changed her expression for the first time to gawk at me. "I honestly didn't know how long it'd been since I died. That's why I asked. I just ... faded out, and then I kind of felt like I was floating in nothingness for .... I don't even know how long. Like I'd been there forever and for no time at all. Almost like I was in space. There were some light spots around me that kind of" —she stared out the window — "faded in and out. I don't know. I felt like I was levitating. It was like that one time I took a gummy and meditated for like two hours. And then I just— I don't know— I heard you crying from somewhere in the distance and then it was like a window had opened up into what you were doing. I crossed through it and I ended up in here ...and was greeted by you destroying your goddamn *arm*."

I looked down into my lap. I felt immense guilt and shame. Since her death had truly settled in as reality for me, I held such anger toward her. After all of the loss in my life, it felt like a slap in the face. Not just to me, either, but to everyone she loved. I saw her death as dishonest and selfish. There was the emptiness and deep sadness that accompanied losing a close friend, but if she were present, I'd have screamed at her and slapped her across the face. Now, there we were. Nothing was as it seemed.

We should've known her better than to think she'd harm herself out of the blue like that, with or without a note. She wanted nothing other than to protect us and try to keep me safe in my home. I blamed myself for her death then. If she'd never met me, she'd be alive.

"It's my fault you're dead," I whispered.

"No it's *not*," she rebutted confidently.

"If we'd never met, you'd be here."

"I am here."

"It's not the same."

"Remember what I told you." She gazed directly into my eyes.

"*You're dead*," I hissed.

"Em, I hear you, but—"

Joel interjected, "There are things I wish I'd done differently, too. I wish I'd woken up that night and checked on you." He reached to place his hand on mine.

"Guilt doesn't change anything. All we can do is accept this … and go from there."

"What about the note?" Joel posed.

"I knew in my gut from the day we met, Em. It's one of the things I saw when we locked eyes. It's why I bolted. All I saw was a noose in front of me. And that night when we slept over here— when Carlson came into the picture— I saw you both at my funeral. I had a vision of the floating. I felt the sadness and the fear, but then the unexpected relief that it was over. I knew it was death."

Joel sighed sadly. "You still could've told us."

"Are you kidding me? Why? So you could freak out for months?"

"But we could've—"

"What? We could've what?"

There was silence.

"What about the cemetery?" I asked.

"What about it?"

"How did you know they were all buried there?"

"Who?"

"The Salleys." I bit down hard on the inside of my lip.

"I didn't until just now, but there's that, I guess."

"Why did you ask to be buried there?"

"I just kept seeing flashes of it here and there. I'd never been there, but I put it in the note because I hoped it would've meant something."

"I met Nancy there," I muttered.

"Woah, the friend? She's *alive*?"

Joel nodded solemnly. "We met with her once."

"And?"

"Nothing about it really matters." I stood up and shook my head, then dragged myself over to my bed. I plopped down on my side in a ball and closed my eyes.

"Em, I still need to wrap your arm or something," Joel piped up.

I didn't move or open my eyes to acknowledge the comment.

"Anyway, I'm sorry. I wrote the note the best way I knew how. It was all in my gut but I didn't know when or why it would all happen, and I obviously didn't know what would lead up to it. I just knew my time was limited, and I didn't want anyone worrying about me."

"You could've had support," Joel whispered.

"I did. I knew you two would have each other until I could come back. That's all the support I needed. No one could've seen it coming. If anything, I was the idiot for getting so messed up that night. But in the moment, I was happy. I had my pals. I had food. It was breezy. I was …good. So if my death somehow involved a noose, I didn't think it was going to happen anytime soon … I was wrong, and that's on me."

"God." Joel's devastation was crystal clear. "Wills, I … I don't know what to—"

"Stop. You don't need to say anything else right now. I don't want apologies. I'm … fine. I'm here because I want to be. But you both need rest." Willow speech was monotonous, but she softly laid one hand on each of our shoulders.

With my eyes closed, I couldn't tell the exact moment that Willow left the room to go wherever she went when she wasn't with us. She left quietly.

Joel exhaled. "I assume we'll talk more later." I heard him walk around the bed to the opposite side. The bed creaked as Joel climbed up into bed next to me. I was too exhausted to process or care that he was lying with me, or that he spooned me with his arm over my side to hold my hand.

"Please don't hurt yourself again," he whispered behind me.

I squeezed my eyes shut tighter.

"I can't lose you, too."

I sniffled.

"I want your life to exist alongside mine." He shifted slightly. "I don't want yours ending any sooner. Whether I can still see you or not. Willow's doing what she always does, acting much less bothered than she probably is. It wasn't her choice to leave us. You shouldn't even come close to deciding to do the same."

"I wasn't gonna—"

"Emma, I don't care."

I inhaled deeply.

"And the way she…" —his velvety voice trailed off— "she shouldn't have provided the details to you the way she did. I have a major problem with that."

"It was … so bad." The image of the dark forest floor from Willow's hanging point of view flashed in my mind again and I shivered. "It wasn't even instant. It took—"

"We can talk about it later." He swallowed.

I nodded. Willow was back; I should've been relieved, maybe even grateful. But nothing felt any different from before she'd returned to us. Her life was still over, in this phase, anyway. She wouldn't age. We couldn't hug her anymore, couldn't drink coffee or tea with her. She wouldn't have a career, a relationship, kids. Not everyone had our abilities, either. No one else would be able to communicate with her the way we could. She could likely show herself to her parents if she used enough energy, but it'd be harder to come across to them than it was to us. She'd be more of the standard translucent apparition or book tossed off the shelf like people reported in ghost hunting shows.

She'd be less of a familiar likeliness to the someone they knew and loved. There would be such a separation from the Willow they watched grow up.

As I wondered if all of this made our sensitivity a gift or a curse, my mind started slowly transitioning through short clips of memories I had with both Willow *and* my mom, like a slideshow. But joined by those pleasant memories, was the nagging worry that at any moment, I could be attacked by Carlson, too. The anxiety started to creep up in my chest, and although extremely tired, I started to doubt that I'd be able to get any real rest. Before I drifted off, I could've sworn I heard Joel whisper that he loved me. I didn't have the capacity to think too much of it, and instead simply found that protection enough to finally fall asleep.

***

"I'm gonna get goin' now, darlin. Be good for Jack." I brushed Lynette's rosy pink cheek with my fingertips.

"I will," she sang.

"Don't be out too late," Carlson warned from the front living room. He sat in a brown reading chair with the paper. His sharp jawline jutted forward slightly as he glanced up at me.

"I won't," I declared simply, then shifted back to see Lynette holding the front door open for me. My tone changed immediately, "Thank you, doll."

Lynette and I stood outside on the wooden porch. "Stay in tonight. Looks like it may rain a bit."

Nancy approached the front porch steps. "Well, *hello*, ladies," she greeted us. "Let's go. I'm starving. She'd better have some *real* food for dinner and not just some lousy cheese and crackers."

"That sounds yummy," Lynette chirped.

I patted down my lavender skirt and hopped down the steps. "Jack will make you some supper soon. I love you." I smiled up at Lynette. "Behave yourself."

"I love you." Lynette waved and spun around to go inside, closing the door softly as Nancy and I headed down the sidewalk.

"Did you get Astrid a gift?"

"If a card counts, then yes." Nancy shrugged as we walked. "My goodness this weather is dreary. Here, though. I brought my umbrella for the walk back."

"Good, I don't want my new dress getting all wet and wrinkled up."

"Hopefully we won't even need it. *Ugh.*" She sneered, adjusting the red pocketbook on her shoulder.

"It's such a nice pattern, though," I remarked, admiring the red and navy plaid. "Matches your dress. That's a lovely blue on you, Nan."

"That dress doesn't look too shabby on you, either." Nancy winked.

DECEMBER

264

31.

MOXIE

December arrived only a few days after our first postmortem hang-out with Willow, and with it came the freezing cold chill of winter. Along with the moderate snowfall was the obnoxious cheeriness and warm excitement of the holidays felt by probably everyone in Newport except for us. For them, December meant colorful twinkling lights lining the streets on houses and trees. It meant festive, cozy outerwear worn by the tourists who strolled down Thames Street and Bellevue hoping to experience a picturesque east coast Christmas. For them, Newport was a magical Hallmark holiday movie. For residents, it was just a pain in the ass to shovel snow off their driveways and deal with the expensive oil bills.

But for us, December meant nothing. It was just another month to get through. We expected a repeat of November, except far less time spent in my house after the shower incident. For Joel, that was the final straw. He'd put his foot down. We were leaving.

We decided to move camp to his place. It wasn't any happier, but it felt safer. Joel returned to his part-time job waiting tables at a restaurant downtown, and I reluctantly went back to Beach Brew despite having to relive my morning coffee dates with Willow. Joel and I agreed that having something else in our lives— other than each other and the comfort of our small bubble that was his apartment — would be the healthy but difficult choice. I felt guilty leaving Lynette alone in the house with Carlson, but Joel was right; she'd existed without me before, and it was smarter to stay away until we had a solid game plan. So far, we had nothing. I wanted to tell her why we were leaving but she never showed. So I left her a little note that didn't feel like enough.

Encounters with Willow were here and there, but not much was said. No one wanted to have the hard conversations that needed to happen. Each time she'd shown up, it'd last a few minutes and was sprinkled with uncomfortable silence and awkward small talk. No one was upset anymore per say, but no one knew how to navigate this new relationship. Willow said it didn't have to be new, but we felt very differently. It was a challenge to have hang-outs together like we used to. Simply being together was really hard when I had to look at the ligature mark around her neck the entire time.

I lied and told Aunt Liv that I wasn't living at the house because I needed time away from where we lost Willow. I told her that at that point in the grieving process, it felt good to be surrounded by some of her old belongings that remained at their place, and that it was comforting to have a roommate who was facing the same struggle as me. Of course, she didn't question me. She wasn't skeptical of paranormal activity keeping me away, nor did she care why I needed to be out of the house; she simply respected my wishes if it meant healing of any kind was taking place. It was very clear, however, that she was skeptical of something else going on.

"You know ... you can tell me anything, right?" Liv blurted one day at work.

"Yeah, why?"

"I dunno. Just— I know that mutual grief can create special bonds, and that your living situation is" —she cleaned a mug very thoughtfully for a little too long— "co-ed."

"*Huh?*" I jerked.

"Oh, honey calm down. I'm not giving you a silly little talk or anything. You're an adult. I just— well— I think Joel is just darling. Your mom would've *loved* him," she almost sang. "But I wanted to make sure that if anything was going on between you two that—"

"Well there's not—"

"That it's built on a healthy foundation and not just trauma, you know?"

"Liv-"

"I know. I'm sorry. You're more than capable of making your own decisions," she said in a hushed tone.

"This sounds exactly like a silly little talk." I sighed.

"Well … I'm definitely not trying to lecture you … and I'd be happy for you if you *were*—"

"I get it. But there's nothing going on between us," I stated bluntly.

"Okayyy." She cleared her throat. "But if there *was*, I support you as long as it keeps you both happy and healthy."

"Liv" —I raised my voice slightly, then whispered quickly— "there is *nothing* going on with Joel and me other than depression."

Aunt Liv sighed deeply, gently placing the same mug down on the counter. "Then in that case, I really do think we should get you into some therapy. We can ease into it. Even once a month."

"I … will call tomorrow." I wasn't going to call tomorrow.

"Okay honey. If you want, I can come over to the house—"

"*No,*" I interrupted.

Liv paused to stare at me, blinking once as she set the clean mug down on a small shelf behind the counter. "Oh … kay."

"No, I didn't mean to be rude, I just—"

"No no, it's fine. I'm just…I'm really trying to navigate and respect your boundaries right now." She blew air up toward her bangs and looked out toward the window with the wharf-view. "I was just going to say that … when you're ready, I'd be happy to be there with you in case you have any questions or just need support," she offered warmly, placing her hand on mine and rubbing it softly.

I feigned a smile, hoping to disguise the couple tears I fought back. "Your substitute mom is showing."

"*Good!*" she shouted enthusiastically. "That's my job and I don't take it lightly." She chuckled to herself, lifting her hand off of mine to rub my back. "You can clock out a few minutes early if you want," she whispered. "I won't tell boss."

"Thank God. I've had enough of you today, anyway." I smirked and hugged her briefly before taking off my royal blue café apron. I grabbed my bag and peered into the tip jar to see what my bonus was for the afternoon.

"Do you want it? It's basically rent." With a shrug, I held up a five and a one.

Aunt Liv stood up straight with her hands pressing against the counter across from me. "*No*," she snapped.

"Keep the change, then." I managed a wink. There were three pennies and a nickel left in the jar.

"You aren't paying rent if you aren't staying there. Go use it to buy a self-care journal or fudge or something."

"Those are two very different things." I turned around to face the entrance.

"Not really," she argued playfully. "Hey," she started as I headed out.

"Yeah?" I turned around to face her again, grabbing my thick red wool coat from a hook near the clearance used books by the door.

"Before I forget … would you want to go to a small book signing with me in Salem in a few weeks?"

"Mmm." I crinkled my nose. "Salem?"

"Yes, honey. A town other than the one you live in."

I glanced around to see if any nosey customers were paying attention. Luckily, the one patron in the back of the cafe was an older regular reading the newspaper. The second customer from a few minutes ago must've snuck out while we were talking. Typical traffic for a weekday afternoon. "I'll think about it. Can I text you?"

"You need a change of scenery. So I'm changing your answer to a 'yes' and I'll buy you Dunkin' for the drive …lunch afterwards, too. It'll be fun."

"If I'm not being given a choice." I exhaled, my heart leaping in my chest subtly. Was it anxiety or anticipation, or both? I'd distanced myself from Liv since we'd butted heads over the house, and after Willow's death I emotionally disconnected from everyone. She'd tried for weeks to get through the barriers I'd put up, and I'd given her close to nothing to work with. That day I felt generous, or maybe I needed her. Something in my subconscious was tapping on my shoulder to chip off a small chunk of that stone wall in my spirit.

"You don't," Aunt Liv crooned over the sound of Thompson's old bells jingling on the door as I walked out into the cold.

***

On the drive home in Willow's beloved blue Prius, I gazed out the passenger window. We passed the art museum and boutiques along Bellevue on our way to pick up Mama Leone's calzones for an early dinner. He always made sure to pick me up promptly from work, and he was usually early. That day he was right on time.

"Do you want to go anywhere else after we pick up the food?" he asked.

"No."

Joel turned into the parking lot of Stop & Shop and found a spot right in front of the Italian restaurant we loved.

"Kay. Should I grab a two liter?" He turned off the ignition.

"If you want." I shrugged. "I don't need it. I have my water."

"Got it." Joel cleared his throat and got out. He scratched his head as he locked the car behind him.

While I waited in the car, my attention was pulled toward my house, which was further down Bellevue and to the right. An inexplicable invisible thread gently tugging on my ear to get me to look in that direction. It was a sad yearning to stand in that house again, to feel the energy in its walls. A buzzing whisper to go check on Lynette … but I didn't want to go.

I itched my ear and shifted in my seat, watching Joel through the windows as he waited for our order. He turned to check on me and waved. I returned a dampened smile and looked out the window to a woman walking with her little girl down the street. The child's wavy blonde hair bounced as they strolled through the thin layer of snow in their boots.

Joel made his way back to the car with two boxes and a small bottle of soda for himself, "Miss me?" he joked dryly.

"Tremendously." I stared into the side rear-view mirror.

"Well that's a big word." He leaned toward me and grinned playfully. I didn't play along any further, so he straightened up awkwardly to look ahead and start the car. "Man, I'm hungry."

"Hey," I spoke up as he reversed. "I think we should actually stop somewhere first."

"No problem. Where?"

***

"Um," Joel contemplated, staring out the windshield up at the front door. "I know I said 'no problem' but—"

"Just for a minute."

"Do you want me to go in with you?"

I shook my head subtly, gazing out the window from our parked spot on the street in front of the house.

"Why not?"

"I don't think he'll hurt me. … not yet," I inhaled deeply and scratched my scalp.

"You don't know that," he cautioned quietly, placing his hand on my knee. "You remember what he said to you in the show—"

I moved his hand off of my leg. "*Yeah*. I do." I glared at him.

"She'll be fine. I'll step in if I have to." Willow appeared in the backseat and looked around. "Oh. Thanks for vacuuming back here, Joel."

Joel gripped the steering wheel and bowed his head with a deep sigh.

"Not sure what you mean by 'stepping in' but okay." I unbuckled my seatbelt. "I'll be quick."

"What if she doesn't show up?" Joel asked.

"I'll give it five minutes. If there's nothing, I'll leave. Promise." I stepped out of the car and before I closed the door behind me, I heard Joel and Willow bickering briefly.

"I didn't vacuum, your parents did … before they gave me car."

"I should've known. Car looks great, of course it wasn't you."

Joel leaned back in his seat, shifting the car into park.

"Well, tell them I said 'thanks.'" Willow nodded coolly.

"Yeah, right. I'm sure they'll handle that well."

"Don't be dumb, Joel. I'm kidding. Duh."

"Are you gonna poof out of here or what? Go with her." Joel shook his head.

Willow vanished from the backseat with a stiff eye-roll. Could things with her ever become a new normal, or would it always just be paranormal?

I walked up the front porch steps, careful not to slip on any ice. My hand shivered as I unlocked the door and creaked it open. I should've worn gloves. The house was chilly since the heat hadn't been run in days. I was hesitant to walk any further than through the front door. "Lynette?"

I stood in place waiting for a response, but I wasn't confident I'd get one.

I wandered into the living room to the right and peeked into the dining room. As if I'd sensed it— and maybe I had without realizing— a small body stood in front of the bay window, looking out at the snow-kissed driveway.

There was the wavy, wet mess of blonde hair I'd missed, whether it was matted with blood or not.

"Lyn?" I whispered, shifting my weight carefully. The floor creaked under me.

"Gwen and I used to pull up chairs and watch the snowflakes fall from here." Her sweet voice was soothing to my ears.

"Yeah?"

"Yes." She kept her back to me. "Where did you go?"

I opened my mouth to answer.

"I'm not mad … just curious."

"I'm sorry." My chest heaved up and down as I took a deep breath. "It's been complicated. I wanted to talk to you but you never showed … There's a lot going on."

"I'm sorry about Willow."

"I'm sorry I lost my temper with you." I took a few steps toward her. "You didn't do anything wrong. I was just scared and you didn't deserve—"

"Did he hurt you?"

I bit my lip and exhaled. "Yes." Intense vulnerability washed over me, "I was very scared. And very sad. But I shouldn't have treated you that way, and I'm sorry." I cleared my throat. "He hurt Willow, too."

Lynette turned around slowly to face me, her mouth gaping open for several seconds. "Is that why she's dead too?"

I nodded. I tried to push back the urge to cry by opening my eyes wide.

"How can I be happy here if he's still hurting people?"

"You wanna stay?"

"I've been waiting for Gwen so long that" —her shoulders drooped— "if she can't come home, I just wanna stay as close to her as I can. This was our house once."

"Okay."

"Is that alright?"

"I would actually … love if you stayed."

A small smile crept upon her little lips.

"Are *we* … okay?" I mustered. "Do you forgive me?"

"Of course I forgive you." Lynette approached and gently held my hand. "That's silly."

I shivered and let go instinctively. "Sorry, it's just already so cold in here and—"

"When will you come back home?" she asked, looking up at me with her big doe-eyes.

"Soon. As soon as we can" —I paused, cautious of who could be listening in— "as soon as we know how to keep ourselves safe."

"But you already tried," she whispered, her inner brows raised in disappointment.

"Then we will again. Until we get it right," Willow spoke up from behind me. She walked into the dining room and stood next to me.

"You're here now," Lynette piped up.

"I'm here and there." She chuckled. "I could probably be at Walmart if I really wanted to."

"What's that?"

"A big store."

"Like Ley's?"

"Sure…"

"Do they have toys?"

"They have everything but good aloe vera gel," Willow explained plainly.

"Wow." Lynette stood looking up at Willow in awe.

"We're gonna figure something out." I redirected them quickly, scanning my surroundings.

With a tender smile, Lynette turned toward the window once again and faded as she approached it.

"Where does she go?" I asked Willow in the cold, quiet dining room.

"I mean, we need to recharge … just like we need sleep, right? So I kinda just … watch from further back. In that spacey void I mentioned before. It's like watching a concert from the shittiest seats. I don't know if it's the same for her or not, but … that's where I go."

"Hm," I crossed my arms.

"Yeah. Not looking down from the heavens or anything, just like looking through a window, but the window is either far away or foggy sometimes. I don't know. I'm trying to explain it in alive-people terms, but I'm still learning it, so…" She shrugged. "There's great power in metaphor, I guess."

"Right." I clicked my tongue and turned around to leave the house.

"Em," Willow started.

"Yeah?"

"Let's go to our spot again soon."

"Sure." I swallowed and opened the door. "Why though? I'm not sure if you noticed, but it's a bad time to go sit out there." I looked back but she was gone.

I bit the inside of my cheek, pausing to look deep into the house, all the way back to the steps down to the landing between the basement and patio doors. Was I being watched?

With a fiery jittering in my chest— like hot oil sizzling and shooting around a frying pan— I remembered the shower again. I couldn't even bathe in my own home. I couldn't do anything there while he was lurking. He could've killed me, and he still could.

Is he gonna kill me?

I clenched my fists.

You're too strong for those thoughts, right?

After all the loss, after the assault, I still managed to stand up off the wet shower floor— even if I needed help. I looked down at my arm and, through my thick coat sleeve, I patted the long scab underneath. Then I tensed my jaw and ground my teeth. As if one huge, hiss of oil had leapt out and landed on the center of my chest, I felt a piercing sensation deep in my lungs, heat spreading throughout my body. I stared down at the dim back stairway and shrieked, "*Fuck you!*"

He wasn't gonna take me with him.

I turned and swung the door open but before I exited, Carlson appeared at the top of the stairs. I took one look at his long smug smile, his tilted head peering down at me, and exploded.

Dapper douchebag.

"Get out."

He furrowed his brows for a moment and then chuckled, "Maybe if you mind your temper."

"I said 'get out.'"

"Yet you're the one running away."

"You better pray that I don't come back into this house again any time soon because when I do—"

"I leave prayer to the feeble-minded."

"When I come back, you're done. You want me weak but you're gonna get the opposite."

"All I see so far, my dear, is weakness."

"I'm not," I replied through my teeth.

"I wasn't made aware that the definition had changed."

I shook my head, gripping the doorknob. "Willow was right. You fucked up."

"Let's not escalate this into more profanities. That language doesn't complement you. The truth of the matter is— and it seems you're somehow still struggling to comprehend this— you ruthlessly took my life, but you clearly need me. You couldn't cope without me, you still can't. Look at you now..." he shook his head. "You're not leaving me again."

"Your sense of entitlement makes me sick to my stomach."

"Your ignorance does the same to me, doll." He growled, all the while remaining composed on the steps.

I blinked. "I *am* leaving. Right now."

He chuckled and vanished halfway down the stairs.

I turned around and took a step out the door.

"I'd be lying if I said this moxie of yours didn't turn me on … just a little bit," he whispered into my ear from behind me. I felt a freezing sting against my left hip. "but it still burns."

"Maybe that's because I set your body on fire with a smile," I spat, slamming the front door shut behind me without looking back or acknowledging his disgustingly frigid hold on my side. I zipped down the front steps as quickly as I could without slipping, and flung the car door open. I threw myself onto the seat and, with my chest heaving, glared straight ahead.

"What happened?"

"Drive," I whispered.

"Em—"

"I'm fine, let's go. I'll tell you later."

32.

GOD FORGIVE ME

That night I slept on Joel's couch, again.

Not long after closing my eyes, though, there I was … staring down at the frothy white waves below, my attention lost in the rising summer evening tide.

I planted my feet firmly on the edge of a cliff, feeling the cool hard rock beneath my bare feet. I looked down beside me at a pair of short cream Oxford heels placed tidily next to each other.

Forgive me.

I knew this was the end of Gwen's story, and I didn't want to see it. No matter how hard I tried to wake myself up, I couldn't pull myself away from the edge.

The heartache was familiar. The only difference was that she had to live with the guilt of killing a man— not an innocent man by any means but not guilty of directly killing her sister as she'd initially assumed. Her aching guilt held hands with the clarity of hindsight. She'd given a predator the keys to her home, her heart, her family. The pain only mounted in her chest as she revisited the moment she'd discovered his trophies in the basement that fateful night. She'd found the back doors open, the gate leading to the woods gaping and broken. Everything had become unhinged, and it was too much to bear. Her family had been reduced to excruciatingly silent suppers with only her father, listening to the clock tick from the fireplace mantle. They waited for life to find its balance again, but that never came. She thought about how her relationship with Nancy had been strained by their secret. Although there was no threat to the friendship ending, there had been some distance between them since that night.

It was difficult to be together and not discuss what had happened, and they couldn't risk anything being overheard. They needed quiet, and she'd expected that. Nancy would never tell a soul, but the sin of involving her most trusted confidant in murder weighed heavily on her shoulders.

I didn't have to kill him. I could've called the police, she thought back on that cliff. *I should've.*

No, she backtracked. If she'd phoned the police, they'd have found Lynette and ruled the death an accident, as it was. Carlson would've either gotten away before their arrival or smooth-talked his way out of any trouble. No one would've believed a such distraught young woman over an intelligent, charismatic man five years her senior. After that, well … with Gwen's knowledge of the truth about him, Carlson would've either done her harm or trapped her in an even more hostile relationship.

I did the right thing killing him. He'd have abused her…threatened to ruin her if she'd left him, if she'd told a soul about his devilish extracurriculars. He would've hurt another little girl. He would've hurt her…

No, no. I'm a murderer. Nothing justifies that. She'd plunged a knife into the man who would've made her a mother. She'd bathed in his blood.

I thought he'd killed my baby sister, though. Perhaps he intended to, anyway. She couldn't stand the wondering … what had he done to that other poor girl? *It was self-defense.* He could've killed her that night. She simply beat him at his own game. He had to die. There was no other way…

But she'd loved him once. She'd killed the only man she'd ever loved … and his blood was on her hands. It was her fault. She could've saved Lynette if I'd never let him in, if she'd never left the house that night, if she'd listened to Nancy.

Her blood is on my hands. God forgive me.

The thoughts didn't stop. They went on and on, repeating over and over until she just couldn't take it anymore. She needed quiet.

Let me see her again.

With that, Gwen took one last deep breath and with the next breeze, she gracefully drifted off the rocks with it. Her bare feet gently pressed off the ground, her arms outstretched as if to offer her life to divine justice. She was righting her wrongs in the best way she knew how, the most permanent way.

She dove down into the salty deep blue below, surrendering to the waves as they got closer and closer to her face. She felt the ocean spray kiss her cheeks farewell right before her body hit the water quickly with heavy impact. Under the water, she moaned deeply at the pain in her abdomen and legs as everything slowed down for a moment. Her arms fell limp, her vision was blurred. Flashes of light sparkled around as her head violently bobbed above and below the waves. She gasped as the crashing water slapped her face. Her brain throbbed against her skull.

Flash.

The painful tension behind her eyes tightened each time the light blinded her. Her ears were plugged with cold water, her mouth overcome with the taste of sea salt. Gwen's eyes burned and she could no longer open them. Her limbs wouldn't move the way she wanted them to anymore. She'd lost control of her body as the Atlantic Ocean took it. She tried to cough the water out, but even more water was swallowed down into her throat each time. She finally went completely lax under the water as her consciousness faded with exhaustion. Her full lungs and collapsed airways pushed against her ribs and expanding until it reached a peak pressure and everything went black. Only small specks of light blinked faintly, like twinkling stars. Her mind was finally, at least in that moment, at rest.

Gwendolyn Salley couldn't swim. She died wondering if God would accept her, or if he'd leave her soul stranded in a cold dark abyss like the one she'd chosen to end her own life in. She drowned in less than a minute.

***

I woke up choking and gasping hysterically, springing up from my pillow. Joel jolted from his spot on the couch and jumped to my side.

"Hey, hey, hey breathe!" he held one hand against my back and the other on my shoulder. I opened my eyes to his worried face.

278

"God!" I gasped with my mouth as wide open as possible. I could breathe; thank goodness it was air and not ocean that filled my lungs.

"Are you okay?" His voice cracked.

"It was Gwen!" I cried as I tried to even my breath.

"What do you mean?" He patted my back.

"I'm so *sick* of dying."

"Emma," Willow said from the doorframe of her bedroom.

I leaned my head on Joel's shoulder and faced her, "Did *you* do that?" I whimpered.

"No, why would I?" Willow shook her head. "She did."

"What?" I sighed exasperatedly.

"Go to our spot today … when it's actually … today."

I glimpsed at the vintage clock on the coffee table. It was only four in the morning.

"Will we get answers?" Joel nodded subtly.

"Yeah, but she should go alone."

"Why?"

"Girl time." Willow winked mechanically, like a baby doll with messed up eyelids.

"What?"

"Em, do you trust me?" Willow ignored his inquiry.

"I mean— yeah, for the most part." I wiped my eyes with my sleeve.

"Okay. I'll be there whenever you are." Willow gave a sympathetic smile. "I just wanna show you something there. Things will start making more sense after that, kay? I promise … I'm sorry I left you guys. But I'm gonna help us fix all of this somehow. Then you and Joel can move into a spirit-free house together and live happily ever after," she teased dryly.

"*Will—*" Joel hissed, but before he could finish scolding her, she was gone. He threw his hands in the air.

I dropped back down onto the couch and shut my eyes.

"Why were you out here?"

"Couldn't sleep."

"Were you watching me?"

"No, just on my phone. I saw you tossing and turning, so I kept an eye out. Just wanna make sure you're okay."

I nodded and melted back under my blanket. "Kay."

"Night, Em. Hope you can get some more rest."

Me too. But it won't be enough.

33.

CLOVERS

"I look whacked out of my mind," I muttered to Willow. Although I knew I was standing next to my best friend, to any passersby, I was completely alone in the middle of a snow-covered field. She'd shown up after I'd parked the car in the Brenton Point lot and gotten out of the car.

"I'm sorry you feel that way." Willow stood in her same old hoodie and jeans, not at all bothered by the temperature, of course.

"Why are we out here?"

"Because our bench is covered in ice." She shrugged, gazing out at the ocean across the street.

"Willow, why are we standing … *here?*"

We stood silent for a minute in the frosted grassy area. Willow glimpsed around and then pursed her lips. "I need you to know something."

"Okay. Tell me."

"I'm not gonna to tell you. I just need you to know."

"Couldn't I 'know' in the car?"

"No." She shook her head. "You really think I'd just fuck with you out here?"

I scoffed and rubbed my gloves together, looking out past the field into the trees that made up a small forest. As a kid I'd wander through it to find the ruins of the stables that belonged to the old Bells estate. The mansion itself was abandoned in the 1920's and demolished in the 1960's, so only the stables were left. Some people claimed it was haunted, but I just thought it was beautiful. Over the years, more and more people added to the vandalism on its walls, and then it just looked sad. I zoned out on a wooden beam that had the words, "Is existing the same as being seen?" spray-painted on it in bright yellow.

Willow stared at me stoically.

"You said Gwen showed me her own death." I cleared my throat. "How?"

"I'm about to show you."

"Again, I don't know why you couldn't just show me right then and there last night."

"I'm a ghost, we're cryptic. It's a vibe."

"I'm gonna to catch pneumonia out here. Start explaining or I'm going back to the car." I held the keys in my hand and jingled them once in the quiet white field.

"Okay, okay. All jokes aside…"

"Mhm."

"You aren't gonna like this, but I know something about you now that you've forgotten."

"You're phenomenal with prefaces." A gust of icy wind hit my face.

"I brought you here so you would remember. You need to remember. It's the reason why you've been having visions of Gwen's life. It didn't make sense to me before, but when I projected my death onto you, I also got something back. And now I want you *here*, as close to that memory as possible."

I sighed.

"So stand here in this field, and remember."

"Remember *what*? I can't just stand out here until I remember if I don't even know what—" I felt a lump in the middle of my chest.

"It was summer. Your mom and Liv were at the car grabbing the picnic stuff, but you stayed here." Willow gestured to the ground on which we stood. She held my hand, and even through my gloves, I felt her chill.

"Close your eyes and let yourself go back to that day. You were making a crown out of those tiny white flowers in the grass."

I closed my eyes hesitantly, but trusted Willow. "The clovers. My mom told me they were actually weeds, but I fought her on it because weeds were *ugly*. I insisted that those were flowers."

"Good. Go back to that … It was a little humid, right?"

"Yeah." I gave my best effort to focus. I wanted answers, even if they were hard to unearth and swallow. "I hated when the air felt sticky. I still do."

"I'm right here. Remember the…" Willow's voice faded and trailed off slowly.

***

"Clovers," a sweet smooth voice cooed from behind me.

I looked up, blocking with my hand the bright beams of sun that shone through the clouds for a moment.

"That's a beautiful headdress you're making," said a young woman in a wet light blue dress. She knelt down next to me, her stringy hair hanging down past her shoulder.

"Did you go swimming?" I asked.

"Yes, I did."She smiled softly.

"But it's not that hot out today." I giggled.

"I suppose I love the water a little *too* much," she joked back gently. "Isn't that silly?"

I gazed back at the car, where my mom met my gaze and waved to me. I assumed that meant it was okay to continue talking to the beautiful but drenched stranger, "What's your name?"

The lady replied, "Gwendolyn. And yours?"

"Emma." I blushed and continued knotting the clovers together.

"Well hello, Emma." She watched as I continued my project in the grass. "It's very nice to meet you."

"You, too," I replied shyly, glancing up at Gwendolyn's face in the sunshine peeking through the clouds again. We caught eyes with each other, and I froze. She had the lightest eyes I'd ever seen, like snowy crystals, the softest baby blue. They were icy, and so glossy that they seemed to twinkle in the overcast light. They didn't look quite right, but they were mesmerizing. "You have pretty eyes," I awed.

She tilted her head softly and grinned tenderly. "Thank you, sweet thing." She reached out warmly, but touched my shoulder with a freezing cold *ping*. "Oh," the nice lady gently pulled away. "Oh my goodness."

"You're really cold." I shivered.

"I'm sorry."

"Do you need a towel? I can go ask my mo—"

"No, no that's quite alright." Gwendolyn looked down at my clovers and smiled, letting her hand gracefully rest on her dress. "I'll dry off someday."

"Okay."

She paused, looking down at her hands in her lap, "You seem like a *very* bright young lady."

"I got all A's last year."

"Well then" —she straightened her back, still kneeling beside me— "you must be *very* gifted."

"Maybe." I shrugged, swallowing as I looked up at the woman again. She stared into my eyes strikingly, never blinking or breaking away from my gaze. I should've been alarmed at this from a stranger, but her gentle energy radiated toward me like a warm, safe blanket despite her chilly, wet appearance.

She reached both of her hands out to me with a kind grin. "May I?"

I glanced around nervously, not because *she* made me anxious, but because I was worried someone would try to stop me from talking to her. Something felt unconventional about our exchange, but I couldn't place it. I placed one hand in her palm. A soft breeze fluttered past.

"Emma, I believe I've been sent to be your guardian angel."

"What's that?"

"Someone who watches over you as you grow up, and keeps you safe."

"Oh, wow."

"You remind me … of someone very special." She gently held my hand in both of hers now, her voice like honey. "She was very kind, *very* smart, just like you. And with a sweet smile. I used to be *her* guardian angel."

"How come you aren't anymore?"

Gwen stared off toward the coastline then spoke slowly, "I still am. I just— well … we were playing a game of hide-and-seek and she just— well— she did a very good job hiding. So good that I'm *still* searching for her. Maybe you can help me find her someday," she oohed.

"Oh." I gazed down at the clovers in my hand. "Can I make her one, too?"

"Of course. She'd love that."

I nodded and kept tying.

"How old are you?" The lady asked.

"I'll be six soon," I piped up. "I'm gonna have a mermaid birthday party! Do you wanna come?"

She paused. "That sounds wonderful."

"Okay, I'll give you an invitation."

"Well, I won't need one if I'm already your special angel. Isn't that neat?"

"Yeah," I said.

"Would you like that, Emma?"

"Yes."

"I'm so glad. Okay … I'd like you to do something for me, then. Don't worry. It's very easy," she reassured. "Are you ready?"

"Okay."

Gwen looked down at my crown. "It looks about finished. Would you like to wear it?"

I nodded, and quickly tied it closed in a knot. Then I laid it on my head and looked to Gwen for approval.

"It's beautiful but—" She beamed, straightening it on top of my head. "There we are" She winked.

"How ya doin, hun?" My mom called from the car. I whipped my head back toward them and gave them a quick thumbs up. They never mentioned the woman with me, and I'd never thought twice about it.

"Can you close your eyes, and keep them closed? I know my hands must be cold, but try to feel them lightly on yours and pretend there's a magic little string tying us together …first at our wrists, and then aaalll around us like a great big *hug*. Can you do that?"

"I think so." I squeezed my eyes shut tightly, trying to concentrate.

"Good, good. What is your favorite color, Emma?"

"Blue."

"Excellent choice. Focus on imagining that sparkly blue string around us, and breathe deeply, in and out slowly." She spoke almost as if she was reciting a lullaby. "Now, I want you to imagine that I'm becoming small ... like a little fairy, shrinking down all the way into the palm of your hand."

I nodded, breaking to giggle slightly, then quickly resumed my breathing. "My mom taught me how to take deep breaths." I felt the fresh air flow all the way up my nostrils and down into my chest.

"Beautiful. Once I'm so teeny tiny that I'm just a little ball of bright *blue* glittery light, cup your hands around it and hold it close to your chest. Three deep breaths ... You're doing so well." Gwendolyn's voice got softer and quieter.

I felt a cold ball of air in my hands, soft like a snowball.

"Now, hold it close to your heart" —she whispered smoothly in my ear— "and try not to forget. I'll see you again one day, little."

With one last deep breath, deeper than all the rest, I felt that sparkly, icy air melt into my chest as shivers spread throughout my body. With a gasp, I went weak and fell back onto the grass.

After that, I woke up very confused. My mom and Liv must've rushed over to me once they saw me faint. They stood over me in a panic.

"Emma, honey. Oh my gosh, are you okay?" my mom spoke quickly.

"I'm okay." I looked around slowly.

"What happened?" Liv asked.

"I don't know, but my head just hurts a little." I rubbed my temple. There was a throbbing pressure on both sides and a tightness in my chest that I wasn't quite as familiar with at that age.

"Should we take her in somewhere?" my mom furrowed her brows at my aunt.

"Up to you, Jen. I think she'll be okay, but..." They examined my eyes and felt my forehead. "Em, do you think you can stand up and walk around a bit?"

"I don't know if she should yet," mom argued in a hushed tone.

"You're right, you're right."

"I think I may call anyway."

"I'm okay, mama," I comforted. "I think I'm just hungry."

My mom sighed and looked to Liv, "Let's keep an eye on her during lunch and see how she does."

"It could be the humidity. You wanna go back?"

"No, no! I wanna stay. Can I have my sandwich? I'm hungry," I repeated, not at all fazed by what had just happened. I'd noticed that I'd dropped my clover crown in the grass, but it wasn't crushed like I'd feared. I quickly picked it up and placed it back on my head.

Mom and Liv kept a close eye on me while they set up the picnic blanket and food. I continued tying clovers together for a second crown, but I couldn't recall who I was making it for. I ended up just wearing two little white clover crowns home that day.

***

I opened my eyes and found myself kneeling down in the snow. My jeans were soaked at the knees and shins. My hands were empty. Willow stood beside me with her hand on my shoulder in the still, silent winter air. Waves crashed in the distance.

"Do you remember?"

"How could I have forgotten?"

34.

MIRROR IMAGE

"**W**ell it makes a little more sense now." Joel slumped back on his couch later that day. "I mean, as much sense as it can, I guess." I shrugged, then shook my head. "No, still … none of this makes sense. I have too many questions."

"Ask 'em then." Willow sat stiffly on the chair across from us.

"So … *what*? I absorbed her *into* me?"

"Ish," she replied.

"Ish? So she's a part of me now, or what?"

"Well that's a sweet way of thinking about it, but she's still a separate energy with her own awareness. It's just shared from time to time," Willow elaborated. "Shithead probably sensed her energy in you and assumed you were one and the same."

"Like … reverse possession."

"Sure." She nodded.

"So she's trapped in there … in *here*." I gestured to my entire bust.

"I mean— I wouldn't call her 'trapped.' Clearly she wanted it," Willow added. "She must've seen *something* from touching you. Like how I knew—" Willow stopped herself. "Sorry."

"For what?"

"I don't know. Everything."

"Well, how?" I asked.

"'How what?"

"How did I do that?"

Willow shook her head. "I just work here."

"Like Gwen said, Em. You're gifted." Joel gazed at me.

"I don't want another gift."

"Well I guess that's too bad." Willow shrugged robotically.

"What it means now, though, is that we can access Gwen for help getting rid of Carlson. Maybe she knows a way to weaken him," Joel proposed.

"Bingo." Willow tapped her pale nose.

"Okay, but I obviously don't have control over this. I didn't even know I could *do* that. How did I forget? I have no idea how to *un* … reverse … possess her." I paused. "I feel like we need a simpler, less cheesy term for this."

"Consume," Willow shot out.

"I didn't eat her."

"Take in?" Joel suggested.

"That's boring. *Boo*, lame." Willow stared blankly at him.

"Can we just worry about this later, actually?" I shook my head.

"Ooh. *Collect.*" Willow smirked. "You can be the Collector." she nodded confidently.

"That's worse," I grimaced.

"Isn't that a movie?" Joel asked.

"No. It's weird." I glared at Willow.

"Is weird bad, though?"

"I don't need a superhero name."

"But do you *want* one?"

"No."

"It's like you adopted her into you." Willow quickly came back with another suggestion.

"*No.* That's stupid, too. Stop." I sniffled.

"God, I'm just trying to have fun. I'm dead. Let me have fun." Her eyes rolled to the back of her head somehow. Maybe it was just a projection of her melodramatic tendencies.

"We need to focus on getting rid of him. I still just don't know how she can help us. She knew him as a living person. What made him weak then is completely different from what makes him weak now." I shook my head, staring down into my lap. I readjusted the blanket on top of me and hid my arms under it.

"Is it?" Willow stood up. "What choice do we have but to try?" I looked up as she tilted her head and stared down into my eyes. Although the attitude behind the look was the same, there was a new vacancy in her eyes that took away from her scolding.

"Don't look at me like that." I scoffed.

"You're in no position to shoot down any ideas here. You're being too negative."

"Can you blame me at this point? Seriously?"

Joel's eyes widened and he bit the inside of his cheek. Had he picked up my bad habit, or had he always done that? "Guys."

"How do I just yank her out and talk to her?"

"I don't know. It's not my gift. I just knew you had it," Willow explained.

The clock ticked from the table.

"I feel stuck." I buried my face in my hands. "I don't know where to go from here."

"Maybe nowhere," Joel suggested. "Maybe just stay here and work with yourself to figure it out. Focus like you did with Gwen. A gentle focus."

"Maybe." I let out an exasperated breath, got up, and went into the bathroom.

"Em, don't be so hard on yourself … please." Joel started to stand up to follow me, but then sat back down.

"Let her go. She just needs space," Willow whispered.

I locked the door behind me and leaned up against the sink, staring closely at my own eyes in the mirror while I searched them desperately. I glared into my pupils for any sign at all that there was a second presence within me, a glimmer of Gwen staring back at me. There was nothing but my fatigued reflection in the mirror.

I glared into my pupils and turned on the overhead bathroom fan so Joel and Willow wouldn't hear me talking to myself.

"Gwen?"

The fan hummed loudly.

"I know you're there. I remember now. Talk to me … please. I need help."

Silence met my request.

"Please."

I sighed and sat on the toilet, burying my face in my hands. As the fan droned on, I let the comforting white noise lull my eyes closed. I didn't even need to go to the bathroom

I just need a minute to clear my head before I … I just need a break to…

***

I woke up a few minutes later, greeted by the bathroom light, which was way brighter than before. I must've dozed off long enough for my eyes to need readjusting. I stood up, rubbed my eyes, and looked in the mirror one more time, expecting to see my hair disheveled from sleeping with my hand against the side of my head.

Instead, a small elegant smile greeted me. Her rosy cheeks lifted slightly, shimmering like fresh strawberries. Her vintage-styled curls were a picture perfect light chestnut. She wore a pretty short-sleeved baby blue dress that had buttons down the front and fitted at the waist. The skirt billowed gracefully down just below the knees. Her lips parted softly as she spoke to me. "*This* is how I wish we could've met."

"Gwen." My chest caved in a bit.

"Hi, Emma."

"I remember."

"I'm so glad. Life has thrown so much at you. I'm proud of you."

"Why?"

"You're very resilient."

"I don't know. Am I?" I shrugged.

She gestured down at my arm. "You're stronger than that. It broke my heart to watch you do that to yourself."

"It broke my heart to watch you do what *you* did."

"I was so worried you'd do the same. I'm glad she stopped you. You can't take that choice back."

"It felt like I didn't have a choice."

"You have *so* many, Emma." She spoke with the same buttery smooth voice that she had when I was five.

"Willow says everything that is meant to happen is already going to happen and we can't change it."

"That doesn't mean we can't make choices." Gwen stood still across from me, as if there was only a window between us.

"I forgot about you."

"I couldn't have expected you to remember me at such a young age, especially with how much it took out of you to hold onto me that day. But thank you for having such a strong imagination … and my goodness, how you've grown."

"Thank you," I mustered, listening for any voices outside the bathroom door. "Why didn't you show sooner?"

"I've been with you every day, but I never wanted to intrude on how you lived your life. I just wanted to watch the world through your eyes until I could understand why you stood out to me that day. I've whispered to you from time to time … from wherever in your subconscious you've kept me … mostly when you were asleep at night. Just little sprinkles of encouragement. Sometimes you needed it. You just thought they were good dreams. I was just what I'd hoped to be, a guardian angel."

"But that was a lie."

"Not at all. I just spoke to you in terms of what you could understand at that age."

"You knew I'd end up here."

"No, but I knew I wanted to be with you. I touched you and I felt Lynette, your gift … I felt home. I didn't know what exactly that meant but I knew I wanted to watch you grow. I'd seen so, so many people there over such a long amount of time. I watched the world change. But then I saw you, and everything stood still. You sparkled the same way she did."

"Wow."

"And I didn't scare you. Not one bit."

I shook my head.

"Why did you turn a blind eye to your gift for so long?"

I inhaled deeply, the scent of apple cinnamon air freshener filled my nostrils. "Not everyone who came to me was as approachable and warm as you. I … didn't know what to do with it. I still don't. I'm just … confused."

"That just means you're learning."

"I feel lost."

"You're not lost, you're still finding your purpose. You underestimate yourself."

"This is more than just a self-esteem issue."

"With *that*, we can both agree."

"I don't think I can handle the responsibility this 'gift' puts on me."

"I think you've taught yourself to expect the worst from the challenges life presents to you. You're more than capable."

I dropped both arms to my sides, "Did you do it all on purpose? The visions? Or was I just tapping into you?"

"I wish I could've explained it all to you like this, but the telephone lines were down until now. It was never my intention to pain you, but I had to push outward a bit and show you the important parts. I needed to help you to understand how we got here with what energy I had."

"I'm sorry." I exhaled deeply, trying to gather my thoughts.

"Don't you apologize to me." She paused, "We've both experienced a whole lot of hurt. It's time to make things right. You deserve your peace."

"So do you." I wiped a tear that had escaped quickly down past the bags under my eyes.

"I just want to start over. I just want a new life here."

"Oh no, no. Not a whole new life, Emma. Same book, new chapter."

I nodded.

"Well," she patted the sides of her skirt and perked up.

"How do we get rid of him?" I swallowed hard.

"It's simple, Emma. He wants me," Gwen asked.

"And?"

"Then *that* is what we'll give him," her plump lips curled up delicately.

"No."

"Yes."

"No. I don't know how to get you out. I don't even know how I got you *in*. And even if I did, I wouldn't hand you over to him like … He—"

"I meant it about being your angel, so please let me."

"Not like that."

"Let him have *Gwen*. Just give it some thought, please. I have to go now."

"*No,*" I snapped.

"Wake up, Emma."She grinned subtly, but her eyebrows drooped and her gaze fell to the floor as she knocked on the inside of the mirror.

"No, I can't do that," I argued.

"Emma," Gwen knocked on the mirror harder, her bright blue eyes shooting up to glue themselves to mine. "*Emma!*" she shouted at me and pounded on the glass repeatedly, all the while keeping her face soft, her eyes piercing, and the rest of her body completely still.

"*Emma!*" Joel knocked on the bathroom door relentlessly.

My head shot up and my eyes opened, again. I stretched out my arm from its bent position under my head. Forearms didn't make very comfortable make-shift pillows. The toilet tank provided cool, hard back support as I blinked aggressively. The blur in my eyes wouldn't go away, so I rubbed them with my fist.

I looked up to see Willow appear in front of me, looming over and gazing down. Her deep maroon hair hung in her face a little. "You can have your space, but you need to tell him if you plan on disappearing for an hour." She leaned over and unlocked the bathroom door, then disappeared.

"Emma, you okay?! *Answer* me, please!" Joel's voice cracked from the other side of the door.

I stood up and rushed to the door, glancing at my *own* tired reflection in the mirror before grabbing the doorknob and flinging it open. Joel almost fell forward into the room, and me.

"I'm sorry, I'm sorry. I fell asleep." I yawned and scratched my head.

"*Jesus*, Em. I thought you'd gone and hurt yourself again. You can't just lock yourself in there and not at least text! I mean— I'm sorry for being so worked up about it but you freaked me out so much I almost called—"

I lunged forward and hugged him, wrapping my arms tightly around his abdomen. He smelled like ginger and patchouli. "I'm sorry."

He took a deep, deep breath. "I forgive you."

"I won't do it again."

"Thank you. I was really worried." he whispered, holding the back of my head.

"I talked to her," I muffled into his shirt.

"What?"

"Gwen." I looked up at him. "I talked to her."

He jerked back and held my shoulders. His deep green eyes stared into mine. *"Really?"*

I nodded. "She wants to help us. I just don't understand the last thing she said to me."

"What did she say?" His eyebrows raised quickly.

"She told me that if he wants her, we should just give him what he wants."

"It was through a dream?"

"Yeah, I guess technically but" —I cleared my throat and itched my nose— "I know it was her."

"Why would she say that? She wouldn't want that, right?"

"I don't know. That's why I don't understand. I wanted more explanation but then I heard you pounding on the door and she was gone."

"You're sure it was actually her?"

"Positive."

"Okay." He sighed in disappointment. "Well, let's get you some rest and then we'll think about it some more, okay? Want some hot chocolate?"

"Sure." I smiled shyly and sniffled.

"Kay. I'll get that started for you. Let's just … try not to worry tonight. Let's forget for a bit, maybe watch a movie. Whatever you want." He patted my shoulder lightly and turned to head to the kitchen.

I went to the couch to resume my new default position—burrito-ed under the biggest, coziest blanket available with only my head exposed; my feet were not simply under the blanket but the blanket was tucked tightly around and under them for maximum comfort. I grabbed the remote and searched my options for our evening distraction.

"Hey, Em?" Joel piped up from behind the compact kitchen counter.

"Yeah?"

"I love you." The words flowed out of his mouth as smoothly as whipped cream melting into my coffee.

My eyes widened at the tv. I was expecting him to ask whether I wanted a bunch of mini marshmallows or one jumbo marshmallow on top of my cocoa. I blinked and took a deep breath to soothe the sharp ping in my chest. Then, as simply as he'd spoken to me, I replied, "Love you, too."

We didn't say much the rest of the night. For just a little while during the mindless comedy we picked, everything felt like it was going to be okay, maybe even normal. Nothing was even near that in reality, but there was a glimmer of hope that it could be … eventually.

***

Tick, tick, tick, tick…

The clock in the living room quietly sounded in the background as I read a hardcover novel on a firm red-orange, velvety upholstered art deco sofa. The front door behind me opened slowly and creaked closed.

"Hello?" I sang, uncrossing my legs and peering back into the foyer from the family room.

"I meant to sneak up on you." A familiar deep voice chuckled as he hung his coat by the front door. "Is your father home?"

I felt warmth in my cheeks. "No, he's gone to work."

"Perfect." The man snickered, stopping to stand in front of me. As I closed my book, he caressed the underside of my chin and lifted it up to look at him.

Carlson's smug smile shone on his freshly shaven face, his hair parted on the side and slicked back with a shiny gel. His blue eyes looked me up and down like I was a steak dinner. He wore brown tweed trousers with a white button-up tucked into them. I should've been furious, yet I found myself uncontrollably delighted by his presence.

"You missed breakfast. You didn't tell me you were leaving so early this morning."

"Where's Lynette?"

"Upstairs playing," I responded lightly. "Why?"

"Stand up." He ordered, squeezing my chin before letting go to grab my hand.

"Well, since you asked nicely," I joked dryly, shaking my head and slowly rising from my place on the couch.

"Look at that dress," he purred.

"Oh, do you like it?" I patted the skirt down softly. "I picked it out the other day for the book club meeting Sunday night. I don't wear much of *this* color, but I figured I'd try it—"

"I wish you'd wear more red, but the purple will do."

"It's lavender."

"Well whatever color it is, I don't want you wearing it out. Why would you want all the men in town drooling over you?" His eyes pierced into mine.

"Ah … Well, it's only the walk to Judy Dornan's. I doubt I'll be snatched up, not with Nancy beside me. They'd much rather take her up first."

"Don't be silly." He stepped closer, grabbing me around the waist with a strong arm.

"Jack," Gwendolyn giggled.

"Say my name again," he whispered in my ear.

"I see you're feeling frisky today." She shook her head, "You'd better not be, Lynette could come bouncing downstairs at any moment."

He glanced at the staircase behind us. "Let her see it," he growled passionately.

Gwen gasped and whacked Carlson's shoulder lightly with her book. "Jack *Carlson*! Don't be so brazen." She scoffed.

He gripped her waist harder. "You like it."

Gwen chuckled, looking down at the ground. "Not when it involves *her*, I don't," she spat quietly, gripping the book in her hand. Then she cleared her throat and reached up to pat his cheek, "I'm sorry. I'm going out to work in the garden for a bit."

"I want you." Carlson gazed into her eyes.

"Well" —she swallowed— "so do my petunias."

"You tease." His brows furrowed.

"I do not. I just know that—"

"You know I hate it when you play hard to get. I'll have you whenever I want," he said in a deep hushed tone. "Right now. I can make it quick." He nudged his head behind them toward the bathroom beside the top of steps to the back patio.

"Lyn—" She sighed before being interrupted.

"I don't care."

"Well I *do*, Jack," she whispered as she flattened her skirt shakily. The fabric was crisp and new. "She's wide awake right now. Can't you wait until tonight? Honestly."

He reached out to grab her forearm. "*No*," he growled.

Gwen jerked her arm away right as she felt his grip start to tighten. "Well you're going to have to." She huffed and turned away to go upstairs. "In fact, I'll check on her now. I've got to change, anyway."

He took her hand before she could make it far enough away from him. "*Gwendolyn*. It's not my fault you make me feel … so weak I could melt into the floorboards." His eyes glared lustfully into hers, then moved down to her waist.

She inhaled deeply as she turned around to face him.

"You seem distant lately. I don't like it one bit." He tilted his head.

"I'm not. I just want to go outside. The weather's nice."

"You've been reading a lot, too."

"Well I can assure you the books haven't made any advances towards me."

"Going out more."

"Am I not allowed to have friends?"

"This club is taking up more of your time."

"It's once a week."

"I can't lose you."

"You aren't." She took a step backward.

"I just won't, Gwen."

"I *just* … want to go … outside, Jack."

"Don't keep me waiting."

With a sigh, Gwen let go of his hand. "Mind your temper," she whispered.

As Gwen walked up the first few steps, Carlson quickly added, "When is the book club?"

Gwen stopped. "Nine o'clock this week."

"That's late for a women's book club."

She ground her teeth. "Judy won't be getting into town until evening and Astrid isn't able to attend if we were to move it to Saturday. Is that a problem?"

He took a couple steps closer into the foyer. "How long do you suppose you'll be out?"

"Couple hours. We're having dinner for Astrid's birthday, and then some coffee with those little tea cakes."

"Cake?"

"Yes," she replied. The usual."

"You know, if you keep attending these book clubs they'll start to look more like dessert clubs on you ladies."

Gwen paused before she spoke. "My father will be out of town for conference until later that night. Are you able to watch Lynette while I'm gone?"

"Of course."

"Good." She nodded once and continued up the stairs, feeling Carlson's eyes on her with each step, "And I'm still wearing this dress to book club."

"Don't forget who put that *ring* on your finger, Gwen."

***

I woke up, gently slapping my face to get the image of a seductive Carlson out of my head. Although it was gross enough to cause me even more nightmares, it was one of the first dreams that didn't jolt me awake, but left me itchy. Luckily, Joel was asleep next to me. I'd fallen asleep during the movie but I knew he was still awake when that happened, so he must've fallen asleep out there to stay with me. Maybe he wouldn't even deny it, and I didn't think I wanted him to.

I didn't bother to wake him. He deserved rest just as much as I did, if not more. He'd been taking care of me when he'd experienced just as much emotional turmoil as I had. Most of the time, I'd been so deep in my own head that I hadn't stopped to realize all he'd been doing for me. Joel sleeping out there— sitting upright and sharing space when he could be in his own full size bed— spoke volumes.

I grabbed a notebook from Joel's shelf; he had several empty. I didn't think he'd notice if one basic college-ruled one went missing. I jotted down as many details as I could from the dream. Was it something that was said? Was it something in the room? Was it just the dynamic of their relationship? There had to be a reason for that dream. It was clear that he was possessive and twisted; nothing was groundbreaking on that front. But maybe it was the fact that he mentioned to Gwen that she *was* his weakness. What was I supposed to do with that? I wasn't letting him have her back, even if I knew how to give her away. I didn't need more details about anything. All I needed was a way to get rid of him on my own.

After purging all of the details I could remember onto the paper, I went back into the bathroom quietly to try and summon Gwendolyn back into the mirror— this time while I was awake. Nothing came of it but a headache from staring into my own eyes in the dark like a creep.

Discouraged and endlessly exhausted, I went back to our home-base couch and covered myself with the blanket again, brushing Joel's foot on accident. I felt the temptation to curl up next to him for a depressed hug, but didn't want to bug him. Instead, I stared up at the ceiling of the old house-turned duplex, studying the small cracks here and there until my consciousness started to drift. The moment my eyes closed, a voice in my ear jolted them open again.

"I told you you guys were a thing."

"Jesus," I snapped in a hushed tome, expecting to see Willow standing behind the couch when I sat up, but there was no one there.

I tried to close my eyes once more, and felt a light pat on the top of my head, "I miss Beach Brew. Let's go tomorrow. Goodnight," my dead best friend whispered.

35.

DRIVE SAFE

John Lennon played overhead as we sat quietly with our coffees.

We'd taken Willow's advice that day, although we didn't know exactly what to talk about. Joel looked out the window toward the dock at a few elderly carolers in Victorian garb practicing their songs. I glanced away from the group and took in all of the holiday decorations around the cafe. We'd been so lost in self-exile— except for work— that we'd forgotten Christmas was only a few days away.

"Ugh." I scoffed, looking at the little fake Christmas tree near the entrance.

"What?" Joel asked, moving his attention to me.

"I haven't gotten you a Christmas gift yet." I bit the inside of my cheek.

He chuckled.

"What?" I took a sip of my gingerbread latte.

"You're really worrying about *that* right now?" He shook his head. "Having you here and alive is enough."

"I know, but" —I swallowed hard, feeling butterflies in my stomach— "you've done so much for me ... you've stayed my friend and supported me through everything."

"I don't think that's something I need to be rewarded for." He raised a brow.

"Well, are you getting *me* something?"

"Of course I am."

"Then—"

"I don't need anything, Em."

"That's not fair."

"This is a stupid argument." He rolled his eyes playfully and took a sip of his coffee.

"No, I just—"

"Aw, your first fight," Willow chimed in, appearing in what used to be her usual seat between us. "So cute."

"No," Joel and I said in unison, staring into each other's eyes.

"I feel tension here … of the sexual sort."

"Shut up, Wills," Joel muttered, returning his gaze out the window.

I simply glared at her.

"Looks nice in here." She nodded. "Toasty. I don't remember them having this many decorations up last year."

"Can you even feel anything?" I wondered.

"I can feel the holiday spirit," she sang in a fake dazzled tone. "*No*, I can't. But it looks toasty. Can I at least pretend for a second? Damn."

"Sorry," I grumbled, looking down at the lid of my coffee.

"Where's your aunt?" Willow glimpsed around the place, "I miss her."

"She's not here today."

"Damn. You gonna go to that book signing Saturday?"

"Huh? Oh. Uhhh, I hadn't thought about it. How do you know about it?"

She cackled. "The same way I know that you guys said you love each other last night." She winked at me.

Neither of us reacted.

"Didn't know I wasn't allowed to be excited for you guys."

"There's nothing to be excited about. Hasn't been in months," I whispered.

"I watch over you guys more often than you know, okay? Despite popular belief, I'm not *always* asserting myself into your conversations, so don't give me such an attitude … *Anyway*, I think you should go, Em. It'd be good for you. I love Salem."

"I'm already going … for Liv."

"Good." She stiffly nodded once.

"So, Gwen gave you another vision last night? I saw the notebook after you fell asleep." Willow changed the subject quickly.

"Yeah." I looked at Joel. "I can't figure out what to make of it — like— what her reason was for showing me that particular memory. She told me she uses her energy to project specific things to me. But I can't figure out how to draw her forward again to ask."

Willow stared across the coffee shop. "Maybe nothing. Maybe she just wants you to see it."

"Yeah … but no." I shook my head. "She told me last night that we should give Carlson what he wants, and he wants Gwen. There must've been a reason."

"What if" —Joel piped in— "she's fine being stuck with him as long as she can be with Lynette again?"

"Are you kidding? No. I'm not letting that happen. I'm not letting them exist their entire *afterlife* with *him*," I snapped. "And I'm not staying in the house if he's in it, whether he gets what he wants and leaves me alone or not. He's a predator … and a killer."

"Oh yeah. Forgot about that." The sarcasm in her voice was clear as her favorite quartz crystal.

"I understand, Em," Joel reassured me. "I'm not suggesting we let that happen. I'm just saying that might be her reasoning."

"I don't care. She deserves better … Gwen, you deserve better," I repeated to myself. "I know she can hear me."

"Kay," Willow said. "Hear me out…"

"What?" Joel and I spoke in unison yet again. To an onlooker, we may have looked insane having this conversation.

"Look, we tried burning him. We burned the box. We may need outside help for this one. From someone who *won't* judge you guys." She raised her brows.

"Huh?" Joel sneered.

"Joel, come on. You've seen my room."

"What about it?" He glimpsed between the two of us.

"Emmaaaa," Willow stretched my name. "Why do you think I want you to go to Salem so bad?"

"Because I need to leave my bubble."

"Well yeah, that too, but…"

"Oh." Joel yawned.

"What?" I looked to him with my jaw jutting forward.

"Willow was into some spiritual stuff."

"Um. Still am, thanks," she replied quickly.

"Remember that other book I was holding the day we met, Em?"

"No." I squinted.

"That's disappointing."

"It was on herbal healing."

It took me a second, but I did remember vaguely. To my surprise, I busted up laughing for the first time since Willow had died.

Joel shrugged at her.

I tried to contain myself. "Halloween was two months ago, Willow."

"I have a friend," Willow said confidently.

"You're *joking*," I slapped the table.

"I'm not, though." Willow's pale face was stone. "I'm dead serious."

"No, Wills, you're kidding. me. Come on. I mean, I'm all for people being into that stuff for visualization and positive thinking but … that's not gonna do *shit* to help this situation."

"I get you, Em. I do. But let's not discredit her. I've seen some shit from her practices."

"Just trust me," Willow stared into my eyes.

"No, this is too much. How is this real life? First ghosts … Now you're saying we need the help from a——"

***

"Hi." I approached an employee at the same bookstore Liv's signing was at. "Sorry to bother you, but I'm looking for a…" I hesitated. "Zuli."

The young employee turned away from the shelf she was looking at to gape at me. "Who's asking?"

"Um, my name's Emma. I'm a friend of Willow's."

"Willow?"

"Yeah, Willow Graham," I said her full name, a twinge of sadness hitting my gut.

"Mm." The woman nodded. The long raven-black curls on the half of her head that wasn't buzzed bounced. "My condolences. I was deeply pained to hear about her passing." Her royal blue lipstick was applied flawlessly.

"Who'd you hear it from?" I asked.

"I'm Zuli." She held her hands together in what looked like a prayer, and bowed her head to me. "Very nice to meet you. Willow was an old friend of mine. We had a lot of nice conversations but it's been *so* long." She smiled sympathetically. "What brings you to Bishop's?"

"Well, my aunt's here for a signing." I pointed over to the table at the front of the shop. "But I was more specifically looking for you," I explained.

"What divine intervention." She gazed sweetly at Liv, setting up piles of books on a small fold-out table. "Hm," she hummed softly.

"Yeah, I guess." I nodded. "Anyway, this might sound crazy but—"

"Nothing sounds crazy to me, love."

Bells chimed as a customer walked in. Zuli didn't address them. Instead she kept her gaze fixed on me. "Go on."

I sighed, and whispered, "My friend Joel and I—"

"Oh yes, Joel. She mentioned him a lot."

I stared at a shelf of science fiction books. "Yeah." I gathered my thoughts. "Uh, we need help. I need help. I—"

"Emma, I don't mean to interrupt. But why don't we go chat somewhere a little more … private?" Zuli suggested, turning to walk down the aisle toward the back of the shop, and behind a curtain of sparkly black beads. I followed her into a smaller room of first editions and rare books locked behind a single glass case. The old light in the room flickered.

"Am I allowed to be back here?"

"Yes, don't be silly." She chuckled. "It's just that no one cares to venture all the way back here most of the time. We just need to keep our voices down. The owner is very protective of this space. Likes it quiet in this room." She put a finger over her lips and winked.

"Oh, okay."

"So … continue." She adjusted the name badge on her brown leather vest that gave Stevie Nicks vibes. "How can *I* … help *you*?"

"Okay. I know you're a" —I leaned in closer toward her— "witch," I whispered.

She giggled. "Yes? So are half the people in Salem. It's no secret. You don't need to whisper about it like you're plotting a murder." She grinned adoringly.

"Well, I live in … a haunted … home."

"Mhm."

"And one of the spirits is a really sweet little girl, but the other is— well— fuckin' evil. Willow told me to ask you for your best … banishing spell."

"Willow did? When?" She looked surprised.

Shit. "Before she died," I answered quickly.

"No need to lie, Emma." She sat down in a black velvet chair. "I see them, too. I can feel it in people. Sensitives stick together." She winked.

"Oh." I took a deep breath, trying to move onto my point. "Well, okay then. She told me about you a couple days ago. This man … we tried burning his remains, we tried burning the belongings that he left in the basement. But we can't get rid of him." An odd trust in Zuli settled in. "Long story short, he had something to do with Willow's death, and then he assaulted me in the shower, and he's threatening to hurt more people I love if I don't give him what he wants, which is his ex … who he thinks *I* am but I'm not and—"

"Ah." She gazed down, seemingly unfazed by everything I had just spewed at her. She twirled her evil-eye necklace between her fingers, "That's fine, Emma. Save your energy. I don't need the whole story. But that *does* sound very unpleasant."

"To say the least," I muttered.

"I can give you a banishing spell. But I can't promise you it'll work."

"Why bother then?"

"Because it could work."

"What makes the difference then?"

"You," she said simply.

"Can you come help us? Maybe it'd work better if you did it yourself."

She cringed and looked away to a shelf containing two old first editions, *The Wizard of Oz*, and *Carrie*. "I would but I have an extremely busy schedule that keeps me tied to the store pretty much 24/7."

"Okay, well then I'll take the spell, I guess."

"Do you have any practice grounding and setting protection for yourself?"

"Uh, no," I answered. "But I can learn."

"I have no doubt you could, but a spirit like him is dangerous, especially if you're threatening real banishment on him."

"I don't have a choice."

"Well…" she turned to a cabinet and tried the handle. It was locked with a key, but she opened it with three simple knocks.

"Banishment to where, though?"

"Well, not here."

I pursed my lips as she rifled through some papers and journals. She finally found and pulled out a small leather bound notebook with a pentagram on it. "This was mine. Page 57 is where you'll find my notes for the ritual."

"*Ritual?*"

"Mhm." She held out the notebook, gesturing for me to take it. "It's just a word. Brushing our teeth and blowing out birthday candles are both ritual but we don't all panic about *that*, do we?"

"Don't you need this?"

"No … I have other others. I have no use for this one anymore."

"Wow, thank you."

"I'm assuming Willow is going to help you?"

"I mean— as much as she can." I shrugged.

"Good. You won't be alone."

"No, but … I have a question," I started. "Would burning the remains have ever worked? Or was he just too strong willed?"

"Yes, and no. Spirits are just as different as the living. What works for some won't work for others. And yours … of course wouldn't give you an easy time if he's just as territorial in death as he was in life, if not more so. He's probably attached to a lot of things here. And doesn't plan on leaving any of it."

"Makes sense."

"He seems strong, but you seem stronger." She winked.

"Thank you." I gripped the book. "I didn't know witches were a real thing."

"Oh yeah. Very real."

"Is it like … a new-age thing, or…"

"We've always been around."

"So are you, like … born one?"

She chuckled. "Witches aren't born. They birth themselves."

"Interesting."

"Very." She studied me. "Always take the left-hand path if you're lucky enough to run into a fork in the road."

I nodded. "I'll remember that."

Zuli gestured behind me to the beaded doorway. "Shall we?"

"There's nothing else you can recommend to help?"

"No. It's all you from here," she explained.

I rolled my eyes and walked out of the back room.

"Don't go into it as if you've already failed, Emma. Read what I wrote. Not just the one page, but take a look at the whole notebook. At least read what I wrote on grounding and protecting yourself."

"Can you just tell me?"

"No, we don't have time for that today. The signing's about to start. You'd better go join your aunt. She'd probably appreciate your help."

"Okay," I agreed as Zuli followed me down the aisle.

"Good luck, Emma. Come back and let me know how it went. I'll be here," she stopped in her tracks. I turned around just in time to see her smile and whisper, "Blessed be." She turned and headed around the corner of the left shelf. I watched as she emerged up some stairs that had a sign next to them: *EMPLOYEES ONLY.*

With that, I took one deep breath and returned to Aunt Liv at her signing table. In front of it sat about two dozen chairs filled with eager customers. How they fit that many people in such a cozy little shop, I didn't understand. Witchcraft.

I sat beside my aunt as everyone hushed up and looked to a sophisticated middle-aged woman who had *really* curly black hair— curlier than Zuli's— and big round glasses standing next to Liv with a hand on her shoulder.

"Welcome, beloved patrons of Bishop's Books. If we haven't already met, my name is Enid Bishop, and I am, as you can guess, the owner of this magical little nook. We are delighted to welcome a very talented author today, Olivia Cain. She's here today to grace us with a passage reading of her most recent book, *Hidden Spirits of Salem*, which beautifully captures the haunted history of some of Salem's most famous haunts, of course, but focuses primarily on the lesser known shops— one of which is our very own." Enid's eyes widened with excitement. "*But* before we begin this morning, I wanted to say a quick word to you all, but mainly to you, Olivia. My daughter … *adored* your books. She loved all things spooky, which would come as no surprise to those of you here who knew her. She was very much a Salem girl, and quite the fan. She would have been incredibly excited to meet you, and if she's watching over us today, I'm sure she's very pleased to have you in our shop. To my little Lauren Lazuli." She held onto her necklace.

I quickly cocked my head up at Enid and darted my eyes back toward the area I saw Zuli last. Above the shop, and behind the railing of the loft upstairs, I caught her eyes.

She stood with her hands gracefully resting on the old oak banister. Hey eyes almost glowed neon blue in the light of the warm wall sconces around the store and the dim light of the overcast day coming through the windows. She simply winked, waved, and backed up further into the loft full of books and boxes, vanishing beyond my sight.

"What's up, honey? You okay?" Liv patted the top of my thigh.

I turned back to face her, "Yeah, fine" —I whispered— "just really sad."

Enid must have heard me, as she gazed down at me and nodded, "Yes, it is. She was taken from us much too soon," she whispered as she trailed off, clearing her throat. "You are *so* very lucky to have your child with you today, Olivia." She smiled warmly. "Zuli was a light. A very strong soul. I'm sure she is exactly where she wants to be now. So … don't let me bring this event down! Let us be joyous and dedicate this day to her, *and* the furthered success of your career! If I don't get a chance to speak with you today, everyone, *please* … drive home safe."

***

Before we left the signing that day, I approached the graceful owner behind the cash register.

"Mrs. Bishop?"

"*Please*, dear. Call me Enid," she said before looking up from her notebook. "Ah, Emma. How can I help you? Will you be leaving soon?"

"Yeah." I nodded. "I just wanted to say I saw the photos of Zuli on the wall up front. She was beautiful."

She chuckled sadly. "Thank you. You're too kind, and quite beautiful yourself. I had no idea Olivia was your aunt. You look almost identical."

"Thanks. We get that a lot."

"Of course."

I tried to think of something else to say, "May I ask how long ago she passed?"

"Just three weeks ago."

"Oh my God, I'm— I'm so sorry."

"Don't be. We don't end when we end here. She firmly believed that."

"I agree." I nodded, feeling the side of my bag to make sure the leather-bound was still in there.

"Please let me know if you two need any help packing up."

"Will do. Thank you for hosting her. You have a wonderful shop."

"You have a wonderful aura. Be mindful not to let anyone dull it," she responded.

"I'll try." As I walked away to help Aunt Liv pack up the last of the books she didn't sell, something compelled me to stop and turn

310

back to Enid. "I think Zuli would've wanted to stay here. I think this is exactly where she is."

Her head shot up at me. She put her hand to her cheek and blushed, but she didn't respond; she didn't need to. She nodded softly, the one tear that trickled down past the frame of her glasses to meet the small smile on her lips was enough to know that I may have helped someone find a small fragment of peace.

"Merry Christmas, Enid."

"Drive safe, Emma," I heard her say under her breath as I walked away.

36.

GIFTS

Christmas Eve came within the blink of an eye and seemingly without warning. It just seemed to show up at the end of the blur that was December. It was snowing softly outside on the street through the window of Joel's living room. We had a fireplace ambiance video playing on the tv; only the downstairs tenants got the *real* fireplace, which provided us the warmth upstairs without the cozy comforting glow of the flames.

We sat on the couch sipping gingerbread coffee under thick plush blankets, staring at our tiny fake tabletop Christmas tree. Neither of us had had the energy to go pick out, transport, and decorate a full size one. It was cute, though. We'd found mini ornaments along with a mini tree skirt and a strand of gold beads at Walmart for cheap and threw them on it. That was as festive as we were gonna get.

"Hey." Joel cleared his throat after a sip, gazing down at the two small gifts next to our tree on the coffee table. They'd barely fit on the skirt. There was one from Joel to me— as he'd promised, of course— and one from me to Joel. I'd spent the day before strolling downtown searching for a gift to bring him. There was no way I was going empty handed when he'd given me such a sweet birthday gift. I'd expected my Christmas gift to be just as heart-warming, after all we'd gone through in just two months.

"Yeah." I leaned back further into the couch.

"I see gifts." He nudged his head in the direction of the tree.

"I see dead people. What about it?"

"Wanna open 'em tonight?" He suggested with a wink.

"That's cheating." I scoffed.

"Nuh-uh. We need some kind of excitement, *right* now. And we're both leaving early in the morning, so…" He readjusted on the couch to sit up a little straighter. "Come on."

He was right. We needed something fun to do other than watching movies, and I was going to be at my aunt and uncle's house the next day while he spent the holiday at his parents. "Okay, fine. But you open *mine* first because I don't want to open an awesome gift from you and then have you disappointed with yours."

His eyes narrowed. "You've got yourself a deal, Reilly."

With that, he leaned forward and playfully snatched the small rectangular box wrapped in royal blue shimmery paper off the table. He gave it a light shake.

"Shit. You just broke it," I joked dryly.

He raised a brow. "Hm, what disappointment awaits me in this box?" He carefully unwrapped the folded and taped sides as he made goofy faces at me. "Kudos to you for actually wrapping, by the way. I'm impressed by the lack of gift bags I see here."

"Bags are for lazy people. I wrap *everything*. My mom didn't train me to be a loser gift-giver." I chuckled, briefly but fondly looking back to a memory of my mom and I wrapping all of our family and friends' gifts together in front of our tree. Back then, we'd have to pack all of Liv and Ken's gifts in a big box and take it to the post office to pay an astronomical amount of money to ship it. We'd get dinner afterward in Mullein Creek's old downtown area. It was *very* different from downtown Newport, but no better or worse— that'd be comparing apples to oranges; gold-rush old was very different from colonial old.

"She did *not*." He nodded and flashed me a smile before darting his attention back to unwrapping the gift. Under the paper was a basic white gift box that he popped open. He moved aside the tissue paper, and once he caught a glimpse of the actual gift, he pursed his lips and took a deep breath. "Emma."

He pulled out the small figurine of a willow tree made from golden wire and crystal chips. I'd found it in a small metaphysical shop down Thames Street toward the very end of the shopping strip. It was the only one there, and shimmered in the warm dim light.

"It's citrine?" Joel asked for confirmation.

"Yeah. How'd you know?"

He tucked his chin into his neck and raised both brows, "Willow had a *crap* ton of crystals. She still does … in a box in her closet. They let me keep 'em because I liked them, too. I just tucked them all away after she … I'm not a fanatic like she was, but…"

"Oh," I said softly. "Well, you probably know, then. Citrine is supposed to help with finding joy and clarity. At least that is what the little card next to it said. Um, I figured that Willow would want us to find both of those things."

"Yeah, you're right. I wonder where she is."

"Probably eavesdropping." I sniffled and itched my nose.

"Probably," he snickered. "It's perfect, Em. I love it." He placed his hand on my knee over the blankets and, in silence for a second, his rich green eyes met mine completely.

"I'm glad." We smiled empathetically at each other.

"Your turn," he piped back up, quickly lifting his hand off of my leg as he grabbed the other gift from the table. "This time I don't think I'll be able to follow *your* gift."

"Uh-oh. I don't think I even want it then," I whined jokingly, taking the gift from his hand. I opened the tiny red box to find a dark-wood engraved circle and three rose gold angel wing charms attached to a rose gold keyring. I held it in my hand and read the engraving in my head: *You are never alone.* "Wow."

"Each angel wing is one of us— me, you, and Wills. *Or* … it could be Wills, your mom, and like, Lynette … or your dad. I don't know. Whoever you want it to be."

"I want it to be us," my voice cracked. I coughed to disguise my emotion as my cold. "It *is* … us."

"You're not alone. You may feel like it. But I'm still here, and so is Wills … kinda."

"Kinda," I repeated, gazing down at the keychain and holding it tightly in my hand. "Hey."

"Yeah?"

"What was the story Willow mentioned the night we burned Carlson? She never told me."

"About what?"

"About why we don't let you near fire."

"Oh…" He shook his head. "It's so stupid. She was burning shit in a cauldron once—"

"A *cauldron*?"

"Yeah, a mini one. It's in her closet."

"Hm. Okay." I yawned. "Go on."

"It's *actually* nothing. She was burning her herbs or whatever on the coffee table and I scooted by to sit on the couch and the— my — the butt of my pants caught the flame for a second because I brushed too close to it."

"Oh crap."

"It was small, and we put it out quick. But you know her … She has to go and make everything dramatic. She would've given you a way more exciting version of that story. It was her fault, anyway … doing that on such a small table…"

"Your butt was on fire, dude."

"You *could* say I had a hot ass," Joel chuckled.

"Oh my god, stop!" I whacked his shoulder jokingly.

"What? It's true." He smiled brightly after he noticing that I was.

We laughed together for a minute and then settled back down into quiet calm.

"You know, it's weird." Joel exhaled.

"What?"

"We met— when? June?"

"July."

"And it feels like I've known you for years."

"Yep. Trauma and being a freak will do that to people, I guess." I took a sip. I noticed that my whipped cream had melted. "Boo," I moaned in disappointment.

Joel looked down at the mug. "I'll go get you more. Emma, I'm serious. I'm so glad we met."

"Willow said everything that happens is meant to happen and always was."

"Well, she did know *everything* so that must be true."

"I mean, it's encouraging … in a way, right?" I spoke hesitantly.

"Is it?"

"I don't know. Yeah. Knowing that you can't control everything takes the pressure off a little, right? That's how I'm trying to force myself to see it. Otherwise—"

"We'll just keep blaming ourselves," he whispered.

"Yeah," I nodded, listening to the fake fireplace crackling.

"You shouldn't force anything. It's okay to feel the negative emotions. Normal, healthy, even. Just as healthy as feeling the positive ones." Joel leaned his head into my shoulder. "Thank you for my gift."

"Thank *you*," I responded.

The fireplace continued on in the background while we held onto our gifts and laid together silently under the blankets. We finished our coffees, and set them down on the coffee table with the empty gift boxes and balled up wrapping paper. Our little Christmas tree glimmered and reflected small sparks of light with the movement of the flames on the screen.

"Em?"

"Yeah?"

Before he stood up and took my mug for me, Joel studied my face intently and said, "It's … okay … to feel the good feelings, too. We shouldn't feel guilty about that, either."

***

On Christmas morning, Joel and I got ready to go our separate ways for the day. We met in the living room with the gifts for our families piled in a large reusable bag. Outside the window it was sunny, but the snow remained piled up on the sidewalks, bushes, and curbs outside.

"Hey, you ready?" Joel walked into the living room, throwing his thick, plaid, maroon jacket on.

"Yup." I zipped up my coat and threw a scarf lazily around my neck.

"Right-o." He clicked his tongue. "Thanks for dropping me off this morning. You sure you won't be late?"

"No, I won't." I chuckled. "They live like fifteen minutes away and they aren't eating until, like, two anyway."

"Cool." He nodded and adjusted his hood.

I licked my bottom lip as I zoned out on him, but turned away quickly once he looked up at me.

"You good?" he asked.

"Yep." I cleared my throat.

We locked up with our thousand layers on, and Joel carried the bag of gifts to the trunk of the car. I got in the driver's seat to turn the heat on and felt the car jolt as he slammed the back shut. He bolted to the passenger door and sat down quickly, rubbing his hands together. "Let's go!" He smiled excitedly. I wished I could've felt as joyous as he seemed that day. Why *was* he suddenly so chipper? Could it have been because of our exchange the night before?

A few minutes later, we pulled up onto the driveway of Joel's parents'. I put the car in park but kept it running.

"Have a nice time." I looked down at the steering wheel. Part of me wished we could've stayed together that day. I'd become dependent on him, and wondered if the feeling was mutual.

"You too, Em." He hesitated to unbuckle his seat belt.

"Do you need help grabbing your gifts out?"

"No, I got it. You stay here in the warmth," he responded promptly.

"Okay."

We both sat in the car for a moment with Christmas music playing quietly on the radio. He shifted and put his hand over the button to undo his belt. "Try to enjoy this day with them, okay? Don't think about the house, don't think about the people in it. Think about family, and think about us."

"I'll try," I reassured him. I wondered what "us" meant, but didn't have the courage to ask.

"I'll see you tonight."

"Want me to pick you up?" I hadn't considered how he'd get home.

'No don't worry about me. I'll get a ride from my dad. I'll be back by the time you are."

"Kay." I nodded once and gripped the gear selector.

"Let me know when you get to your aunt's."

"I will, but I have to do an errand first."

He cracked up. "What errand? What place is open for errands on Christmas."

I shrugged.

His smile faded, "What errand?"

"Don't worry about it."

"I can't stop you … but please, *please* be safe. Text me when you're done with your 'errand'."

"Okay, I will." I looked away from him as I answered.

"Em?"

"Yeah?"

"Text me all day, actually. I'll reply every time." He undid his seatbelt and opened the passenger door. The car whirred. He got out and stood in the same place for a moment. I popped the trunk and expected him to go straight to the back because of how cold it was. Instead, he bent over and popped his head and torso back into the car. He looked at me for a second.

"What?" I furrowed my brows inquisitively.

"Nothin," he replied.

"Okay." I chuckled anxiously and turned to look out the windshield. The second I did, I felt a warm soft pressure against my right cheek. My heart leapt into my throat and I straightened my back against the seat.

"Merry Christmas, Em." Joel smiled shyly and stood back up quickly, closing the car door. As he rifled through the bag of presents in the trunk, I stared wide-eyed out the windshield, watching the exhaust clouds flow by around the car. I felt the trunk slam shut again, and Joel's light knock with his fist against my window. He waved to me with a warm grin and hurried up the steps of his porch.

It wasn't until a couple minutes after he'd disappeared inside his family's house that I backed out of the driveway and drove off to my next stop.

***

I pulled up to my house and turned off the radio, sitting in the car for several minutes debating whether or not I really wanted to go in by myself and do this. But my heartstrings were pulled inside. I sighed with the low hum of the car in park, looking up at the cold, sad looking home. Snow sat in clumps on the sides of each of the front steps, and the mailbox was full. The lid to it wouldn't close all the way. All of the lights were off, of course, and if I didn't know any better I would've thought it was completely dormant.

"You know, Joel's gonna be pissed when he finds out you did this without him." Willow's sudden presence made me jump.

"It's not like he doesn't already know." I turned off the ignition and threw myself back against the headrest.

"So why are you doing this now?"

"I don't want him to worry, and I want him safe. He deserves to enjoy his Christmas."

"So do you," she challenged.

"But I can't until I do this. It feels right ... and necessary. I've been feeling awful for not being here for her."

"She's fine."

"Yeah, I'm sure she's 'fine.' But I know she's lonely."

"She knows why you haven't been here, Em."

"Okay, well we love her. So leave me alone and let me do this, okay?"

"We?"

"Gwen and me."

"Oh. You're a 'we' now?"

I scowled at my friend.

"Here's the deal before I go pay Joel a visit. I'm gonna stay back while you do your duty to Shirley Temple. But I'm not leaving you alone until your ass is back in this car driving to Jamestown. Ight?"

I simply pursed my lips and flared my nostrils. I couldn't make her go away, but I didn't really want her to, not completely. I just wanted her to butt out and be quiet for this. Before I got out of the car, I glimpsed over at Willow in the passenger seat. The marks on her neck remained. I swallowed. "Why didn't you come visit us last night?"

"And interrupt *that*? No *way*. I'm no cockblocker." She smirked and shook her head stiffly. "I gotta say though ... I'm a *little* jealous."

"*Of me?*" I screeched. "What the fu—"

"Of Joel." She winked mechanically and chuckled. "Merry Christmas, Em." Just as quickly as she'd come, she'd gone.

I took shook my head and took a deep breath, muttering under my breath. "Love you, too."

The door creaked open as I stepped in, and the crisp air in the house hit me with a chill. I held her gift in my hand and teetered on my heels while I scoped out the house. There was no sound, no movement.

I walked up the stairs and into Lynette's room.

"Hello?" I wasn't sure if speaking up was wise or not; I didn't want to attract the attention of the wrong person, but I wanted her to know that I was there and thinking of her. There was no response, so I slowly and quietly walked upstairs to the spare bedroom. The wood floor groaned beneath me as if I were disturbing its slumber.

"Lyn?"

I ventured further into the room and decided I'd merely place my gift for her in the corner of the room by the window and leave. I gently put down the glittery pink box with a pearlescent white bow and turned to go back downstairs.

"Is this a Christmas gift?" a voice squeaked from the same corner behind me.

"Yes." I exhaled and spun around slowly.

"I haven't gotten a Christmas gift in- well, I don't know how long. The last Christmas gift I ever opened was … well … I think it was a Slinky."

"Well those are *still* cool. I guess I should've gotten you one of those … They make pink ones now."

"I didn't even know it was Christmas again." Lynette smiled sadly.

"Of course … it's for you."

"Thank you."

Lynette moved toward the gift shyly. She gently peeled the wrapping paper off the gift, the scraps floating off the sides and onto the floor below it. She lifted the box flaps and delicately unfolded the tissue paper inside it. She peered into the box and gasped.

'Do you like it?"

"I *love* it," she swooned, picking up the miniature bookshelf ornament. She let it hang from her pointer finger.

"It reminded me of you instantly. Little. But full of wisdom," I explained.

"I miss you." Lynette spoke clearly across the room.

"I miss you, too." I paused. "There's something else in there, Lyn."

"Yes?" She searched through one more layer of tissue and uncovered a small figurine of a small angel dancing with a taller angel.

"You and I?"

"Or you and Gwen."

She said grasped it tightly in her hand. Quietly and shakily, she spoke. "If I could cry, I would. Happy tears, though."

I nodded and crossed my arms.

"Please come home soon," she whined longingly.

"I will, I promise. I think I may have found a way, but we'll have to wait and see if it works."

"I trust you." She placed the two gifts on the windowsill. "I'm gonna play with them all day. The two angels can read all of the books together. Until you come back." Her matted damp hair slightly shone in the snowy sunlight that came in through the window. The deep crimson blood on the side of her head acted as a twisted and sorrowful bow on the odd gift that she was to me.

"Love you, kiddo." I sighed. "I have to get going now, but I'll see you again soon. Enjoy your presents. Remember that you're not alone. Even if I'm not here, I'm thinking of you. I hope I've made that clear."

"You have." She grinned. "I hope Gwen is thinking of me wherever she is, too."

"I have ... absolutely no doubt."

Lynette rushed over to me and wrapped her icy being around me in a hug. Somehow, it was just as warm as it was freezing.

Right before I reached the front door from the stairway landing seconds later, Carlson appeared in front of me.

"Where's *my* gift?" He shook his head playfully. "Surprised? No. But disappointed? Yes."

I responded with silence, simply glaring at him before taking my step off the landing.

"Why are you still hiding from me?"

"I'm not."

"With that pansy boy, too," he hissed. "We both know where you belong."

"I do." I stood tall, putting forth my best effort to seem unbothered.

He took a step toward me, and I could feel the unnerving bite of his energy. It was the same cold vibration as Lynette's, but inexplicably worlds different.

"Then why don't you come back?" He brushed the back of his hand against my cheek and I immediately saw the water-blurred vision of the shower incident.

While I wanted to collapse and cry, I found strength within myself to remain stone. "I do belong here, but not with you."

"Don't be like that, darlin'." He exaggerated a whimper, feigning empathy.

I scoffed.

"Come back to me. I already told you, and I'm getting sick of repeating myself. I won't lose you again."

I took a glimpse into the mirror on the opposite wall from the staircase. Not only did I see Carlson's reflection, but my image replaced with Gwen's.

She tipped her chin downward at me and nodded. *Give him what he wants, Emma.*

No.

"I won't hurt you this time." He reached out to grab my hand. I yanked mine away.

"You've hurt *everyone*."

His glazed eyes narrowed on me. "Well, I'll never do it again." he uttered coolly as if his predatory behavior were a minor infraction. "I *just* … wish you'd come to your senses and stop fooling around with this new life. Leave it behind. You've lost so many people as Emma, anyway. What's the point of staying in that life? You're exhausting my patience."

"You're exhausting mine." I declared, wishing I could drive a knife into his chest, too.

He stared into me for several seconds. I wanted to look away, but refused to show any sense of intimidation by him.

"Despite always preferring the ... receiving ... in our relationship, I'd hoped you'd come today so I could give *you* a little gift," he teased, pointing to the table by the side of the stairs. On the narrow table was a folded up piece of clothing.

I didn't touch it. "What is it?"

"It doesn't look familiar to you?"

"No." I thought back on what I was missing, or if this was something he was convinced I'd recognize because he believed me to be Gwen. "That's not mine."

"Of course it isn't yours, *Emma*. If it were already yours, it wouldn't be a gift."

I studied the garment from a distance, remembering the fabric and color, then realizing that the brown stains peeking out of the folds weren't part of a pattern. "It's Gwen's."

"Ahhh." He nodded with a sick smirk. "Atta girl."

"How did you get this?"

"For such an intelligent young lady, you— or Gwen ... I'll play along— didn't hide it very well. You should've known better than to stuff it under a weak old floorboard. You should've burnt it, like you burnt me."

Why wouldn't she have burnt it?

"You watched her do it."

"Of course I did. I watched you all the time. You knew I was there, too. Don't you remember? I'm sure it's one of the reasons you left. Why you *ran* away like a lost puppy."

"She didn't just run away. She was tortured by what she did ... even though you deserved it. She was too good, too pure of a person to live past it."

"So you're acknowledging that you know what she did?"

"I—"

He winked.

"No."

"How else would you know what she did? How else would you know that was hers … if it weren't also *yours?*" His smug smile conveyed that he was convinced he'd caught me in a lie.

"Why?"

He walked over to the dress, unfolded it, and held it up in front of himself. It was covered in old blood stains and splatter, tattered with dried mud and dirt smears. She wasn't able to get it all off in the shower. The beautiful original color was barely visible, and what remained uncovered was faded. "I want you to wear it … That is, if it fits that body." He looked me up and down.

"No."

"You will. You'll wear it, and you'll do … what I need you to do." He paused, looking at me as if I were a freshly prepared, pristine piece of steak. "For us."

"*You* can go wear it. I'm not coming close to it."

"Do you not realize that you owe this to me? To your sister? If you hadn't abandoned her that night, would she have died? Would you have done something so unspeakable to me? Stop *running* from it. Own up to your part in this."

"Gwen didn't abandon her. She doesn't owe you shit for thinking she could trust her *fiancé* to not attempt to *rape* a child! Her *sister!*"

"You shut your mouth."

"We owe you nothing. None of us. I gave you a chance to leave on your own … to do what's *actually* right … at least, the only thing you could possibly do to even slightly redeem just a *fraction* of the atrocities you've committed. And *still*, you refuse. This is *my* house. Whether I'm here or not. Don't mistake my absence for running. You take up too much space, but I don't fear you. Your ego just makes me sick to my fucking stomach. Don't worry, though. I will come back, but when I do … it won't be to wear this dress for you. I told you before and nothing has changed, so I'm getting sick of repeating myself, too. The next time I walk into this house, it'll be to evict you." The conviction in my voice shocked me, and the words that flowed out of my mouth hit like pouring, pounding rain.

For once, he had no cocksure response cued up.

I gripped my keys in my pocket so tightly that it hurt, and probably left an indent in my palm. "I'm *not* Gwen. But I do admire her for getting half the job done." I flew right past him, grazing the electrifying current that was his side. Before I opened the door, I stopped and glared into his evil, dormant eyes. "Merry Christmas, Jackie boy."

His head went from a slight tilt to completely erect and his brows furrowed furiously as he caught the door in one hand and gripped my shoulder with the other. "You don't call me that, you understand me? You call me *Jack*, you little *bitch*!"

"I'll call you whatever the fuck I want. Pretty soon you won't even be worth a mention." I pulled away and grabbed the door knob. With all of my strength, I slammed the door shut, making eye contact with him until the door obscured him from my vision. I locked the door as quickly as I could and bolted back to the car.

Once I was in my seat with the doors locked and the heat on, I let it all out. I released all of the fear and anxiety I'd shoved desperately to the back of my consciousness during that confrontation. It must've been adrenaline or pent up anger that allowed me to go there. I should've been horrified by him; he was capable of causing harm whether he was dead or alive. Should I have held my tongue? Had I made things worse for myself? For Joel? Lynette? Had my words put us in even more danger?

I broke down in my dead best friend's car outside of my own home on Christmas. It took several minutes to catch my breath. To see clearly again. As I was finally starting to slow my breathing down, Willow appeared in the passenger seat again.

"You killed it back there with that piece of shit. So proud of you … but you should really text Joel and tell him to stay with you today. I don't like what I'm seeing right now."

"No, that's so selfish of me," I cried.

"Tell him what happened. His family will understand. They know how much he cares about you and how close you two have gotten."

"No."

"Fine. I will. Bye." She shrugged stiffly and vanished.

I let out a loud muffled scream into my sleeve, and gave the steering wheel one big bang. Then I shifted into drive— probably too early— and drove off through Newport to the Pell bridge on my way to Liv's.

I did get a text from Joel just after I arrived at my aunt and uncle's house:

Hey... u ok? surprise visit from willow. she pulled me away and told me wat happened... do you need me to come to you???

I responded quickly to try to alleviate his worries:

no im fine. at liv's. ill text you if i need you. don't worry about me...just enjoy your day. tell your fam i said hi.

My phone dinged almost immediately after:

Ok... <3

I took a deep breath before I got out of the car.

c u soon...
Relief washed over me as I sent the text and stared down at his last message to me. I did my best to wipe my eyes dry and enter the house with my strongest attempt at holiday cheer.

37.

RESOLUTIONS

People usually celebrate New Year's Eve with wine and parties, watching colorful fireworks at midnight. While I would've greatly preferred these typical celebrations, I had more urgent business to attend to. I sat criss-crossed on the living room floor of Joel's apartment with Zuli's hefty leather-bound notebook in front of me open to page 57:

Banishing Ritual for Evil Spirits

Cast the circle, surrounding yourself with a ring of salt. Prepare the following:

Light a black candle south of the circle.
Burn sage in the air and place down north of the circle.
Place clear quartz, smoky quartz, selenite or any crystal used for protection and/or banishment east of the circle.
Place a small dish of water west of the circle (either salt or fresh will work).
Light a white candle in each of the four directions of the circle.

Recite:
Guardian spirits, I call on you.
Of the north, of air
Of the east, of earth
Of the west, of water
Of the south, of fire

Make sacred this space.
This circle is cast, protection unbroken.
Blessed be, magick spoken.

Grind together and mix a pinch of sage, wormwood, mugwort,
peppermint, and rosemary.
Burn the herbs in the cauldron and recite the following:

I call upon you, evil spirit (or spirit's name if known)
May your negative force be banished from here to whence you began
May your exit leave no trace
From darkness to light
Be gone from this place

Blow the ashes of the herb mixture outside of the circle, careful not to
disturb the circle of salt.

Blessed be.

Remain silent in the circle for a several minutes to meditate on your
intention and honor the workings of the Divine.

Close out the circle:
Guardian spirits, I thank you.
Of the south, of fire
Of the west, of water
Of the east, of earth
Of the north, of air
Now I close this sacred space.
This circle is closed, yet protection remains unbroken.
Blessed be, magick spoken.

Blow out all candles, put away crystals, sage, and water. Do not
disturb the salt circle until ready to depart from the ritual area.

I buried my face in my hands. *This* was my next attempt at
getting rid of Carlson?

I stared down at Zuli's bubbly handwriting on the page, wondering how she'd even gotten this information. Had she made it up, or was it given to her by someone else? Was this actually supposed to work? Herbs, pretty rocks, candles, and poetry?

I tried to be positive, but because I didn't subscribe to those beliefs, that was hard for me. I had no doubt that crystals and herbs had calming energies and benefits to the user. However, using it to get rid of a very powerful, very evil spirit was different from finding remedies to improve sleep or spark some self-confidence.

I sighed and closed the book, wondering how I was going to find all of those herbs and crystals in the first place. Then I remembered Joel mentioning the collection of crystals Willow had in her closet. She must have had at least one of those rocks mentioned in this spell. The herbs could probably be found at the fancy spice shop downtown— although I'd *never* heard of wormwood or mugwort before. Those sounded like ingredients only found in an old cottage in the woods or a potion class.

I had gotten one thing out of this study session, however. I felt the sudden desire to light some candles in front of me and meditate in silence; maybe I'd even burn some of the sage Willow had left in the center of the tiny dining table. Joel wasn't expected to be back for about an hour, anyway. He and Elliot had gone to visit his grandmother for a bit that evening. I had some time to try to clear my mind, even if just to quiet my worries down a notch.

I turned the fireplace ambiance video on just for the constant crackling sound in the background. There I sat, alone in the middle of the rug on the old wood floor, struggling to settle in and keep my body still. It took several minutes to redirect myself and stop shifting and itching.

Finally, I was able to steady myself in a comfortable sitting position. I forced mindful deep breaths and attempted to focus on the inhales and exhales. This was way easier said than done, but after a while, my mind started to sync with my breath and the crackling of my fake fire.

Am I ... relaxed? I'd forgotten the feeling.

In the quiet calm of the white noise, I heard a whisper in my head. Not in my ear, no. It was as if I were having thoughts that weren't my own. I tried to quiet them because I was trying to focus. I couldn't make them out at first, but then they got clearer. They weren't louder, nor were they intrusive.

It's okay, keep relaxing. You're doing wonderfully. Don't change a thing, and don't open your eyes. But I do want you to see…

Okay.

Thank you.

I tried to imagine opening my eyes without actually doing it, like a layer of vision within my mind. When I did, I found a vivid, *real* fireplace in front of me. The log popped while it burned in the bright orange-yellow flame. This fireplace wasn't one I'd created in my imagination during the meditation, but my own, at home. I sat on a blanket on the wooden floor in front of it, taking in the smell of sweet vanilla and spicy ginger wafting in from the kitchen.

"I can't wait to eat our cookies," a soft, familiar voice squeaked in excitement beside me.

I turned from the fire to face Lynette, who sat right next to me, cuddled up against my arm.

"They *do* smell wonderful, don't they?" I spoke in that angelic smooth voice.

"Gwen?"

"Yes?"

"What's a resolution?" Lynette's eyes widened as she picked at the fringe of the deep maroon woven blanket beneath us.

The small clock above the mantle ticked.

"As in a New Year's resolution?" Gwen chuckled.

"Mhm," Lynette nodded.

"Well, it's a sort of goal, or a promise to yourself for the new year. For instance, mine is to read more … and get married. So once that clock hits midnight tonight, I need to start working on those two things."

"Hm." Lynette looked down at the blanket and pursed her lips deep in thought, and after several seconds, she piped up. "Well, I think I know what mine will be!"

"And what is that?" Gwen posed enthusiastically.

"To learn how to bake cookies as good as yours!"

Gwen giggled and put her arm around her little sister, "They'll be ready very soon. Be patient."

"I *am* being patient," Lynette's soft curls shimmered in the warm glow of the fire as her rosy lips and cheeks rose into a smile, "Gwen?"

"Mhm?"

"Are you going to marry Jack?"

"Well, if he asks me. I believe he will." I felt a warm flush in my face as Gwen spoke.

"Wow," Lynette awed. "He's nice."

"Yes, he is. I think he may even *love* me," Gwen gushed, laughing.

"Well I love you more," Lynette harrumphed jokingly.

"Oh there's no doubt about that." Gwen felt butterflies in her stomach as she gazed down at her sweet baby sister. "Do you want to know a secret?"

"Of course," she tee-heed in a whisper.

"There's no one I'll *ever* love more than you. But *shhh*, don't tell Jack. He may not propose if he knows that." Gwen winked and nudged Lynette gently.

The little timer in the kitchen rang to alert us that the cookies were done baking. Lynette gasped and jumped up off the blanket and onto the hardwood.

"Now calm down, little. I need to take them out and let them cool." Gwen shook her head and stood. "You are most definitely *not* being patient!"

"Am, too!" Lynette exclaimed as I glided into the kitchen. I felt a floating sensation, and time seemed to blur past me as I took the cookies out of the oven, left them on the counter, went back to the blanket on the floor, stood back up, grabbed a plate of warm cookies, and returned to Lynette. It felt like I was living inside a time lapse video until we both sat together again in front of the fireplace with fresh soft gingerbread cookies in hand.

"These are delicious!" Lynette shrieked with a full mouth.

"Thank you, thank you. My apparent claim to fame, isn't it?" Gwen smiled humbly and gazed at Lynette lovingly.

After a few slow minutes of munching on cookies together in front of the flames, the grandfather clock in the living room to our left chimed.

Lynette gasped excitedly.

"Happy New Year, little." Gwen set her napkin and half-eaten cookie down to hold Lynette tight, giving her a long kiss on the top of her head.

"Happy New Year," Lynette muffled into Gwen's chest, taking in the hug as the clock chimed twelve.

Gwen rested her head on Lynette's, continuing the cuddle. She gazed back out the dining room window at the softly falling snow in the light of the street lamps.

"I love you so much," Gwen whispered. My eyes closed with Gwen's and as I took a deep breath, I felt myself drifting away from the cozy hug and back to the present.

Thank you for sharing that, I thought.

Thank you for letting me.

I know you want to be with her again, I kept my eyes closed.

I do.

I want to help you.

I told you how to help us.

I'm sorry. I couldn't give you over to Carlson even if I knew how.

Give him what he wants, and we'll sort out the rest later.

There has to be another way.

You'll find it in yourself to do the right thing. I'll be ready when you are.

After that thought, my eyes opened slowly back to Joel's living room. The clock ticked, catching my attention. I looked over to see that it was 11:30. I sighed, realizing I'd been out for about an hour. Thinking back to the bittersweet memory I'd just experienced, I wished I could go back to that place with Lynette.

I heard a rustling outside the door to the apartment. Joel walked in with his arms full. I squinted from the floor to try and figure out what he was holding.

"Hey, I made it back just in time," he cheered.

"What's all that for?" I stood up and patted my legs anxiously.

"Us!"

"Huh?"

He walked into the kitchen nook and pulled two bottles of wine out of a paper bag, followed by a whole Tupperware container of huge chocolate chip cookies. He held the container up and added, "Oatmeal."

"Even better."

"I know, right?" He laughed.

"Glad we're on the same page with that ... the *right* page. Thanks, Grandma Quinn," I grinned and stretched.

"I want some." Willow's bedroom door opened and she strolled out.

"Sorry Wills." Joel inhaled deeply. "You can still celebrate with us."

I took a seat on the couch to wait for Joel to bring me a sizable glass of rosé and a plate with two giant cookies only seconds later. "Why thank you."

"Absolutely." he smiled and joined me on the couch. "Whatcha wanna do?"

"When are we doing that spell?" Willow inserted.

"Not tonight, Wills." Joel said quietly.

"Well, duh."

"No, I mean we aren't talking about that tonight. We're relaxing."

"Okay … Just a question. I just want you to feel safe again, Em." Willow's gaze fixed on the floor.

"It's okay. I know," I reassured.

"Still," Joel took a bite of his cookie, "No more talk of anything stressful…" He paused, then exclaimed, *"Em!"*

"What?"

"What's your New Year's Resolution?"

"Um…" I thought back to my vision of Lynette and Gwen. "I think it's to get those two sisters back together."

"Yeah, but for *you*," Joel clarified. "What do you want for yourself?"

"Peace, I guess." I took a sip. The warm wine trickled down my throat. "To get my home back … You?"

"I think" —Joel spoke pensively— "that I'd like to focus on our friendship. Take a trip somewhere when this is all over."

"Mhm, your *friendship*." Willow remarked from the corner of the room.

"You can leave whenever you want." he glared.

"That sounds nice. We'll plan something. Maybe the Smithsonian. That'd be awesome … Wills, what's your resolution?"

We both turned back to look at Willow, only to find that she had disappeared from where she stood.

"Did we piss her off?" I asked.

"No, she'll be fine." Joel shook his head. "She knows she's loved," he declared loudly into the air, then put his arm around me playfully. "Let's bring in the New Year drunkenly."

I chuckled. "Yeah, okay."

"No, no. I'm kidding. Just tipsy … Okay. Let's watch something." Joel went to reach for the remote.

"Wait. Can we play something fun instead?"

"Sure." I watched as Joel's eyes drifted over to the bookshelf in the room. His eyes lit up. "I know exactly what we'll do."

We spent the next two hours playing Disneyland Monopoly together. We didn't even notice when the clock had reached midnight. It wasn't until we finished the game that we even considered the time. After celebrating my win by chugging the rest of the rosé, I stretched and took a peek at the clock. It was past 2 o'clock in the morning. All of the cookies were eaten, and both wine bottles were empty.

"Congratulations, Emma Reilly. You've won the new year." Joel cracked himself up. "C'mere."

Joel stood up and stayed in place with his arms outstretched toward me, a goofy smile on his face. His auburn hair was a scruffy mess. He'd grown it out a bit since I'd first met him, and he wore beanies most of the time, so I wasn't used to seeing all of that wavy hair. He'd taken off the beanie halfway through his bottle, and messed with it a lot when he was drunk, or relaxed. I couldn't tell which.

I chuckled and walked up to him so he could wrap his arms around me in a very intense hug. It wasn't tight or painful, but genuine and intimate. He rubbed my back and rested his head beside mine. I leaned in on his shoulder.

"Joel," I mumbled. "Go to bed. You're drunk."

"Happy New Year, Emma!" He exclaimed lightheartedly with a twinge of a slur.

"Happy New Year," I replied, releasing myself from the hug.

"This is gonna be a great year. Don't even worry about it."

We met each other's eyes for a moment. His were slightly squinted as he wobbled in place. I caught his chestnut eyes and forgot to look away.

"*God* ... you're beautiful." He didn't break from my eyes, nor did he drunkenly stumble on his words.

I smiled, unsure of whether it was Joel or the alcohol was talking. "Thanks."

"*No.* Thank *you.*" He placed his hand on my cheek. The contrast between his touch and Carlson's was wild. Joel's warm palm felt safe. It *was* safe.

"Okay." I blushed, but remained calm. "Let's get some sleep."

"Here, here ... You take my bed. Really," he offered.

"No, Joel. I'm okay." I laughed.

"No. I know what happened last time we all got drunk. I'm not letting you out of my sight, so you decide where we sleep. My room or in here," he explained.

I sighed. "Okay. Sleep out here with me," I reasoned, clearly more talented at holding and handling my liquor.

"Shhh." He put his finger over my mouth. "No."

"No, what?"

"Okay, okay. I'll sleep on the couch." He mosied over and lazily flopped onto the cushion. "Come lay down, Em. Do you have any idea how *late* it is?" he muffled into one of the blankets.

"Move over then." I shoved his leg lightly.

"Ri— right." He quickly adjusted his position and made room for me to lean against him. He put his arm around me, and pulled two blankets over us. He wasn't even in pajamas, but it was too late to convince him to change. After he lovingly brushed his hand down my hair, he passed out.

It took me longer to fall asleep, but the alcohol definitely helped speed up the process.

Before I closed my eyes, I thought again about my resolution. Willow had asked when we would do the spell, and I wanted to achieve my New Year's resolution as quickly as possible.

"Willow," I whispered into the room. "Let's do it this week … as soon as I have all the stuff … Let's try." I stared into the dark doorway to her room. She never showed up to me, but I felt a reassuring pat on my head right before falling asleep.

JANUARY

38.

THIS IS WHY WE'RE HERE

On the third of January, Joel and I pulled up to the house. The snow had gone away except for a few small clumps here and there on the streets, but it was so cold that a thin and foreboding layer of fog floated above the ground around the house. We parked in the driveway, but stayed in park with the heat on for several minutes.

"Are you sure you *want* to do this?" Joel asked.

"No, but if there is even the slightest chance of it working, then yes." I bit the inside of my cheek, staring into the window next to the entry door. It gave a frosted peek into the front living room.

"Yeah, but … do you think it will?"

"We don't have much of a choice but to just hope it does." I shrugged.

"Well" —Joel took a deep breath— "whenever you're ready, we'll go in."

"We have to move fast and quietly. I don't want Carlson confronting me the second we walk in."

"Yeah." He nodded. "Hopefully he won't. I'm here if he does. We'll start with the salt and hope that it actually does the trick."

I sighed. "We're saying 'hope' a lot, but I'm not feeling too much of it," I said dryly.

"Don't be such a downer." Willow popped up in the backseat.

"Are you staying for this?"

"Duh. Of course." She nodded stiffly in the rearview mirror.

"This is my home. Why does it feel like I'm breaking and entering to do a Satanic ritual?"

"Um. Offended. A lot of us don't even believe in Satan."

"Sorry."

"And come *on*, Em. It's witchcraft, not crime."

"Sadly, some people would view it as the same thing," Joel shook his head.

"It's just a little … different … for me." I tilted my head.

"Yeah, so was burning a child predator's remains in the middle of the woods at night but hey— been there, done that." Willow made a valid point.

"Let's go," I decided, turning off the ignition and reaching toward the backseat to grab our bag of supplies. Willow was right next to my bag and I felt her freezing energy on my arm. It broke my heart.

"See you inside," she said and vanished after I turned back around.

"I'm not sure I'll ever get used to that," Joel whispered sadly.

"Neither am I."

Joel and I got out and made our way through the cold up the porch steps and into the silent, still house. Joel stopped to glimpse around, but I marched straight into the empty dining room. I speedily removed the box of salt out of my backpack and got to work pouring it in a circle like we had the night we burned Carlson. It didn't work then, but maybe it would this time.

Maybe.

My black faux leather combat boots planted into the middle of the circle as I searched the backpack for Zuli's book. I wasted no time. I wanted this over with as quickly as possible, and I wasn't going with any theatrics. I knelt down on the wood floor with the book open to page 57. Joel walked into the room and stepped into the circle with me.

"I don't see anyone. Not even Lynette."

"Good. I don't want her to see any of this. That'll lead to more questions that I don't want to answer and don't have the answers *to*." I shook my head, removing the small jars of herbs from the bag along with the candle, small cup, water bottle, large cluster of clear quartz, and bundle of smudging sage.

"Do you at least want a light on?" Joel asked shyly, likely picking up on my no-nonsense approach to this.

"If you want," I murmured. My focus was on setting the items in the correct direction of the circle to start the ritual. Once everything was in place, I took a deep breath and told Joel to sit down next to me. He never did turn the light on. We were doing this by the light of the four white candles surrounding us and the one black candle in front of me.

I burnt the sage and wafted it around us, then set it down behind me to the north. "Okay."

"Where's Wills?" Joel asked anxiously.

"I don't care. I'm starting." I hadn't even taken the time to remove my fingerless scarlet alpaca gloves, my beanie, or my thick black denim jacket.

Don't upset him. Don't let him find out you're here. Be careful.

I pushed that thought— Gwen's thought— out of my head and began reading quickly from the book, "Guardian spirits, I call on you. Of the north, of air. Of the east, of earth. Of the west, of water. Of the south, of fire. Make sacred this space. This circle is cast, protection unbroken. Blessed be, magick spoken."

Joel cleared his throat, as quietly as possible. A freezing gust of air expanded behind us. It could've been one of three people, but I didn't take the time to look back to find out who. Instead, I began mixing the sage, peppermint, wormwood, mugwort, and rosemary together with the mortar and pestle Willow had used to use to make tea. Thank God she'd had all of those herbs with the exception of rosemary, which was easily found at Stop & Shop. I came to realize while preparing for this that Willow was much more into witchcraft than she'd let on, at least to me. Joel explained that she didn't quite hide it, per say; she just kept it close to her chest. She didn't bother opening up about it. It was her personal practice, and most people wouldn't understand or even attempt to, anyway.

"Sorry I'm late, guys," Willow whispered, making me jump slightly as I crushed the herbs together.

"How can *you* be late?" I acknowledged her solely by scolding her.

"I don't know. Still navigating coming in and out of this veil, I guess. But I'm here."

"Emma, just go ahead and I'll keep an eye out for—"

"*Don't* say his name yet," I growled. "Sorry." I realized how I was behaving.

"Em. Relax or it won't work. Be present," Willow suggested.

I didn't respond because I knew I'd end up taking my stress out on her. Rather, I finished mixing the herbs and transferred it to Willow's small iron cauldron. On my knees, I lit the herbs with a lighter and watched it smoke. I closed my eyes slowly and took one deep breath before reciting the words written by Zuli, "I call upon you…*Jack Carlson*," I hissed his name. "May your negative force be banished from here to whence you began. May your exit leave no trace. From darkness to light. Be gone from this place."

At no point during my recitation of the spell did Carlson show up. It almost angered me that I had to say his full name for nothing. There was no movement or noise in the room for several seconds. I felt safe enough to close my eyes with both Joel and Willow next to me. I took deep breaths to focus on pushing Carlson's energy and spirit out of the house.

"Emma." Joel nudged me softly.

Thud thud, thud thud, thud thud.

"Is this really necessary?"

I opened my eyes at the sound of the footsteps entering the dining room from the kitchen. They stopped right in front of me. I looked up to see men's dress shoes. Carlson stood right outside the salt circle with his arms crossed.

"This somehow seems … even *more* excessive than burning my body."

I felt a ping in my chest. Neither Joel nor I moved.

"I gave you one last chance." He glowered down at me.

As I continued the steps, I decided to ignore him as long as he didn't attempt to enter the circle. Maybe there *was* something to the salt protection. I took one more deep breath, finally locking my eyes with him, and slowly leaned forward to blow the ashes of the herb mixture outside the circle toward him. I didn't break our stare as I spoke as clearly as possible. "Blessed be."

I leaned back and placed the cauldron down. Carlson didn't speak.

"Guardian spirits, I thank you. Of the south, of fire. Of the west, of water. Of the east, of earth. Of the north, of air … Now I close this sacred space. This circle is closed, yet protection remains unbroken. Blessed be, magick spoken."

I blew out one of the candles gently, so as to not disturb the circle of salt.

"This … is…" Carlson chuckled furiously, placing a hand on his bloody torso.

"Done," I finished.

"Foolish," he corrected sternly.

I blinked, simply said, "Okay," and blew out each candle while maintaining eye contact with him the entire time. This front of confidence was my best attempt to mask my worry that this spell had, in fact, failed.

I did look away for a moment to make sure I'd closed out the ritual completely and when I did, Carlson was gone. This was a momentary relief, yet not very promising.

"Em." Joel cleared his throat. "Is that … it?"

I sighed. "Yup."

Willow was so abnormally quiet that I'd almost forgotten she was there. Her chilling presence had become regular, and the very least of my concerns.

I continued to pack the supplies up into the backpack again, full of doubt in my gut, and dread about leaving the circle. Part of me wanted to stay in the ring of salt for a while to see if Carlson showed back up to rub his persistent presence in my face. The larger part of me wanted to leave, but then there would be no way of knowing whether the spell truly worked or not.

"I mean, he left before the ritual was completely finished, so…" Joel shrugged.

"I don't know." I zipped the backpack and anxiously chugged the rest of the water in the bottle I brought. I sipped whatever water was in the ritual dish, too.

"Wills?" Joel noticed her unusual silence.

We both looked up at Wills, who was frozen in a standing position, looking forward. "I'm sorry, guys."

"Huh?"

"Why?" My lip curled up in fearful anticipation.

"I still feel him here."

I threw my head back, gazing emptily up at the ceiling with a shaky exhale.

"Could it just be residual energy?" Joel wondered.

"No." Willow looked down at us suddenly.

"How do you know?"

Before Willow could answer, I stood up and stomped outside of the circle, smearing the salt with my shoe intentionally. "Let's go."

I looked into the large rectangular mirror above the mantle. Under my black pom-pom beanie and tired eyes were dark circles that seemed to have become a permanent fixture on my face.

"Em, are you sure you wanna—"

"Joel, let's *go*." I couldn't stay in the room any longer.

The sun was starting to set outside, giving off a light reddish glow through the front windows. "Sorry, mom," I whispered to the urn below the mirror.

"We'll find something else, Emma," Willow said solemnly.

I grabbed my house keys out of my jacket pocket. "I'm tired of dealing with this."

As quickly as put my hand in my pocket, my arm was ripped out of my jacket and the fireplace burst on from behind me.

"So am I," Carlson growled in my ear. "Take the jacket off. Make yourself comfortable. You aren't walking out on me this time." Carlson appeared right in front of my face. His pale eyes were like a mirror into a distorted, uncanny reflection of myself, his lip fixed into an angry smirk.

"*Emma!*" Joel shrieked.

"All of this…" He shot his eyes around and stuck his arm out, bending unnaturally at the elbow toward the salt. "All done."

"What, then?" My balance shifted uncomfortably.

Carlson froze, his eyes penetrating mine. The barren, icy evil in his eyes was what I'd imagine Hell freezing over to look like.

"What? Are you gonna kill me? I'm a little older than you like your victims," I spat.

Jack took a step back, chuckled with his head tilted, and then craned it back to look at Joel. His eyes darted sharply from me to him. The twisted smile from the night I first encountered him distorted his blue lips. Willow stepped back to stand next to Joel, placing a hand on his shoulder. The only sounds were Joel's and my anxious breaths.

Without warning, Carlson bolted toward me in a blur and pushed me back against the mantle of the fireplace. My shoulder blades banged against it.

"*Hey!*" Joel wailed.

In the split second before Joel was knocked to the ground, we made eye contact— both horrified, but trying to comfort each other. Once Joel was thrown onto his back against the hardwood floor by an unseen force, Carlson zipped over toward him and held him by the collar of his shirt. Joel was unconscious, his neck flopping back as Carlson pulled at him viciously. Joel gasped only once, loudly and painfully. Before I could process what had happened, Carlson was gone and Joel was limp on the floor.

"Joel?" I whimpered.

"Emma, you need to leave right now." Willow spoke sternly into my ear.

"*No.*" I shook my head and scrambled over to his side. The floor was cold around him. "Joel?" I shook his chest. "*Joel!*"

His eyes were open just slightly, rolled back to reveal the whites of his eyes that peeked out from his fluttering eyelids, "He's breathing," I told Willow.

"Good, but you need to get the hell outta—"

Joel's eyes popped open and he sat up robotically, staring into my eyes.

"Oh my god. Are you— are you okay?" My heart pounded against my chest as it heaved up and down. My face was red hot with fear. "Is your head okay?"

He didn't blink.

"Joel."

Instead of responding with reassurance or a request for help, the corners of his lips slithered upwards.

I knew that grin.

"Shit."

I scurried up quickly and tried to run into the kitchen.

"Go!" Willow screamed in my ear.

I wasn't fast enough. Joel caught up to me and yanked me back by my hair. I yelped, trying to twist around to fight back, but he pulled me forcefully with one hand and clawed at my neck with the other. I gagged from the pressure of his hand as he threw me down to the floor by the fireplace. My head hit the wood and I lost my beanie. Several specks of light danced in my eyes.

"I told you he was a pansy," Joel snarled, drooling angrily over me. He straddled me, crushing my chest.

"Stop," I groaned. "Joel, please."

"*Shhh.*" Joel held one finger over his lips as he pushed his hand into my neck harder. "I've had enough of this. We're done playing games."

I struggled to dig my fingers into his legs, but my thick gloves made it hard to get a strong enough grip. He held my arm down, my wrist banging into the now heated floor in front of the flames.

"If you aren't going to come to me on your own, I'll just have to take you … I gave you time. I gave you choices, gentle reminders." He choked me, pushing my head down when I tried to lift my neck. "And now … I'm done waiting."

"Sto—"

"*Shut up!*"

Willow tried to push him off of me, but it was no use. He shot his head up at her. "I thought I got rid of you," he barked.

Willow shook her head stiffly.

"Go ahead." He squeezed my neck as he stared at Willow, "Try."

Willow took a step back, dropping her eyes to the ground.

My vision started to blur. Willow was gone. In my ear, I heard her say. "I'm so sorry. I don't have the strength."

"Leave her alone!" Lynette appeared above me. "*Please* Jack!"

"Don't you want her with you?" Joel howled with frenzied laughter as he looked down into my eyes. I could've sworn I caught a glimpse of guilt and powerlessness in his eyes. *That* was my Joel.

Everything had happened so quickly that my heart hadn't had time to break until that moment.

"Joel" —I gasped— "it's oh … okay," I gurgled.

More specks of light appeared like snowfall until my vision was completely white.

Emerging from the blank white space was a stand-alone angel in her flowing beachy dress. She smiled sadly and extended her hand out to me.

Mom.

I wanted her. I really did.

"Hi baby," she spoke as smoothly as warm fluffy sand in the summer, but before I could follow the urge to run toward her, another voice spoke.

Not yet.

My mom faded away from me, drifting backward slowly and gracefully like a child's lost balloon in the sky. I went from white nothingness to the slightly blurry image of Carlson mounted on top of me. *This* wasn't Joel, but Carlson, in a plain white shirt. He thrust against me violently, sweat dripping down the sides of his head. He gripped my neck, digging his nails into my skin and grunting ferociously. I weakly lifted my arm to put my hand against his disheveled, gelled hair, separating in stringy clumps over his forehead. I tried to pat him to get his attention but it failed.

"Baby, *please*," Gwen's voice cracked as her body was pushed back and forth. "Please, you're hurting me."

I closed my eyes tightly, going numb from pain. I wanted it all to be over. Then Gwen's voice echoed in my mind.

No more.

My vision rushed back to the present as his name exited my mouth like hot, acidic vomit. "*Jack!*"

Give him what he wants, Emma, or you're going to die.

"Jack, *stop!*" I choked on my words.

Everything became crystal clear.

Carlson froze, as if he himself had seen a ghost.

"Jack, please." I hacked. "Please, I'll give you what you want just *please…*"

He sat up straight, still mounted on top of my chest. He cocked his head to the side and raised a brow.

"Get off me, please." I struggled to breathe still. "Jack.."

"You *killed* me," he boomed, slowly lifting the pressure of his body off of mine.

"You broke my heart, Jack … Why— why her? Why *any* child … any person?" I let the words flow out of my mouth like a blood-gushing, slit throat. "Why me? You killed me."

"I watched you fall apart. You were weak without me."

"I was weak with you, too," I inhaled brokenly.

Joel glared down at me, lifting his body off of me only to remain on all fours with his face directly over mine. Those green eyes…

"You were right," I cried. "I didn't even realize it until recently. But you're right."

"About?"

I exhaled deeply and scrambled to steady my breath enough to elaborate. "Gwen has been with me all along. You knew it even before I did. She's been there, reminding me … I didn't want to acknowledge it. I didn't know how. But now I do … Jack. I'm ready to accept who I am. I'm ready to be … with you, again."

The same villainous smile crept up on his lips. "Gwendolyn?"

Smart girl.

"I never should've gone to book club that night. I should've stayed with you. All this time, I think I've forgotten whose home this is … who I belong to." I gulped. "Jack, I needed you to remind me of who I am, and you did."

"You…" Carlson was at a loss for words. "Finally."

"I see it clearly now." My chest still heaved. "Clear as day. Le — let me wear the dress for you." I stammered, trying to focus on Joel's eyes as I made the effort to caress his head with my shaky hand. If he was witness to what was happening, he'd hate himself forever for hurting me.

"*You're* not a pansy. *You* are a real man." I stared deep into his eyes and gulped. "Let me put on the dress for you. Let me come to you the way I want. Leave this body, Jack. Be with me. I want to see you … I want you to watch me."

Joel didn't blink. He simply smirked. "Get up, then."

"I need you ... to get up first," I whispered.

The devilish man inside of my friend harrumphed, pleased, and stood up. He reached for my hand to help me up. For my sanity, I could only hold his hand if I closed my eyes and imagined our time together on New Year's Eve.

"Come." He led me into the foyer where the blood-stained dress still sat on the shelf. I stared down at it for several seconds while Joel's usually gentle hands gripped my shoulders aggressively. I focused on the stains, the difference between the blood and the mud. The mud still looked separate from the dress, resting in thin, cracked layers on the fabric, even after all those years. The blood had completely merged with the dress to become part of the garment itself.

"What are you waiting for?" the deep voice boomed.

"Just thinking back to that night," I answered quickly with a sigh.

"Put it on," he whispered in my ear.

I hesitantly reached for the dress. It was cool and fragile, like it could've fallen apart at any second. I held it in my hands, my chest riddled with what felt like electric zaps one after another.

"Smell it," he ruffed.

"Why?"

"That's my blood on your hands. It was then, and it is now. Breathe it in. Go back and remind yourself why we're here now. You owe it to me."

"Jack." I ignored his demand and turned around to face him. One hand held the dress tightly in a ball against my chest and the other I placed softly on Joel's chest. "I'm gonna go put it on now."

"No," He said as I took a step toward the living room. "No. You're gonna put it on right now, in front of me."

My slow blink was accompanied by a harsh gulp. I didn't want to be humiliated— desecrated— like that again, especially when I knew Joel could see what was happening and couldn't do anything to stop it.

"Do it," Carlson snarled through Joel's lips.

I shook my head and gulped. "Jack please."

"Should I just take care of this all myself? Because I will, Gwendolyn."

"No, I—"

"Then put ... it ... on." His gaze felt like hundreds of knife wounds to the chest. "Now."

I nodded.

"Good girl." His eyes fixed thirstily onto me as I bared myself almost completely to change into the raggedy dress. It smelled like musty, rusty old iron. It fit, albeit snuggly.

"Hm." Joel's head tilted sideways against his shoulder. "Doesn't fit like it used to."

"It's an entirely different body." I glared, holding my tongue.

"Turn around."

I obeyed, sick to my stomach.

"It won't button all the way in the back," he groaned frustratedly.

"It doesn't need to. It won't be needed for long, anyway." I spoke through my teeth.

He straightened his head promptly. "What a nice point of view. That'll do, then."

"It'll have to," I snapped.

He took me by the throat within the blink of an eye and squeezed. "Don't get fresh with me."

I took a deep breath and remembered my goal. "I'm sorry."

He looked me up and down, then placed his hand on my cheek. I swallowed, searching helplessly for any semblance of Joel in those eyes. They were the same rich evergreen, but had an entirely different soul puppeteering them. They were calloused, deviating completely from what I'd seen them to be. In the hopes that Joel was indeed somewhere behind them watching consciously, I whispered, "I love you. Whatever happens, I love you."

"We both know exactly what's going to happen. So tell me ... how do you want this to end?"

I took no time to respond. I'd prepared my answer already. "I want to go where Lynette took her last breath."

"You're insane." He chuckled. "It's freezing outside."

"Not for you. You told me it's my decision. Let me be with her."

I waited for a response as he scanned my face.

"You can push me" —I added— "if you leave this body."

"Why?"

"I just want to see you. Let's go together, just me and you. You don't need this body, just like I don't need this one." I gestured to myself in the blood-stained dress.

His sneer transformed into a look of ease. "Okay."

With a wink, Joel's body went limp and collapsed to the floor like a ventriloquist dummy.

Carlson appeared standing triumphantly above and behind Joel's unconscious body. I wanted to leave before he could wake up. Carlson's sharp but empty eyes stared into me like a deadly icicle hanging above me. One false move, one gust of wind or slam of a door … and I could be dead.

"Well." I nodded. "There you are, Jack."

"Let's make this quick."

"Of course."

***

The journey with Carlson to the clearing in the freezing dead of winter was the coldest I'd ever felt in my life. Lucky for me, though, he let me wear my boots outside— and *only* my boots, aside from the bloodied dress and underwear. I'd told him I'd meet him there, but there was no way he was letting me out of his sight. I didn't plan on fleeing, but he didn't know that. He didn't know nearly as much as he thought he did.

As we reached the eerie quiet of the clearing, my boots crunching on the frozen fallen leaves alerted the few sparrows in the trees of our presence. Startled, they all flew off.

We were alone.

No you're not.

Once we reached the very center of the empty circle of space within the trees, Carlson stood stiff as a board, staring at me. When I reciprocated the stillness, he began pacing around me like a starved shark. My heartbeat quickened. I hadn't been back there since we'd found Willow.

"Well." He gestured up at the tree.

"Stay with me." I extended my hand.

"I'm not going anywhere until your breath leaves that body."

"Please." My hand stayed stretched out in front of me.

"You've experienced death before. What's one more time?"

"I'm still … afraid." My voice cracked; it wasn't a lie.

Don't be afraid. Focus.

I glimpsed up at the tree. In my mind's eye, I saw her hanging there, swaying ever so slightly. Her pretty eyes were robbed of pep and sass, her skin drained of its warm honey color. Her hair's vibrant shine was completely stolen away from her.

I looked around to see if she was with me, but she was nowhere. Why had she left me? To tend to Joel? Where was she? I needed her.

Emma, focus.

"Jack, take my hand." The clearing was silent. "I want to share this moment with you before I see you on the other side. I don't know how long it will take to come back to you."

He took my hand reluctantly. It stung. "Only a woman would let all this emotion prolong business."

"Jack, what if I'm … reincarnated again? What if I don't come back to you?"

"Then *find me* again," he growled.

"Jack, please. Give me this before I go. I'm so afraid to be without you. Now that I've accepted that we were brought back together, I don't want this to end."

Carlson slowly stepped toward me. He took my face in one hand and kept the other interlocked with my fingers. It was even colder than it was outside, plus the uncomfortable zip-zapping of energy on my skin, as if I could *feel* television static. Pins and needles, frostbite.

Emma.

"Did I make you feel weak, Jack?"

"Always."

"Do I still?"

"Yes."

"How weak?"

"I could melt into the snow."

I took a deep breath. My vision of Wills faded away from the branch she hung from. A vision of Lynette's small mangled body appeared briefly like a single film frame on the ground next to the large established rock that killed her.

Focus.

I inhaled deeply, gazing around at the twisting bare branches around and above me. "Okay. I'm ready."

"Then do it." He nodded once.

"Jack?"

"Yes?"

"Do you love me?"

"I need you."

"Then remind me of what I did to you before I go."

He placed one of my hands on his abdomen, where his dress shirt was absolutely covered in thick clots and deep red pools of blood. Between his chest and stomach were the deepest illusions of gashes that ripped his shirt clean open in a few spots.

"This is why we're here, Gwen." Carlson pushed my hand harder against his icy being. "Because you killed me."

"I plunged the knife ... right into your heart." I whispered, looking down at his chest, a tear dribbling right down my cheek. It wasn't guilt or regret, as he might have hoped, but trepidation.

"Right in the heart. You stabbed me, and you *just* ... kept ... going."

I pressed my hand even more deeply into his freezing energy, taking several steps forward toward the tree. "Jack?" I spoke sweetly, looking up into his eyes. I studied both of them for a second, partially hoping to find some sliver of humanity in them. There was nothing, not even a reflection of myself. He was an abyss.

"Yes?"

"I just kept going."

Without warning and without anymore begging, I approached Carlson as closely as I could and slammed my face into his. It felt like kissing a block of ice ... that was also on fire. It hurt. It stung. It burned and shocked my lips. It nearly destroyed me to have to get so close to pure depravity. My heart and lungs leapt into my chest— tight, painful, repulsive. Shivers shot throughout my entire body, so many sensations thrown onto me within a fraction of a second.

I opened my eyes briefly to see his, wide and unexpecting. Furious. Before he could process what I said, I slammed my lips harder against him and closed my eyes tightly, focusing on keeping his energy exactly where it was.

Deep breath in.

I inhaled so deeply I felt like my chest was going to burst. I imagined breathing him in, reducing him from a wildfire to a tiny pathetic flame that I could easily snuff out with one shallow exhale.

Deep breath out.

I kept breathing, feeling the burn move through my body, radiating from my chest, expanding out to both the top of my head and the bottom of my feet. I felt his energy pull away from me, but I deepened my inhale and struggled to pull it right back in.

Emma, breathe out!

I felt a frosty, sharp rush of electricity zap through me, and I fell backward to the ground. Intense pressure filled my chest, pushing up against my ribcage. My spine curved as my chest reached up toward the sky. I saw a flash of Carlson above me, but it wasn't in any human form. I was simply seeing red. With a loud shrieking gasp, I gathered my strength and inhaled painfully. My head pushed into the ground so hard my vision went white again as I screamed.

Then everything went to black for a moment.

***

"Jackie, come 'ere," a woman called from a distance.

"Comin' mama," the voice of a child rang out in my ears.

My vision was blurred, but was cleared gradually to see a woman reclining in an old clawfoot bathtub. She beckoned me, steam rising up over her face, "It's time to take us a bath, baby."

"No, mama. Not today, please."

"Did you just say 'no' to me, boy?"

"Mama, I just——"

"You just' nothin'."

There was silence as the thin woman fanned her face and stood up slowly. The water sloshed around the tub as she stepped out onto a small thin rag that was lying on the olive green tile floor. Paralyzed, I watched as she approached me without a towel covering her body. She grabbed my hand in hers and yanked me over to the bathtub.

"I *said* it's time for us to take a bath."

With that, the woman took the back of my head and slammed it into the piping hot water. I gasped for breath, water rushing up into my nose and down my throat.

She jerked my head up out of the water. I wheezed, crying as my face throbbed from the intense heat.

"Next time ... you don't argue with me. Take your clothes off."

***

The pressure pinged back into my sternum as my back was thrown against the ground. My vision quickly flashed back to the present, the fiery heat transforming back into the bitter winter chill. The pressure mounted in my chest as if it were about to either combust or completely cave in. I finally exhaled and felt warm tears stream down my cheeks like a river.

With that single breath out, I imagined a tiny sparkling ball of light escaping out from my mouth. Some of the pressure left my body. The rest compacted and settled somewhere deep in my core.

I stared up at the gray clouds drifting by. My arms and legs went from stiff to deflated, poked by sticks and leaves. My entire head throbbed as speckles of colored light appeared, disappeared, and reappeared in different spots in front of the sky and the bare branches looming over me. The sound of sparrows crept back into the trees of the clearing.

There *was* another way.

With that thought echoing inside my head, I smiled as I let my eyes close softly, and allowed my body to go completely limp. It was a whole new sensation, release. It was over.

This is why we're here.

39.

SNOW AND SAND

"Is she gonna be okay?"

"Ssshhh, everything's alright, little."

"Should you call 911, Joel? She's not moving."

"You said she'd be fine, Wills!"

"She will, but like … maybe she needs a hospital to get … fine."

My eyelids felt so heavy as I listened to the slightly muffled voices around me.

"Em, *please* wake up," Joel begged, holding onto my shoulders. "I'm calling."

"Oh no," a soft voice whimpered.

The voices sounded clearer.

"Give her a moment … Joel, call if you feel you need to," a familiar angelic voice spoke.

"G— Gwen?" I slowly opened my eyes. My vision was still blurry, but I could see that there were four figures surrounding me.

You … bitch.

My eyes locked on one very familiar figure and my vision focused on him. "Oh thank God you're okay!" I shot right up to hug him.

"Woah! Woah! Easy." Joel buried his face into my hair.

Warmth. Just warmth. No burning, no stinging. No shocking cold. He held me tightly and rubbed my back. Everyone else was quiet, except for Willow.

"She needs to lay down and rest."

I closed my eyes again. They felt strained just from being open for a few seconds.

"I'm so, *so* sorry." Joel squeezed me gently and comfortingly.

"It wasn't you."

"I never should've let that happen." He shook his head, letting go to look at me. "I'm so happy you're okay."

I rubbed my eyes and squinted. "My head hurts."

"You overexerted yourself." Gwen smiled sympathetically. "I told you to breathe out."

"No, I couldn't. I would've lost him."

"Perhaps you're right." She gazed down into a toasty light.

I caught a glimpse of the flames reflecting in Joel's eyes and realized I was back inside the house. I'd been situated gently next to the fireplace to warm up. "What happened?"

"You first." Joel held my hand.

"Emma took Carlson in, and let me go," Gwen explained. "Don't exhaust yourself any more by telling the whole story. All that matters is that you're safe with us."

Joel leaned back, "Holy shit."

"Yeah, well … now she has *him* trapped inside her," Wills asserted. "I don't know if that's much better."

Joel locked eyes on me, his gaze moving between each of mine.

"I don't know. I did what I had to do. He was gonna try to kill me, Wills."

"You really think this is a permanent solution?" Willow spat.

"I don't think I had much of a *choice*, Wills." I sat up straight and snapped back with a glare. "Unless you wanted one or both of us over on that side *with* you."

"Hey, relax. Breathe," Joel reminded. "We'll figure it out together, okay?" He held my face with both hands.

I nodded. Willow stayed staring at me, but I shook my head and looked over to Lynette and Gwen. "Hi. Wow."

"I knew you'd do the right thing." Gwen nodded. She still appeared in the same damp nightgown, with the same damp hair. But death never took away from her timeless beauty.

"Was it, though?" Willow asked.

"If 'right' means alive, then yes." I glanced back toward Willow only to find that she'd disappeared. I sighed.

"It's okay." Joel rubbed my back. "If she wants to go right now, let her."

"You kept yourself and Joel as safe as you could, and I believe you're strong enough to keep Carlson at bay until you can find a way to release him without putting yourself in harm's way."

"Keep him at bay," I repeated.

"He's persistent, and he isn't going to be as quiet a guest as I was … I think Willow is just concerned for your well-being …That's all."

"Well, for now he can't hurt anyone else, so…" I trailed off.

"That's right, and this house is your home again."

"Yours, too," I reassured.

Gwendolyn smiled gently at me and looked down to Lynette, who was beaming at both of us, "Little, I believe it's time we went exploring."

The words hit me like a ton of bricks. "Oh … You mean you're gonna—"

"To be quite honest I'm not too sure what I mean." She chuckled daintily.

"Don't be sad. We'll check in on you! Right, Gwen? We'll come visit?" Lynette exclaimed.

Gwen and I exchanged a nod of understanding. "Of course … if we can from where we're going."

There was silence in the room aside from the soft crackling of the firewood.

"I'll miss you," I whispered to my young housemate. I held her hand, the familiar cool breeze of her energy welcoming me back home.

"I'll miss you, too." Her eyes slowly drifted to the wood floor. "Thank you for keeping your promise to me. And for reading with me at night. You made me feel not so lonely anymore."

"You made *me* feel not so lonely, too." I smiled in an attempt to keep her positive. But I felt the inevitable burn that came with goodbyes and tears rushing to my eyes.

"Emma?" Lynette started.

I felt Joel let go of my other hand to check what time it was on his phone.

"You can be my honorary second big sister," she squeaked. "I don't think I can take the Christmas presents you got for me, though. They're in my room. You can keep them there to remember me until I get back!"

"I won't move them, promise. Those stay in your room." I took in her comforting chill— a walk on a beautiful, brisk, summer morning.

Lynette's eyes stayed with mine for a moment. They appeared more vibrant than ever before. Hopeful.

"I have no doubt you'll take care of the house." Gwendolyn nodded softly up and down, gazing into the flame.

"It belongs to my aunt," I reminded. "But I think I'd like to stay here. I'll talk to her about buying it someday."

"Will you tell her the truth?"

"I don't know."

"She loves you as if you were her own. Tell her, and trust that she'll respect our story. I do. And if she ever *does* choose to write about it, try not to be upset with her. She's a sweet lady. In fact, I think I may like to be the main character in one of her books."

"We'd be famous," Lynette piped up.

"I'll talk to her. Maybe not tomorrow, but I will."

"Make her purchase worth it. Oh. And tell Nancy I said the wine at book club really did taste like dirt." She winked.

"I will," I laughed nervously as the realization hit me with the feeling of emptiness, "You're not with me anymore. I feel like a part of me is gone."

"Oh, no. No, no. Quite the opposite. *You* ... are such a strong young woman. And you'll come into your gift. You already are. I *will* say I'm tempted to stick around just to see where you go." She looked to Joel. "You take good care of her."

"Absolutely."

"He's your guardian boyfriend." Lynette giggled.

Gwen stood and took my face in her hands. "I am *forever* grateful to you ... for being so amazing to her. Don't be so scared of life. None of the small stuff matter in the end. What matters is very simple." She leaned down to kiss my forehead. It lasted for what felt like eons, and made the throbbing in my head stop. Before she stood back up, she whispered in my ear, "There is a letter … under the floorboards of your bedroom. That's where the dress was. Look for it … and give it to Liv." She paused, studying my eyes. "I am so, so happy … that I got to watch you grow up." She straightened up, and gestured for her sister. "Come on, little."

Lynette bent over to kiss my hand softly and let go for the last time. As she turned to join Gwen she shouted. "Wait!"

"Yes?"

"Emma, can we dance one more time?"

Joel blinked slowly.

"Oh, Lyn. I— I'm not feeling too well right now."

Lynette looked down at the floor forlornly. The deep maroon bow of blood remained on her head.

"You have your original dance partner right here anyway," I added, tasting the bittersweet tear that trickled down my face and into my mouth. "But we will when you get back."

With that, Lynette gave me one last sweet, sweet smile and pranced over to join Gwen. She bounced excitedly as she reached out for her sister.

"I have waited so long to dance with you again," Gwen said.

Lynette giggled, beaming up at her.

Gwen brushed Lynette's cheek and glanced over at us. "Play us off?"

Joel sighed and nodded. "Of course." He cued up a jazz playlist and, almost too perfectly, the song "We'll Meet Again" by Vera Lynn began playing on his phone.

Gwen closed her eyes and hummed softly, taking her sister in her arms and swaying in front of the dining room window, where the street lamps outside let in the soft glow of winter moonlight.

I rested my head in Joel's lap as we watched the Salley sisters turn into two sparkling spirits, twirling together until they dissipated into one gentle, breathtaking burst of misty bright light. They were like tiny glowing snowflakes, soft iridescent grains of sand in my dining room. They lingered like fireworks for a few seconds until all the little twinkles drifted down toward the floor and vanished.

***

On January 6th, the waves crashed toward the sand on Second Beach. Joel and I needed some peaceful quiet after spending three days inside my house resting together. The way he'd been caring for me made it seem like I'd been recovering from open-heart surgery. He was basically an in-home nurse and butler combined, whether I needed it or not. He'd argue that he was simply honoring Gwen's last wish.

That morning before heading to the beach— to find a patch of sand that wasn't covered in snow and just sit— we'd put together the blood-stained dress and Gwen's note in a box. We knew exactly what to do with them. I did, in fact, find the letter under the floorboards in my room, just like she'd said. Joel's sharp eye had found the loose piece of wood. The box was waiting for us in the trunk of our trusty blue Prius while we sat on the thickest beach blanket we could buy with our Christmas gift money.

"You sure you're ready to do this?" Joel sniffled, wiping his cold red nose with his sleeve.

I gazed out at the horizon where the gray clouds met the sea. "Yup."

"I'll be right there with you."

"I know."

The waves roared up onto the shore and back, in sync with my deep breaths.

"She'll believe us," Joel reiterated.

"Yeah."

"Do you think she'll write about it?"

"Probably."

"What are you gonna do, then?"

I sighed, looking out toward the waves. "Gwen gave her blessing ... It's Liv's house, anyway. I can't really do anything."

"But it's your home. Are you ready for that kind of attention?"

I shrugged my shoulders, staying bundled in my coat. "I'll have time to prep, I guess. It could be worse."

"I'm proud of you, Em."

I nodded, thinking back on Gwen's note. I'd read her handwriting a million times over since finding it:

March 13, 1951
To whomever may find this someday,

I made a terrible, awful mistake in doing the only thing I felt was right.

I was distraught to find my sweet, sweet Lynette dead, and after having found evidence prior of his abhorrent crimes that same night, I murdered my fiancé Jack Carlson. I stabbed him to death with his knife and buried it with him in the woods behind this house. It is a relatively shallow grave. By the time this note is found, he may be long gone, as well. I can only hope.

It has come to light that my sister's death was an accident, though I know he was involved. I believe he meant to harm her that night had she not fled. What I consider to be evidence of the kidnapping, assault, and murder of Betty Remington is hidden in the basement. I have not touched the box since that night, and I couldn't bring myself to turn it in. I'm so sorry.

I acted alone, and I've tried to live with it for too long now. I am utterly incomplete without her, and I am ashamed that I allowed such unholiness into my home. His blood is on this dress, and while I am guilty of homicide, his blood is on his own hands. Lynette's blood is on mine. I am responsible for her death at the end of the day. Now I just want to be with her. To tell her I'm so sorry.

If you should find this, do what you will. I find some peace in knowing that eventually the truth may be uncovered. But that day is not today, and I don't have the strength or courage left in me to tell it to the world myself. I have hurt too many people. The last thing I want to do before I go is hurt my father with the truth. I never wanted to leave you alone, daddy, but I just can't live with my sin anymore. We both did our best, and you were wonderful. I will see you in heaven with Lynette and Mama.

Please forgive me,
Gwendolyn Salley

"When are we meeting with Nancy, again?"
"She's meeting us at Beach Brew with Liv."
"Oh, a two in one," he bit his lip. "Yikes."

"Yeah."

"You nervous?"

"I'm a badass now, remember?"

"So ... no?"

"No. I'm very nervous."

"Have you heard from Wills?" Joel furrowed his brow.

"Nope." I shook my head. "If you haven't, I haven't."

"She'll come around."

"She's probably pissed at me."

"She can go be pissed off if she wants." He raised his voice slightly in case she was watching from behind the veil. "You followed your instinct and saved both of our asses."

I cracked up slightly, but pushed it down. "For now."

"Em."

"It won't be forever right?"

"What? *Him* ... in there?" Joel nodded down at my chest. "No. I'm telling you, Em. There's a way, and we'll find it. We'll be handing him another eviction notice sometime soon."

"Okay."

"Don't sweat it today. Certainly don't fear him anymore. You took him, not the other way around."

"Easier said. I feel him there. I've already had one nightmare ... thoughts I *know* aren't mine ... What if it turns into more? I freed everyone but myself." I swallowed hard.

"No, you freed everyone but him. He's *your* passenger. You're in the driver's seat, and you are now the strongest woman I know. Just keep him right where he is, and we'll get on it after we tell Liv everything and after the dust settles for a bit."

"Ugh ... I'm anxious."

"Don't be. Just tell the truth ... except for the——"

"For the *him* ... of it all." I blew a raspberry and placed my hand on the middle of my chest. "I don't know. I don't feel good."

He rubbed the knuckles of his tight fist with his other hand. His nose scrunched and he took a deep breath of salty ocean air.

"I don't like it, Joel."

"I know." He licked his lips and hung his head over his lap.

"What?"

"I'm sorry."

"For what?" I asked.

"I don't know…"

"Stop … Don't be." I crinkled my brows and caught his green eyes staring off into the distance. I was grateful for them. "Please," I chirped.

"Yeah, okay."

"It's not your fault." I ground my teeth.

"Okay."

"Joel?"

"What's up?" He looked over at me and into my eyes.

"Thank you." I allowed a small smile to creep up on my lips.

He nudged my shoulder with his, and I propped my legs up on his lap and leaned into him for a friendly hug. We sat in silence, watching the ocean come and go against the soft, winter sand as I fiddled with the pineapple bracelet around my left wrist.

365

FEBRUARY

40.

DEVIL IN THE DEEP BLUE SEA

I stared down into the dark roaring ocean from the bottom of the stone steps. The water crashed angrily up on the rocks below me that day, and my emotions crashed angrily against each other within me. The wind picked up, and when I cleared the hair out of my face, he was there.

Where I wished to see a glimpse of my mother someday in the reflection on the water, I saw him, bursting in and out of the sea foam as the waves raged against Cliff Walk.

I could almost hear his cackling, his taunting. It was faint, in the back of my head, but it was most definitely present.

He wasn't going to ruin this place for me, though.

I turned around and made my way up the forty slippery steps, gusts of cold air brushing past me. I found my new car parked by itself along the uneven cobblestone sidewalk ahead.

After I got in the car and situated myself, I turned on the ignition and checked my rearview mirror. To my relief, the figure staring back at me was only Willow.

"Nice car."

"Hey," I mustered, buckling my seatbelt.

"Nice jacket, too."

"Thanks, it was on clearance at some thrift shop. Guess no one wanted it cuz it's so fuckin' ugly." I chuckled dryly and slid my hand down the sleeve of Willow's old yellow suede jacket she'd left behind in her closet— the same one she'd worn the day we met.

When I'd stumbled upon it on my couch on a few days before Valentine's Day, there was a small blue sticky note on the sleeve, written in her handwriting:

Now you can also go to the library in style.
                                        -Wills

She'd still had her ways of giving interesting gifts— or of having Joel leave them for me. It didn't zip in the front, but I didn't need it to.

We snickered together for a brief moment, then Willow returned a stone-faced stare at me through the rearview.

"Emma. Go home."

"No." I shook my head solemnly with a sniffle. My leg shook on the car floor.

"Where are you going?"

I turned the heat on low. "Just for a drive."

"Emma, *where?*"

"I'm not dealing with this anymore. Not here."

"Don't do this."

I stayed quiet, biting the inside of my cheek. "I don't feel good."

"I'm telling Joel."

I squinted into the mirror. "Go ahead, he'll enjoy the visit from you. It's been three weeks … So thanks for checking in."

"*Seriously?*"

"Dead." I raised my brow and shifted the car into drive with a quick sharp yank.

"You suck … *ass* … Em," Willow growled and vanished.

As I pulled away down the street from Cliff Walk, I looked in the rearview again to make sure Willow hadn't nosily gone through my luggage in the backseat to sabotage my getaway.

I drove past the spot where I'd first met Willow, and gently smoothed over one side of the jacket collar as I noticed a light fog rolling in.

"That's a nice color on you. Still not red, though." He appeared in the middle of the mirror a couple minutes later.

I ignored him.

"Where *are* we going, Emma?" His eyes glowed yellowish, like warning lights on my dashboard.

"Road trip."

"How exciting." He spoke passively.

"You shouldn't be excited."

"That'll be nice. Just the two of us."

"Not for much longer," I shot him a savage glare, to which he smiled and disappeared.

At the next stop sign, I banged on the steering wheel and growled through my teeth, closing my eyes tightly for a second to push him away.

Uh oh. Don't snap your cap, darlin.

"Shut up."

Why don't you just go home.

I took a deep breath and focused on the long road ahead. I turned right onto Farewell Street toward Pell Bridge to leave the island. "I am."

370

NOT THE END

ACKNOWLEDGEMENTS

I want to first and foremost thank my backers on Kickstarter for showing support so early on in this process, and for believing that this book would be worth your while. I know that it took much longer than expected to get this into your hands, but I am forever grateful for your patience and kindness.

Thank you to my parents for encouraging me from a young age to go with my gut. I was raised to pursue my passions. Although some passions came and went in no time at all, you always took interest in *my* interests, no matter what it was. I am so lucky to have parents who fostered my creativity and imagination from such a young age. Thank you for keeping so many of my drawings, handmade magazines, picture books, and letters. I look back on them now and *know* that writing was my calling. I think you knew all along, too. I wrote my first children's book when I was four years old, and I'm positive that it is *somewhere* in your garage.

Nana and Papa- thank you for always having something for me to craft or design at your house. Our times creating fashion catalogs, pretend-school worksheets, and stories in the living room will never be forgotten, and are my fondest memories of that house in

Newport. I'm tearing up writing this because that house is so special to me. Thank you for choosing to live in *that* house, in *that* town. Without that, this book wouldn't exist, and Emma wouldn't have had such a beautiful new home.

Thank you to Aunt Renee and Uncle George, who showed me incredible support, and from such a distance, too. Your messages have helped me push through these last steps of publishing my book. I look up to you both, and I couldn't have published this without you. Big Renee, I am proud to share a name with you.

To my *entire* family— my wonderful in-laws, my siblings, aunts, uncles, cousins— I want to thank you. Whether it was about the book or something else, the encouragement and love you have given me has carried over into my writing process and has helped me grow more confident— slowly but surely. I love you.

I have few friends, but the ones I have are wonderful. Thank you for listening to me worry about my book: *Will I ever even finish this? Does this sound right to you? I'm worried no one's going to read this. I'm never going to be a successful writer. Read this sentence and tell me if it sucks.* Thank God I have had you in my corner rooting for me.

Lilly, you've been supporting me with this book since I started writing its earliest drafts a decade ago. I have so appreciated your feedback as a fellow writer. We were kids when I first told you about *The Sensitive.* Since then, we have changed, our friendship has changed, but our love for writing has not. I hope it never does. To my chosen sister, let's be authors together and then retire in Newport.

Tiffany, thank you for being encouraging during my final writing stages. You and your motivational quotes have helped me feel more capable of doing this. You have given me new ideas and insight on how to get my book out there, and it felt like a defibrillator on my creativity.

And of course, my acknowledgements wouldn't be complete without mentioning my personal assistant, graphic designer, at-home barista, creative consultant, errand boy, and business partner Dustin Lee Richardson. I am truly blessed to have you by my side with each of my projects. This gorgeous book cover, my website, and my tech support have all come from you. While our greatest collaborative work will always be our beautiful Charlotte, I look forward to our future projects with excitement. You are beyond talented, and your kind heart and dedicated work ethic will go far. I can't wait to see it.

FINALLY, I have to thank YOU, the one who read every single page of this book, including this acknowledgement section. Wow. Not everyone makes it *this* far. Usually "the end" is where we close the book. You must love reading, and I'm so grateful you chose to pick up my book. I hope you found something valuable within this story, even if it was just pure entertainment. I'm flattered. I have more coming, I promise.

Much love,
Renee Richardson

Stay tuned on social media for updates on *The Sensitive,* and feel free to reach out with any questions or comments by contacting me via my:

Instagram: @reneerichardsonbooks

E-mail: reneerichardsonbooks@gmail.com

Website: reneerichardsonbooks.com

Much more to come...

ABOUT THE AUTHOR

I was born in Visalia, California, but spent several years of my early childhood living in Newport, Rhode Island. After moving back to California, my fondness for Newport only grew during the multiple summer vacations there visiting my grandparents. During the summer of 2009, I found my first little spark of inspiration for *The Sensitive* while visiting Newport. My grandparents have since sold their home in Newport to follow us out west. I've stayed in California, where I graduated from Sacramento State University with a degree in Art Education. I currently reside Sacramento with my husband and daughter. In my free time, I love spending time with my family, watching ghost shows, meditating, listening to podcasts, and— of course — writing.